# Ex-Wives of DRACULA

## GEORGETTE KAPLAN

# ACKNOWLEDGMENTS

Big thanks go out to Janine, Sean, Mina, and the whole crew at Ylva Publishing, without whom this book would be much longer and have much more "teh" instead of "the."

# DEDICATION

For my Grandmother:
I hope you've found as nice a home as the one you always made for us.
Sorry about all the swearing.

# CHAPTER 1

Mindy was not a happy delivery driver. Her pizza place, Dragon Pizza, had scheduled too many drivers for a Thursday night. The shop was barely big enough to fit all seven of them and the in-store employees. It was a box of a building with no counter, just a window with a big sill like they all worked in a broken-down taco truck. Thankfully, the window was always open, which meant a cool breeze. Essential in a building that was pretty much a temple to the big oven in the middle of the room. Everything else was squeezed off to the sides.

Mindy had had a double all lined-up. Two deliveries and two tips, close enough together that it was one trip as far as her gas tank was concerned. But because her idiot manager had overbooked the evening shift, he'd split the order between her and Freddy just to get them out of there. Even though the deliveries were three blocks apart. Even though Freddy drove a pickup truck to deliver pizza. A Ford F-150. How could he possibly make any money with that thing's gas mileage? And with twice the gas being burned on what could've been one trip—it was like she was the only one who'd ever heard of peak oil.

Her only consolation was that the order she did get was on her block—no need to futz with her GPS and its touch screen that hadn't worked right since a babysitting charge had spilled a Happy Meal's worth of soda on it.

And it'd be a short trip. She lived roughly half a mile from Dragon Pizza, which meant it was impossible for her to be late. A good thing for a high school student. As long as she remembered to change clothes, she could come home from school, sleep in her work uniform, wake up ten minutes before the start of her shift, and get there three minutes early. It could've been five minutes, but she just couldn't sleep with her shoes on.

Mindy's car was cool and sleek and fuel efficient—back in the eighties. In the year of our Lord 2016, her Ford Taurus had all the class of a Segway. It turned over after thirty seconds of her pleading with the ignition to stop messing with her, instantly starting up a localized dust storm in the immediate vicinity of her tailpipe.

Speaking of peak oil, she should've bought a moped. Those things ate up gas like supermodels did milkshakes. But there was no way she would deliver pizzas in Carfax, Texas without air-conditioning. The rest of the country had weather; the great state of Texas had oven settings.

The heat-retaining bag of her order rode shotgun. All it held was a rinky-dink twelve-inch cheese pizza. Surely not the kind of delivery worth a decent tip. As she took the few turns between Dragon Pizza and her destination, Mindy rested one hand on the warm bag in the passenger seat. Hitting a speed bump and sending her order flying out the passenger-side window that was stuck halfway up would be the perfect end to a perfect day.

Trying to keep at only five miles over the speed limit but often going as fast as ten over, Mindy made it to the house so fast that her boss Dario could've done a "Fifteen Minutes or Less" sales promotion if the other drivers didn't still get their directions from road maps. But seeing the golden house number confirming her target, Mindy checked the receipt again. Yes, 214 Whitby Lane. Right beside 212, her own house. And the name on the order was Lucinda West.

*Well. This should be interesting.*

Mindy didn't remember the last time they'd talked. Probably wouldn't remember this time either, since a blank smile and a signed receipt didn't quite count as a conversation.

Leaving the motor running, Mindy pulled a pen from her pocket with one hand, scooped up the pizza with the other, and held onto the receipt with her mouth. She jogged up to the front door, rang the doorbell, and juggled everything into a vaguely efficient configuration before it was humanly possible for anyone to answer the bell.

Lucinda West opened the door, and Mindy felt automatically underdressed for the *Fuck Off* mat, clad in her shapeless red polo shirt, black work pants, and a logoed ball cap that was doing unfortunate things to her lack of hairdo. Lucia had always looked good—taking the hit of puberty like Rocky Balboa and emerging into a Michael Bay version of womanhood. The woman was all long golden hair, lean legs, and boobs that were, frankly, just not fair.

Mindy ran crisply through her recitation of corporate malarkey. It was missing half a dozen keynotes like "Let me know how else I can provide you with great service today" and "Thank you for giving us a chance to value our customers once more," but Mindy didn't think she could spew that bullshit on an hourly basis without bashing her head against a convenient wall hard enough to leave a gray matter stain.

"Hello, ma'am, thank you for ordering from Dragon Pizza, I have your twelve-inch pizza here in only twelve minutes, and your total today is only $11.92. If you could just sign here, please." She held out the receipt and pen and immediately thought that she'd been doing this job too long. She had to have been, going through that whole spiel before she even noticed that Lucinda was bleeding. "Mary, Mother of God!"

"Nah, you can call me Lucia." Wobbling a little from reaching over while she stood on one leg, Lucia quickly rebalanced, pressed the receipt against the doorframe, and signed by the X. She even put a considerate *3* on the tip space.

Grabbing a piece for herself, Lucia called back into the house, "A-team, pizza!" Two little towheaded boys came running. They snatched the box away before Mindy could even warn them how hot it was.

Lucia continued, "You better save me a piece or I'm throwing one of you off Tate's Creek Bridge. I'll still have a spare, don't test me!" She turned back to Mindy. "Don't worry about it, I just dropped a glass. And stepped on it. And pulled it out." The foot she was very much not standing on dripped. "I think I'll take a shower. I always do that when I have a bloody nose."

Mindy had been taking shop class way too long to be freaked out by the sight of blood. "Here, let me see—let's go inside, sit you down…"

"No!" Lucia said quickly but emphatically. She followed it up with a quick breath. "Don't you guys have rules about going inside customers' houses?"

"Yeah, don't go inside serial killers' houses. I don't see any satanic altars; you should be fine."

"They're in the back." Lucia hopped out onto the porch. Before Mindy could help her, she'd sat down on the swing. Its rusted chains barely moved. She folded her leg across her opposite thigh. "Here. Feast your eyes, pizza lady."

Mindy took a look. There was more blood than when her cousin had gotten her first period at their sleepover, and Cousin Betty had heavy-flow issues. "Damn. It really went in deep. That must've been a big chunk of glass."

3

Lucia grinned as if with pride. "It was one of those Burger King collectible glasses. Now I'm out a drinking container that shows my love for *The Lion King*." A little playfully, she shoved Mindy away before the examination could go any further. "It'll be fine. I'll wrap a towel around it. I've had worse."

"Doing *what*, sword-fighting?"

"Shaving my *legs*, drama queen. Shoo, already. Your car looks like it's toking some bad shit."

Mindy looked across the yellowing lawn to her even yellower ride. As usual, the Taurus's exhaust had turned from a wistful gray exhale to a vomit of phlegmy gray molasses while she wasn't there to massage it into compliance.

"Wait here. Right back. Enjoy your pizza."

Not giving Lucia time to reconsider, Mindy ran at undignified speed to the Taurus. She reached through the open window to flick the ignition off and then zipped around back to pop the trunk. Inside were a change of clothes and a cache of supplies that could've come out of a zombie movie. A worried mother's work. Mindy's mom had probably spent more on the go-bag in the trunk than Mindy had spent on the car.

After a few seconds of looking, Mindy found the first aid kit. She ran back to Lucia, who showed the same nonchalance both in eating a slice of pizza and dripping blood onto the timbers of the porch. "You got any, like, crushed red peppers?"

"You got a hose?"

"Side of the house. Watch out for raccoons, there was one hiding behind a bush there the other—"

Mindy was already around the corner of the house. She came back, yanking at and untangling the hose as she went, until she'd finally wrestled it up to the porch. There, she tried the trigger, shooting a torrent of warm water into the ground. She modulated the pressure she put on it, quickly working out a strong but supple flow of water.

"This could sting a little," she warned Lucia.

"You mean the big bleeding cut on my foot could *hurt*?" Lucia asked in faked wonderment. She held her slice of pizza up and away from herself. "Don't get my dinner all soggy."

Mindy was careful not to as she cleaned off the cut, even though she had already been tipped. Then she opened the packet of antiseptic wipes from her kit, using them to scrub Lucia's wound clean. Lucia winced. She even whimpered despite her tough façade. But when Mindy was finished, there were no tears. She sat thoughtfully as Mindy blocked up the cut with gauze and adhesive tape.

"Sorry to be keeping you from your job," Lucia said finally. "You're probably losing money."

"It's a slow night anyway," Mindy reasoned. "If I went back, I'd probably just be cleaning something."

Lucia viewed Mindy carefully, like Mindy had been set in front of her by some eccentric artist and Lucia was trying to figure out what the work *meant*. Realizing she was being stared at, Mindy looked down. She wasn't used to being a work of art.

"But still, I should go. You never know when half of Carfax will decide they need both melted cheese *and* marinara sauce in equal quantities."

"Hey, wait a sec," Lucia piped up. She offered Mindy her half-eaten slice of pizza. "Have some pepperoni."

"I'm not hungry."

Lucia's perfect eyebrows quirked, an expression of curiosity designed to make its object like when she was curious. "Listen, I'm sorry to put you on the spot like this. I ordered *before* I managed to impale my foot. I didn't know you were an emergency room on wheels when I called."

"All part of the job. I volunteer with the peewee football league: iodine, cuts, bruises, it's all good practice for the occasional customer who answers the door with no blood pressure."

Full lips formed a smile that seemed amused but not *too* amused. "Hey, I'm having some people over later. I don't mean to impose, but is there any way you could make a quick round-trip to the store? It's just one mile up the road. I was going to go myself, but people might look at me funny if I hop the whole way there, and I do not have a car." Reaching into her pants, she managed to retrieve a twenty-dollar bill from one of the uncanny imitations of a real pocket that the fashion world was convinced women's clothing needed. "Here. If you could just get some chips, some salsa, and a Redbox of anything with Ryan Gosling in it. Consider the change an extra tip."

A strong, rational instinct told Mindy to say no. Last week, Jenny had gotten fired for buying her customer cigarettes on a run, and she'd been working there forever. But there was something about Lucia that made her different from all the people Mindy could say no to. The look in her eyes was confident. So were the tone of her voice and the set of her expression.

But the way she sat lengthwise on the swing, foot drawn up awkwardly to keep the bottom from coming into contact with anything painful, screamed vulnerability. She wasn't milking it, and she wasn't hiding it. It was more like camouflage. Indiscernible unless you knew where to look. And Mindy had always known where to look.

Her car started readily, as eager to impress Lucia as she was. And with a slightly bloody twenty crumpled in her fist, Mindy was on her way to the store.

Seeing Lucia up close had been a shock. Mindy had seen her at school, of course, but it was like they were zoo animals in different enclosures. That John Hughes teen movie stuff about cliques was bullshit now, if it ever had been real. There were the same two Hogwarts houses there had always been. Cool kids and everyone else. Lucia West was the queen of the school. And Mindy was very firmly not. It was part of them, blood deep, growing out into their physical appearances like a mighty oak from roots deep in the earth.

Lucia was beautiful. No, she was sexy. It was all in the way she dressed, Mindy supposed; the makeup she put on. Lucia didn't want people to think how lovely she looked, how elegant, how well bred. She wanted people to picture her naked, and she wanted it enough to give them plenty of hints. Most of her shirts exposed her tanned, flat belly. If she wasn't wearing a skirt, she was wearing Bermuda shorts or even hot pants, in the summer. When Lucia had her face on and her ensemble polished, she was a fearsome sight. Mindy had read enough YA books to know Lucia's species roamed the entire American continent; maybe even overseas. She could've been the villain in a high school movie; the rich bitch that made the quirky heroine's life a living hell. Or at least the girlfriend of the villain, who put up with her psycho-ass boyfriend's shenanigans until the nerdy hero won her over because it was a movie. Lucia was a fine specimen of those girls who saw no difference between dating a jerkass bully and a sweet, good-natured underdog. Popular girls.

And if they had a hive mind, Lucia had to be their queen. Almost as tall as a man, she looked like an actress, if not a model: when she stood straight, the gap between her thighs was a narrow view, her breasts swelled from her slim chest in perfect symmetry, and if her belly dipped inward, it was more likely because she was wearing a corset than because she'd had two ribs removed. She was Megan Fox. She was Jessica Alba. She was the woman that women hated and boys loved.

But Lucia hadn't always been beautiful and sexy and fuckable and dangerous and all the other things villains in high school movies were supposed to be. Once, she'd just been cute. She'd had dimples and lived next door to Mindy. They'd been inseparable. BFFs before that saying was a thing, at least in their neck of the woods. Then Lucia had gotten boobs, her blonde hair had turned a shade of gold favored by fantasy movies, and her legs had refused to follow Mindy's example and *stop growing*. The cuteness had drained out of her, leaving only sex appeal. Now Mindy's childhood friend was almost gone. All but her smile. A kid's smile.

The smile Lucia had worn when asking for Mindy's help.

Mindy parked outside the grocery store and went to get what Lucia needed for her party. It was a good tip, after all. That was more than she'd gotten the last time they'd parted ways.

"Thank you, thank you, thank you!" Lucia cheered when Mindy came back with a bag of groceries and a $1.99 Ryan Gosling DVD from the bargain bin. Each repetition was a little louder.

Mindy was uncomfortable with how much it looked like Lucia would hug her. Thankfully, pom-poms didn't have much reach with her busted foot. "Yeah, well—I needed the money. New One Direction album coming out."

"Yes, good sir knight, I think this does call for a reward." Drawing a fiver from her pants—okay, were those *real pockets*?—Lucia straightened the bill before Mindy's face. "Here. Found it between the seat cushions. All yours."

"Thanks." Mindy took it, trying to think of a way to tell Lucia she was actually acting pretty cool without letting on how *uncool* she'd been since the first day of class freshman year.

Before anything occurred to her, they heard rolling thunder under the horizon. Teenage boy. Football team. Ford F-250. It was loud enough to rattle Mindy's teeth from there.

"That's Quentin," Lucia explained. "My boyfriend, who I love. He's not so bad. You should stay and meet him!"

"No, no—I've gotta get back. Even *my* boss isn't going to believe I got this lost on the way to my own house."

Lucia planted her hands on the sides of Mindy's shoulders, like she was locking her in place for a hug or sizing up the dimensions of her head for praying mantis jaws. It was hard to tell, but it seemed to be meant in a friendly manner. Who could tell with praying mantises, though? "Hey, when do you get off work? You should come over. It's gonna be an epic party."

"Nah, I'll… I'll still be in my work uniform."

"But you live right next door. Just change and *get over here*." Lucia gave Mindy a little shake. "It'll be fun. You'll be fun."

"Maybe if I get off early," Mindy said with all the flavor of a promise, but none of the actual calories.

"Cool. You're so cool." Lucia slapped Mindy on the back as she turned away, sending her off. "Go deliver good pizzas!"

As she got into her Taurus, Quentin nearly ran her over. Mindy was getting used to the near-miss sensation.

The rest of Mindy's evening was too dull even for her blog, and she had posted more than one "What *Star Trek* captain are you?" quiz. She went out on another run, this one up north. Got stiffed, shoveled the receipt into her glove compartment for later, and when she got back, the manager finally cut her. She tallied her tips, brought in her car topper, and started home. And all the way there, she thought about Lucia's party.

Assuming the offer was even genuine—assuming the party hadn't dissolved because someone couldn't bring ice cream sandwiches or something— assuming it wasn't already over because she'd driven five miles up the road and back again with nothing to show for it but a corporate-mandated twofer for gas money. Assuming all that, go or no go?

If she went, Mindy could pretty much guarantee all she'd do is hang out in the corner and snarf all the snacks she could. Was that really any better than an evening of decompressing, updating her blog, maybe a movie on Netflix if she could stop herself from just endlessly scrolling through the new releases?

Then again, she was a fucking teenager and she'd never sent a drunk text. She hadn't even used chatspeak. That was screwed up. She should be spontaneous and fun loving and easygoing. And in a week from now, she would be sitting in her room, bored out of her mind, wishing she had gone to the party. Because maybe at the party she'd meet a boy or whatever, and maybe they'd go to a movie. Then maybe in a week's time she'd be thinking, *Hey me-a-week-earlier, I'm kissing a cute boy because you went to the stupid party like a great big normal!*

She was going to do that. She was going to get home, put on something cute, maybe grab a quick shower, and go over. She could bring some of her mom's dinner rolls. They were still in the Ziploc bag by the fridge, right? Everyone loved dinner rolls.

Then Mindy got home and felt, right through her Goodyear tires, a thumping LMFAO song from the backyard of Lucia's house. The words FUCK THIS were suddenly installed in big neon letters on the inside of Mindy's forehead. She went in through the front door, leaving her hat in the car and ruffling her freed hair from back to front. Her parents were on the couch watching *American Kid Swappers* or whatever. They gave her, "How was work?" and she gave them, "Good," and trudged upstairs to her bedroom, where with the windows closed, the party music became a subsonic transmission straight to her fillings.

Too tired to undo her shoelaces, she folded down onto her bed and kicked off her shoes before looking over at the window. Through it, she had a view of Lucia's house and just about nothing else. Usually, Lucia's blinds were down, leaving her with "nothing else." Tonight, they were open. And Lucia herself sprawled across her bed. Not at the party. Not with some guy. Just lying in bed.

As if feeling herself being watched, Lucia's gaze crossed the seven feet between them. She saw Mindy's slumped posture, so close to her own, and smiled wearily. She even gave a modestly excited wave. Mindy returned it, not sure what to think. Before she could figure anything out, Lucia had turned away again. Mindy did the same, staring up at the ceiling and the baby platypus poster she had up there. Baby platypus always looked like it was having a good day being a baby platypus.

She was a little tired, but she felt like she'd waste the evening going to sleep now. She wondered how she could wake herself up enough to watch some TV, read a book, or photoshop some bees into that GIF she'd found of the Pope waving both his hands. That'd be funny. Probably get her a thousand likes on Facebook. She yawned. Did people still use Facebook? Did Lucia use Facebook?

Her phone trilled—a meow from Burt Reynolds the cat, who she'd house-sat for three weeks last summer. They were BFFs. She checked her phone. Not a garbled mishmash of Spanish or a butt-dial, for once. It was a text from Lucia.

*My mom's too much of a neat freak to let strangers in the house*, Lucia had sent.

As if Mindy had been wondering about the carnival in her backyard. Mostly, she was just surprised Lucia still had her number.

Surprised, but oddly touched.

The next day, Mindy drove past Lucia's bus stop on the way to school. Lucia wasn't looking her way; she had her back turned while the wind played with her flaxen hair. She really was pretty, in unguarded moments.

# CHAPTER 2

Mindy didn't know why everyone hated on the school lunches. Everything on her tray tasted fine, in that it was tasteless, which was an improvement on her mom's cooking. Mindy didn't know what kale was supposed to taste like, but it probably wasn't like the flesh of a dung beetle that had died screaming.

The cafeteria was basically just a very big classroom, without the TGI Fridays educational posters and such that the teachers put up. It was featureless except for the brick pillars that held it up, the bulletin board which shed extracurricular fliers like dead skin, and the glass doors that let the students see when a stray dog wandered onto campus.

Mindy ate alone, as usual, or she might as well have. The lunch room wasn't crowded and she sat far from the vending machines, so she had her table to herself except for the couple who tried to kindle a fire with their jeans. Mindy toasted them with her carton of chocolate milk and went back to her homework. Last question and…done. She decided to give her brain a rest before moving onto her World History assignments. Digging out the library's copy of *A Great and Terrible Beauty* from her backpack, she set about reading.

Her eyes rolled over the words like they did when it seemed like a book was beaming its story right into her brain. She wasn't aware of her eyes running along the lines of text, didn't know she was turning the pages, didn't even look at her food as she worked it off her plate and into her mouth. The peas, the mashed potatoes, the pudding, they all disappeared bit by bit until—*kritch*! Her spoon scraped against the mesh of the tabletop. Her lunch tray was gone. Mindy looked up from her book to see Lucia sitting opposite her.

Lucia pushed the tray back into place. "Sorry. Could not resist." She gave Mindy a slightly apologetic smile. "I don't suppose you're not really reading but simply desperately shy and secretly hoping I'll hit on you?"

Mindy reared up. "That was a lot of adjectives."

"I'm just fucking with you." Lucia hovered her hand over Mindy's little bowl of baby carrots, begging silently until Mindy made a permissive gesture. Lucia took one and crunched it. "That's a good book," she said, her mouth full but her voice still clear.

"Huh? Oh, oh yeah—I guess so." Mindy rubbed the dust jacket self-consciously. "I haven't finished, so, uh…"

Lucia wagged an eyebrow. "Surprised I know how to read?" She took another baby carrot.

"No, of course you can read…" Mindy said a little too apologetically for what she now realized was a joke. "You're in high school," she finished lamely.

Lucia let her off the hook. "Plus, I'm a cheerleader. We need to know how to read to spell out words. Otherwise how will the football players know what to do?"

Mindy giggled. She'd forgotten how *bright* Lucia was. High school seemed so monochrome, and Lucia was like a little splotch of color even when she wasn't doing anything. From a distance, you couldn't see it, but when she was up close, Lucia was just so alive.

Lucia kept going, picking up one more baby carrot and rolling it between her fingertips. "Not that I've seen you at the games."

Mindy hid behind her book. "I'm not big into sports."

Lucia preened up to look at her, so Mindy dropped the book to look back. Lucia gave her a brief smile. "Well, there's a game this weekend, and I will be there wearing something I can't blame men for jerking off to. Why don't you come? Give contact sports a chance."

That, more than anything, took Mindy aback. Lucia was surprisingly easy to talk to; it was even easier still to slip into their childhood friendship like it was a set of old clothes. Actually having Lucia proposition her set off a little pang in her. She remembered all the distance between them. And she didn't know if Lucia was closer than she'd thought or if all that space just made her feel safe throwing stones, since Mindy was too far away to hit back.

"I don't know…" Mindy said at last. She wavered in the face of Lucia's expectant look. Her words got chopped up into some needed order. "If you're there, okay."

Lucia happily chomped the carrot she'd been playing with. "You know, you look so smart in those glasses, but when you don't speak in complete sentences—totally ruins it." She plucked just one more baby carrot as she rose. "See you Saturday."

The next time Mindy saw Lucia, she was trying to kill someone.

Mindy was coming out of class the next day, going to her locker, the one with *No weed here* written on it. She was about to exchange one back-breaking load of textbooks for another when she heard all the sounds of a fight stampeding down the hallway.

Squeaking shoes, grunting, high-pitched profanities, and the arrhythmic slap of flesh on flesh.

Mindy wasn't immune to interest. She waded through the crowd that always gathered at these things, expecting to see another gay kid standing up to a bully because *Glee* had done a song about it.

Instead, she saw Lucia had jumped on Quentin's back, one hand buried in his curly locks and pulling hard, another punching him in the shoulder in a not-at-all-friendly way.

Their words overlapped as they spun around, Lucia's high and shrill, his pained and slightly hysterical. *"Get her off me fucking cheating asshole calm the fuck down I'm gonna kill you crazy bitch fucking shiv you!"*

Mindy's brain popped open the thought that it was only a matter of time until a teacher or school safety officer put in an appearance, separated them, and as the school system's approach to violent behavior was more enlightened since Columbine, treat them both as if they were Nazi war criminals. And just like that, she'd thrown herself through the onlookers, grabbed Lucia by the waist, and pulled her off Quentin.

Lucia was slimmer than her, but she helped hold up three people at every cheerleading practice. The fact that they were probably bulimic didn't take away from that. But Mindy had more body mass, and she'd taken Lucia by surprise. She dragged Lucia back six feet before she started resisting, digging her feet into the linoleum floor.

"Seb, little help!" Mindy called. Sebastian Brewster, Seb, a foreign exchange student from Romania or thereabouts, pulled out of the crowd. Mindy remembered being mock-UN partners with him last semester. He'd found it really funny whenever the Bulgarian delegates said something, and they got a B+ on the assignment. That was his entry in the Encyclopedia Mindy.

He wound his arms around Mindy's waist and helped her pull, a Human Centipede that managed to overcome Lucia's berserker rage. Pulling against Mindy's grip, she slipped and slid on the floor, banging her knees on the tiles multiple times as Mindy tried to calm her down.

"Hey, hey, it's me, I've got you." She barraged Lucia's ear with whispers, trying to talk her down like she was doing a show on Animal Planet. "He's not worth it, okay? Let's go—"

Lucia caught her breath. Mindy still felt her heart going a mile a minute. There was a feverish heat coming off Lucia, but she stopped struggling against Mindy, letting herself be held. Seb let go. Mindy didn't. So they just stood there, Mindy now embracing Lucia from behind, as the cheerleader jabbed a finger at the recovering Quentin like she could fire a bullet from it.

"Just so everyone knows, he cheated on the hottest girl in school because he had an *away game.* Enjoy your sluts, genius motherfucker!"

"Let's go," Mindy repeated, pulling at Lucia, getting her to take a few steps back with her.

Quentin wiped at the blood from where she'd clawed at his cheek. "I gotta get some suck action before a game. You knew! You should've come to support the team, but thanks for putting your boyfriend-girlfriend shit before the Dragons!"

"Fuck you, Quentin!"

Mindy heard big, official footsteps coming down the halls. She tugged insistently at Lucia. "Bathroom, Lucia, *let's go.*"

Lucia barely let herself be led away.

"Listen, Mindy—" Seb began.

"Daisy McDowell would've let Billy get a beej if he needed one!" Quentin shouted after them.

"Daisy McDowell's a fucking A-cup and Billy's into dudes!" Lucia shot back before Mindy could shove her into the nearest restroom.

Seb tried to press on. "Mindy, I was wondering…"

"Hold that wonder," Mindy told him, following Lucia in.

The bathroom was empty, thank God. Mindy barely had time to look for Lucia before the blonde ran past her, kicking the wall hard enough to put a dent in the plaster. "Fuck!" she screamed.

"Hey, Lucia, hey…" Mindy tried to think of something to say, but someone came through the door then. "Use the boys' room!" she ordered the intruder.

"This is the boys' room," he stammered.

Mindy took a closer look at him. He had very long hair for a boy. "I like your hair."

Jabbing a finger at the row of urinals Mindy had failed to notice, he left. No sooner was he out the door and a few muffled words were exchanged on the other side than there was a knock from outside. Mindy gave Lucia an awkward pat on the head, mouthing promises to be right back, and went to answer it. It was only as she was actually pulling the door open that she realized how weird it was to knock on the door to a public restroom.

Coach Bakula was Mindy's favorite teacher by a factor of a million and one, and he wasn't even a teacher. He was the coach of Millarca High's seven-time championship football team, but if that weren't enough to make him small town royalty, he also volunteered to teach English class.

He was handsome in that ageless Hollywood way that seemed to be a constant from year thirty to year sixty, but without the Botox or plastic surgery, just a weirdly orange tan and some white in his hair and goatee. The business suit he wore everywhere was slightly undone, tie loosened and jacket hung up on the back of a chair somewhere.

"Everything okay in here?" he asked gently, sneaking a look at Lucia before averting his eyes respectfully.

"Yeah," Mindy said. "We just need a minute."

"Take all the time you need. I've got Quentin doing sprints until he learns some manners. Or vomits. Whichever comes first. Meantime, I've got a feeling this bathroom is going to be out of order for the next few minutes." He flashed her one of those yellow folding floor signs before splaying it out at his feet. "Put it away when you're done. You've got me next, so I'll just forget to take roll until you get in."

"Thank you, Mr. Bakula. Big time."

"Go. Be a good friend." He shut the door.

Lucia had slid to the floor, back against the wall thumping her head rhythmically against it. Mindy sat beside her. She offered a handkerchief before Lucia started crying.

The sight of the white cloth in her hand got Lucia started. Hot tears leaked out of her, under too much pressure to stay inside. "Fucking asshole," she murmured.

Mindy put a hand on her shoulder. She didn't know quite what to do. She'd never had a friend breakdown in front of her. She didn't even cry that much herself. She'd seen a hundred movies and TV shows where someone cried, still looking sexy and perfect and beautiful, and someone comforted them, looking caring and masculine and confident. The women in those shows didn't cry like Lucia, with her face all blotchy and her eyes bloodshot.

Mindy took out another napkin from her purse and held it under Lucia's nose. She'd grabbed a whole batch of them at work. Lucia instinctively blew. Mindy wadded up the napkin and tossed it into the trash bin. Three points.

At least she'd stopped crying.

Mindy used another napkin to wipe under Lucia's eyes and rub off her runny makeup. Lucia sat there passively, letting Mindy mop her up. Then her head fell to one side, and Mindy almost got out of the way before she realized Lucia meant to rest it on her shoulder.

"I really tried with him," Lucia said. Her voice wasn't rattling with emotion any more, it was just quiet. Which was even worse. "I really thought I was a good girlfriend. I was gonna—wash his clothes and fix him pies and shit. I would've done anything to be a good girlfriend."

"You were a great girlfriend," Mindy assured her. "He's just an idiot. He's an idiot who never even got to know you well enough to know what he's gonna be missing. He's gonna be big and fat at the high school reunion, and you're going to be super-hot and married to a senator. He won't even know why he let you get away."

"I did anal!" Lucia cried to the florescent lights. "What more is a girl supposed to do, huh?"

"Nothing. You're pretty and smart and funny and own a cheerleader outfit. He's just a goddamn idiot. He's like the guy who dates Diana Prince and crushes on Wonder Woman, but he doesn't even know that Diana Prince *is* Wonder Woman with glasses and a different hairdo. Screw that guy. He doesn't know he's dating Wonder Woman."

Lucia gestured for another napkin. "It's the week before Valentine's Day," she said listlessly and blew her nose.

"You don't have to even *do* Valentine's Day. I don't."

"Yeah, but you're, like, a hobbit. I have to do something. That fucker's not taking Valentine's away from me. That's the one holiday that is all about women. You never hear about a woman getting shit because she forgot to get her boyfriend something. Feminism, Mindy."

Mindy felt a little like resting a head on Lucia's shoulder herself, she felt so drained catching the shockwaves of Lucia's explosion. She sat there beside her, a lump.

"We should have a fucking Galentine's Day." Lucia nodded to herself. "Yeah. We'll go shopping and eat at a fancy restaurant and go see a romantic movie—they're for us anyway…"

"You…wanna spend Valentine's Day with me?" Mindy asked.

"Yeah, what, like you have plans?"

"My parents book a suite at the Renaissance on Valentine's Day. I get the house all to myself, so I watch *Game of Thrones* really loud in my underwear. I don't even fast-forward the naked scenes at all. I've caught up on whole seasons that way."

Lucia was staring at her. "Bitch, you want bloodshed, nudity, and midgets, you go shopping with me."

Lucia's and Mindy's houses were almost nothing alike, except they both had first-floor additions in almost the same spot, extending toward each other like they were going to lean on one another. The roofs almost touched, so when Mindy saw Lucia sitting on the little "balcony" outside her bedroom window, she thought for a dumb moment that Lucia was actually in her room.

Lucia waved at her. Mindy waved back, but gave her a confused look.

Lucia shrugged.

Feeling awkward, Mindy picked up her closest textbook and gave it a little shake.

Lucia rolled her eyes but in an understanding way.

Mindy lay down on her bed and pyramided her book on her tummy. It was a little nice knowing Lucia was there, almost watching over her.

Then she heard something fly through her open window and flap onto the foot of her bed. Mindy sat up. Lucia had disappeared back into her room, but she'd left a card.

It was a Valentine's Day card, a picture of Bane from *The Dark Knight Rises* on the cover saying, *You think being my Valentine gives you power over me?* On the inside, another bit of Tom Hardy stock art said: *It does.* There was a bit of text seemingly intended for Quentin that Lucia had Xed out so thoroughly nothing remained except an ellipsis. Then Lucia had penned in a new message: *You're the only good thing about this week*, followed by a smiley face with a wobble for a mouth.

# CHAPTER 3

Carfax Mall was all done up with flowers and pink and hearts in a way that was almost tasteful. Budgetary constraints. Had to be.

What surprised Mindy was how thrifty Lucia was. She'd brought her credit card, expecting she'd be cutting it up by the end of the day, but Lucia walked right by the boutiques to go to smaller businesses, thrift stores that all seemed to know her by sight. Once she had Mindy in front of the staff, it was like a general giving his lieutenants a battle plan. Dresses started materializing, skirts and blouses and jeans and belts that everyone said would look great on her. But only those Lucia okayed went into the dressing room.

"Those glasses have got to go," Lucia told her. "We need to LensCrafters your shit…it's like from the feet up, girl, girl, girl, eighties stockbroker."

"I like my glasses."

"I like singing Macklemore songs, but I know better than to do it in public." Lucia rushed them into a well-sized dressing room like it would fortify them against a zombie apocalypse, giggling as she threw the lock closed. "Alright. We need to know your dress shape."

"You mean size?"

"No, shape. They can be higher or lower. Depends on the girl. Pull your shirt up."

It all happened so fast, Lucia running her from one store to another, showing her how to dress and what to wear, all the tricks of the trade. It was like a movie montage more than Mindy's boring little life.

INT. DRESSING ROOM 1 - DAY

LUCIA, our heroine, heartbroken but sexily
so, runs her hands over the sides of her
comedy sidekick, MINDY: a GINGER with round

cheeks, freckles, and a bulb of a PUG NOSE
under a curly mop of hair. She finds the
narrowest part of Mindy's WAISTLINE. A
shitty single by GREEN DAY plays on the
soundtrack because our CORPORATE OVERLORDS
declared it so.

INT. SHOE STORE - DAY

Lucia and Mindy try on HEELS. Lucia shows
her friend how to walk around in them. She
exaggeratedly SWINGS her hips, then puts
her hands on MINDY'S HIPS to show her how to
shift her body weight the right way.

INT. HAIR SALON - DAY

LUCIA explains to Mindy that her THICK CURLY
HAIR will look a lot better if she DOESN'T
BRUSH IT and washes it only EVERY FEW DAYS
instead of every twenty-four hours. Mindy
agrees to TRY IT.

INT. DRESSING ROOM 2 - DAY

LUCIA tells Mindy about properly fitting
her bra, because if she's got it wrong,
her BREASTS WILL BE SORE, she'll look TEN
POUNDS HEAVIER and the girls WILL NOT BE AS
PERKY AS THEY COULD BE. Borrowing a TAPE
MEASURE, Lucia checks Mindy's underbust while
STANDING, BENT OVER, and LYING DOWN. It TAKES
A WHILE. This is a subject Lucia IS PRETTY
PASSIONATE ABOUT.

And then the eighties movie montage was over and Mindy realized she was in a makeup store. An actual *makeup store*, where the employees wore matchy-match outfits and name tags and hats and you had to bust out a credit card to pay for stuff. And Lucia had bought her some eye shadow with a French name, along with a bunch of other stuff, and had taken her into the cramped employee space in the back to put it on her. She was so intent that Mindy would've giggled if Lucia hadn't been so insistent on her holding still.

"The key," Lucia was saying, sounding like she had an IQ of 240, "is to separate the socket line up top from the crease. We do not put shadow on our creases unless we're, like, Asian or something. Really Asian, too, not *Last Airbender* Asian." She stopped to check her work, then smiled like it was the shape her mouth was made to fit into. "You're so pretty."

Mindy looked away. Why did people feel the need to humor her—condescend to her, really? She knew what she looked like. "No I'm not."

Lucia grabbed her by the chin, holding her still to work her lips with some gloss. "Shut up, you're cute and sexy, deal with it."

But Mindy knew she wasn't. Lucia was the one who was pretty. This close, she could see it in every pore. She was made of awesome. Especially her lipstick. The last time Mindy had tried to put on lipstick, she'd looked like Ronald McDonald, but Lucia's lipstick was amazing. It was so red. Red and red and red.

Mindy looked away again. This time Lucia let her.

"Okay, done! Ready to start your modeling career? Wait, wait, no, not yet! I want to see how you look in that Matthew Williamson dress."

Mindy's ears grew even hotter, which seemed impossible without them achieving nuclear fusion. "Good, I can look *completely* ridiculous."

"Well, true, you're no *me*, but that's not so bad." Lucia gathered up the spoils of the hunt into one of their shopping bags. "It's always the best food that has flies buzzing around it, y'know? Guys like Quentin." Lucia realized her thoughtlessness in one epic contortion of her face. "Oh. Oh! Not that you look bad or anything. You always look great—I mean you belong with someone who likes you even with your awful fashion sense. For your heart and shit. Come on."

They drew the attention of mall security, going into the nearest boutique with a bunch of shopping bags already full, but Lucia just laughed when Mindy pointed it out to her. They were only going to use the dressing room, after all.

Inside the coffin space of a dressing room meant for one, Mindy held the dress over her body again. Light olive-green with white daisy lace embroidery, green bead raffia and sequin embellishments. It didn't grab the eye like Lucia's wardrobe did, but Mindy liked how it looked on her. Lucia was right about that much.

"I'm stealing this from you," Lucia said, dragging a pink Alexander Wang crop top from one of Mindy's bags. She held it before her chest in the mirror, looked undecided, then peeled off her Famous Last Words tee to try it on.

Her bra was Armani—one of those things you saw on girls who were someone's thinspiration. Mindy was staring. She hated that she was staring. Then Lucia unhooked her bra. Unbroken by straps, the expanse of her back was long and smooth, and you just wanted to touch it. Like it was a dolphin or something.

"Hey, you sure you want to do that?"

"Why? You think there's a hidden camera in here?" Lucia turned to her, and Mindy thanked Isaac Newton that physics kept her bra in place. Mostly.

"No," Mindy said. "Wait, is there? No, I just mean, in front of me."

Lucia smiled fondly as she took her bra all the way off. Mindy shut her eyes. "Mindy, besties share everything. Including what their nipples look like."

Mindy gestured blindly, but stopped when she had a nightmare vision of accidentally grabbing tit. "It's just…Would you take off your clothes in front of a straight guy?"

Lucia snorted. "Yes. Obviously."

"I mean, a straight guy you weren't dating."

"He'd have to buy me a drink, but—"

"Is there a situation where, like, you'd take off your clothes in front of a guy because he was gay and didn't care but not in front of a straight guy because he'd be perving?"

"Well, I'd have to be wearing cute underwear, because those gays can be vicious when it comes to ladies' undies, but—whoa, do you think I'm gay?"

"No! Me, I'm—maybe."

"Maybe you're gay? What, did you just see Olivia Wilde?"

"Like, maybe I'm gay, maybe I'm straight, maybe I'm bisexual, maybe I'm demisexual—"

"What is that? That sounds like one of Luke Skywalker's friends. And would you open your eyes already? I promise I'm decent."

Mindy opened her eyes. Lucia had put on the pink shirt.

"That looks really cute on you," Mindy said.

"Thanks. I know. Tragically, I am ninety-nine percent heterosexual. I am entirely into dicks and Olivia Wilde."

Mindy took a deep breath. She felt like she should be panicking. Why wasn't she panicking? This was the first person she'd told about being less than straight, which also happened to be the first chapter in all those books about kids who got run out of town or lynched or burnt at the stake. And Lucia made her feel so *calm*. "The point is… I don't know where I'm going to end up. So I'd understand you being, like, concerned to take off your shirt and end up in my spank bank or whatever."

"Mindy," Lucia put her hands on Mindy's shoulders, "I would be honored to be in your spank bank." She pulled her jeans a ways down her hips. "Look how cute my underwear is. Look at my gay guy underwear. This is the underwear RuPaul would wear if he didn't have a dick."

Lucia had her laughing again. "Stop it! You're gonna make me pee."

"*Do not!* I just got that outfit right. Well, wait, not quite right—" Lucia took off her necklace, a simple gold cross, and put it over Mindy's head. "You're not, like, waging war on Christmas or anything?"

"Mm?" Mindy found a mirror, looked at the little crucifix in the hollow of her throat. "Oh no. Just not sure if God really cares about someone…eating sushi or whatever."

"Well, take that off if you're going to eat sushi, just in case." Lucia straightened it. "It looks nice."

"Yeah," Mindy agreed. "Wouldn't be disappointed to find this in a Cracker Jack box."

Lucia slapped her arm. "Ho. It's my grandma's. She gave it to my mom, and my mom gave it to me before—anyway, it's official. You're my baby. I've adopted you."

"Can I have a pony?"

"No."

Cut. Print. Fade to a Jamba Juice bar, where they waited in line because every boy and girl that had ever shared a boob felt compelled to also split a smoothie. Mindy had been pretty quiet. She'd had a lot of mental versions of this conversation, where she told someone and they had a big fight about slumber parties and yelled at each other and threw stuff, and it was all very dramatic. There was Linkin Park music, and she had a good cry.

Now she'd told someone, and there was no drama. No accusation that she was perving on them or planning to "convert" them or any of the other horror stories she'd read online. Lucia seemed more curious than anything else. Maybe not bi-curious, but...

"So!" Lucia whispered in her ear. "You don't know if you're straight or gay. There a word for that?"

"Questioning," Mindy whispered back.

"Got it, got it, simple. How does one becoming "questioning" anyway? You weren't, like... I mean, you didn't walk in on your parents doing it or anything?"

"No, just lucky, I guess."

They got to the front of the line. Lucia ordered something with enough ingredients in it to sound like a magic potion. Mindy ordered the same. When Lucia brushed her elbow along Mindy's ribs, she paid. Galentine's Day was killing her allowance, but spending time with Lucia was worth it. *Someone should figure out a way to pay cute people to keep you company. Oh, yeah. Prostitution.*

Most of the couples left the store as soon as they got their drinks, on their way to one PG-13 activity or another, so they stayed, sitting in a booth near the back of the store. Lucia and Mindy and all their bags. Lucia was looking at her with that look that'd been seared into Mindy's brain ever since she'd told her parents. Someone who had questions but didn't know if it was pushy to ask.

Say what you would about Lucia, but she wasn't indecisive. "But how's that work? People either like pizza or they don't. They don't look at a slice of pizza and ask if there's a third option." Then Lucia drank from her smoothie like it wasn't a big deal either way.

Mindy blew out a gust of air that brushed the fine hairs on her forearm. "You've never looked at a girl and thought she was so pretty, you didn't know if you wanted to be her or…the other thing?"

Lucia grinned at her like Mindy was a kitten that'd gotten tangled in string. "Fishing for compliments now?"

"Not me, obviously!"

"Why obviously?"

Mindy shook her head to clear it. "Or a guy. Okay, a guy. A guy who looks really hot, and you know he's hot, but you still wouldn't screw him."

Lucia looked away thoughtfully. "Mads Mikkelsen," she said under her breath, nodding.

"It's like that. Kinda. Sorta." Mindy picked up her drink and turned it around in her hand. "I'm explaining it bad."

Lucia picked up her drink and held the lower half against her head, the ice helping with the Texas heat. "Is it weird that I'm asking? If you don't wanna talk about it—"

"I don't mind. It's just…" Mindy paused. She watched Lucia put the smoothie down. "Whether I'm going to be marginalized and persecuted for the rest of my life or whether I'm going to be normal."

Lucia's eyes sought hers. Lucia's were so blue that they seemed to glow. They stared at each other for a moment. "Are you scared to be gay?"

Mindy looked away. "Okay, that—"

"Sorry," Lucia said quickly.

"That's an okay question, but…we're at a Jamba Juice."

"We are at a Jamba Juice!" Lucia said, changing the subject very naturally. She picked up Mindy's empty cup. "You want another? Anything with seaweed is good. Seaweed is the chocolate of the smoothie world."

"Get me another one."

Lucia got back into line, leaving Mindy with her thoughts and a small panic attack. She hadn't pictured telling someone going like this. Telling a friend. Having a friend. It'd always just seemed…kinda obvious to her. Of course she wasn't *normal*—she wore horn-rimmed glasses and plaid pants and big, baggy T-shirts and Timberland boots like she was going to hike her way from Home Ec to Calculus. People saw her that way; so what did Lucia see her as?

Lucia returned, shoving Mindy's smoothie into her hand. "Okay, we've gotta book. You took a hella long time coming out of the closet, and *Frankenstein* starts in two minutes."

"*Frankenstein*?" Mindy asked, trying to remember if Boris Karloff had been scheduled for the local Alamo Drafthouse that month. She thought it was all Christopher Lee.

"*Frankenstein: Rise of the Prometheans*," Lucia said in her best trailer voice. "I've been looking forward to it all month. Haven't you been paying attention to me?" she asked, throwing in a fake pout.

They reached the theater just in time, so there were ten minutes of previews, commercials, commercials for previews, and public service announcements that were really commercials to sit through *before* the trailers started in earnest. Mindy guessed people had liked movie trailers too much for the powers that be not to mess with them.

At least she still had her smoothie. Lucia had said "please" and had bent over really far, so the ticket-taker let them take their "outside food or drink" into the movie. She slurped it loudly, in competition with Lucia. The movie they were about to watch had opened as counterprogramming to *Valentine's Day 2: The New Breed* and a Ryan Gosling movie, so they had the theater to themselves. Between that and being teenage girls, they resumed their conversation.

"So, if you woke up one night and Chris Hemsworth was in your bed, naked and shit," Lucia began, "you'd kick him out because you might be gay? Follow-up, same question, Natasha Henstridge."

"Natasha Henstridge?" Mindy asked.

"You don't know who she is?"

"I know who she is, just—wow, dated much?"

Lucia stretched out, kicking off her flip-flops and putting her bare feet up on the seat in front of her. "I saw *Species* as a kid, and it gave me a total lesboner for her. She's cute, and it's an analogy, work with me."

"I don't know. I have no idea what I'd do with a naked guy or a naked girl. Good thing it hasn't come up much." Mindy followed suit, putting her Timberlands up on the seat in front of her, though she worried about breaking it. They were good-sized boots.

Lucia poked her in the side, right below her waist. "Because I could set you up, if you were looking in the guy department."

"I'll think about it."

"I could get you a picture of the dude's penis first, if that would help. Because you can just ask and they'll send you one. Boys are such sluts."

Lucia laughed. It felt good for Mindy to join in. Like they were singing a duet.

Mindy trailed off into another drag on her smoothie, slurping on the icy dregs at the bottom. "You were right about seaweed. For something that is one part weed and one part sea, it is not bad."

"Here." Lucia took Mindy's straw and put it besides hers in her smoothie. "Case you get thirsty."

The lights dimmed, and the stereo system got louder to signal "We're starting for real now." Even with no one else in the theater, Mindy spoke softly. Or maybe it was just what she had to say.

"We'd still be friends if I were gay, right?"

Lucia faced her in the sudden darkness. "Of course. I'd just start calling you my lesbro."

"Okay." Mindy sat back in her chair as the green of an MPAA-approved trailer finally came up. "Strong reason to be straight."

During the obligatory scary part of the movie where the heroine went into a dark and spooky apartment despite knowing there were monsters running around and it turned out there were monsters inside, Lucia grabbed hold of Mindy's hand. She didn't let go, even after Frankenstein saved the *Maxim* cover girl.

Toward the end, after a battle that broke most of the laws of physics that Mindy could name, the main bad guy lay defeated on the ground, his katana knocked far away. "You can't kill me!" he said, with all the gravitas a British character actor who hadn't managed to be cast in Harry Potter could muster. "You're Frankenstein... You're a hero! And I'm an unarmed man!"

"I'm not Frankenstein," said the guy with the conspicuous but not unattractive scars. "I'm his monster!" Then he dropped a refrigerator on the poor bastard.

*Frankenstein: Rise of the Prometheans* was the worst movie Mindy had ever seen. She had never had a better time at a theater.

They walked out of the mall, pausing briefly, regretfully, at the window of the jewelry store. Inside was a heart-shaped necklace that could be broke in half so two people could wear it. One half read *Best friends*, the other half read *Forever*. Lucia groaned lustfully as Mindy led her away.

Mindy drove them back home, where Lucia kissed her on the cheek and took back her necklace before she scurried out of the car to her own house. Mindy watched Lucia disappear through the front door before ambling to her own house. She noticed her parents' car in the driveway.

A sewer main had burst at the hotel, so the romantic evening had been cut short. Her dad was saying maybe they were getting too old to make a big to-do about Valentine's Day anyway, and it'd become one of those mild arguments that Mindy supposed cropped up when people had been married since the dawn of time. They suspended it, like halftime in a football game, to gently waterboard Mindy as to who she'd been with for Valentine's Day: Had she been with a boy? What was his name? No need to be embarrassed.

And Mindy pretended to look through the fridge for something to eat, replying *no*, it was just her friend Lucia, *yes*, just a friend, not a lesbian, a *cheerleader*. Her parents were ex-hippies and considered themselves pretty liberal, and maybe that was so for Texas, but Mindy thought they were more *ex* than *hippie*. They'd prefer Mindy be friends with gay kids, not be one of them.

They were great, really. She'd known one boy at school who'd kissed another boy and had been sent to a gay cure program that might as well be called Camp Lobotomy. Compared to that, her parents could lead a gay pride parade. But it was *so* obvious that their vision of their little girl hadn't been so butch, and they were still holding onto that picture in their heads. Like it was a losing lotto ticket, with them hoping the gambling syndicate was gonna call and say that there'd been a mistake, it really *had* won. That grated on Mindy, despite all the love and tolerance. All it took was one kernel between your teeth to ruin a tub of popcorn.

But wouldn't it be great if just a few more people could be like Lucia? Make bad jokes and ask questions and look at this whole *thing* that even she hadn't figured out as just another part of her, not some terrible secret like she was the Green Goblin or a Martian from *Invasion of the Body Snatchers*?

She saw Lucia again at school the next day. The cheerleader looked perfect as ever. Perfect face between heart drop earrings, perfect breasts under a zip-front hoodie covered in little pink hearts, perfect ass in J. Brand skinny jeans, perfect toenails exposed by her wedge sandals. Perfect boyfriend holding her, kissing her, playing with her hair like it was his.

Mindy didn't cry. She didn't feel sad. She wasn't angry. But all of a sudden, she was driving home, and she didn't know why it was so hard to fill her lungs with air and just breathe.

Lucia was next door when she went into her room. Mindy didn't look at her. She needed to study. She didn't even notice her, not even a little bit. Not until she heard the voice outside her window.

"Knock knock."

Lucia was straddling the little bumped-out addition on Mindy's house that almost touched the little bumped-out addition on Lucia's house. *Shit, she's gonna fall.* Mindy ran over and threw open the window.

"You're gonna break your neck."

Lucia rolled her eyes. "You're supposed to say 'Who's there.'"

Mindy stepped out of the way and gestured for Lucia to come inside.

"Knock knock?" Lucia repeated meaningful.

*Deep breaths, Murphy.* "Who's there?"

Lucia grinned as she answered: "Easily offended bear."

"Easily offended bear who?"

"Fuck you!" Lucia laughed at her own joke, perching herself on Mindy's windowsill. "Next-door neighbors," she said wonderingly, looking into Mindy's room. "You ever watch me get dressed in the morning?"

"You don't get dressed in there."

"Ha! You checked. You're such a perv."

Mindy smiled, but she didn't really mean it. Didn't smile with her eyes, as Tyra Banks would say. "Speaking of pervs… Heard you're not on the market anymore, West."

Suddenly Lucia wasn't smiling with her eyes either. "Lots of couples have fights, Mindy. It's not like me and Quentin broke up. Not officially. Officially-officially."

"He cheated on you."

"It was a blowjob."

"You can get herpes from a blowjob. It counts."

Lucia tried not to laugh, but her cheeks ballooned up until she just couldn't take it anymore. She giggled, and Mindy giggled with her because she didn't have any words to *tell* Lucia how special she was, how beautiful, how funny and clever and amazing she could be. How could she not know?

Mindy stopped laughing before Lucia. "Just tell me one thing. Why him? You could have anyone you want. Why someone who—why Quentin?"

Lucia spoke lightly, but it took an effort. Or maybe that was just Mindy's imagination. And she just *wanted* it to be hard for her friend. "Girls like me are supposed to date guys like that, you know?"

Mindy shook her head.

"C'mere." Lucia pulled her into a hug without waiting for an answer. "You're going to find someone. And it won't be like me and Quentin. It'll be easy. It'll be really, really easy for you two. How hard could someone have it? Being in love with you?"

The phone rang back in Lucia's room, a million miles away, and the ringtone was as harsh as a dentist's drill.

"I gotta take that," Lucia said as she slipped out of Mindy's hands. "It'll be Quentin. He said he'd call. He says we need to work on our relationship."

"You shouldn't be the one doing the work," Mindy said, but Lucia had already turned around and stepped over to the little balcony of her house and acted like she hadn't heard a single word of it.

# CHAPTER 4

"Hey, Minz, got a live one for ya," Dario called up from the front.

Mindy hustled out of the backroom, barely grabbing a paper towel to dry her hands off. "Yeah?"

"Yeah." Dario routed her on the computer, futzing with it as it tried to do everything but what he wanted. "214 Whitby Lane. Order asked for you by name and said there's a ten dollar tip there if you bring…" The receipt finally printed. "ten hot wings and a twelve-ounce Sierra Mist."

Mindy ripped the receipt out of the printer. She was smiling to herself. "Driver out the door, ten minutes."

"You don't have a stalker, do ya?"

"Ten bucks is worth someone watching me pee."

Mindy didn't think she lived in Carfax. She was just kinda there, the way Carfax just *was*. You lived in NEW YORK, you lived in SAN FRANCISCO, but in Carfax, she just drove along, in and out of the forestry that pressed in on the city limits like a cancer—or maybe white blood cells. It wasn't a bad place to live, she knew. Way better than places like Peniel or other East Texas towns that seemed like little more than storage units for people who couldn't be anywhere else.

Mindy turned on the radio, shuffling between the two stations she got with real regularity. Imagine Dragons and Blurred Lines. She shut the radio back off. She was almost to Lucia's place anyway, dipping into the dirt roads that wound through Carfax like holes in a cork, trees throttling the road, before she hit pavement again and saw the house. Lucia was sitting on the curb, wearing jean cutoffs and a gray top from the Gap with the sleeves rolled up.

Mindy pulled to a stop a few feet from her. Lucia got up, parked her hands on the roof of Mindy's car, and leaned in on the driver's side as Mindy rolled down the window. "I checked out that singer you told me about. You're right, she's not a tranny, she's just British."

Mindy offered her the receipt. "Quentin not picking up the bill?"

"No, I got it." She took the receipt and the pen and signed atop Mindy's car. "Pop the passenger side, I'm hitching a ride."

"You're what?"

Lucia practically sashayed as she wound around the hood. "You heard me. A blood vessel in my brain is going to pop if I spend any more time staring at a Calculus textbook. It's true. I checked WebMD. So I'm going to ride with you a while. Road trip!"

Mindy pushed open the passenger door, but her mind gave the order under protest. "That's not how road trips work."

Lucia moved the heat bag from the passenger seat onto the dash. "Sure it is. C'mon. Bring Your Bestie To Work Day. You can't tell me it doesn't get lonely."

"I have books on tape. And the radio. You like NPR?"

"Does NPR have fresh hot wings they're willing to share?" Sitting down, Lucia opened up the box and presented it to Mindy like twenty-four karat gold.

"Not with present technology," Mindy sighed.

Lucia cheered as she buckled her seatbelt. "This is gonna be just like *Thelma & Louise*!"

"They died. And I think almost got raped. And one of them was Susan Sarandon."

"Okay, then it's like *The Heat*. I'm Sandra Bullock," Lucia added quickly.

"You don't want to be Melissa McCarthy just a little?"

"I did until I watched *Identity Thief*. Then I wanted to die for a while, then I wanted to not be Melissa McCarthy. Or human." Lucia picked up a leg and offered it to Mindy. "You drive, I'll feed."

Lucia was right about one thing, and it wasn't Melissa McCarthy. Driving with her was a lot more fun than working alone. Usually, Mindy just let the road hypnotize her, getting to her destination in a haze of pizza smell and Top Forty hits, but with Lucia, she actually felt her neurons firing.

"No, what sucks about this town—besides the fact that we let a website pay us a couple million dollars to change the name of our shit to *Carfax* and then spent all the money on a new football stadium—is that it's *fucking hot*. All the time. Other places have weather. Remember weather? Being a meteorologist here must be like getting sent to the gulag."

Mindy laughed along with Lucia. "I think this place can't decide if it's a city or a town. I think we might have more deer per capita than people. Like a...like a tattoo on the forest, or something. Did they really have to build one shopping center, go two miles down the highway through nothing but grass and trees, then build a Blockbuster and go another mile for a Wal-Mart? I visited my grandparents in Cleveland. They can actually *walk* places. If you have two legs over there, you can get groceries, you can see a movie, you can get a dog. It's like a superpower!"

She looked over to see if Lucia thought she was funny, but she was resting her head on the window, staring out at the dark pavement made darker by the setting sun. The cat's eye highway markers were just starting to wink at her.

"I could take the heat," she said, "if only there were something here. There's nothing here once you scratch the surface. If you're just passing through, it's *idyllic,* but that's just because people project—they see what they want to see. They make every generic small town into *Gilmore Girls*. But when you live here, it never stops being just...anonymous."

Mindy saw the *NOW BAKING* sign in the pizzeria's window coming up. It shot out light that dappled onto the scrubs and trees surrounding the place. "Hey, you'd better hide. There's probably some BS corporate rule that says you can't ride with me."

Lucia ducked down into the footspace. "Okay. I'll just stay here and eat your hot wings."

"You paid for them. Hey, let me know next time you want something. I'll give you a discount."

"You spoil me."

Mindy parked. As she left, she heard a canine whine as Lucia pouted and pawed at the window. She looked back briefly, but only to insist Lucia hide again.

"Sup." Mindy clocked back into the computer, saw a new order was available across the bridge, and logged it out. Freddy, working oven, shoved the stack of pizzas into the bag she opened up for them.

"Go make some money."

"Buckle up, drive safe," the manager said as she breezed out the door.

She got to her car. Lucia pushed open the door from inside and made a little "ahhh…" expression when they came face to face. Mindy dumped the heat bag on her lap. "Here. Keep those warm. You're the firecrotch here."

"Anything else you need?" Lucia asked, batting her eyelashes.

"I suppose it'd save a little time if you typed the addresses into the GPS." Mindy handed Lucia the receipt. "Top right corner. I already know that it's up north, so that could get us into traffic earlier and whatever. Oh, and keep an eye on the GPS. It likes to slip out of the holder."

"GPS…" Lucia muttered, looking at it as Mindy demonstrated how to punch in the address. It was a little Garmin the size of a notepad, stuck to the console's AC vent by a set of claws that gripped the ventilation slits. Only it wasn't very tight, so the GPS slid down with every button press. "Hey, would these help?"

Lucia turned two pegs on the bottom of the holder so that instead of being parallel with the holder, they stuck out and kept the GPS steady.

Mindy stared at it. "Either you're a genius or I'm an idiot. I'm an idiot."

"Does this have to be an either/or situation?" Lucia leaned over and kissed Mindy on the cheek. "C'mon, let's go. My vag can feel the pizza getting cold."

At the end of the night, Mindy counted out her tip money. She'd driven them home, it was raining, and they were taking their time before making the dash from the Taurus to their front doors. Most nights she made about fifty dollars. Tonight it was sixty-six. Mindy could only attribute it to Lucia being good luck. She peeled off a ten and a five and gave them to Lucia once she'd driven her home.

"I can't take this," Lucia said.

"You earned it. You helped fix the GPS and everything."

"Oh, that's how we're going to remember it?" Lucia took the money. "You could at least put it in my G-string."

"Like you're wearing a G-string."

"You're right." Lucia's grin was feral. "I'm not."

They ran to their houses, screaming and laughing as the rain drenched them well and good. Then they were inside, upstairs, and in their rooms to

shower, dry off and put on warm clothes. The rain was coming down too hard
to open the windows that bridged between them. Almost too hard to even see.
But Mindy saw the message Lucia wrote in big bold letters on a piece of paper
held up to the glass.

*Sometimes I feel like you're my only friend.*

Mindy almost reached for her phone, but she quickly felt why Lucia hadn't
sent her a text. The words were too big to fit on a tiny electronic screen. So she
dug through her closet, found a marker and the notebook-sized dry-erase board
that her mom had used to assign the kids chores for six weeks one summer.
Shortening Lucia's name to something from childhood, she wrote out:

*You have a lot of friends, El.*

She held it up, but Lucia already had another piece of paper written out
against the glass.

*It would be okay if you were.*

The next week, Mindy forwarded her new schedule to Lucia. Lucia wasn't
always waiting at her car when Mindy came out in her smart uniform, ready for
a day's deliveries, but she was there often enough for Mindy to get used to it.

Fun became novelty, routine, ritual, comfort. They talked about everything
in that car, with the sole exception of Quentin.

Eventually, Dario brought up that a customer had mentioned Lucia to
him. Mindy told him it was a friend of hers who wanted to know what it was
like to work for Dario's. She might apply someday. Dario nodded. Then he
asked what Lucia liked on her pizza. He sent one home with them that night,
free of charge. Lucia was grateful as hell. She was babysitting her brothers and
hadn't had a clue what to do for dinner.

The Taurus surged along the empty highway, up toward the bridge, a five-mile drive to the northern boundary of Dario's delivery range. It was an unlucky order for Mindy to take—the northies tipped for shit and still expected their pizzas on time, as if they lived in civilization. But she didn't mind, not with Lucia for company.

Lucia reclined in her seat, her right leg dangling out the open window, bare foot catching the wind between its toes. She looked like Mindy felt. It was the Thursday after the dinner rush, the last lazy gasp of the week before Friday and the weekend rush.

"You wanna get drive-thru?" Mindy asked. "The guy can check your uterus when we pull in."

Lucia's head lolled in Mindy's direction. "Is that a comment on my skirt?"

"It's a comment on your bajingo, which your skirt is pointing at."

Lucia aimed herself straight ahead. "Drink it in. Don't need an ob-gyn anyway. My bidness is in perfect working order. I should know, I've used it often enough."

A car passed in the other lane, its light flying over Lucia. The strength of the beam turned her thin skirt transparent where it was bunched on her inner thighs. Mindy could see black panties caressing her fair skin.

"Can I ask you something?" Lucia said. Her voice was faraway, like a fairy tale.

Mindy pondered it. You never could tell where a conversation would go with Lucia, now that she was back with Quentin. It was like walking through a minefield. If Lucia asked her for relationship advice, Mindy was swerving into oncoming traffic. "Only if I get to ask you something."

"That's fair. You wanna go to church with me on Sunday?"

Mindy gave her a look. She'd noticed the crucifix necklace that was part of Lucia's look, but she'd kinda thought it was just there because it looked good with her boobs. She winced at herself before considering the offer. "I don't know. The…orientation going to be an issue?"

"No, no, it's not that kind of church. They're cool. I mean, they're not a rave—" Lucia made a desultory gesture, like she was describing a movie she'd enjoyed but was trying not to oversell it. "But they're cool. And, like, it's fine if you don't want to—"

"It's not that I don't want to, it's just—ya know?" Mindy winced again. "I'm not an atheist. It's just I'm not that religious. Honestly, I kinda thought you…"

The conversation was moving ahead in fits and starts. Lucia couldn't do anything to smooth it out. "What, because I don't march around an abortion clinic? I used to be in the children's choir, remember?"

"Oh yeah." Mindy vaguely recalled seeing Lucia in a weird-looking Victorian dress thing on a few Sundays. "Did you quit?"

"Didn't really have time. Work and…stuff. Anyway, some of the people there were really helpful with my mom."

"What about your mom?"

"Just some stuff. She's fine now. Hey, what'd you want to ask me?"

"Just…you know how in *She's All That*, Freddie Prinze Jr. made that bet to make Rachel Leigh Cook prom queen and they started dating…That's not us, is it? Like, there isn't some bet or…or prank…"

Lucia turned to stare at her. "You think I'm being nice to you to set you up for, what, some YouTube video?"

"The thought had crossed my mind," Mindy said weakly.

"No. No, I wouldn't do that to you."

"Well, people don't just start being nice to other people all of a sudden—"

"Nice people do—"

"Usually they want something."

The heel of Lucia's hand met the orbit of her eye. She ground it in. "I don't want anything from you, okay? Do you think this is some *Carrie* kinda thing? Like, just because I have more than five Facebook friends, I must be some kind of sadist?"

"I don't think you're a *sadist*—"

"Mindy, I would never hurt you." Lucia was staring at her so hard that it was almost uncomfortable—only it wasn't. "If I'm being nice to you, it's because I like you. Okay?"

"Okay," Mindy repeated. Noncommittal.

"Why wouldn't I like you, Mindy?"

The GPS indicated one last turn to their address. Mindy whisked her fingers across Lucia's calf. "Put your leg down. We're here."

Lucia put her feet down in the car, smoothing out her skirt as Mindy switched off the radio. They came up on the lit house on a dark block. It was a good neighborhood but bland, too manicured—lacking that lived-in feel Mindy saw on her own street. *White people farm,* her big brother would call it. Mindy took her flashlight, double-checked the house number with it, then gathered up the customer copy and merchant copy of the receipt. "Call him. It says he wants to be rung when the pizza arrives. Guess his bell doesn't work."

Lucia's eyebrows knitted inward. "He didn't promise a tip, now we're going to put him on our phone bill?"

Outside the car now, Mindy gestured for Lucia to hand her the pizzas. "Just call him."

"I'll call him collect."

"No, *call* him!"

"Bad enough if we drove all the way out here for nothing but the wear on our tires…"

"Fine, use my phone." Mindy nodded to it, sitting in the cup holder. "Slide to unlock." Then she turned and walked up to the house, ending the discussion.

The last thing she saw was Lucia dialling the number on the third part of the receipt, a long scrap of thermal paper that included the customer's full address and order.

Mindy, meanwhile, trudged upward. Mr. Louis Card's house was one of those that sat on a little hill with a steep driveway and a set of stairs going up the front lawn. She could never live in a place like that. Make her neurotic backing out of the driveway every morning.

At the front door's pale and lonely light, a welcome mat read, *Enter Freely, Leave Safely, And Leave Some Of The Happiness You Bring.* Mindy restrained herself from knocking, just unwrapped the pizza and presented it along with receipt and pen for inspection. The door didn't open, though she heard Lucia in the car below, introducing herself brightly as "Dragon Pizza Delivery Service!"

Another long moment later, Lucia cupped the phone to her chest and yelled up, "He says it's open."

Mindy turned the knob and gave the door a push. The hallway was dark, the illumination from the porch light slicing into it and revealing only dirty tile, then carpet and a hint of stairs. There was a smell of butterscotch.

"El?" Mindy called down, turning.

Lucia leaned out of the driver's side window, phone cupped. "He says come in."

"Tell him I can't."

"What?"

Mindy came down a few steps, out of the porch light, the butterscotch smell receding. She said again, not raising her voice, "I can't go inside."

"Oh right, because he might be a serial killer." Lucia nodded.

"No, because it's corporate policy."

"Corporate policy for dealing with serial killers."

"Just tell him I can't come in."

Lucia put the phone to her ear again.

"Because corporate policy!" Mindy insisted.

Lucia gave her a thumbs up as she spoke. Mindy turned back around. She could see something stirring in the darkness now. She walked back up the stairs to get a closer look, but when she came to a stop on the door mat, all was still again. Just a door yawning open and a bunch of shadows. Mindy held the pizzas.

"He wants to know who he's talking to if you're at the door!" Lucia called up.

"You can answer that!"

"Right, right…" Mindy heard Lucia jabber at the level of polite conversation while she stood there rocking on her heels and feeling the heat coming off the pizza. Always comforting, that warmth. No one wouldn't tip for pizza you could *feel* was hot.

He came out of the shadows suddenly, fast and low, his footprints only sounding as he came off the carpet and onto the tiled landing, big meaty feet slapping on the tile with an almost moist sound. He was big, a six-foot-big number, dressed in boxer shorts and a wifebeater that revealed an equal number of dark hairs on his thick arms and legs. Fat neck and broad shoulders led down to a barrel chest and to an impressive belly that bulged over the elastic waistband of his boxers. He looked like he could've been a wrestler gone to seed except for the head curiously perched on his neck.

It was dominated by cleaver cuts for eyebrows and a mustache, ruddy cheeks, and a fat, flat, broken nose. A smug face made for aviator sunglasses, a coach's whistle, and a Cuban cigar.

"Yeah? Hi there," Mr. Louis Card said, his Texas accent broad. Not a cartoon, but almost proud in its curling consonants, its cut-off vowels. "You couldn't just bring me the pizza?"

Mindy wished people would just let her do the spiel. They let cashiers do the spiel. "Uh, no, sir." She handed over the pizza. "Corporate policy, ya know."

"Yeah, yeah, because I'm a serial killer or something." He looked at her accusingly.

How had she not noticed his eyes before? They protruded, big and bloodshot from under his bushy eyebrows.

"No, sir. I think it's more to do with stealing. So, if something goes missing in the next few days, you'll know it couldn't possibly have been your…humble delivery driver," she finished in a self-effacing rush.

"But the door was open. You could've walked right in and taken anything. Maybe I oughta search you." Then, eyes blazing at her, Mr. Louis Card laughed with his mouth opened as wide as his jaw would go.

Mindy didn't like it. It seemed too loud. Like when people in movies turned up the music to cover the sounds of a murder. She didn't join in his laughter.

"Where's the receipt, anyway?" he demanded, sounding as defensive as a cornered animal.

"Here, sir." She handed it to him, along with the pen, and moved to help hold the pizza boxes as he signed. Holding it against his prodigious belly, he gave her a sharp glance at her gesture. She withdrew her hand, shocked at the sheer *rancor* in his look. Close to him, the butterscotch smell was almost overwhelming. If it was cologne, he must've slathered it on.

"Thanks," he concluded gruffly, shoving the receipt back.

"And…my pen?"

He dropped it on the pizza box. She swiped it and the receipt up in one pass. "Have a nice night." Then she was down the first step, the second, the third—

"You didn't have to be afraid."

She stopped out of politeness, turning around to see those bare feet—their thick, yellow toenails—padding out onto the porch. Big, almost moist sounds against the pavement with each step. "I wasn't."

"I'm a cop, you know. State trooper. You should be more trusting."

"It's corporate policy. Sir," she added belatedly. She slotted her pen into her pocket for something to do with her vacant hands.

"It's rude. Feels rude. Might not order from you guys again."

"Sorry. Sir." Then she remembered Lucia watching. Imagined her jawing on the way back, telling Mindy she should've punched the guy in the balls and ran, because who would've taken some middle-aged weirdo's side over a teenage girl? Or Lucia jumping out of the car and doing it herself. "If you'd like to call my manager, I'm sure he'll explain why he thinks it's a good rule."

Mr. Louis Card just stared at her, his eyes with that casual rage, his eyebrows twitching, his mustache bristling. "You drive safe now."

"Always do." She turned and went down the steps, not especially fast but definitely not slow, telling herself she would not stop if he told her he had burst into flames.

Lucia opened the door for her, slid into the front seat, tossed the empty pizza bag onto Lucia in the other seat, dropped the signed receipt into the cup holders, and hit the gas. A block later she thought to buckle her seatbelt.

"How much we get?" Lucia asked, breaking the silence and swishing up the receipt. "Motherfucker! Zip?"

Mindy glanced at it briefly when Lucia held it up for her. "He didn't give me cash."

"Aw, and he put a big fucking zero in the tip section! That fucking burns me, man. Like we would put a number there and get fired over, like, five bucks. He's saying we don't deserve to get paid for our labor *and* we're cheats. Dickwad!"

"Put it in the glove compartment."

"Huh?"

Mindy opened up the glove compartment. "It's that thing."

"I know what it is, I just don't—" Then Lucia looked inside and saw that along with the tire gauge, the car's manual, and a rubber-banded assortment of insurance information, there was a rat's nest of crisp and wrinkled receipts.

"Put it in already, I don't want them to spill out."

Lucia shoved the receipt inside and shut up the compartment again. "Okay, sensing a story there, Mindy."

"It's nothing. Some dumb therapy thing—"

"Is it voodoo? Voodoo would be awesome. You could get, like, a paper cut from them signing the receipts and then—"

"It's Twitter."

"Mm?" Seeing a receipt caught in the door, Lucia opened the glove compartment again, pushed it fully inside, and sealed it back up.

"I…" Mindy put a finger to her brow, rubbing at the throbbing vein she felt there. She hated confrontation. Felt like she'd failed at polite society, not whatever asshole was confronting her. "Someday, when I'm rich and famous, I'm gonna tweet those dicks' names and addresses, and everyone's gonna know they—are—lousy tippers!"

"Holy shit," Lucia tittered.

"It's gonna be one of those Twitter accounts that go viral. Whenever anyone gets a bad tip, anywhere in the US, they're gonna post the receipt there. Name and shame. I wonder if that handle's taken…" Mindy wondered, liking the sound of it: @nameandshame. Then she shook her head. "I'm probably never going to do it."

"You should. You should do it. I like the sound of that."

They came out of the white people farm, out of the inverted shadows of yellow streetlamps and onto the highway, the only thing darker than the night that surrounded it. Finally freed of the thirty mph limit, Mindy pumped them up to forty-five, fifty, fifty-five, sixty. Only five miles over the speed limit, though. That was the real limit in Texas.

Lucia rested her head on Mindy's shoulder. "I love it."

The smell of Lucia's hair erased the butterscotch from Mindy's memory. "Thanks for coming along with me."

"Anytime, girlfriend." Lucia snapped her finger.

"No, I mean it. He may still have his two bucks, but I have someone to call him an asshole with. So, who's the real winner?" Lucia rubbed her hand on Mindy's knee in answer. Her hair trickled down Mindy's short shirtsleeve like a beam of sunlight wisping at her bicep. "You know what you are? You're my good luck charm. Even if I don't get a tip, you make me feel really—fortunate."

Lucia turned the car stereo back on. The jazzy music was warm coffee poured down their throats. Invigorating and relaxing them at once. And Lucia's head on Mindy's shoulder was just heavy enough, just warm enough, just right. Lucia reached up and smoothed out the hem of Mindy's sleeve where it had folded back on itself. Her fingernail traced briefly over Mindy's skin.

This fast, highway markers and lane dividers became a hypnotic blur in the headlights lulling them into a trance. Then, like a snap of the fingers, a stray dog appeared in the road. It came up so fast, it was like they were standing still and the dog was speeding toward them. Mindy spun the wheel, braked. The car veered to the side with the dog full-on in the headlights. It slipped into the darkness down below. There was a bump as they swung into the turn lane. Then they were surrounded by empty night. The dog had disappeared as fast as it'd arrived.

Mindy broke the silence before it was fully formed. "Did I hit him? I turned... *I fucking turned!*" She pounded the steering wheel. "Shit! SHIT!"

More than anything else, she felt frustration. She'd seen it, she'd reacted— why hadn't that been enough? Why did the dog have to be there, *right there,* just when she was too close to do anything about it? What the fuck was she supposed to do? Just... She'd hit it.

"You didn't hit him," Lucia said vehemently. "It was...the brakes, the gears, they make noises when you turn too fast—"

"I hit him! He was in the fucking road and I was going fast like a fucking idiot and I hit him!"

Mindy's foot twitched on the pedal. The speedometer rose like water coming to a boil. She was beginning to cry.

"Mindy, slow down."

She hit the wheel like it was at fault, like it hadn't turned fast enough, like it hadn't responded well enough. Her fist hammered at it, setting the horn off. "Fucking—"

Wind shrieked in through the cracked window, roaring against the rear windshield. Mindy screamed with it, frustration becoming anger, anger the only thing bigger than her sadness. She kept thinking of, kept hearing that *thump.* The brief glimpse she'd had of the dog circled in her mind, spinning in her like a top—a border collie, it'd looked like.

Big and cute and majestic and she'd killed it. She'd *slaughtered* it without even looking, hadn't even thought about it, just *stepped on it* like she was a big evil monster and it was her victim. What was even left of it now? Scattered meat, a smear on the roadbed—what was left after she'd murdered it?

As the speedometer climbed to eighty, Tate's Creek Bridge loomed ahead of them, its iron trusses aimed at them like sawblades in shop class, ready for them to be run through.

"Mindy, we're gonna get pulled over…"

She felt the tears drip off her jawline—they'd made it all the way down her face without her knowing. Her throat felt like someone was choking her. She was a dog-killer. A fucking monster.

And then Lucia's hands were on the wheel, holding it steady as she said in Mindy's ear so it went right to her brain, "Stop. Stop the car. Stop the car now."

As clumsy as a woman drugged, Mindy picked her foot up off the gas pedal and set it down on the brake. Where it belonged. She applied the pressure steadily, constantly, and they slowed in little gulps. At twenty miles per hour, Lucia eased them off the road and onto the dry brown grass that was the new desert in Texas. There they came to a stop, a stone's throw from the drop-off of Tate's Creek. Its waters laughed a good seventy feet down.

Gently, so gently, Lucia took hold of the gear shift and pushed it through neutral, through reverse, into park. She let it go. Mindy closed her eyes, heard Lucia turn the key in the ignition and kill the engine. The great beast of the car—the murderer, the murder weapon—sighed and cooled and slept. Only the headlights stayed on, shooting into the night to expose the bridge's iron trusses. The bleached white bones of some long-dead monster.

Lucia got out of the car, slid around the hood, and opened Mindy's door. She undid her seatbelt and pulled her up. The frustration and anger had abandoned Mindy. All she had now was the sadness. And that *thump*.

"Please don't—" Lucia said, pulling Mindy away from the car. "Don't go into your head. It wasn't your fault."

"I was driving too fast."

"Bullshit. Five miles over the speed limit." Lucia shook her head. "No. No."

"Poor fucking dog—fucking dog didn't ever do anything to anybody."

Lucia sat Mindy down on the hood and looked around, desperately checking the wheels, the bumper. "There's no blood, okay? How can you have hit him if there's no blood?"

"I crushed him. I'm a stupid fucking jerk, and I put a tire tread through his belly like it was nothing—"

"No!" Lucia said it as emphatically as a curse. She stood there in the headlights' glow, a performer in the spotlight. Her shadow shot out behind her like it was fleeing from her. "This is not your fault! You listen to me! It's not!"

"I hit him! I saw him, and I didn't, I couldn't—whose fault is it if it's not mine, huh?"

"Dog catchers!" Lucia took a step closer to Mindy, her shadow growing bigger. "It's their job to pick up dogs so this doesn't happen! Why are we even paying those guys if they can't find a big dog like that? Huh?" She came even closer as Mindy wiped the tears off her blotchy, reddened, murderer's face. "And we have leash laws! We have fucking leash laws, Mindy! If that dog belonged to someone, and we don't know that it did, but *if it did?* It's *their* job to make sure he doesn't get out. They need a fence or an electric collar thing and a fucking leash! And if he did get out, they should've gone after him. We're—we are a long way off from houses. We're in the middle of nowhere. A dog shouldn't have gotten this far if its owner gave a crap. He should've been driving around *looking*. It's his fault, not yours. Please don't cry Mindy, it wasn't your fault, it's not fair."

And she kissed Mindy. It was like being set on fire. One moment Mindy was so cold, a chain of thoughts wrapped around her, biting into her, and then Lucia's lips were against hers and her body was so close and her hands were right there, on her face, in her hair. Lucia replaced everything. Put herself in all the places where Mindy felt sad or alone or awful. Became a little world for Mindy to feel safe in.

Mindy lay back, relaxing into, then away from Lucia's lips. Her hands lay on the hood, feeling the heat of the slumbering engine. It seemed like it would burn her. And she shimmied up the hood as if she were fleeing from Lucia. Or daring her to follow.

And Lucia crawled up the hood with her, on her hands and knees, kissing Mindy again, again, until the back of Mindy's head was on the cool glass of the windshield and the front was all lips, being kissed and licked and held. She felt like she would freeze and she would burn up and she would explode.

Until Lucia rolled off her, out of breath, speechless for once, and they laid there on the hood of Mindy's car with their backs to the windshield. Lucia's left hand was lying next to her right hand. Mindy joined them. She couldn't believe how quickly a set of lips could cut through her sorrow. It was like Lucia had hijacked her mind. Stolen her.

"Sometimes death is inevitable," Lucia said at last. "It's not anyone's fault. It just happens. So you go on. It's not a story, but—it happens."

"Okay," Mindy said softly.

Lucia looked at her again. With the headlights under them, her face was all shade and stars. Except for her eyes. Those Mindy could see. They looked brand-new.

There was one last tear on Mindy's face. Lucia reached out, wiped it away.

"I'll drive," Lucia said. Nodding to herself, like that was who she was talking to. "You just have to sit in the passenger seat, and when we get back, you tell Dario you're not feeling well and I'll take you home. You get some sleep. In the morning—"

"Can we stay here a minute?" Mindy interrupted her. "Just a minute?"

"Yeah. Of course."

They laid there. Mindy put her arm under her head and Lucia turned on her side, doing the same. Their bodies didn't touch, but there was an electricity, a vibration Mindy knew Lucia felt too. The night was cold. The engine was still warm underneath them, but it would cool soon. If they stayed there long enough, the light from the car battery would flicker and go dark.

Then, like fingers playing a cello's strings, the darkness pinned down by the headlights stirred. It shook and broke apart, and Lucia sat up to see it clearly. She smiled.

"Look," she said. Her voice was still gentle, so unlike how she usually talked but so *her*. "Bats."

They were coming out from under the bridge, streaming out, not in an apocalyptic flood, but in a steady flow of twenty or thirty at a time, a scarf that wound down the river and emptied into the night sky. Mindy sat up too. She saw her breath frost in front of her. "I thought they only had those on Congress Avenue."

Lucia shook her head. "That's the big colony—two million—but there are smaller ones all over. Like this one. Maybe a couple hundred thou. The bridge must have those deep, narrow little hidey-holes they like. The mommas come up here from down in *Mehico* to give birth and stay spring through fall, hunting together. Binge on thirty thousand pounds of insects a night. Then in October, they go back down south." The swarm had formed up now, become a storm cloud of crying, chittering bats. They were everywhere, but Mindy wasn't afraid. Not when Lucia was so calm. "They make such beautiful music…"

"You sure know a lot about bats."

Lucia looked at Mindy. Her eyes were still tiny stars in the dark. "I love them."

Lucia drove them back home, even though Mindy said she was okay to drive. They got out and went into their houses and up to their rooms. Lucia got there first. She must have rushed. The blinds were drawn when Mindy got up there. They would be down in the morning too.

In the bathroom, Mindy finally noticed Lucia's lipstick had left a wound smudged on her mouth.

# CHAPTER 5

Everyone always left Coach Bakula's class so quickly. Mindy thought they were intimidated by his intellect. He was the one person in Millarca High who called people on their shit, whether they were the star quarterback or a Hufflepuff.

Last class of the day, the halls became a mild riot, everyone headed for their cars or the buses, but Mindy stayed in her seat. She shuffled her things into her backpack with care before slinging it onto her shoulder and approaching Bakula. He leaned back in his seat, looking at her with a big smile.

"Ah, Ms. Murphy! I saw you at the game this Saturday," Coach Bakula greeted her. "I hope you weren't planning to be there when history was made and our streak ended." He faked a sigh. "Yet another victory."

"Yeah, it was pretty boring," Mindy shot right back. "No wonder the crowd had to cheer so much. Otherwise they'd fall asleep."

Bakula put the finishing touches on some paperwork as Mindy leaned against her old desk in the front row. The past few weeks, she'd been sitting a few rows back with Lucia. Things shuffled. Sometimes they sat next to each other, sometimes there were a few people in the way…it'd been a while since Mindy had been up front. The view was getting unfamiliar.

"Now, Ms. Murphy. What can I do for you?"

"I was just—I mean—you've been around, right?"

"Oh yes." Bakula nodded. "I'm practically ancient."

"Stop. You're not that old."

He tilted his head to the side in a tiny gesture of reconciliation. "Well-regarded teen movies to the contrary, we don't have a wise old janitor to offer illumination—not to disparage Senor Navarro. Please. Ask me anything."

Mindy took a deep breath and checked the open door. The hallway was clear, the scuffle of shoes and the murmur of voices having moved down the school. "How do you know if someone—a boy—likes you?"

Bakula sorted through the papers of his desk, came up with one, and held it out to Mindy. It was the essay she'd turned in last week, a red A added to it. "They give you good grades."

"I'm serious," Mindy insisted, though she tucked the paper into her backpack with a bit of pride. "There's this friend of mine..."

"Ah," Bakula said perceptively.

"Don't 'ah' yet. It's not like that. It might be. I don't—just listen."

Bakula leaned back in his chair. Mindy sat back on the desk as well, hugging the backpack to her chest like a shield. She paused for a long moment, trying to conjure Lucia's name, or maybe a pseudonym. Nothing came. Not even the name of a boy.

"My friend," she said at last, "is really great. Really...great. S—smart, funny, pretty... good at *Mario Party*."

"Marry them," Bakula said quickly.

Mindy laughed, nearly dropping her backpack. She scooped it back onto her knee. "Sometimes it feels like we're almost the same person, you know? Like we're two halves of—I don't know. Batman. And then it's like we're a million miles apart. I just want to get on the same wavelength. That would be enough! Just *understanding* each other. I don't want a kiss—well, I do—but if we just had, like, I don't know—" Mindy waved her hands around each other, like she could say it in sign language. "I think there's a connection trying to be made, but I don't know if it's just on my end or if she's trying and just can't— maybe it's my friend, maybe they can't make a connection." Mindy rolled her neck, staring up at a dead florescent light in the ceiling. "Course, makes a connection to the ol' bf just fine..."

"Boyfriend?" Bakula asked. "Wait, are you interested in Billy Carlyle?"

"No! Wait, maybe. This is all anonymous. It could be anyone. Don't think about it. Yes, it is Billy."

Bakula tapped a long fingernail on his desk a few times. "Mm. I know it's difficult. Seeing someone you have feelings for every day, and not being able to tell them. Planning it out...seeing it in your head...then...the not knowing." He stood, pushing his chair back, his bones gracefully erecting themselves to their full height. His long legs stretching out in their gray Dickies. "You see it going off without a hitch—your love returning all your affection, your only regret that you did not ask sooner. And almost more enticingly, you see it going the other way. Raised voices. Tears. Recrimination. Hate."

Mindy shivered, winced. It was hard to picture Lucia hating her, those warm eyes gone cold and her lovely face twisted into anger. But Bakula made it sound almost inevitable.

"Have you told this…Billy, how you feel?" Bakula asked, coming around the desk at last to stand across from her.

"No. But I think—he knows. We kissed."

A thick eyebrow steepled on Bakula's face. "I see. But you don't yet know where you stand, so to speak?"

Mindy looked down. "He could never see me again, and I wouldn't be surprised. And he could be right outside that door, waiting for me, and I wouldn't… I love…him. Way too much to be in love with him. I'd only mess it up."

Mindy's breath went away as Bakula's finger caressed her chin, raising it softly until her eyes met his. "In my experience, the heart is not so willful a beast. It can be tamed. This person, the feelings you have toward them—they wouldn't exist in a vacuum. Your friend has encouraged them. Kindled them in you. They belong to him. They are his responsibility. Now that you burn for him, you mustn't let him ignore that. Go to him. Win his heart. Do not let him give up on what he himself has started. And you don't give up either."

"What if he doesn't feel the same way?"

"My dear girl, how could anyone not be in love with as sweet a young woman as you?

Mindy wasn't Lucia's only friend, of course. Lucia was friends with practically the entire school, except for the inevitable backlash minority, and they were smart enough to save it for people who were more self-evidently heinous. Her two chief cohorts were fellow cheerleaders, Pammy and Tera.

Pammy was an African-American woman so light-skinned and straight-haired that Mindy suspected most people thought she just had a great tan, while Tera was even more fashionable than Lucia—she wore berets. If she had an ounce of sense, she probably would've taken Lucia's place as queen bee.

Mindy noticed them behind her when she ducked into the restroom. Pammy and Tera's kitten heels rocked on the tile floor as they went to the sinks. Makeup kits were opened, blouses were adjusted, a little soundtrack of feminine upkeep.

"You see Mindy Murphy in class today?" Pammy asked, her voice snappy and a little musical, like a comedian warming up. Mindy cringed in her stall. "She looks like a Wal-Mart shopper sat on someone."

Tera replied in her own spacey drawl. "Yeah, heard when she eats alphabet soup, she chokes on the *D*."

"As if she even likes the *D*."

Mindy drew her legs up so they couldn't be seen under the stall. It made her feel better to pretend they couldn't notice her. The girls laughed. Maybe they'd seen her retreat. "You think she's really a dyke?" Tera asked.

"Might as well be. Not like she could get a man anyway."

The door squeaked again, and a new set of Keds popped the floor. Mindy tightened her arms around her knees. Her legs pressed into her chest like a vise.

"But do you think she's… I don't know. I wouldn't change if she were in the locker room with me."

"Me neither. I heard she kissed Becky Davis."

"Who hasn't kissed Becky Davis?"

"Sup?" Lucia called, and through the tiny side gap in the stall door, Mindy could see the glow of her at the sinks. She did nothing more than give her hair a brush in the mirror. "So, who kissed Becky Davis?"

"Mindy Murphy," Pammy said.

Mindy thought that blur of motion through the slot was Lucia shaking her head. "Bullshit."

"It's the word—"

"The word is wrong."

"Don't tell me you're buying that straight act of hers."

"Did you have breakfast today?" Lucia asked. "You know you're a jerk when you don't eat breakfast. Go get some waffles." Pammy began to protest. "WAFFLES!"

Keds on the tiles. The door squeaked twice, once when Pammy opened it and once when Tera shoved it to keep it open. Then Mindy heard the bubblegum pop of Lucia's sneakers coming to her stall. She knocked on the door. Mindy wiped at her eyes, wondering if she was crying. She wasn't. Not yet.

"Mindy, come on… If it's not Mindy, I'm going to feel really awkward."

Mindy undid the lock. Lucia opened the door. Her smile was weak, but it was genuine and reassuring nonetheless.

"These two, I cannot. So tacky I could stick them to a wall."

Mindy was silent. The wave of relief that washed over her, just hearing Lucia talking shit about her dumbass friends was so *immense*. And yet it hurt at the same time that Lucia could love her in some way or only so much, and then… There was a part missing, and without it, she was incomplete. And how, *how* could she put that on Lucia when she was probably straight, probably in love with Quentin, probably going to get married and have five kids and be the happiest fucking housewife in Texas?

None of which Lucia could see in her red-rimmed eyes. Or maybe all of it. "Are you gonna cry?"

"Not that desperate for you to kiss me again."

Lucia's eyes swiveled to the door. It was safely shut. "That's not funny."

"Sorry," Mindy said quickly, with the biological instinct of a chronic apologizer.

"It was just to make you feel better, you know? Like kissing your sister."

"You kiss your sister?"

"I don't have a sister. Get the point?"

Mindy didn't get her point.

"I've gotta go," Lucia said, turning to the sinks to wash her hands. "You should too. Class is about to start."

Mindy tried to stand, ended up putting her feet down on the tile so hard that the sound was like a rifle shot. Lucia looked over her shoulder at her, and Mindy felt six inches tall. "Lucia, I'm not gay. I mean, I might not be gay. I'm not going to gay on you. We're still friends, right?"

Lucia worked the air dryer. Her voice emerged haltingly from under the thick sound. "Yeah. We're still friends."

"I just don't want you to stop hanging out with me again. Because you think that I'm…or because you…"

"We'll hang out," Lucia said after the dryer cut off. "Soon. But Quentin's taking me out a lot, so it's hard to find time. And there isn't a lot we can do together. We don't have much in common."

"Yes we do."

Lucia looked at her and her eyes were almost fond, like she almost understood how much it hurt for Mindy to not be able to figure out what she was supposed to say—what Lucia wanted her to say. "What are you doing tomorrow?"

"Work," Mindy sighed.

"All night?"

"I get off at eight."

"Perfect. I'll call you."

"Promise?"

Lucia smiled, lifted up her hand, and crossed her fingers in front of Mindy. "Promise." She uncrossed her fingers. "Keep your phone charged, 'kay?"

"'Kay," Mindy replied dully as Lucia swept out of the room, leaving Mindy alone with the cracked mirrors.

Without Lucia in it, the Taurus felt lopsided. Off-center. Even getting a ten-dollar tip on an order of eight large pizzas did nothing for Mindy's mood. When her phone rang, it was like a drug kicking in. She nearly swerved into oncoming traffic fishing it from her car's sunglasses holder.

Lucia's smiling face on the incoming call screen, right along her own, a selfie they'd taken. Mindy answered. "You know, before you, I never took a personal call on company time."

"Company time?" Lucia scoffed. "They pay you minimum wage. They're legally not allowed to pay you less."

Not that Mindy wanted to hang up, but she didn't want the call to be all her…blubbering over Lucia. "I'm driving."

"So go slow," Lucia said. "Are you almost off work?"

"Almost." Mindy nodded, not that Lucia could see it. "I already did my deployment, I just had one last run—"

"Cool, cool. Listen, I am at a lake house on Lake Travis—"

"As opposed to a lake house on the set of *Veronica Mars*?"

"Oh, nice burn. Keep talking, bitch, see if I watch the next *Hobbit* movie with you."

"But it's gonna have the Battle of the Five Armies!" Mindy pouted, not that Lucia could see that either. Funny how just five minutes ago, that pout could've been real.

"We're partying like it's 2099. Get your ass over here, but before you leave work, use your employee discount, get us like ten pizzas, we'll pay you back. Okay? Ten. Put whatever you want on them, but I'm trusting you not to get pineapple. Or olives. Hey, do people actually order olives on their pizza, or is that just like a way of secretly asking for drugs?"

"No olives, no pineapple. Got it. Wait, are you inviting me to your party?"

"Duh."

"Well, do you have a dress for me to change into or—"

"Not that kind of party, Minz. There's a guy here in jean shorts. It's anarchy."

Mindy hid her phone for a moment as a cop car passed her by. She kept it down until she hit a red light, then raised it quickly.

"—passed out already," Lucia was saying.

"Listen, I'm not sure I wanna go to a party if it's just you high school one-percenters and none of my friends are there."

"You have friends? I'm jealous. *I'll* be there, dum-dum. And so will a bunch of cute people. We'll see if we can find you a boyfriend. Or whatever you're into. There'll be cheerleaders there. Don't you wanna kiss a cheerleader? Know you do, slutty."

Mindy was trying to parse this statement with Lucia being a cheerleader when her bestie followed up: "I'm gonna hang up now. I can't text you the address and talk at the same time. If you're not here in forty-five minutes, I'm gonna assume you pussied out."

"You know, the vagina is actually, like, superstrong as an organ."

"Goodbye, Mindy."

"Love you," Mindy said without thinking, at about the same time Lucia interjected, "No onions!"

What was wrong with her?

Twenty minutes later, she was at the store, and thanks to a quick game of phone tag, they were already taking her pizzas out of the oven when she got there. She got her money, loaded her pizzas up in the trunk, and was off, her hair blessedly free of the Dragon Pizza ball cap.

It was about a thirty minute drive to Lake Travis. The drive passed quickly. Breathlessly.

When she crossed the great gray bulk of Mansfield Dam, one of those eternal Texas sunsets had laid in. Like the sun was a quarter someone had flipped, and now it was spinning on the ground, not sure whether to come up heads or tails.

Lake Travis had changed since her girlhood visits with the folks. There was a parking garage now. And she was old enough to go to Hippie Hollow. Her actual destination, though, was a turn-off she'd never taken, circling the lake through a road lined with verdant trees to finally hit a sign that said *Private Beach*. There was a fence that looked like it could keep a rhino out, but it was swung open for the truck up ahead to jaunt along the semi-paved road. She followed it, grateful for the tour guide.

The pavement ended in a field of gritty rock. Several cars were already packed off to the side on the gray grass. The gravel led straight to the water, where it became a wind-worn boat ramp. Even with her windows mostly rolled up, Mindy could hear the party music blaring from a nearby pickup truck with roided-up speakers in its wide-bed. On the ramp, a two-engine racing boat was being filled with coolers, wake boards, and a few life vests as an afterthought. Next to it, jet skis were lowered from their trailers straight into the water.

That wasn't Mindy's destination, not according to Lucia. There was a car trail through the woods that looked like it had already been aggressively pummeled by trucks and jeeps, the tire treads well-worn in the dirt, and the tree branches and shrubs bent back and broken.

Slowing down, Mindy took the path, hoping her sedan could handle the twin ruts in the earth. What really worried her was the uncut section in the middle, with its much-abused grass. If the ruts dropped low enough for her undercarriage to hit— But the journey came off slick and smooth. Mindy went through the punched-out flora and found a nightclub had exploded in front of her. The party spilled out onto the big swath of pavement—the elite few cars there looked to be the football team's, judging from their soaped-in messages from the rally girls: *Go Dragons*, *Beat The Wolves*. But they were parked off to the sides, letting the interior serve as an open-air dance floor where a storm of young, tanned flesh stretched all the way to the sandy white beach.

The trees were sparse near the water, dead and dying, but where the water had receded there were plants as green as jade. It was an open corridor between the dance and the parking lot Mindy had come from, the two mainly separated by a thin claw of rocky land leading out to the island. Mindy remembered it from childhood summers, the spit of rock in the middle of the lake accessible only by a hard swim. The hard drought exposed the ridge that connected it to the mainland—its bones poking through the watery skin like a sick farm animal.

A girl whose breasts could double as life preservers was jumping on a trampoline, with onlookers following the balls like they were at a tennis match. Another passel of wild bikini girls rollerbladed past Mindy. She dialed Lucia just as a couple pounced onto her hood, girl on top of the boy. They made out furiously. Mindy tried flashing her lights.

"Guys, you're not making good choices!" she said, just before Lucia picked up. "Lucia?"

"Pizza!"

"Yeah. It's pizza." The couple had gotten to second base on her bumper. Mindy turned on her windshield wipers, with the fluid, but they were out of range. "Where are you?"

"I'm in the house! I'm waving at you!"

Mindy looked up. The mass of people tapered down the hill like an octopus tentacle extending from the lake house—its glass walls shining out light and pumping out music so all Mindy could see were darkly flaring shapes, the lightning inside a storm cloud. "I don't see you."

"I'm waving!"

Mindy plugged a finger into the ear that wasn't against the phone so all she heard was Lucia's voice. "No one's waving."

"Well, I'm waving. Come on, get up here."

"The next season of *16 and Pregnant* is gearing up on my car."

"What?"

"If I were driving a Transformer, it could file a sexual harassment suit."

Lucia started laughing—Mindy thought it was at something else—and the call got dropped a moment later. Bracing herself, Mindy locked all the doors and stepped out. It was like stepping out of the eye of the storm. Sound hit her in one great rush: music, dancing squeaking shoes, a thousand conversations like the hooves of a stampede, screaming boats out on the water, phones, lighters, kissing, fucking. A thousand people, all so desperate to prove they were alive that they'd cut their skin to watch themselves bleed.

Mindy wished she were one of them. But she slipped through the crowd feeling like a dog around a vacuum cleaner. This should be her idea of fun. *Was* fun. But something zigged in her head so she read cold as hot, this party as a dungeon.

With a combination of ducking, dodging, pushing, and unmeant apologies, she made her way up the impromptu obstacle course of the casa's stairway and onto the deck, where an entire wall opened into the house. It was slightly more sedate than the lower party. The music was a racing heartbeat in the background that broke against the house's glass walls, no one dancing to it, just letting it animate them like thunder on the night of Dr. Frankenstein's experiment. Everyone was smoking, drinking, kissing, chilling. Lucia was no exception.

She was sitting on a coffee table in True Religion denim shorts and a flower-print tanktop, it not covering her body so much as occasionally interrupting its flow. Top pulled up to her bra, bottoms unbuttoned and unzipped so Mindy could see the crease of her pelvis. She was a vision. Mindy almost couldn't breathe, seeing her like that. There was usually a casualness to her sexuality; it wasn't as direct as this. This was directed at her. Maybe at everyone else in the room, all her fawning worshippers, everyone who wanted to be or fuck her, but also at Mindy.

Her belly button was filled with tequila—lemon wedge in her mouth like the pin of a grenade. Quentin Morse…he of the square jaw, blond hair, blue eyes, all the necessary ingredients for an American Apparel model, or a Hitler Youth, poured salt on her breasts like it was money at a strip club, ran a trail of it down her stomach.

He knelt to her breasts, just missed them, licked the salt down to her belly button, drained the tequila like a tornado sucking up a pond, then went back up to get the lemon from her mouth. There wasn't one part of her he'd leave untouched.

*Injustice!* The word shot through Mindy's mind like the hook to a song she couldn't remember the rest of. She was hungry, starving, and someone was eating a banquet in front of her.

Lucia kissed him, let herself be kissed, it didn't matter, until she pushed him away to collect a shot glass from a nearby tray. Seeing Mindy, she grabbed another. Attention sloughed off her as she ran to Mindy; the new center of attention was someone doing a keg stand.

"Hey! Hey, hey, hey, hey, hey! Hey! Heeey!"

"Hey," Mindy replied.

"I waved at you!" Lucia said enthusiastically, demonstrating by flopping her right arm from side to side and spilling most of the tequila from the shot glass.

"I'm sure you did." Mindy tried not to sound judgmental. It was hard when she felt like such a bitch. "Are you high?"

"Noooo! No, no, Mindy, no. I'm *drunk!*" Lucia passed the empty shot glass to Mindy, carefully closing her fingers around it. "There's a difference, ya know!"

"I think you've had—" Lucia knocked back the shot glass like it was a Flintstones vitamin. "I think you've had enough and then a shot."

"I'm not drunk!"

"You literally just said you were drunk."

"You want me to do a tuck check?"

Lucia turned, scouring the crowded room until she saw Pammy Dupree grinding on a guy. "Hey! Hey, Pammy! Tuck check!"

"Tuck check!" Pammy confirmed, elbowing clear of the guy, conversations breaking up as people cleared a circle around her. Then she did a standing backflip, making a neat roll in the air before coming down on her feet.

"Cheer, cheer, show no fear!" Lucia chanted, shoving Mindy back before doing her own 360. Even the sound of her feet hitting the floor was pitch-perfect. "Hey! Hey!"

*Not this again.* Mindy said, "How many drinks have you had?"

Lucia counted on her hands. Thumb, pointer finger, middle finger—which she then turned around, aimed at Mindy. Lucia broke out into gales of laughter, clapping her hands, with riotous applause coming from a few onlookers as well. Then she straightened so fast, she might've taken an electric shock. "How many shots are in a drink?"

Mindy tried very hard to hold in a sigh. "You told me you'd pay for the pizzas?"

"Huh? Yeah, yeah, *currency*." Lucia clenched her hands together, which seemed to help her stay upright. "I put it—I put it—I didn't want it to get lost, so I put it—microwave!"

Lucia shoved the other empty shot glass into Mindy's hands, then pulled her by the wrist into the kitchen. Like the other room, it was a tile floor with thick walls and little else. That room had some furniture, this room had metal appliances, but just a few. At the exterior wall, a guy was mooning the dance party below. Only from the way he was resting on his shoulders and knees with his ass in the air, he'd passed out before the moon could wane.

Giggling her little heart out, Lucia opened the microwave to reveal an upside-down cowboy hat, stuffed to the brim with dollar bills. Some ancient and wrinkled, some so new Mindy was surprised they didn't have Hillary Clinton's portrait on them.

"Here! Here, here, here!" Lucia said excitedly, proudly presenting the hat to Mindy. With a huffed breath, Mindy took it, set it on the counter, and started counting it out.

No sooner had she turned her back on Lucia then she came up and tickled her ribs. Mindy stopped trying to hold in her sigh.

"Would you quit it?" Mindy demanded. "God…"

"It's a party, Minz. Lighten up." Sobering up, or doing a good impression of it, Lucia heaved herself onto the kitchen island to play with a dangling set of cooking knives. She chuckled to herself, then reached out to prod Mindy with her toe. "Sorry, my friends are poor. And you can kick in the last five yourself, right? You're eating too!"

"It's fine. I'm fine. We're all…" Putting a pause on the count, Mindy turned over the hat. A small avalanche of coins poured out onto the counter. Some quarters. Mostly not. "Yup." She gave up on the counting, turning to Lucia, who preened. "So where the hell are we, anyway? We're not just breaking into someone's house cuz they're gone for the weekend, are we? Because this is Texas. You get shot for that."

Lucia waved her hand like she was bitch-slapping that idea away. "It's Coach's vacation home. He lets the football team use it if they make a three-point shot with the puck or whatever. Oh!" She slapped her forehead. "That's why I wanted you up here! Rules! Like, don't break shit."

Mindy had turned away from her to count out the money. "Really? I thought he was cool."

"You can't break shit!" Lucia insisted, missing her sarcasm. "And food stays in the house so you can put the dishes in the sink and the trash in the…the… the…"

"Trash cans?"

"That! Oh, and don't go into the basement."

"Why, what's down there?"

"I assume porn."

With a noise that made Mindy jump, Quentin careened into the room. The front of his shirt was stained and stunk of beer. After a kiss somewhere nonspecific on Lucia's head, he went to the stainless steel sink to wash himself off. The process involved stripping his shirt off and watering it under the tap. "Hey, L, where's the pizza? Beef's getting hungry."

"Mindy's got it," Lucia promised him. She clapped her hands. "Mindy! Keys! Pizza's getting cold."

A bit nonplussed, Mindy slid her keys down the counter to Lucia. Lucia collected them and bobbed into the other room. Through the glass wall that separated the kitchen from the dining room, Mindy saw Lucia be picked up by a quartet of beefy quarterbacks and borne outside like the priestess of some native religion.

Behind her, Quentin twisted the water out of his shirt. "So hey, I hear you're bi-curious or whatever."

It was amazing how you could be a person with thoughts and dreams and favorite Phish songs one moment, then the next, you were an animal caught in the headlights.

"Who told you that?" Mindy asked. Her voice sounded very steady to her.

"Hell, you know—saw it next to a dick on the bathroom wall. So, how about it?"

"How about what?"

"You have a…" Quentin lost his train of thought. He was soused, but able to hold his liquor. Out of the corner of her eye, Mindy could see him wincing in blitzed thought. He smiled as he got it, "A lick-her license?"

"No." Mindy turned around, faced him, dared him to say differently. The setting sun glinted off the cooking knives and into her eyes as she turned. *No more than your girlfriend does.*

She stared at him. He was so handsome, so smiley—muscles. Everything a girl could want in a guy. He twisted a little more water from his shirt into the sink. "That's cool. If you were, you know… A lot of these girls, they get drunk, they want some attention, you could probably get to second base. They're not, uh, lezbos—is that offensive?"

"I wouldn't know."

Quentin's train was already barreling forward. "They're straight, but, you know. Wouldn't surprise me if that rumor about you got started by a real Lebanese, *lesbian,*" he corrected himself. "Trying to turn you, maybe. You hear about that? Lesbians trying to convert straight girls. Like Mormons."

"Just like Mormons," Mindy said. She could feel a bead of sweat dragging between her shoulder blades.

"But I get it. You girls with the push-up bras and the dresses and the high heels—normal girls, I mean. Like Lucia. Of course, if you're into chicks, you'd be into that. But some of these lezbos," He hit the word harsh, knowingly. *Offensive.* "They dress up with the suits, the business suits…short haircuts… shave their heads. That I don't get. If you're into women, how come you go for women that look like men?"

"I guess," Mindy's mouth was dry, "they're attracted to the lady and not to her hair."

"Yeah, yeah." He nodded, almost to himself.

"Hey, what's the Wi-Fi password for this place?" Mindy asked him.

That's when Lucia and her jocks returned like a Viking longboat laden with spoils of war, piled high with pizza boxes. Lucia wrestled around a small mountain of breadsticks.

As soon as they were inside, they were set upon by the party mob. They couldn't defend a single slice. Boxes were ripped open—pulled apart like a black guy on *The Walking Dead*—a veggie pizza fell to the floor and was trampled underfoot. Mindy winced. What a senseless waste of mozzarella. Between the mob and the floor, Lucia lost her breadsticks, but she was able to beat everyone back with one last, steaming-hot box. She got to Mindy, shadowed by an orgy of finger-licking, lip-smacking Italian cooking. "Hey! Ask me how many drinks I've had!"

"No!" Mindy replied, shouting to be heard over the music, which had cranked up another level of THX.

Lucia gave her the finger. "This many!" Then she laughed like she'd been telling the joke to a split personality.

"That's so funny, I would hate to disrespect it by laughing."

"C'mon, I rescued us a pizza. I don't think it has any olives on it. It'd better not!"

"Lucia, can I talk to you? Alone?"

Lucia took Mindy's arm, nearly fumbling the pizza box before Mindy steadied it for her. "Come along, come along, let's get me alone."

# CHAPTER 6

They swam upstream against the tide of partygoers who smelled pizza like blood in the water. Bodies juddered against them like moving speed bumps. Mindy was jostled and rocked, nearly carried away with the mob, and only Lucia's grip on her hand kept her from disappearing downstream. She felt the edge of a hand skating over her breast. Impossible to tell if it was deliberate or accidental. She looked around for the culprit, but in the dark and the music and the pounding lights there were more masks than faces.

Lucia pulled her through a door, seemingly chosen at random, and Mindy nearly fell. They weren't on level ground anymore but on a staircase enclosed by solid concrete walls. The stairs, made up of faded cement, shot down a good thirty feet, so far that the light from the bulb over the door became just a lazy stirring at dark outlines near the bottom.

Lucia steadied her, then as one they started down the steps, the music fading behind them, becoming a dull cacophony filtered through the walls and then trapped between the concrete. It now sounded slowed down, drawn out, strangely organic, like they were in the belly of the beast hearing the workings of its organs. Mindy followed Lucia down into the dark, grateful for the rest.

Something hissed over her shoulder. Mindy jumped and dropped the pizza box before seeing it was the light bulb Lucia had turned on at the bottom of the steps. It came on flickering before the light solidified. There was no basement, just a few feet of floor that ran headlong into a door that took up the entire wall. A big, metal, and padlocked door. It reminded Mindy of the door to the cooler at her restaurant. Except for the padlock.

Lucia picked up the pizza box, turning it over, and opened the top to reveal the Freddy Krueger of pizzas. But it was still edible. She took a piece and playfully fed it to Mindy, like a bride smearing her groom with cake at their wedding. The casual thought set off a landmine in Mindy's head. Thoughts of

Lucia were a minefield now. Anything was likely to set off an explosion in her heart.

"You look nice," Mindy said helplessly, sitting on the last cold concrete step with her best friend.

Lucia laughed through a mouthful of feta cheese. "I look like a Russian stripper. I'm not built for classy. Now you—if you shopped anywhere other than Goodwill, *you* would look nice." She swallowed, went for another bite, didn't. Frowned instead. "Why don't you ever wear something that shows off your legs? Do you have hideous scars or something? Prison tattoos from juvie hall, even?"

Mindy rolled up one of her pant legs. And she'd even shaved.

Lucia pouted. "No butterfly tattoo on your ankle? Guess that wild-child reputation of yours is all bullshit."

Mindy smiled ruefully. It was so easy sometimes. Sometimes she could almost resent how easy Lucia made it. She ate her deformed pizza slice and let the bass upstairs filter down the cement and settle into her bones. Lucia, buzzed, maybe even a little high, collected spaghetti strands of stretching cheese with her manicured nails when they tried to escape her slice and licked them up. Offered one to Mindy, who acted more grossed-out than she was.

"I'm gonna take you upstairs and I'm gonna dance with you." Lucia picked pepperoni off her pizza to eat individually. "People just look hotter dancing with me, it's a fact. We'll find you a girlfriend. Or a boyfriend. Or a vibrator."

"Actually, could we just go home?"

"Go home?" Lucia sneered a little saying it, like it was something she'd translated for French class.

"Yeah. We've had some laughs, made some new friends, had some pizza. Once we're finished, how about I take you home?"

"What? No! The party's just started! Sun hasn't even set!"

"Yeah, but it's late, and we have school tomorrow, and you're drunk."

"No I'm not," Lucia replied, smiling guiltily.

"You're drunk," Mindy insisted, her voice taking on a teasing lilt almost against her will, "so I will drive you home and get you into bed so you can sleep it off. Okay? Before something bad happens?"

"What's gonna bad happen?" Lucia demanded, her mouth briefly full of marbles. She rolled her eyes at herself and took a huge bite of crust.

"Police? Police could come." Mindy followed suit with Lucia's gaffe. "Police find underage drinking. Bad."

"Yes, they're going to arrest the whole football team. Get real. Get *real*, Mindy. Stay here and have fun with me."

Mindy brushed her greasy fingers on her pants. She'd lost her appetite. "I'm in my work clothes. I can't, you know, wreck 'em."

"So take 'em off. What are you wearing under that monkey suit, anyway?" Lucia got a finger in the collar of Mindy's shirt and pulled it open, looking in at Mindy's camisole. "Not bad."

She swung away before Mindy could push her, laughing, against and the railing.

"I'm serious, El. I really have a bad feeling about this and I really wanna go and you should come with me. Just come with me, Lucia. We can watch a horror movie or a Britney Spears documentary, whatever you want. Just at home. Let's just go home."

Lucia leaned forward. Wavering. Her smile a little lost on her face. "You want me all to yourself."

Mindy was about to say no—figure out how much of that was a lie—when something hit the basement door. The other side of the door.

They looked at the dull metal, scuffed and scratched in the bare bulb's harsh light.

"What was that?" Mindy asked, her own voice louder than the impact had been. Reassuring. The noise had been so sudden; now its absence lingered, filling the air with electricity.

Lucia burst out giggling. "Coach's sex slave! Didn't I tell you about him? We've all met him, the one day a month Bakula lets 'im out for a haircut."

"That's not funny."

"Some poor QB wannabe who was too cute for his own good! He wears these tight little leather shorts and his nipples are pierced; taught me how to give a blowjob."

"It's not funny!" Mindy insisted, hating how Lucia was taking advantage of her bad vibe to scare her. She wrapped her arms around herself and Lucia laughed, a little ruefully, taking Mindy's hand and shaking it a little in apology.

"It's just the house. It's an old fucking house. Like, it has a furnace and that makes noise?" Lucia shrugged in confusion. "No one's in there. I'll prove it."

She raised her hand, fingers curled into a fist.

"Lucia, don't!"

Lucia rolled her eyes at her. She tapped out a little pattern. "Shave and a haircut—my tits." Then she waited a long moment, her hand cupped to her ear.

The door was silent and insoluble; the monolith from *2001: A Space Odyssey*. Mindy stared at it, seeing her foggy reflection in the old metal, and thought that it was just a door. Just a stupid door. Probably nothing on the other side but Bakula's man-cave.

"Two bits," she said at last.

"Hmm?"

"It's 'shave and a haircut—two bits.' Like, you pay two bits for the shave and the haircut."

"What's two bits, like, Canadian money? It's my tits, because it's a guy. He's getting a haircut and his chest shaved. Why would a guy pay someone to shave his face? What, is it a kinky thing?"

The hum of the light bulb suddenly coarsened, hissed, clawed at their ears. In half a second, the bulb popped with a flash that left lingering colors in the new darkness—little creatures fluttering in front of Mindy's face. It'd burnt out.

"That's not funny," Lucia said.

"Up the stairs. We'll just—work our way back, one step at a time."

Lucia said nothing, but when Mindy grabbed her hand, Lucia squeezed it. They took a step backward up the first stair. They kept facing the darkness like it was a rabid dog, and it grew stronger as they went up another step, another, another, fumbling with cold concrete ledges that were never as wide as they seemed they should be.

Lucia's thumb rubbed at Mindy's knuckles. They'd gone up eight steps. The dark was *thick* now, thick as honey. Anything could be in there. The door could've opened, even. Mindy imagined someone at the foot of the stairs, looking up. He'd be able to see them, the working light bulb at their backs, but they wouldn't be able to see him.

Mindy blinked. Her eyelids slid closed and open, like they did a million times a day, and it was like *he* had jumped forward while her eyes were shut, then back when they opened again. So she only caught his face as it was sinking back into the dark.

*It's your imagination.* She muttered it to herself. *Just your imagination, your imagination*—"Did you see that?" she asked out loud, and Lucia *crushed* her hand, startled by her voice.

"What?"

"I saw someone down there. He's watching us."

"Shut up."

"Didn't you see him?"

Lucia growled. Outright *growled*. "This is retarded, okay? You keep looking down, I'm gonna look up, and I'm gonna walk us right outta here, okay?"

"Lucia…"

Lucia looked at her. Really looked at her. "Just a fucking light bulb," she said, and turned to look up the stairs.

She screamed.

Mindy screamed, the sound shooting out of Lucia and into her, and she nearly lost her balance as she backed up the stairs, then fell on her ass, hitting a cement edge as cold and hard as a straight razor. Lucia pulled at her arm, and finally she looked away from the blown light bulb to see Quentin at the head of the stairs, a longneck in his dangling hand.

Lucia appeared to bite down on her Marion Crane scream. "You fucking asshole! Don't sneak up on people!"

"Sorry. That was about the funniest thing I've ever seen."

While Mindy gathered herself, Lucia stared at him like they were two gunslingers about to draw. "It's not funny! Mindy was really scared! She saw something!"

"I wasn't *scared*, I was cautious."

Quentin was already sliding his phone out of his pocket. He turned the bright screen on full blast and aimed it down the stairs.

Nothing but a closed door and a half-eaten box of pizza.

"I think it has anchovies on it," he said, reaching out to tickle Lucia as she climbed to him. "Spooky!"

"Fucking asshole," she repeated under her breath. "You wanna go get it?"

"No, I'm busy. The bonfire's about to start. You coming?"

"Yeah. Sure. Just let me get a beer first."

"Alright. I'll be looking for you." And Quentin disappeared through the door, letting in the sound of a milling crowd and a new track on the party mix. Mindy recognized it, just barely. A remix of an old band called Bauhaus. "Bela Legosi's Dead."

With the house emptying out, the scratchy goth noise stirred and stuttered with authority. It drove them out with the stream of people taking shelter from the noise out in the night air where the faded music pulsed and throbbed almost sexually. Mindy was buffeted by the crowd into Billy Carlyle, who held a big cardboard box full of hardcovers in his meaty hands.

"Take two," he said, canting the open-topped box their way.

"And call you in the morning?" Mindy quipped as Lucia obediently took two copies.

"What?" He hadn't heard her over the music.

"Doctor joke."

"What?" Then, not caring, he moved along to hand out more copies of the book.

Lucia handed her one. They were both copies of the same book: *Guilty As Charged: How A High School Football Coach Made A Fiefdom Out Of A Small West Texas Town* by Benson Mears.

"'Fiefdom'—there's a word you don't see in titles very often," Lucia thought out loud. "Except maybe for Daniel Craig movies."

Mindy paged through the book. She couldn't speak to its quality, but its length was evident. "So why are we getting books? Is that just how men flirt now?"

"You would love that."

"Yes, I would. I'd have to recommit to straightness." As Mindy sniffed the new-book smell, Lucia put an arm around her waist and guided her the rest of the way out to the back patio. "You remember three years back, that newspaper guy went around town asking about our football program?"

"Must not've talked to me—wait, no, I remember getting a permission slip asking if it was okay to interview me around my English teacher."

"Yeah, that was this guy." Lucia held up the back cover, tapping the author's photo. "He was supposed to be writing, you know, about how we won at State and brought home two dozen rings. Instead, he did a hatchet-job. He went in on the town's renaming, the new stadium…"

"I never heard of it."

"Yeah, the Town Council's putting their head in the sand, but to everyone else—I mean, he said Coach Bakula had sex with an eighteen-year-old at his old job in Dakota."

Mindy's eyebrows darted up. She didn't know what to say. "I was born in Dakota." Probably not that.

"Yeah, well, it's total muckraking bullshit. Nowadays the girl said it never happened, public hysteria or something, but you think this douche-canoe Mears puts *that* in his book?"

"Yes?" Mindy tried.

"No! Keep up, Minz. That prick fucked us over. Made us look like a bunch of… Lifetime movie…" Lucia flicked a middle finger at the air. "Who do I hate? Him, Satan, Adolf Hitler, Justin Bieber, that janitor who keeps telling me my shorts are too short, and Justin Bieber. Those five people. I have a literal handful of people I hate, and Benson Mears makes the list."

"Well, don't you hate, like, Stalin?"

"Yeah, obviously, but he's friends with Hitler, so I hate him automatically. Keep up. If I hate someone, my hate extends to people who refuse to disassociate themselves from my enemy, even if I've tweeted about it. I mean, I just can't with Selena Gomez anymore. Can. Not."

"You hate Selena Gomez just because she dated Hitler?"

They came out to the backyard, where the forest had been cleared back for maybe a hundred yards, making room for not only a standing swimming pool but a barbecue pit. Now, the gray pit only held a Jenga tower of logs, twenty feet tall and festooned with paper dolls like a Bizarro World Christmas tree. Squinting, Mindy saw that all the dolls were cutouts of Benson Mears from magazines and newspapers. "Okay, so we're making our own *Wicker Man* movie. No bear suits, so we're off to a good start…"

Lucia shushed her. Quentin was in front of the pyre, wearing his letterman jacket and holding a torch. The torchlight turned him red.

"Kill the music!" he shouted up to the house, and a moment later it went dead. A moment after that, the music from stereos down on the beach died as well. The new silence was like going deaf. You knew you *should* hear something, but there was nothing to hear.

"Three years ago!" Quentin started in a loud, team captain voice. "This town opened its doors to a man. We let him ask us questions and get to know us because we thought he was our friend. And that all he wanted was to tell people a little about our nice town. But that isn't what Benson Mears wanted. It isn't what he wanted at all. He wanted to humiliate us. He wanted to take our power. And most of all, he wanted to hurt the Coach!"

There was a rabidness to the crowd as he spoke—feet shuffling, weight shifting from side to side, jaws and fists clenching. Mindy felt it on all sides. Even Lucia stared with an anger so Mindy barely recognized in her.

"The Coach made this town great. He gave us something to be proud. Sugar Bowl three times, championships twice. He made all of you winners. He made the Dragons your defenders. And this fucker—Benson Mears—he wants to take all that away. With his lies. With his bullshit. So you enjoy the party. You drink your beer and you dance and you do whatever. That's what you're here for. But don't you forget all the Coach has done for us, and let's not let Benson Mears forget how the Dragons feel about 'im!"

Cheers exploded the night like fireworks as he touched the torch to the pyre. It went up fast, kerosene taking the flame and growing it into a bonfire so hot and so bright it hurt Mindy to look at it. She saw the Dragons around the fire, featureless shapes in their lettermans and jerseys. Copies of the Mears book had been passed out to everyone, and all at once, they threw them into the fire.

Book spines cracked like bone, lamination hissed, covers burst into sparks that bum-rushed the crowd in little stinging clusters. Pages curled and came loose, flying up as if trying to escape before they curled up into dead, ashen bugs.

The crowd pressed in, throwing books at the fire like stones at a martyr. Mindy was pushed forward by the crowd. She dug her heels in, letting them jostle her, clutching her copy to her chest as the mob swarmed by her. Lucia flowed in front of her like a shadow, not fully caught by the mob but stirred by the wake of its passage.

"Lucia, no."

Lucia turned around, her copy looking leaden around limp fingers. "Don't embarrass me."

"Don't embarrass *me*. I'm not burning a book."

"Mindy, this guy—"

"*No.*"

Either Mindy meant that much to her or Lucia wasn't crazy about the idea in the first place. Radiating frustration in all directions, she relented and tossed the book to the ground, where a passing foot kicked it to the outskirts of the crowd.

"Happy?"

Mindy was not, even in the slightest. She grabbed Lucia's hand and pulled, not caring if she ripped her arm out of the socket. Lucia, barely complaining, trailed her as she pushed her way through the glow of the bonfire and the people standing around like statues entranced by it. Until they were in the woods alongside the house, the trees sheltering them from the noise and the light. The darkness was cool and calming, and the lapping of the lake water below was easy to hold onto, like a pulse.

They had a great view of the lake to the islands, all with their own mini-parties. The sunset glinted off the empty beer cans floating in Lake Travis. On the nearest boat, a conversation drifted up about someone's first beer bong. The inner tubers were beginning to come in as the water chilled, some abandoning their flotation devices like little acne outbreaks on the face of the lake.

They sat on a rocky crag. Lucia coughed. "Wanna see a set video for the new *Frankenstein* movie?"

"No."

"That's exactly what Hitler said when I asked him."

Mindy let herself get drawn out of her funk. It was easy with Lucia, like going to bed after you'd taken Nyquil. "Hitler has good taste in movies." And the sun set. Big and powerful, the clouds one kind of jewel, the sky another, the water another.

As far away as it was, as small and tiny as its part was, it seemed like it was theirs. Lucia sagged against her, Mindy's arm around her waist, and they sat with dead leaves spun around them like party favors as they watched the color drip out of the world. The night turned cold, and the music came back on louder and more unbearable than ever.

"Feels like it's not gonna come back up," Lucia said. When Mindy looked at her, her eyes were darker than the night. "You're not having fun."

Mindy said nothing.

"I have a prescription for that."

It was in her sock. A little envelope, like the ones that held fake rattlesnake eggs that scared Mindy when she was a little girl. Inside this was two little plastic baggies; inside those were two speckled-blue gelcap pills. Mindy didn't say that they looked like robin's eggs to her.

"Gimme your hands," Lucia said, her voice slurring a little. She corrected herself, sounding like an honor student. "Give me your hands."

Mindy held them out. Lucia put a baggie in each one, then pushed Mindy's hands behind her own back, leaning into a little embrace in the process. She rested her chin on Mindy's head.

"Would you trust me if I told you which one to take?" she asked.

"Yes," Mindy said, into the hollow of Lucia's delicate throat.

"Maybe I don't trust me. Pass them around, Minz. Mix 'em up."

Mindy switched the baggies in her hands. Thought better of it and switched them back. "What's in them?"

"One's poison…and the other's the antidote."

"You're not making any sense, babe."

"I don't wanna make sense." Lucia smiled. "Hold out your hands."

Mindy brought her hands in front of her, closed, palms down—classic one or the other. Chicken or the egg, life or death, live or Memorex. Lucia tapped her right hand, and like she'd seen in all the movies, Mindy spun it around and opened it up. Quick as a thief, Lucia snatched up the baggie, opened it, and dumped the pill into her mouth. She dry-swallowed.

"Your turn."

Under Lucia's expectant eyes, Mindy opened up the little elastic band on the baggie. She pinched the bottom of it between her fingers and wiggled the pill out onto her palm. It sat there like a pet that refused to do a trick. She met Lucia's eyes, heavy on her, and saw her irises blooming. Lucia grinned, seeing how Mindy wanted it.

"What's in it?" Mindy asked desperately.

Lucia picked the pill up between slender fingers meant to paint masterpieces, play sonatas. "Trust." She brought the pill up and Mindy felt it on her chapped lips, brushing the tiny cracks and crags. She parted her lips, and Lucia slipped it inside her with two fingers. Mindy tasted Lucia's nail varnish—coppery. Lucia took her fingers away slowly and didn't drop her hand until Mindy gulped like a cartoon character. It took a moment for Mindy to do it. She thought of spitting it out in her hand and telling Lucia she couldn't. Or waiting for Lucia to step out and then making herself vomit it up. She'd never actually made herself throw up, but how hard could it be if supermodels did it?

But Lucia was trusting her to do this with her, and she trusted Lucia that it would be fun, just like the football game, just like riding shotgun delivering pizza. Just like the kiss.

"Do you feel any different?" Lucia asked, with her supernova eyes.

"No."

"That's good. Means it's working. It doesn't change you, you know. It changes the world. Haven't you ever wanted to change the world?" Lucia looked at her forefinger, her middle finger, the tips wet with Mindy's saliva. She brought them to her mouth and tasted them. "C'mon. Let's dance."

Mindy nodded.

"I just wanna dance," Lucia said. "I just wanna dance with you."

Her hand was bright white. It swam in the darkness like a little piece of the moon just for Mindy. How did you talk to the moon? How did you say no to it?

A few tiki torches were scattered about the picnic area, and the light from Bakula's house shone bright, but real illumination only came from the cloud-strewn moon. The dancers going at it on and around the bolted-down tables were smeared with Day-Glo gels in a variety of styles, a dance floor of art projects. One person had cyberlocks—synthetic dreadlocks that glowed with LED lights. In the near-total darkness, they were anonymous bodies identifiable only by the radioactive paint on their bare skin. They reminded her of Dona Dolorosa paintings, *Dia de Muertos*. Spirits of the dead, given life for a day. Or night.

Mindy held tight to Lucia, only identifiable by how unidentifiable she was. No Day-Glo, no cyberlocks. The only thing on her that shone was her teeth when she smiled. In the ultraviolet light someone had set up, they glowed with florescent toothpaste. A Cheshire cat smiled grafted to her best friend.

"Follow my lead," was Lucia's only advice.

The flickering torchlight and the blasts of illumination from the house made the world shift in and out of darkness. Mindy was stepping out of her body, taking smoke breaks from her head. She saw herself step up behind Lucia and was there suddenly, right behind her, molding to her body like a shadow to a statue.

A beat, a moment of light and dark, a note of music, and Lucia was behind her. Mindy stood still now, like a mouse hypnotized by a cobra. Suddenly she felt Lucia's hands sliding around her hips, bringing her to life, resting on her stomach. Lucia's hips swayed. Mindy felt them all the way in that firm grip. The hands sashayed under her shirt, pulling her just a little closer, encouraging her to move just a little with Lucia's rhythm.

Mindy wondered if the pill had kicked in. Was it supposed to mellow her out? She didn't feel mellow. She felt like there was snow drifting down inside her body, blown back up by a hard wind, a storm wind, blown out to her arms and hands, fingers, legs, toes, sweaty palms…

But it didn't feel bad. Lucia didn't feel bad either. Her body was warm down Mindy's back, the snow melting against their merging skin, tingling, dripping wet—Lucia dragged her lips across Mindy's neck and it *burnt,* a hot shaft of summer sun in the middle of her winter.

Lucia's hand on her arm turned her, or maybe steadied her as she turned in Lucia's arms. Her own arms were shot through with snow, prickled with icicles. She lifted them, put them around Lucia's neck for warmth. "I trust you," she said. They were swaying, holding onto each other—feeling Lucia's breasts press to her own, legs brushing together… Lucia's foot stepping on Mindy's. Mindy yowled a little and fell further into Lucia's arms.

The world was soft and rounded, and its chill was a kind of warmth, the dark colors soothing, letting her eyes relax…all the darkness bled into itself, but Lucia was untouched… Mindy could see her inner light…her features sharp and distinguished in a world without edges… Everyone else was just a shadow, a worshipful fawning around Lucia. Because Lucia was a goddess. She kept it hidden from everyone else, but she let Mindy see. And Mindy was a goddess too.

"I wish you were a boy," Lucia whispered, a sweet little glacier crashing into Mindy's ear. "If you were a boy, I'd date you so hard."

Snow melted. Then it froze again, black ice that covered the street like a cancer, killed you cuz you couldn't see it. "If I were a boy…" Mindy croaked, "what makes you think I couldn't do better?"

Lucia's voice was so sweet to listen to. "If *I* were a boy, I'd be a total slut… sleep with a bunch of other dudes. Pick 'em up at gay bars and on…they have an app. What's the name of their app?" Her lips brushed against Mindy's ear. "No one cares about you sleeping around when you're a gay dude."

The thing about ice was, if you pushed it to a wound, it made the pain numb.

Lucia pushed Mindy away. Black ice on the dancing shadows. Mindy saw Lucia's golden arms raised to the moon, followed them down to the rest of Lucia arching her back like a cat—the hands came down, moving over her breasts, her belly, back up to cup and squeeze her flesh.

Mindy just stared—watched Lucia's bare belly ripple, undulate… She wanted Lucia back. She moved for her, hugged her, tackled her, and Lucia screamed with laugher and Mindy screamed back, and they were falling off the rocks, into the water.

Drowning was the most peaceful way to die. Mindy remembered hearing that as she and Lucia sunk down, in their billowing funeral shrouds, staring at each other. It was cold—instant numbness—but there was a transcendence in the sudden shock of the water on them. It brought clarity. It was very Zen.

Lucia swam closer, golden hair billowing all around both of their faces like sunken treasure. Mindy hadn't noticed before how blue her eyes were. Then Lucia's lips jumped to hers, burnt through the cold, melted into her skin like a brand. Hot, but a good hot, born from lax warmth—sparks jumping off a fireplace. Mindy felt a core of molten heat inside her, like a living flame in her mouth strummed by Lucia's tongue. Like Lucia had more control of it than she did.

Then Lucia was swimming away, long legs flashing in the moonlight—so beautiful, clothed in the moonlight shining over the rippling water. Mindy followed her down a tooth of land that bit into the lake with bare, stark stone. The cold and the water sobered her. She felt almost entirely back in her own head when she came to the end of the rock, where a solitary tree grew out between two boulders. Its black leaves formed a rune of starless black in the sky.

Mindy felt sand under her feet, wet satin, then a fallen log on the lakebed. It was overrun with slimy moss. Mindy stood on it, slippery, precarious, waves blowing on her with puffed cheeks. Trying to knock her off. In the distance, a speedboat and water-skier sawed through the middle of Lake Travis, making the water choppier.

Lucia clung to the lip of a boulder protruding from the water, hanging from it as the waves stirred her. "I'm sorry. I shouldn't have done that. You're really easy to kiss." She didn't sound sorry.

Mindy fell off the log, got back on as the speedboat circled in the distance. "Why not? That's what people do when they love each other."

# CHAPTER 7

Lucia kicked off the rock to swim to Mindy. "Okay, how many pills did you take? One, right? Did you do some pre-gaming?"

Mindy shook her head and nearly toppled off the log. "I wanna talk. I want to talk. I'm not pressuring you, I don't want you to come out of the closet. I just want you to break up with Quentin. We don't have to be official, I just want us to be…real." Mindy liked the sound of that. Who was it that said *cellar door* was the most beautiful phrase in the English language? A wrong person. She giggled, teetered off the log on one leg, and regained her balance.

Lucia was breathing hard. Mindy could see the little ripples in the water under her nose. "We are real, Minz. We're really—good—friends." It was almost in apology. She climbed onto the log as it shifted from side to side. "Other girls don't do this."

"And I don't do this with other girls," Mindy protested.

Lucia shrugged. "Maybe I do. I do it with Quentin. What do you even want, a celebrity couple name like Bennifer?"

"We kissed, El. We kissed just now, and we kissed before and…" Mindy paused. It seemed like there was something she was supposed to say, some spell she was supposed to cast, and she was doing it wrong. She was messing it up. "It was a good kiss."

Lucia shrugged again, something exaggerated in the gesture, a kind of pantomime. "It was fun. We have fun. That doesn't mean we're in a *relationship*. I'm not a—not even gay. I'm just weird!" Lucia laughed it off.

Mindy felt just how cold the water was again. She'd gotten used to it, but—"You think I'm weird?"

"No, no!" The log wobbled, but Lucia kept absolutely still. "*I'm* weird. You're just confused."

The log kept shifting, but Mindy stopped trying to stay on top of it. She just floated. "Confused?"

The log settled. Lucia was balanced. "Yeah. I mean, you've *gotta* be confused. You don't know if you're gay or straight or bi or *what*. And here I am, just trying to be your friend, and you think we're in love. I'm not even gay. I have a boyfriend."

"Some boyfriend." Mindy struck the water in front of Lucia, splashing them both. "Some boyfriend! He cheats on you! He hurts you! Why do you want someone who hurts you and not someone who loves you?"

Lucia kicked away the log; Mindy felt it roll by her leg. "I don't know, because I'm not a dyke, okay? God!"

In the distance, the speedboat cut in front of an anchored yacht, kicking sea spray into its spectral white hull, proving it wasn't a distorted reflection of the moon.

Lucia straightened her mess of damp hair. "I'm sorry—I don't think there's anything *wrong* with…"

"Fuck you, Lucinda." Mindy walked past Lucia to pull herself out of the water. She got a good look at Lucia as she went by. A memory of her. "You kissed me. I was your friend before that. I wasn't after. And I'm not now."

In the night air, she was so cold it was like walking through goosebumps. She had to get her stuff and her money and get to her car and drive home and get *gas*, even. An eternity didn't seem long enough to do all that. She was so cold.

Mindy got back into the water with tons of rock separating her from Lucia. She held her head under the water. That way, she didn't have to know if she was crying or not.

Finally, when her lungs ached and her molten eyes had cooled, she rose through the veil of her drifting hair and drunk in air. Her thoughts were not her own; she felt tuned to a stranger's radio station. She saw herself kiss Lucia, over and over again, from outside her body. Such a simple thing. A small thing. Just the touch of her lips. But she could remember the touch, the explosion of light that had erased night from her world, like it had left her red-hot and she still hadn't cooled.

She pushed away from the rock, swimming a few strokes out, then letting herself drift on her back. Her body felt numb, alien. How could it just give itself to Lucia, let her *change* it, *rule* it, leaving her brain behind? How could her heart be on fire while Lucia's was stone-cold? Hadn't they met? How could Lucia feel nothing and Mindy feel everything? How could they be oil and water?

Something touched her back. She floundered herself up, putting her feet down into the depths, kicking to keep afloat. She'd drifted out from the shore several yards and, what, brushed against an underwater rock? Mindy looked around for it automatically, but the water was black as ink; the moon had gone behind some of the clouds that mired the sky. She dipped her head underwater. She saw nothing around her. Felt something tap her shoulder, like a person was trying to get her attention in a crowded room.

Her mouth opened, ejected her breath in a swarm of bubbles that flew around her face like bees. She came up spluttering, swallowing some water as she tried to gulp oxygen, just making her cough and choke in the night air. The sound of her hacking traveled over the surface of the water, hit her own ears like weird echoes. There was no one around to hear it. She was far from the party; the speedboat had gone back to shore.

She was about to start for shore herself when the moon came out, giving her some merciful light. She saw a shape like an oil slick on the water in front of her. It flashed silver in the light. She ran her hand through it unthinkingly. Something warm clung to her skin. She looked closely at her palm. Her mind wasn't racing yet; she spent a moment wondering *what kind of water* was on her hand before realizing. It was blood.

Bubbles came up all around her, suddenly, out of nowhere. It was like being in the middle of a boiling pot. She kicked away from them instinctively, backward, further away from shore. A cloud drifted in front of the moon; the light went off and back on like someone was flipping a switch. Mindy felt warmth all over her, tickling her like little fingers. She was swimming through blood.

Something popped to the surface in front of her. It took her a moment to recognize it as a dog. This wasn't because she was complacent. It was because a dog is hard to recognize from only one half.

She turned and swam, cutting through the water, slashing it with her hands and feet. She would not go back to shore. She would not go anywhere near whatever had done that. The opposite shore was miles away, but the glowing white yacht was close by, maybe fifty feet.

She felt it brush her foot. It was not seaweed. It was not a rock. It had *fingers*.

She screamed as she swam, shouted for help, cried for it even as she forced water into her mouth with her speed. The world screamed back. She heard all at once the loud music, the cheering, all the sounds of the world going on without her. All at once the thought hit her: if she died, the world would barely notice. Lucia would barely notice.

The yacht was just ahead of her; adrenaline had slid the time right past her. She saw a ladder on its stern. The white hull filled her vision; reflecting the moonlight. Mindy spared a look back just before she reached the ladder. There was nothing she could make out in those waters, but for a moment, she thought she saw a spot of light reflect red instead of white. Twice. She knew her mind was running away with her, she knew she was seeing things, but the thought burrowed into her head: two glowing eyes.

Mindy hit the ladder, pulled herself up, legs kicking in the water, trying to step on rungs that weren't yet there. In the blink of an eye her fingers were wrapped around the top of the cold metal, her foot was stepping on the first rung. A shooting pain went through her other foot; she pulled it from the water and saw two neat holes, like little dabs of black paint, before the blood came. It crept around her wet foot and the dewy little hairs were like a spider-web being built. But she was out of the water. At least she was out of the water…

She saw the boat's name on a bulkhead as soon as she swung herself up. The *Persephone*. Mindy stepped down on the boat's floor—what was the nautical term for that? Floor. Deck? Floor. Her mind was still racing, still in the water. She had to focus. Think. She looked down and lifted her leg to leave a bloody footprint on the floor. She was bleeding. She watched the blood trickle from her leg, overflowing the lines of her footprint, becoming a tiny puddle. Okay. She needed to find a bandage. Okay.

She put her foot down—it didn't hurt yet—was that bad? One foot in front of the other, other foot in front of the first. She was limping; her leg seemed uncooperative, like it had fallen asleep up to the thigh. But it didn't hurt. She thought: *this must be bad.*

"Hello!" she called into the dark ship. The cabin doors open and dark, she thought of a giant skull leering at her. It was a big vessel, over a hundred feet long, which seemed like the kind of thing that would cost a lot of money. They had to have first aid kits aboard, right? Or at least towels. She had to put pressure on the wound. She could either go up into the tower, or she could go inside and down to the middle deck. She didn't want to be climbing in her condition. Down it was.

Going down the stairs, she fought both the urge to hurry and the urge to be cautious. She had to be quick, but a tumble down the stairs, a broken bone, those would not make her night better. She called out; the sound of her own voice was reassuring, no matter how hoarse and shaky.

"Hello? Anyone here? I was in the water and something bit me—I don't mean to bother you—I just need some help. Sir?" Anyone who owned a yacht seemed like a "sir" to her. "Please? Anyone?"

The emptiness ate her words like it was ravenous. She reached the bottom of the stairs. This main room was a big bowl surrounding a glass floor; there were lights to illuminate the view under the boat. They fired blue light up into the cabin, making things just visible with a dim glow. Mindy could just about see her hands in front of her face.

The interior was packed with furniture, bookshelves, wine cabinets, not freestanding but set into concentric rings leading down to the glass bottom so they formed a series of rings with passages cutting through them: one from Mindy's entrance to the glass bottom, another to the front of the ship, two more to the sides. She was reminded of a Roman coliseum and imagined a shark eating a seal under the arena of glass, like a Christian being fed to the lions.

Then she saw it. A white towel lay in the middle of the glass floor. How had she missed it, *God* was she stupid. Someone had dropped it there. Mindy limped onto the glass, stamping it with bloody footprints, and sank to her knees beside the towel. She wrapped it around her foot, pulled it tight. Now pain flooded her foot, and the towel turned red. She looked down into the spotlight the *Persephone* cast to the lakebed and saw something sleek and dark shoot past. Something sleek and dark and *red*, not all over, just in one spot, a red eye staring up at her. *Seeing* her. It was headed for the back of the boat. Mindy thought of the blood she'd left on the ladder—dripping down into the water. Tempting it.

It couldn't get her. It couldn't get her. She was out of the water, her bleeding had stopped, and she was safe. She just had to find a phone, or a person, and get help. Tell them that something was in Lake Travis. Mindy tried to think *shark, barracuda, crocodile,* but her mind refused to call *it* by one of those names. Sharks and barracudas and crocodiles were animals. They weren't evil.

She stood and immediately lost her balance, smacking her head on the glass floor. The yacht had lurched to the side; no, it had lurched backward. As if something very heavy were at the aft end of the ship. Pulling itself onboard.

*No. No, no, no.* Mindy said it aloud. "No." The word was simple and stupid and useless. Think. She should probably get off the glass. It was still in the water. It had to be still in the water. And if it was in the water, could it get through the glass? Sink the boat? Mindy wouldn't let it get her. She would lock herself in a cabin, stay there and drown before she'd let that thing do what it had looked at her and thought of doing.

It was on the boat. She heard the stairs creaking. They hadn't creaked underneath her weight.

"No. No, please."

The noise stopped, but a tiny reptile part of Mindy's mind felt the threat still oncoming, saw movement through closed eyelids. Mindy resented this low, primordial intrusion into her civilized brain. It felt like she was thinking someone else's thoughts—someone scared and small, someone she wasn't.

The footsteps had stopped, but now she saw a broth of mist pouring down the steps, thick, white, almost liquid in its consistency. It pooled onto the deck like swathes of silk and then, as if it had a mind of its own, oozed to the left. It seemed caught in a gust of wind, a river current, but there was no wind, no water. It just…slunk behind a bookshelf.

Then the rats spilled out. Swarms of them. A hundred sets of beady red eyes, glowing as if the darkness had been stabbed over and over again until something worse could bleed through. The rats squeaked and squealed, moving with one horrible instinct, pushing over and around each other and down a set of steps so they were closer to her, louder, the red eyes brighter. They kept going, slipping from view behind a white leather luxury couch. And then came the wolf—big, huge, six feet long. Growling in the dark, its red eyes flashing, the only thing Mindy could really see besides the bristles of its mane catching the light. It couldn't be there, it was impossible, but its nails clicked on the shining floor tiles like the snapping strands of a rope, *snip-snip-snip*, until the rope broke and whatever was holding it dropped away. It growled, the sound filling the cabin, echoing as the creature dissolved, bleeding into shadows.

"Please go away." Mindy thought she said. There didn't seem to be a difference anymore: whatever fears she imagined, whatever horrible fate she could picture, it was as real as anything her eyes could report to her. *Please go away, please go away, please go away.* Stuck in her head like a song.

*I need to wake up.* The thought dropped into her head like a rope ladder into a snake pit. A way out. She was asleep, dreaming. She just had to make it stop, force it out of her head, out of her subconscious. *I'm going to close my eyes and count to ten. I don't have to keep my eyes open, because it can't hurt me, it's just a dream.*

Mindy closed her eyes. She stopped, turning to face the creature as it flowed from one form to the next, her nightmare spooling out. She still heard it circling her. A wafting noise—a strong exhale of wind like, like... It wasn't important. It was a dream. She just had to count. *One. Two. Three.* It was behind her now, but it wasn't real, was not really there. *Four. Five.* She couldn't hear it anymore. Did that mean this was working? *Six. Seven.* Was it still there? *Eight. Nine.* What was that noise? That little anonymous noise, that bit of rasping that could've been a million things on any other night but for tonight, when it was *that*.

*Ten.*

"Ten." She could open her eyes. It wouldn't be there anymore because this was her dream. She forced her eyes to open. She looked to her left. She looked to her right. Then, all at once, she spun around. It was not behind her either. There was nothing there. Nothing anywhere.

*Just a dream. The drugs. This is what McGruff the Crime Dog warned you about in elementary school, remember?*

She was alone. She was awake. She was sober. She was still on a glass bottomed super yacht. Her foot still hurt, but she had probably just cut it on a rock. She had to stay with the hurt, not with the fear. Pain was real, pain was useful, pain told her what was wrong. Fear just made up what might be wrong. A phone. She had to find a phone, call 911, then she could stop. Then she could sleep and have all the nightmares she wanted.

The voice came from above her. "Unclean."

It was a cold voice, slicing into her hearing like ice. She was half-asleep, she told herself, a waking dream, a bit of the pill still dissolving in her system. But she looked up. She saw the bat.

Oh God, the bat. Clinging to the ceiling, its black mass distorting in the liquefying underwater pattern from below. It was huge, the size of a man, the size of the night, so big it was like a part of her; no, she was a part of it, an extension of its body that had fallen numb and now was being woken up. She stared into red eyes and felt herself slip under.

*A dream. All just a dream. It's a dream.*

The bat opened its mouth, jaws gleaming white with slobber, and for a second she thought it would say her name. She thought it calmly, rationally; it made as much sense as anything else did. But its lips hadn't drawn back to speak. They were revealing a set of teeth that were human, men's teeth in an animal mouth, all except for the eyeteeth. The canines. They were elongated, spearing out from the jaw like a saber-toothed tigers fangs. And beyond those stark white teeth, nothing but darkness. The thing's maw was as black as a tomb.

It came for her, or grew larger, or let the world slip away while it remained, solid and real. But as it fell, it was suddenly not made of itself, it was a thousand million insects, everything that crept or crawled, and they hit Mindy like a heavy blanket. She heard a subwoofer-bass hum in her ears as wings beat around her, felt every tiny leg clinging on her body, saw them, heard them, and was them as they swarmed around her, an impenetrable cloud of locusts wrapping her up. She closed her eyes and shut her mouth and covered her ears, but already she heard that voice in her head and thought it was one of them, in her ear, in her skull, whispering to her. *Unclean, unclean.*

The awful warmth of their bacchanalia ended as abruptly as stepping out of a sunny day and into cool air-conditioning. It wasn't bugs anymore. It was a man. She felt him pressed to her from behind, his arms around her in a lover's embrace, as close as Lucia had held her. Except that Lucia always gave her room to breathe, let her slip away when she'd had enough affection. The man didn't. His arms crushed her to his body, cold and stiff. She was far away and thought she could keep going, into another dream, and leave her body to the bat and its nightmare.

But no. She thought of her shopping trip with Lucia and the cute underwear they'd bought together and she didn't want anything to happen to it. She dug her fingernails into his arm. It gave a little, even if she didn't break the skin. Not so much steel as Kevlar. He lifted her off her feet—tall, he was so tall—but she could still kick at his legs, hit his shins. It had to hurt him. It had to do something.

He was going *shush, shush*, like a father soothing an uncooperative child, and she found herself thinking, *Fuck you, Jack, I'm not unclean. I showered right before I went to work.* She threw her head back, felt a protrusion notch into her skull. His nose. She hadn't broken it, but she still heard a sigh of pain come from him, the exhale of it cutting the back of her neck. His grip tightened. The air shot out of her lungs; she felt it rattle out of her throat.

She screamed, not in words but in thoughts: *Helppleasehelpmeidontwanttodie.* It came out as a word, long and pleading, and he brought his hand up to cover her mouth. She moved first. She bit down on the webbing between his thumb and forefinger. His skin was so hard, it scraped her teeth, but she dug in. She would bite him down to the bone like a rattler. He could cut her head off, and she would still be biting him. He'd have to carry her head right the fuck around with him.

Another piercing exhale to the back of her neck and he tried to pull his hand away; she clung to it. Her teeth hurt like she was eating steak. *You kill me, I'm dying with a chunk of your hand in my mouth.* She thought of detectives in smart suits running DNA tests on his chunk of hand lodged in her throat; a coroner saying what a brave girl she was. *Don't worry, Mindy, we got the guy.*

He pulled. She bit. The skin gave and his blood flooded her mouth. It wasn't warm, it wasn't salty. It was cold and thick, *knotted* like old cough syrup. She wouldn't release her hold on him to spit it out. She swallowed and felt it all the way down her esophagus, cold and heavy. It sat in the pit of her stomach like she'd eaten dry ice.

His arm relaxed around her. She'd done it. The pain had been too much. He was in shock, he was losing consciousness. Another second and she'd break free. She would run and she would swim and she would not stop until she was in her car. She would drive to the police station and park in the fucking lobby.

He let go of her, and her legs were already pedaling, scraping the floor for a foothold. The long fingernail of a long finger touched her neck and broke her skin and curled around her carotid artery and *dug* it right out of her flesh, like an earthworm out of wet soil. She felt the tissue of it hit the outside of her neck, a warm strand of spaghetti, and then the blood came. Hot and fast, spraying like a garden hose. It was down her neck and her underarm and her side, soaking her shirt. A few seconds and it was in her pants, her cute underwear. Her pumping feet caught the ground and she took a few steps before she slipped on her own blood. She was running on air anyway.

Her skull smacked the glass with an impact that felt faint, even to her. It was enough to put a hairline crack in the glass-bottomed hull, like a single perfect tear, but it didn't let a drop of water in. Her blood filled the little fissure quickly. She saw her blood spreading out under her, like a warm blanket for her to sleep on. Her prey-instinct was silent now, given up. Her stomach hurt, but nothing else did.

And she felt him over her, his body as chilled as the first day of winter. She could see his face if only she could move her head, but she was too comfortable for that. Blood made a fine pillow. She did see his hand come down: alabaster white, blue veins like cracks in marble. The pad of his finger touched her blood, and it stopped spreading. It went up his finger like soda up a straw. She saw the pale skin darken, the blue vein redden, and the shriveled flesh grew until the long fingernails fit inside his fingers in a fine manicure.

*When people died, their bodies shrank over time, but their hair and fingernails stayed the same. Made it look like they were still growing.* Her mind vomited up the thought.

It seemed to take a while for her blood to be vacuumed up by that one outstretched finger. But finally it was all gone except for a few molecules of red tint on the glass. He brought his hand to her head, touched her hair. It wasn't a fond gesture; he was just wiping off the last of her blood.

With all her strength, Mindy turned away. Moved her head one half-inch so not a single speck of him was in her sight. She didn't want him to be a part of her last moments on Earth. She didn't want him in Heaven with her, even in memory. She looked down and saw her face in the red glass and the waters of Lake Travis. Only it wasn't her face.

It was Lucia's.

# CHAPTER 8

Mindy never got the expression "woke in a cold sweat" before. She lived in Texas. She woke up feeling she was frying in her skin, her sweat boiling on her like grease on a hot skillet. Her sheets and mattress were soaked with it; they stuck to her like flypaper. A discarded mask of sweat lay on her pillow, lovingly revealed by the moonlight.

She felt grimy and disgusted with herself. She peeled herself out of bed and went straight to the bathroom with no concern for modesty. She turned on the shower as cold as it could go and put herself under the pure, clean spray. Her boxers and Grandma-gift T-shirt became wet straitjackets around her. She stripped them off and let the water rinse off every bit of the dream, wash it out of her hair. She swallowed some to salve her dry throat. It almost hit the spot.

She turned the water off without bothering to shampoo or soap, just swabbed her purified body with a towel. It'd taken her a minute under the frozen spray to remember herself, but she finally had. She hadn't gone back into the water at Lake Travis. She'd gotten out, she'd left Lucia behind, and she'd gone home. Anything else was just a dream.

She thought of herself…or was it Lucia…in the dream. It hadn't felt like a dream. It was like it hadn't *wanted* to be a dream. With her towel wrapped around her, white and clean and soft, she found she worried about Lucia. Trying to picture her put thoughts of cement blocks and plastic wrappings in Mindy's head. Back in her room, she looked through her window to Lucia's. Her room was dark and empty. Mindy thought of crime scenes. She found her phone and dialed Lucia's number before her self-consciousness could prevent her. Three a.m. Great time for some girl talk.

*"Hey, this is Lucia. Guess you finally worked up the balls to ask me out, huh? Probably on a date with one of my other boyfriends right now; make your pitch at the beep."*

"Hey, Lucia, hey." Mindy was talking even before the beep sounded.

"Hey," she repeated when she realized the recording had finally started. "I just wanted to hear your voice, and I guess now I have. Well, sorta. I got your answering machine. Very funny, by the way. Crazy how I hadn't heard your message until…now. Uh, listen—" Mindy swore to herself she would not "uh" or "um" again. She would say what she meant until she was done. "I know we had—*have* our differences, but I just wanted to tell you that I really care about you. And I don't know how many people care about you. Maybe you're some poor little rich girl who doesn't have any real friends, maybe that's just a stupid cliché. But you've got at least one, okay? You've got me. Bye."

Mindy hung up. She dressed. She went downstairs to find something to eat. She tried to distract herself within the funhouse of her own mind, make her thoughts walk the familiar paths, the proper paths…come to the same half-dozen justifications as always. She could have something fattening, but she would skip breakfast, skip lunch, skip dessert, take the dog for a walk in the morning, do something, do anything.

She looked through the refrigerator, the freezer, the pantry, and back again in case anything decided to come out of hiding and surrender itself. She wanted something sweet but not sugar, solid but not thick, meaty but not…meat.

She wanted to stop thinking about Lucia. Yeah, fat chance.

Christ, but that was a weird dream. What'd it even *mean*? She'd been Lucia—and she knew a lot of lesbians had trouble deciding if a pretty girl was a life goal or a wife goal, but that'd never been a problem between them. Then there'd been a shark attack or something. Okay, that was explainable, sharks were scary, even if you were a girl who liked girls. But then that boat, and the mist that turned into rats that turned into a wolf that turned into a bat? What was that, six different Syfy Original Movies at once?

Maybe it was supposed to be how Lucia saw *her*. That made sense. She'd gotten high, so her subconscious had been high as well. It'd been trying to tell her that Lucia saw her as a—shark that turned into mist that turned into rats? This was fucking ridiculous.

Okay, Lucia probably thought sharks were cool, who didn't? And mist was nice. No one was crazy about it, but it wasn't *bad*. She'd been Lucia's friend, then Lucia's uncool friend, then… Rats. Wolf. Bat.

Lucia liked bats, right?

She could feel herself getting a headache, trying to fit this one random nightmare into a message from God regarding her lesbian crush, so she fiddled with her laptop and found an e-mail from Lucia that had gotten caught in her spam folder. Just seeing her e-mail address was enough to give Mindy a lesbian 'Nam flashback.

God, how could she have fallen in love with a straight girl? Especially when she herself was like, half a straight girl? She had straight girl ancestry! Really, Lucia was way out of line letting Mindy crush on her when they were both in the straight girl faction.

"I'm not thinking about Lucia," Mindy said out loud, hoping that her brain would listen. She kept narrating as she went. "I am opening an e-mail *from a friend*. I am seeing that she sent me a video while I was at work with no information other than subject line 'Hey, slut, look at this.'" It was a set video from the new *Frankenstein* movie they were filming, *Frankenstein: Evolution*. "I am wondering why *my friend* is obsessed with Frankenstein. Is it just since she learned MMA fighting, or did she have a thing for Boris Karloff too?" Even Boris Karloff had more pull than her. "Shut up, Mindy. Look at the blurry people fighting in Vancouver."

Was she in the friend zone? Shit, she was in the friend zone. She was the kind of person who complained about the friend zone. She was being totally unfair to Lucia...though that was after Lucia had been unfair to her and generally unreliable, insulting, straight, calling her that *word*... "Which, coincidentally, maybe makes her not dating material, *Mindy*?" she said aloud, to herself.

In shaky detail she watched a black-clad villain confront ol' Frank. "You won't kill me, Frankenstein—you're no killer!"

Frank replied, "No...I'm not...but I have the arms of one..." Several snapping noises followed. Why did people keep saying he wasn't a killer? He clearly was.

She'd gone to the damn party just wanting to know how Lucia felt. Well, now she knew. She knew what Lucia had said, and that was all that mattered. Who gave a shit if deep down, Lucia had some boner for her, because up on the surface, out loud, she had said what she'd said and done what she'd done, and it wasn't all sweet and caring—Lucia wasn't her girlfriend and didn't want to be. She saw Mindy as a shark, or a mist, or a bat—anything but a lover.

The screen of Mindy's phone blinked Lucia's name at her, flashing—*Call her. Call her*—like Morse code. It was just impossible not to hit the *call* button. The screen cleared, filled instead with a selfie Lucia had made of the two of them together. It shook in her hand ringing Lucia's number.

Lucia's phone rang.

On the porch.

Right outside the front door.

Mindy looked at that door like it was about to break down. She cancelled the call on her cell phone. The ringing stopped. The house was silent. Mindy's thoughts were speeding up, pulling her along at a hundred miles an hour. Probably just Lucia. Probably just wanted to apologize for once in her life. So why was she thinking of going to her parents' room, crawling into bed with them like she was a child who'd had a nightmare? No. Couldn't. They were off visiting relatives. She had the house to herself. *Par-tay*, she heard Lucia say.

She called Lucia's number again.

The phone rang on the other side of the door almost before she pressed *call*, and it was louder and closer, right in her ear. A ghost standing right in front of her, heard but not seen. Mindy jabbed *disconnect* with her thumb, hit it until her phone went dead and dark, then set the phone down on the floor like a dead cockroach. She looked through the door's spyhole and saw Lucia. Well, she thought it was Lucia. Her back was turned.

Lucia probably wanted to patch things up, stop this all before it festered, and Mindy didn't want to be the pigheaded one, the one wanting Lucia to grovel and suffer and love her. She wanted to be fair. She wanted to be evenhanded. She wanted to forgive Lucia so much she could've thanked her for apologizing. She threw the door open and saw Lucia in the glare of the porch light.

It wasn't her. Mindy thought that, over and over, more than anything else. Lucia wouldn't be caught dead in tattered, stained clothes like that—though she had been wearing those shorts and that tank top earlier. Was that a chain winding down her leg?

And what could Lucia possibly have spilled on herself to turn so much of her clothes, so much of her *skin* that dark, brackish color…like some kind of *sludge?* And the makeup smeared like melted wax, the bruises making a camouflage pattern of her skin—her skin that was bleached white, but somehow dim, somehow *sallow.* Her hair was a shade of yellow that was nearly white, reaching down her shoulders like pallid fingers. The brightest things on her were the bits of seaweed that tangled with the muck dripping off her. And all of it wrapped in plastic that Lucia clutched to her like a child's blankie.

*Greek ruins.* You saw what was left, and it was enough to make you wish you had been there in their heyday, seeing them as they were meant to be. There was just enough of Lucia left for Mindy to wish that. She couldn't remember what Lucia had looked like just a few hours ago. All she could see was the damage.

Her mind ran a marathon to find something to say. *Anything.* "Lucia," she said, hacking the words up like phlegm, "is this a grunge thing?"

Mindy's brain kept clawing at memories, trying to throw them in front of this walking corpse, blot it out. So when Lucia fell, Mindy remembered how cheerleader stunts went wrong, adolescents fell from the top of a pyramid of girl and broke their necks, and Mindy lunged forward to catch her, snaking her arms into layers of plastic and skin and clothes.

Lucia was slippery, one huge mass of slime, but Mindy wouldn't let her fall. She grasped at her over and over again as the plastic sheeting fell away and the chain unwound, coiling onto Mindy's mom's begonias. The end had a fist-sized chunk of cement attached. Mindy grazed it with her eyes, thought *cinder block*, and finally got a firm hold on Lucia.

She forced her up—how was Lucia so heavy, how could she be at the top of all those human pyramids, how could a bunch of anorexics lift her that high? She was a messy, ungainly weight, seemingly boneless; her head flopped forward, mouth open, and down came a slap of water, then a steady trickle like the flow from a water cooler. Water that hit the pavement in fits and hacks, coming down red, splatting like a lanced boil on the floor of the porch.

The last strings of it swung from out of Lucia's throat like a pendulum. Mindy fought the urge to wipe it away for her. Instead, she got Lucia up, got her head under Lucia's arm like she was a wounded soldier in a war movie, and together they took one big step into the house.

Only Lucia didn't go through the door. Straining under her weight, Mindy looked around to see that Lucia's other arm had somehow gotten snagged on the doorway. Putting more of Lucia's weight on herself, Mindy reached across Lucia's body and pulled her arm tight to the side of her body.

Again, Mindy tried to shoot them through the front door. They ground to a halt like a ship running ashore, no coordination at all. Mindy looked back and saw that Lucia's foot was clawing at the side of the door. She pulled, trying to dislodge it, but it was like Lucia's fucking leg had been nailed to the wall.

"Come on, get in here!" Mindy hissed, and Lucia came loose with her next great heave. They toppled into the house all at once, Lucia landing on top of Mindy. Mindy felt all of her body, and there wasn't a spark of warmth in any of it. Just wet, leaden *stuff*.

She could've been a corpse. *Dead weight.* Except Lucia stood there with her head erect, chin up, eyes aimed at Mindy the same way NASA pointed telescopes at distant galaxies. There was something in those eyes. Mindy didn't know what it was.

Then Lucia's head dropped. For a moment of hell, Mindy thought she'd died. But she was just bowing her head to vomit, another liter of red-tinged water rushing out of her mouth and pushing down on Mindy's chest. It was so cold and there was so much of it; the chill gripped Mindy's torso like she was inside a block of ice. Summoning all her strength, she pushed at Lucia and managed to shove her off so they were lying side by side on their backs.

Above them the chandelier that the Murphys had inherited from Grandma's house tinkled in the breeze from the open door.

*Deep breath. Count to five. One-two-three-four-five. Now recap.* She'd gone to a party on Lake Travis, had a break-up-without-the-relationship with Lucia, total bullshit, and now Lucia was on her landing, soaked to the bone and looking like a virgin at the end of a slasher movie. And throwing up enough water to keep SeaWorld in business. It was just like that dream. That fucking dream. It wouldn't let her go.

*Just go to bed!* The thought was so loud and sudden that Mindy almost held her hands over her ears. She could just go back to bed. Pull the covers over herself and go back to sleep and in the morning—what could possibly happen in the morning? In the light of day?

Call 911? Yeah, and explain to the authorities that a high school student had taken drugs right before college applications went out. That'd go over well. *Only call 911 if absolutely necessary.* Mindy wrote that down on a mental checklist, underlined it, put a star next to it. First she'd check Lucia's pulse. If it was fucked—excuse the medical jargon—*then* Mindy would call an ambulance. She turned to Lucia and didn't see her. Just her bare feet on the linoleum tiles, green with muck.

Mindy scrambled to her feet. Something about being prone before this version of Lucia made her feel she was tempting fate. Like lying on the train tracks while you heard the whistle. But standing before her, Lucia still seemed so much taller than her. Looking down at her from on high—from the top of a microscope with Mindy on the slide.

Mindy didn't know where she got the courage, but she grabbed Lucia's hand. Limp and wet and so pliant it seemed it would run through Mindy's fingers if she squeezed just a fraction too hard. "Lucia? We have to get you out of those wet clothes, okay? Come on. Come with me. Let's get you cleaned up."

She pulled, ignoring the mad picture behind her eyelids when she blinked—the skin of Lucia's hand coming off in hers, like an oversized glove. That didn't happen, but Lucia didn't move either. She was putting up resistance. Limp as she was, she moved only reluctantly with Mindy's efforts, like she was still in the water. At her pace, they went up the stairs, leaving muddy footprints on each step. In the dark, they could've been blood.

In the bathroom, Lucia almost blended into the white tiles, the plaster walls, the linen towels. The light washed her out, made her almost translucent. Only the trail of muck she left behind her on the upstairs carpet marked her. *The afterbirth of being born from the darkness.* Mindy's English teacher would love that one. She should work it into a poem. Wouldn't even have to rhyme.

"Okay, let's just…let's get you…" Mindy barely knew what she was saying. Like some sort of rictus, Lucia's lips had pulled back into a lascivious smile. Like Mindy was a cute boy or something. Mindy turned on the shower, still at a loss. "It takes a minute to heat up. Do you want to take your clothes off?"

It seemed impossible, but Lucia's smile widened. She raked off her tank top, dropping it in the hamper behind Mindy. The motion pressed them together, but all Mindy felt was the nervous sweat under her arms and below her bangs. When Lucia backed away, Mindy could see her cute bra lined with scum and the marking on her belly.

It was right below her belly button like a C-section scar, almost covered by her shorts. Rings of purpling, reddening, *blackening* flesh—the discoloration of a spider or snake bite, as wide as a dinner plate and centered around two puncture marks.

Almost unnoticeable except for the bruised corona that surrounded them. Mindy thought it might've been left there by the chain that'd been wrapped around her. What the chain had been doing there, Mindy would not think about.

Beside them, the shower hissed and drizzled all the way to the drain. Mindy felt momentarily guilty over how much water she was wasting. And during a drought too. "El, you have to take off all your clothes to take a shower."

Lucia giggled coyly, as if Mindy had just said some very naughty euphemism. Mindy realized she'd have to do it herself.

"Okay, okay, I'll do it. You just stop me if you start…whatever."

Mindy undid Lucia's belt—it was on tighter than a vise—and unbuttoned her shorts. Lucia kept giggling, staccato now, in fresh little bursts. Mindy got down on her knees and hauled the denim down. Breathed a sigh of relief; Lucia still had her panties on. The bloody muck, mucky blood had soaked into them as well. Mindy thought about getting a Ziploc bag to put them in but was too worried Lucia would bolt or hurt herself.

So Mindy tried to remember everything she knew about handling blood-stuff: she relocated all of Lucia's clothes to the sink, then washed her hands with soap in the shower spray. All while Lucia stood there, still smiling. Her teeth were brown; she was chewing something. When Mindy noticed, she spat it out like a child caught chewing gum in church.

Was that a flap of skin?

Mindy couldn't think about it for long. Lucia was running her hands over her body like she'd noticed it for the first time. She brushed a finger over her bloody nipple. Raised it to her lips with a keen interest.

"No! Bad! No!" Mindy stopped, realizing she was yelling at Lucia like a dog. And Lucia was growling, also like a dog. Mindy took Lucia's hands, unfortunately smearing her palm with what felt like cold snot. "Listen, Sweet Tarts, I can't see a wound, so I don't think this is your blood, which is awesome, but it also makes me worried that maybe it has something gross in it? Like about that time you told me Pete Wentz had halitosis? Something like that. So we need to wash it off, 'kay? Just, you know…"

She embraced Lucia, and together, they stepped under the shower spray. Lucia stiffened like it'd taken her by surprise, but Mindy stayed with her, petting her face and sides, soothing her.

"It's okay, baby. You're okay. You're safe. Just take some deep breaths and… keep breathing, I guess."

Lucia looked down, watching the muck fall off her and swirl down the drain. It was so black. Mindy wondered if that was normal. Then Lucia was sobbing, loud banshee wails that echoed inhumanly in the shower stall. Mindy wrapped her up tight in her arms, the water soaking them both. Warm now. Almost warm enough to distract Mindy from the hunk of ice in her arms.

# CHAPTER 9

Mindy held her until she went totally still, then a little longer, then gently broke away. Lucia was again petrified inside her eerie silence.

Pulling the showerhead off on its extendable hose, Mindy efficiently scrubbed Lucia of all the blood and dirt she could find. Leaves and blades of grass tumbled from her hair. Mindy was careful with her bruise; with all of her lower belly. But it seemed to have faded a little since Mindy had last noticed it. Washing the dirt away had to help.

"I think I have some clothes that would fit you—" Mindy's eyes briefly flitted over Lucia's slender body. "Yeah, I think I have *all* clothes that would fit you, so I'll just go grab them…"

Lucia grabbed her wrist before she could even turn to leave. "Mindy."

Mindy blinked. "That's right, I'm…Mindy." She brushed some of the hair out of Lucia's face. Her friend was smiling again. "I'll be right back, I have…"

Lucia shook her head slowly, her toothy smile catching new light at every angle.

"Okay." Mindy took off her water-logged glasses and looked around. It took her a second to look under her own damn feet. The bathtub! From what she'd read of her mom's old pregnancy handbooks, taking a warm bath was great with stress.

Mindy turned the shower on again to wash out the bottom of the tub before it could ring, then put in the stopper and turned on the faucet. Steaming hot water. She stepped out of the bath as it rose, crawling up the soles of Lucia's fish-belly white feet. They should be pink. They should be tan. It was like Lucia had frostbite and Mindy just couldn't warm her, no matter what she did.

When she shut off the faucet, the only sound was the water dripping off Lucia. Mindy gulped down a sudden need to look at Lucia. She was the only girl in town who went into Austin for a tanning salon, and it paid off. And now the blood was off her and the bruises had faded, all but the one over her womb. Mindy could barely look, even to find out if the rumors were true about Lucia's pierced clit.

"Okay-doke, artichoke, lie down…just lie…down."

Lucia didn't move.

Gently, infinitely gently, Mindy put her hand on Lucia's shoulder. She pressed. And, satisfied with that attention, Lucia sunk down into the tub. Her head disappeared underwater in a cloud of silvery hair, and for a second Mindy thought she was going to drown. Then Lucia resurfaced, her smile kindled.

"Does that feel good?"

Lucia almost purred, the noise deepening until it could've come from the belly of a jungle cat. She leaned back until she was resting against Mindy's mom's Sears bathtub pillow, her hair spilling out toward the floor. It still had some brambles in it. Mindy grabbed her good comb and began brushing Lucia's hair. Lucia made more purring sounds and Mindy giggled. It felt good to get that kind of response. It was probably great for her blood pressure.

When Lucia's hair was straight, Mindy picked up the small pile of twigs from the floor and dumped it into the wastebasket. Then she squirted shampoo into her palm and massaged it into Lucia's scalp. Lucia rocked against Mindy's hands in absolute comfort, her body kicking up little waves as it thrummed. When she was done, Lucia dunked herself again. When she came up, hair cleaned, she brushed it behind her shoulders herself.

"Are you feeling better?"

"Yes…" Lucia sounded it out clumsily, like a stroke victim.

Mindy grabbed a loofah and ran it over Lucia's back and shoulders. Lucia's mouth fell open and she let out a really porn star sigh.

Mindy paused. "Do you wanna talk about it?"

Lucia pouted and held her hand out of the water, watched it drip. Mindy took her hand and rubbed the loofah down her arm.

"Mindy?" Lucia said, small and cloyingly vulnerable.

"Yes, that's me," Mindy replied, for some reason feeling it had been as much a question as anything.

Lucia picked at the golden cross around her neck, the only thing she wore. "I feel dirty."

Mindy felt tears heating her eyes. "It's okay, baby, you're safe now. I won't let anyone hurt you. Promise. I got a yellow belt at the YMCA."

Lucia moved suddenly. Her perfect breasts emerging from the water like island paradises. She stood. Turned, her hips swinging as gently as a pendulum, her breasts thrust out.

Mindy couldn't not look. She felt her breath trickle out of her chest without replacement. Found herself standing slowly, rising to Lucia's height. Finally, she closed her eyes. The afterimage of Lucia burned white on her eyelids, but when Mindy opened her eyes again, she could look Lucia in the eye.

Lucia reached out to Mindy. Her cold, cold fingers brushing over Mindy's face. Taking away some of the tears she found there. Lucia put her fingers in her mouth. Her fingers trickled off her lips. "I've been thinking about the night."

Mindy misheard. "What night?"

Her voice was small. It seemed to barely make it out of her. "The darkness... what if you could see everything in it? Wouldn't it hurt your eyes? If there were no darkness? Not even behind your eyelids. If everything were just so... bright?"

"Lucia... I think we should call the Girls' Town crisis hotline. You're freaking me out."

Lucia swept one long leg after the other out of the bath and onto the floor. She walked out of the bathroom and Mindy followed her. She could see this violence in Lucia, something barely restrained, and if it were anyone else, she'd worry that when it got out it would come toward her.

Instead, Lucia stood in the middle of the upstairs hallway, dripping dry, her pallor and her bruises and her limpid hair all spooling together into something Mindy couldn't define. Her face was slack. She looked at Mindy like she was begging her for something. Then she smiled. An awful, clownish smile, showing all her teeth, all her "pep".

"Tuck check!" she cheered and swung around her own belly button in the air, barely leaving her feet before they slapped back onto the carpet, wet with old muck and new water.

"Tuck check!" she chorused again to herself and went into another 360 degrees. She landed off-kilter, ripping backward, but another chorus—"Tuck check!"—and she launched again, a propeller speeding up. Landed on her feet again, but like a car with a flat tire, she was steadily being pulled off-course. "Tuck check! Tuck check! Tuck check!" Each backflip took her further down the hallway, faster and faster, covering more distance with each loose stunt. Mindy could only think of a firework going off. It burned hotter and hotter until it exploded.

Lucia crashed into the table at the end of the hall, her body a wrecking ball that took out papers and books and vase and flowers. And she laid there in the wreckage, her damp nymph-body out of a Michael Bay movie, her hair spouting a red ribbon of blood from where the back of her head had struck the wall. In some insane way, the color reassured Mindy. And as she rushed to help Lucia, the cheerleader laughed and laughed. A jagged laugh; it cut Mindy. Cut deep into her.

The bleeding stopped fast, Lucia's body desperate to hoard whatever color it had left deep within itself. Mindy got Lucia dressed in a baggy shirt—everything of hers was baggy on Lucia—and a pair of men's boxers that Mindy's mother had bought her accidentally. Mindy still hadn't figured out how her mother had "accidentally" thought she had a son instead of a daughter. She put Lucia in her bed, wrapping her up in blankets like they could protect her, and said a quick prayer over her. She didn't know if there was a Jesus, but if there was, she couldn't think of anything better for Him to do than look after Lucia.

And though a part of her only wanted to crawl into bed with Lucia, to hold her close and protect her better than God or bedsheets ever could, she knew Lucia would hate that. Waking up with a dyke. So she took her comforter, too warm for all but the winter months in Texas, and dragged it downstairs with her. Wouldn't be the first time she'd slept on the couch. She built a little castle out of cushions, laid her head down on it, cocooned herself in her comforter, and she dreamed.

She wasn't sure if she was herself or Lucia in the dream. She was in her own bed. When she got up, she passed the mirror, but she didn't have a reflection. She was thirsty, though. So thirsty she was made of desert, her mouth and throat cracking, her stomach heaped with sand. Downstairs was water. She could hear it flowing.

Down the steps. Across the floor. The darkness was so…light. Like a spider-web, it was *there,* but she could see right through it. See to the girl on the couch. See it was herself sleeping there, so innocent, so delicious.

Her hand was suddenly around this Mindy, the other version of herself's throat, so strong that she could've lifted her right up off that couch. But that Mindy didn't feel someone's throat in her hand; instead, in her dream, she felt the thumb stroking along her jugular. It felt like an ice cube.

"Your blood's so warm," she said, playing Prince Charming to the sleeping beauty. "I can feel it moving through you." She brought her hand up to Mindy's face, like she was trying to cool the hot blush on her cheeks. "In that big brain—in your cute face…Then it goes down…down…" Her hand moved, and snow fell on Mindy's chin, down her throat, onto her chest, her clavicle… between her breasts. "to here. That great big heart of yours. *Ba-dum. Ba-dum. Ba-dum.* It soaks up your blood like a sponge. Pumping, swishing. It's so warm. I bet it could make me just *melt.* Are you scared?" Mindy asked herself.

Despite her cold words, she was. Scared. Excited. Aroused. Giddy. It all seemed indistinguishable at the moment. "Yes."

"Me too." Mindy moved her lips down to her own body. She was at a feast and couldn't decide what to try first. Whet her appetite with the little vein in the forehead? Or gorge herself lower, at her breast? Her lips brushed through Mindy's hair, over her earlobe. Following the path her fingers had frozen earlier. Down her throat, with its pumping, swishing carotid artery. Between her breasts. To her heart.

Mindy wanted her heart so bad.

"Let's be scared together, Mindy."

Mindy woke up. Her hand flying to her throat, feeling the clear, unbroken skin. Her hand rolled lower, over her chest, her stomach, but there was no blood, just warm sweat plastering her shirt to her body. Then her hand dipped between her legs and she felt it. Heat. She was burning like a furnace, but there was no blood. Just the thought of Lucia…what? *Doing what to her?*

*Doing this.* Mindy let her hand fall into her panties. As she touched herself. As she thought of Lucia and came like a pot that'd finally reached a boil.

It was early morning. The gray light that had just begun tinting the house said as much, even before she found her glasses to see the clock. Mindy felt slick and overwarm; a robot with too much lubricant on one of its joints. She didn't find anything immoral about masturbation, but she'd never come so quickly before.

It seemed sinful, how fast it had happened. It took her longer to wiggle out of her panties than it had to orgasm.

After washing her hands thoroughly at the kitchen sink, she went out to get the newspaper. The golden glow of dawn hadn't come. It was an overcast, drizzling sort of day that blew raspberries at her. She ducked under the sprinkler to get the paper and came back by the front door.

The welcome mat was white. Mindy knelt down to look at it. She'd already brought the plastic and the chain inside, hiding them in the garage; had she missed something? No. The white was mushrooms, springing up from under the mat like the fingers of a hand holding it from underneath. Mindy lifted up the mat against her better judgment, finding several more vestigial bulbs. She took a picture of them with her cell phone. This kind of thing needed to be Googled.

Inside, she started on breakfast. Something extravagant. She fixed pancakes, as excessive as those were for only two people. She made some with blueberries, some with chocolate chips. Finally she had a plate piled high. She put it on a tray and added a tall glass of milk, some utensils, newspaper, and a squat bottle of syrup fresh from being nuked in the microwave. All that was missing was a little vase with one flower, which seemed like tempting fate for people with allergies.

Out in the hallway, she gasped so hard she nearly dropped the tray. The footprints Mindy had so assiduously cleaned up, with Swiffer mops and Resolve Spot & Stain, were still there in ghostly form. They'd metastasized into mushrooms with long, slender stalks and caps the size of tennis balls, with small siblings alongside them. The patches of fungus went up the stairs. One for each step Lucia had taken.

Mindy went up the stairs, careful not to so much as brush one with her Keds. At the very top of steps, the mushrooms were less developed. Shorter, thinner, their white color less glossy, more translucent.

The door was open a crack. She toed it all the way open. The bed was empty. *Déjà vu* struck. Mindy remembered how she'd left the sheets in her dream. It was exactly how they looked in the cold light of day. She set the tray down and forced herself to focus on Lucia. Went to the window and saw that Lucia's blinds were drawn. Called her phone and it went straight to voice mail.

In the bathroom, little cords of moss ran between the tiles, sometimes crossing them through cracks. Underneath the bathtub, they sprang into life. There were at least six heads springing up right where the porcelain tub met the linoleum floor. Ghastly white with black spots on the heads. Mindy took another picture and hurried to her computer and ate the pancakes there.

A lost hour of research, and she had narrowed them down to some kind of Enokitake mushrooms—just really big. One word jumped out at her: *saprotrophic*. They fed on decay.

Lucia wasn't at school. Had called in sick. When she got home, Mindy didn't want the mushrooms in her house anymore. Grabbing a pair of old dishwashing gloves from her mother's box of old things, she ripped each one out and stuffed it into a supermarket plastic bag. The tiles she scrubbed clean with a hefty dose of bleach, and the carpet she sprayed and vacuumed. The welcome mat she threw out. She took the bag to the same garage closet where she'd put the plastic, the chain. Tied the bag shut and left it there.

She tried Lucia's number again, but it went straight to voicemail. She didn't even hear the song of its ringtone in Lucia's lonely house.

Three days without Lucia. Mindy stayed in the gym after school, watching the cheerleaders practice. Gravity was put on a lower setting. They did basket tosses, back tucks, stunts that Mindy couldn't name any more than the dances in a Bollywood movie. But they all had meaning. They were sewed into Lucia's body in sweat and muscle and scars, only Mindy hadn't looked for them. Hadn't seen Lucia jogging by her bedroom in the early morning, or staying late after school, or disappearing to away games. Mindy had always fit in around those gaping holes in Lucia's life. Even back then, Lucia had been a ghost. Now she'd just been exorcised.

When they noticed her, Pammy and Tera asked if she knew where Lucia was. She hadn't shown up for practice. She always showed up for practice.

Principal Haywood was urging the cheerleading coach to kick her from the captaincy. Mindy left the arena of cheers and chants before she started to cry.

When she got home she opened the garage door and a cloud of moths flew out. They'd been near the mushrooms. Mindy could just tell.

In her dreams, she is Lucia, and she wants to see herself, see Mindy, see a mirror. She gets out of bed, the sheet wrapped around herself like a body covered at the morgue, and goes to the window. Just a quick look between their two houses. Even seeing Mindy sleeping will be enough. But she has lost track of time. It is dawn, and when the blind rolls up, the light comes in. Her eyes burn too hot to need this soft warmth; it's too much for her. She sees the light itself, a shower of shimmering needles that stick in her extended arm like a porcupine's quills. Each of them is red-hot. They burn in her skin as she wraps the sheet tightly, protectively around herself. She closes the blinds once more. Her arm is not her own anymore. It has been claimed by the day—

Mindy woke up and needed to see Lucia. With her own eyes, now.

Enough cabin fever, enough stir-crazy, and Mindy could do anything. Even cook.

Mindy found her mom's world-famous chicken soup recipe on page 244 of her seventies yellow cook book. It took some chopping, some slicing, and almost setting a dish towel on fire, but Mindy got two quarts of soup created and poured into a Tupperware container. To that she added a twenty-ounce bottle of Sprite from the fridge. Thus armed, she went next door and she knocked.

It took a while. She rang the bell in case they couldn't hear her knocking, knocked again in case the bell didn't work. After maybe five minutes, she heard the door unlock.

Lucia's mother was like a funhouse reflection of her. The same tawny hair, but not as bright, thinner, framing a crabapple version of Lucia's face—too many cigarettes and too little sleep. Her lumpen upper body was hugged by a T-shirt for a rock band Mindy had never heard, even on the oldies stations, and a pair of stained sweatpants ended in a set of gel shoes. Young and pretty, Mindy instantly felt embarrassed for her.

"Yeah? Whaddya want?" Mrs. West asked. Her words carried a strong brandy scent between consonants.

"It's Mindy? Lucia's friend from school? I live next door?" She raised the Tupperware container, feeling idiotic for putting it in a picnic basket. It'd been the only way she'd been able to carry it, the Sprite, and a spoon. "I heard she wasn't feeling well, so I brought her some chicken soup. To get better. She eats it and then she gets better. Hopefully."

Mrs. West started a cigarette. It was a practiced motion—first she dug a pack out of her pants and slapped at the cardboard packaging like it was an unruly child. "Lucia doesn't like getting company. Not too fond of it myself."

"I know that, but I—" Mindy unslung her backpack, Mrs. West still tapping out bass on the cigarette pack. "I brought her homework. From the school she's missing?"

A phlegmy laugh came up from Mrs. West like a sudden cough. She fetched a single Marlboro from her pack and clenched it in teeth that had seen non-brown days. "School. Yeah. That what she does when she ain't shaking her ass on some football field? C'mon in, can't stand outside jabbering all day, let the cool air out, bugs in. Got enough of both…" She slid back inside. Mindy followed after a moment; she hadn't opened the door more than she had to poke her head out. In the hallway inside, Mrs. West was working a spark from a plastic Zippo. "Sumbitch husband dragged us out here. Looking for work at the bottom of a bottle. Then he up and left us here, Hell's sauna. Joke's on him, though; governm'nt still sends his dole here."

Mindy came inside. Instantly, she was watching her step. She didn't want to walk on anything.

It wasn't like her own house was the cleanest. Before Jon had gone to college, when she was still into *Sailor Moon* and Neopets, the two of them had left clutter all over. That's what her mom had called it. Not junk or trash. Clutter. But they got older, stopped leaving their toys out because their toys were all in their phones, and her mom hired a Spanish woman to come by once a week and tidy up.

Lucia's house had *trash*. It was a subtle distinction—a robot or an alien wouldn't get it. But you just had to look at the pile of bills that'd come through the mail slot and been swiped aside by a foot. The groceries still in bags, not put away—Costco-sized groceries were all store brands, not name brands. Mindy followed Mrs. West automatically to the kitchen, thinking they were carrying on a conversation, but Lucia's mother was talking to herself—keeping herself company as she poured a drink. A social drinker. Mindy left her.

Up the stairs, same story. Down the hall, same story. The door to Lucia's room had the same collection of warning signs and keep-out signifiers that Mindy had once had before she took them down in a fit of maturity. Mindy rapped on a High-Voltage sticker, shaking a hanging pillow that said *The Princess Is IN*.

"Get lost, Bro," Lucia groaned through the door, her voice strained and far off.

Mindy turned the knob anyway, cracking the door the width of a molecule. "It's your lesbro, not your bro-bro."

"Which one? I'm friends with a lot of lesbians, I go to viewing parties of *The 100*." The warmth in Lucia's voice was invitation enough. But Mindy opened the door slowly. Like she would if there were a growling Rottweiler on the other end.

This is being a teenage girl: you bottle everything up. But not all in one bottle. You get a few. You let things out in different circles, to different people. Some to your teachers, some to your friends, some to your besties, some to your family, even some to boys. When it bursts out of you, it's onto your phone, your locker, your room. You don't choose which part of yourself you show to the world. You choose all the parts you don't.

And in Lucia's room was nothing: A dresser (Mindy thought—*junkyard*). A wardrobe (Mindy thought—*curbside*). A sewing station, not just with Lucia's girl-clothes on the rack but with underwear worn away at the elastic, shorts with holes at the groin. Mindy's mom had a whole hobby room for that sort of thing. A few posters so oddly placed that Mindy wondered if they covered holes in the wall, and so normal that they hit Mindy like a hip-check. Chris Hemsworth in a towel, a wrinkled pin-up of the Jonas Brothers, a Spider-Man ad from a magazine that'd been torn out and taped up.

And the oasis in the desert was Lucia. Swathed up in a sagging bed, holes in the mattress pad, mismatched sheets, pillows squashed flat by time, comforter bleeding cotton. Only her face came out of the little burrito she had made of her bedding.

"You've missed five days of school and three Harry Potter marathons on ABC Family," Mindy said.

Lucia grinned blandly. A cheerleader smile-smile-smile! "Hey! Did you know that if your dad ever starts doing heroin, you can stay fashionable by cultivating a vintage look? You keep up on makeup, a little jewelry, some new shoes, most people will never notice that everything else is from a thrift shop. And obviously, you make your own clothes, do a home Gucci knock-off, it's not like anyone will know. Plus, little boys, they can wear the same clothes forever."

"Lucia, stop it."

"Food, food is easy. All those barrels at the supermarket, they go to the church—church people actually buy stuff just to give to you. The craziest shit too. Like, cake mix and green peppers… Hard part there is getting them to just let you pick the damn stuff up, because they'll want you to go to a whole thing and listen to a sermon for poor people and eat salsa dip and you just want to take the food and go because you have a job on the other side of town that might as well be *Mehico* to everyone in school. And I don't eat much to begin with, so…"

"*El*, I don't care that you're poor."

"Of course you don't. You have money; why would you care about it?" Lucia reached over to her nightstand, clearing some schoolbooks off the top. The only other things on it were some cheerleading trophies. Gold-pewter girls flying through the air, only bound to Earth by the trophy stands. "You brought food?"

"Yeah. No cookies though." Mindy set the Tupperware on the nightstand. It was hard to look at Lucia. The aura she put off was of rotting meat, putrid drink. Her lips were thin, and her skin didn't catch the little light in the right way. It made her look gray. Like she'd been burnt into ashes. "Lucia, you look gray."

"I haven't been keeping up with my exfoliating." Lucia unscrewed the bottle of Sprite first. "Need to drink this quick before Abe or Artie find it.

They never get soda, so if they go over to a friend's house and some mommy has Diet Coke, I get little crack addicts for a day. God forbid I don't get them Count Chocula Frosted Shits at the grocery market—"

Mindy had seen evidence of little brothers downstairs. Crayon drawings on the wall that'd only been scrubbed at with water, not Clorox. The faded lines stayed behind like scars. "Lucia, how are you feeling? C'mon, tell me."

"Like shit, Mindy. Simple as that. I feel tired and hungry. So damn hungry. Not the kind of hungry where you just have to wait until your boyfriend shares lunch with you; like he gives a shit—" She smiled condescendingly at Mindy. A tired smile. "Hungry like there's a hole in my stomach. Maybe I'm dying. Maybe that's what it's like when you die. You keep getting hungry, and itchy, and horny. You just can't eat, can't scratch, can't fuck. Can't even sleep. Do you think death's insomnia, Mindy?"

"I think death's what happens when you get old. Eat your soup." Mindy moved to sit down on the bed. Lucia held out her hand, motioning her to stop. It was the first time Mindy had seen her fingernails unpainted.

"I don't want you to catch what I have, Minz."

"Eat. Please."

Lucia pulled the Tupperware into her lap, struggled with the lid, finally got it. The spoon took longer. "I can't afford a doctor."

"I can find one. Someone who'll just come here as a favor."

"I'll be fine, Mindy. I'll get better in a few days. I always do."

"You have to let me do something. Take the boys to soccer practice or whatever. You do that, right?"

"Always so charitable. At first. Takes a while for the resentment to set in. *Why can't Lucia be middle class? Isn't there a form she can fill out?*"

"I don't sound like that," Mindy said to Lucia's nonspecific falsetto. She didn't want to fight. A little voice whispered that she didn't want her last memory of Lucia to be fighting. "Do you remember the night of the party?"

"Must've been an alright party, because *not really*." Lucia's drawl had too much phlegm in it to be properly sarcastic.

"You came over to my house, remember? You were really out of it."

Lucia tried the soup. "What kind of sick are you when food doesn't taste like food?"

"Did you take something or…or could someone have given you something to take…"

Lucia was staring at the ceiling. "Everything tastes like water. Maybe my tongue's messed up. You remember that chart they gave us where it shows what part of your tongue tastes sweet and what tastes bitter…least the part that tastes water is okay."

"That chart's a myth. Your tongue doesn't work like that."

Finally, Lucia looked at her. "You being the expert on my tongue."

"Did you take something?"

Lucia blinked, and in all her brittle hair, her drained face, Mindy could see the blue of her eyes. "Only your heart, darling."

Mindy's teeth ground down on the nothing Lucia gave her. "Let me see your arm." Lucia looked at her. For the first time, those blue eyes were surprised. "Your left arm, Lucia. Let me see it."

Lucia kept it at her side. Under the covers. "I think it's time for you to go."

Mindy stood and wondered why she wasn't so frustrated, now that they were parting. Maybe it was true love. "Get some sleep. Drink plenty of fluids."

She is Lucia, sick in bed. She is wrapped in the cocoon of her sheets, shielding herself with them because the night is too bright and the silence is too loud and the days are even worse. The days bleed. Her arm burns with the venom of the sunlight that stung her. She scratches at it (*it itches it itches it itches*) and peels away a layer of dead skin. And another layer. And another layer. And another layer. Always another layer, peeling and peeling, an onion that doesn't make her cry. Underneath is something the white of bone.

Nothing is a mystery to her anymore except her own body, which has betrayed her for reasons of its own. As a cheerleader, she pushed it to its limits, made it tight and tense and loose and limber. Now it punishes her. It takes her further than its limits. It makes her see everything, hear everything, smell everything.

Because now she can hear the door downstairs open—her baby brother Artie, only seven years old, still so young she has Facebook posts talking about how she got him a glass of water or helped him to the bathroom.

She smells the fear—a bad dream, she wonders if it was of her—and knows with a sister's knowledge that because she is sick, he will not bother her, and because Mom doesn't care, he will not bother her. He goes to Abe instead, who is ten years old. Abe wakes, and she hears them trade curses like Pogs, foul words without the proper inflections to make them offensive, babies playacting arguments.

Abe relents. He takes his brother to the kitchen. Mindy hears the spongy whisper of the carpet absorbing their steps become the slap of the scuffed linoleum deflecting them. Abe strains up to get a glass that was once a jar of grape jelly. He fills it with water but his grip is clumsy; he is still half asleep. The glass falls. It shatters and Artie is too young not to panic. He steps on a piece. There is blood in open air.

Lucia winds herself up in her sheets, makes a straitjacket of them. She thirsts. It's perfume in an unscented world, fresh water on a sea of salt, food in a famine. Not as fresh as Mindy, nothing's smelled as good as Mindy, but it would do. Who wants a vintage wine when they're dying of thirst?

Is this the moment she stops being Abe's sister and becomes his boogeyman? Swallowing him whole. Swallowing Artie and Mom and Mindy and the whole world, to sate her hunger, to choke the black hole.

No.

It's a revolutionary thought: don't find a way to win the game; instead refuse to play. Does her body—the treacherous thing—think she's afraid of pain? Because she's not. She's a cheerleader. She's risked broken bones with every stunt. She's scraped enough skin off her body to make a vest, left blood on the gym floor like semen at a Motel 6. And no one tells her how to finish her routine. She decides for herself.

No, she doesn't bite, she doesn't drink. She gets out of bed. She strips herself bare. She walks naked through the empty house, her house. It doesn't hurt anymore. She opens the doors one last time. She looks in on Abe and Artie. They've fallen asleep in the same bed, Artie's foot swathed in six different Spider-Man Band-Aids. She'd almost yell at them for the waste, if it still mattered.

Her arm burns insistently. Another flap of brittle translucency comes easily off in her hand as she goes to her mother's room. Looks in on her. Maybe this will be good for her. What do they call it, a wake-up call? Shock her back onto the Twelve Steps, give her a good story for those anonymous meetings. She goes to the back door, steps into the backyard with its high fences. No reason to give some early-morning jogger a thrill. The sun is coming up. The sun is coming up, and her skin sizzles like bacon on a skillet. She only wishes the sprinklers were on to help wash the burning newspaper of her skin away. To wash *her* away when she's yesterday barbecue-ash on the back porch. She burns and it doesn't hurt, it really doesn't hurt. It just feels so good to scratch that itch, like chicken pox she can actually dig out of her skin, and it all comes off like a sweaty bra at the end of a twelve-hour shift.

She is burning, and her only wish is that Mindy would understand.

# CHAPTER 10

The PA system crackled in the middle of first period. Mindy was dissecting a frog. It didn't bother her like it did the other girls. Next to the dream she had, it was like a cartoon. She couldn't stop thinking of Lucia burning, even though she'd seen El come out of her house on the way to the bus stop, a huddled mass of hoodie and jeans. She'd run out after her, but by the time she'd come out of her own front door, Lucia was gone. Not answering her phone again. She must've sent a couple hundred texts to Lucia's phone. There was only one she left in her Drafts folder, like a grenade with the pin still inside. It read, *I love you.*

Then the principal was clearing her throat in everyone's ear at once. Mindy knew the routine. Principal Haywood was not newfangled. She only interrupted class for emergencies. Hospital beds. Dead bodies. Finding a copy of *Maxim* on school grounds.

*Please don't let it be Lucia*, Mindy sent out to the universe. She wrote it on her mind in letters too big to be ignored. And the universe listened.

Quentin had been taken to the hospital. He would miss the next game, victim of an animal attack. Something had bit him right in the neck.

Millarca High was abuzz when the bell rang. Electric in the way that only gossip could make it. Mindy noticed glances striking at her, but it was only Pammy who was rude enough to confront her.

She and Tera fell in on either side of Mindy as she hit her locker combination, like raptors preparing for a kill. "You!" Pammy said, "You finally did it. You finally made her like *you.*"

"Did you cast a spell on her?" Tera demanded.

Mindy stopped to look at her. "A *spell?* If you're going to spread rumors about me, can you at least pick one and stick to it? Am I a lesbian or am I a witch?"

"Both!"

"What is this, *Buffy*?"

"*Buffy*? What's that? *Is that a spell?*"

Mindy was about to let her disgust have its way and stomp off, let them pepper her back with insults, but then she heard it. Not a commotion—the halls were still a din of noise. More like a bubble of silence that was traveling, getting bigger and bigger. People sensed it. They clustered into groups, turned their heads to the end of the hall like it was the Blitz and they'd heard an air raid siren. But all Mindy heard was the slap of wedge heels.

Lucia came around the corner not as Lucia, but as someone else. No belly-baring top; no skirt or shorts. Leather pants that could've been borrowed from Catwoman scrolling into sinister-looking boots, red-tinted sunglasses, a snug black-and-white striped shirt under one of those leather jackets every girl wanted after watching *Grease*, all chrome studs and necklaces strung down by the dozen. Meaningless little girl things on chains: coins, lockets, bits of mineral, bits of crystal. But all that was a costume. Shock and awe. What shocked Mindy was *her*.

She was white. Not just pale or pasty, but *white,* a brilliant white, the white of a tropical beach struck by the sun. All her skin was a creamy, milky white, and yet somehow it seemed pristine in its uncompromising starkness after the mottled gray of her illness. Her hair had been chopped to her chin and dyed into a tousle of raven-black bed hair, freshly fucked hair. Her lipstick was dark, her eyeliner wings sharp enough to cut. The blue of her eyes shone entombed in eye shadow.

She walked right by Mindy. Didn't even look.

A few seconds later, it was clear no one was brave enough to follow her. So Mindy did.

"You do something with your hair?" she asked, catching up to Lucia.

"No, I just woke up like this."

"Oh. Because you look like you're either going to sing 'Cherry Bomb' or help Criss Angel with a magic trick. Seriously, what's with all the black leather? We're in Texas. Aren't you hot?"

Lucia stopped to look at her. Her eyes were almost white within all that black. "I'm always hot."

Mindy nodded. The weight of Lucia's gaze was so much heavier than before. "You hear about Quentin? Crazy, right?"

"Maybe it was bad karma."

"He volunteered at the soup kitchen." Mindy tried again. "I dreamt you hurt yourself."

"Like, I wore UGGs?"

"No, you…went out in the sun."

"Are you forgetting which of us is a ginger?" Lucia sighed. "You know you can stop pretending you care now, right? Since I'm not going to eat you out or anything."

And Mindy stood there, staring at her, as Lucia turned and walked away. Maybe she couldn't take that look. Or maybe she was just bored with Mindy. But as she left, Mindy realized the strangest thing of all about Lucia's new look.

All those necklaces and she wasn't wearing her cross.

In her own pre-grief, Mindy hadn't noticed the outpouring of Quentin-love. The trophy case that smelled of him had become his shrine. Someone was selling buttons identifying the wearer as one of the Quentin Morse Support Squad, and the locker room and boys' room spoke of a coyote hunt. And as unnoticed as an asterisk in a magazine ad, the school counselor, Mr. Pletsky, had made himself available for grief counseling.

Mindy thought she was the first person to take him up on it. When she went into his office, she found him building a little house out of trust exercise cards. The top one, the one he was just adding, read *Ask your therapy partner what you can do to make his day more fulfilling.*

"Hey, Mr. Plets," Mindy greeted, amicable as a family reunion.

Mr. Pletsky was a black man, musclebound and gentle as a kitten. He never raised his voice; it was already at the level of a rockslide. "Ms. Murphy! My favorite student!" Everyone was his favorite student. "What can I help you with? Please, tell me."

Mindy sat down across from him and a pillar-card reading *Give your therapy partner a personal item and trust him to return it.* "Well, Mr. Plets, I've been having these nightmares lately? I think it's what happened to Quentin. I mean, he was such a big, strong guy and something just—it makes you afraid to walk the streets at night."

Mr. Pletsky nodded sympathetically. "It's a dangerous world we live in, Ms. Murphy. Dangerous. Dangerous. But there are a few simple steps we can all take to—"

Mindy had to keep him off-balance. Move him, work the mid-section. She heard Lucia urging her on like a ringman in a boxing match. "I keep having these nightmares. There's this animal—sometimes I'm running from it, sometimes I'm fighting it, sometimes it's, it's eating me…"

Mr. Pletsky raised a hand to his lips. "Oh dear."

"I know, it's silly. It's silly. But I thought, maybe if I had some of the facts… I mean, the truth can't be as scary as my dreams, right?"

"No, child. No, never."

"I heard that Quentin lost a lot of blood…" Mindy focused all her Jedi powers on Pletsky. Tried to make him go along with her as hard as she'd ever tried to float a pencil as a kid. "That's not true, *is it?*"

"I'm afraid it is, Mindy." Mr. Pletsky hung his head. "Two whole liters. Thankfully a car was passing by; if someone hadn't called an ambulance… Obviously, we're not allowed to advocate any religion here at school, but *thank Xenu…*"

"And the blood, was it…there?" Mindy asked.

"Excuse me?"

"Was it…with him? Like, on the ground? Around him? Or was it…" Mindy made a butterfly of one hand.

"Ms. Murphy, I don't know if that's really conductive to therapeutic success…"

Mindy edged hysteria into her voice. "Because in my dream, the coyote rips my throat out, and that brings all the other coyotes, and they're all licking up my blood as it runs out of me and there are so many coyotes, Mr. Pletsky!"

A card came loose from its house. *Let your therapy partner know the last way he made you unfulfilled.* "That is just inaccurate, now. All it is, is that animal attacks don't happen in one place. Quentin was probably wounded in some initial attack, then he ran for it, ending up at the side of that road with the aforementioned blood loss. Of course it wasn't *there*. He put up a real fight, Quentin. A real fight."

The edge of hysteria slipped. "So there wasn't any blood where they found him?" Mindy didn't claim to be the best at this.

Mr. Pletsky got defensive. "There was some blood…"

"But not two liters," Mindy guessed. "Not anywhere close to two liters."

Pletsky nodded a little. "Let's not let this dominate our thera-versation. Now, do you do any afterschool activities? Not many people know this, but we have a mock-UN. I've heard from multiple anxiety sufferers that an hour in the UN, and the tension, it just melts away."

Mindy had to be going crazy, because she was thinking crazy thoughts. She was thinking of Lucia walking with Quentin, all boyfriend-girlfriend, teasing him, playing with him. Maybe waiting for it to get dark. Maybe it was already dark. She hears a car coming or she sees the headlights in the distance. So Lucia strikes. Drinks. Leaves Quentin in the middle of the road.

And the next day she's all better. Just needed a little suck-action.

"Well, Mindy?" Mr. Pletsky took her silence for keen interest. "Don't tell me there isn't *one* extracurricular that interests you."

Mindy looked him in the eye. "I was thinking about cheerleading."

"You're in luck, there's an opening. I hear Lucia West just quit the team."

The next morning, they went to their homerooms, and the teachers immediately took attendance. As soon as everyone was accounted for, Mindy and her classmates were lined up and marched to the school auditorium. Principal Haywood had a speech to give, and this time it wasn't about another study on how half a blunt and a sip of vodka could cause eye cancer.

Another animal attack. Joel Shapiro. Haywood didn't linger on the details, but the hushed gossip going through the rows of the assembly covered it. He'd heard his trash cans rustling; raccoons. Went to scare them off with a baseball bat, didn't come back. When his wife went to look for him, she found that someone had bitten a chunk out of his neck and left him for dead. Some said coyote, others said bear. All the while, Haywood kept telling them to use the buddy system, not linger after school, extracurriculars were canceled. That got a few groans, since the football team and cheer squad would still be allowed to practice under supervision.

With Haywood going on and on about staying calm, the assembly stopped paying attention to her. The gory details she wasn't going to supply were more interesting. Pammy said that Dillion Marshall had said that the cops had found the baseball bat broken in half.

Haywood wrapped up and gave them all a chance to use the bathroom or the water fountain. In ten minutes, the police chief was going to say a few words about wild animal safety. Mindy guessed it boiled down to "run."

"Hullo, Mindy," a voice came from beside Mindy, a body dropping into the seat her neighbor had abandoned. Though it was a male voice, she turned, like maybe Lucia's balls had dropped. She caught Seb trying to find a nonchalant lean on the armrest. "Very good to see you. Hope I am not intrude."

He was surprisingly ordinary looking for maybe the only person in Carfax who'd been outside the country. Pale skin on a stick-figure frame, a brush of dark hair, an eclectic collection of T-shirts with Romanian text on them in eye-searing combinations, and seven sets of identical jeans that he bragged were genuine American denim.

"No, Seb, you're fine." Mindy saw a goth, but she was just too emo to be Lucia. She went back to scanning. "What's up?"

"I have heard you were looking forward to newing David Fincher movie, comes out this week, I am think we could see it together?" He laughed nervously. When his teeth came out, they were lined with orthodontics. "You have purse; could get in much more candy than my jeans!"

He pulled out his pockets, like a cartoon character illustrating his poverty.

"Least you have pockets," Mindy replied. "Hey, where'd you hear this?"

"Online? This Tumblr—we follow one another? I am Sebchan7?"

Mindy remembered his tag after a moment. They didn't talk much but he reblogged her often and she returned the favor. "Yeah, yeah, you make those mash-ups... I have 'Black Skinhead' and 'Glory And Gore' on my iPod."

"Yes! Always good meeting fan." He smiled again; it was easy for him. "So, yes-no on movie?"

Mindy smiled back automatically, thinking of the old canard that you never got any interest until you were actually in a relationship. "Are you asking me out on a date?"

He nodded big, like a machine designed for nodding. "Not big date, though. Little date." He held his forefinger and thumb apart a short distance, then moved them around. Making the distance greater, smaller. "*Leetle* date, little date…" He shrugged.

"Thanks for the offer, but I can't. I have this person…" Mindy chanced a look at the empty doorway, just to see if Lucia was a straggler. She wasn't. "It's complicated."

"Alright. Hoping I have not offended. Take it as simple compliment; you seem like you would be very good girlfriend."

She smiled at him again. It wasn't so easy now. "I try to be."

Someone tapped on a hot microphone, sending reverberations through the sound system. Seb's eyes flitted around, seeing the student whose seat he'd taken returning. "I must go! I hope you work things out with your person. And my offer stands if you just want person to help pay for movie ticket. Movie tickets very expensive in America."

The police chief took the stage, announcing a big fat curfew. As groans of dismay filled the auditorium, Mindy got out her phone, looked up Seb's Tumblr, and opened an instant message to him. She left it blank as she locked her phone again. She didn't know what to say to Lucia either, and it felt like nothing could get through that barricade. Without Lucia, she couldn't feel anything.

"You're a dead man!" Mark Strong yelled, stabbing his knife into Frankenstein's heart.

"Yeah," Frankenstein said, before swatting him away and pulling the knife out. "I am."

Watching *Frankenstein* for the second time with Seb, Mindy came to a realization: it really was a bad movie.

In the last four weeks, she'd seen three movies with Seb. The David Fincher one, a showing of *Blade 2* at the Alamo Drafthouse, and now a redux of *Frankenstein: Origins* at the dollar theater.

It'd been a lazy month. The curfew was safe, but it was boring, everyone Mindy knew staying indoors, tweeting about the same dumb shows, the same dumb people. Megan Fox had said something stupid, apologized. Shia LeBeouf said something stupid, didn't apologize. Up in LA, Benson Mears had been admitted to the hospital for anemia.

And in Carfax, Texas, Ontorio Jackson suffered the latest animal attack. He should've been safe. He worked at an auto shop, had waited with his coworkers to all leave together, they'd all gotten into their cars at the same time, and all had driven to their various homes. But for some reason, he'd stopped in the middle of the road, put his car in park, opened the door and… From the blood, they said it was like he'd been shaken around by the neck. Like a dog with a rat.

Mindy had told Seb from the word go that she wasn't looking for a relationship or a boyfriend, and he hadn't tried to sneak his tongue down her throat while she wasn't looking. Seb was actually kinda cool, really. Back in Romania, he'd used to do knife dancing. It was like folk dancing, but people threw knives at your feet. Tonight, though, she wasn't just helping Seb with his English and enjoying his bewilderment at movies that really wanted to be part of the *Underworld* series but couldn't afford Kate Beckinsale in a leather catsuit. She was trying to remember the spot of white she'd seen in the backrow as she'd looked for a seat. Because the longer she sat, the more she was convinced it was Lucia's face. Mindy felt attuned to her. Like a Geiger counter picked up radiation, she felt—what? The pangs of Lucia's heart?

As if Lucia had a heart.

Mindy got up to get a popcorn refill and visit the bathroom. She'd seen the movie already, after all, and didn't feel like revisiting the bit where Frankenstein killed Tom Sizemore with a flamethrower. "Fire bad—for you!"

When she came out of the stall, Lucia was standing at the counter, looking like the Ghost of Christmas Post-Apocalyptic.

"Don't mindfreak me," Mindy said.

Lucia was invincible for such long stretches of time—eons—that when she let herself be small, Mindy never knew if it was a choice or not. "You don't like the way I look?" she asked quietly.

"It's a lot to take in."

Lucia pulled up the belly of her plain white tee, jangling her sunglasses where they dangled on her neckline. Her stomach was a little pale, but mostly as burnished as ever. "It's just makeup." She let the shirt drop back down. "You know, you've got crazy taste in movies."

"How's that?"

Lucia walked to Mindy. Her hand lashed out—it hit the wall over Mindy's shoulder. She was leaning over her now—bearing down on Mindy like a ghost ship ready to run aground. "Well, sometimes you're into really good movies, small movies, not the shit that sells Happy Meal toys. Like you really care what you watch. And then sometimes, you seem to watch movies just to kill an hour and a half. They could be about anything. Just so long as you don't have to *think*." Her hand came away. She was standing before Mindy once more, almost a supplicant in her backing away. "Maybe it's the company."

Lucia's metaphors were no Robert Frost poem. "Seb is just a friend."

"Friend? Sniffing around your panties like a hungry dog—" Lucia gritted her teeth. "You should keep him on a leash."

Something about the way she said it poured gasoline on the embers of Mindy's feelings. They burst into hot anger. She stepped up to Lucia. "What do you even *care?* Maybe I fuck him every night. Is that what you want to hear? That I suck his cock? That I let him jam it in my ass? Is that what you think?"

Lucia's teeth ground down like glaciers crashing together. "I *don't* care."

"Bullshit. I know what I felt. I know what *you* felt. Why can't you just say it? Why can't you just say that you've missed me?" And like that, like a candle being blown out, Mindy's anger was gone. "I've missed you."

Lucia stared at her "Don't put this on me."

"I am putting it on you. Because you talk and you talk and you talk—" Someone pushed through the door. Mindy swiveled on her. "Use the boys' room!" The girl disappeared. Mindy faced Lucia with tears in her eyes. "You act like such a big slut, like such a badass, but you can't even kiss me. You can't even fucking kiss me."

Lucia just stood there. Taking it. "It wouldn't change anything if I did. So why bother?"

"Because I don't want Seb. I don't want some girl—I don't even want Angelina Jolie. I want *you*. But you're a coward. You're not brave enough to be with me—"

"Don't say that."

"You just have to open your mouth. That's all you have to do. That's how fucking pathetic I am—that if you'd just open your mouth, I'd be yours." Lucia's black lips worked over each other, showing Mindy the startling ivory of her white teeth inside her luscious mouth. "Just open your mouth."

And she was kissing Lucia suddenly, her lips tingling, her body singing like an addict that'd finally gotten her fix, but Lucia's mouth was stubbornly closed. Mindy nearly pulled away, embarrassed, but almost immediately, Lucia began to give. Her lips parted and Mindy seized on it, taking it as a gentle invitation to her tongue, and slowly Lucia was receiving, then was giving, and the hands knotted at her sides were rising, opening, ready to draw Mindy to her, to lock their two halves together, to complete them.

Then Mindy felt the sharp pain in her mouth. She threw herself back, her lower lip hurting worse than when she'd let Casey Jaye pierce her ears. She was bleeding. She tasted it, wiping out the memory of Lucia's honeyed taste— everything was the bitter offensiveness of blood.

"You bit me." Mindy didn't accuse, just stated. She wondered if this was what shock felt like? She wiped her mouth. "You bit me, Lucia."

Lucia left before anything else could happen, before Mindy knew how she felt. Five seconds later, when Mindy thought to follow her, she was gone like the sun behind a cloud.

That night, she dreamt of Lucia again. Lucia holding Seb by the throat, saying that if he broke Mindy's heart, she would rip his out.

She woke up. Damp sheets. Warm sweat. Mindy remembered that when she had gone back into the theater, Seb had been rubbing his throat.

Fanning her pajamas out from her body, Mindy went to the window. Lucia's blinds were still drawn, but they were moving. Mindy blinked and saw a white leg, sinewy as an insect's, sliding out from under them. She looked down—and barely saw but *did see*—Lucia crawling down the side of the house like a fucking lizard, headfirst, *slithering*, until she reached the AC unit and dismounted like a cheerleader would, uncoupling her feet from where they stuck to the wall, bending them down over her head to hit the ground, then letting go with her hands and coming upright.

It'd happened so fast that the white football jersey she wore hadn't even had time to be pulled down by gravity; now she smoothed it over her body, down to bare mid-thigh. Her feet crinkled on the night-damp grass as she walked to the sidewalk.

Mindy didn't think at all. She couldn't. She slid her feet into her nearest flip-flops and started down the stairs.

# CHAPTER II

What the fuck was that? What the fuck had she seen? Something—something with shadows, her half-asleep, Lucia just climbing down with a rope or—or something. Mindy had no idea, no idea why she was following Lucia, no idea what she would do if Lucia noticed her, no idea what she was planning or hoping or doing or anything.

Lucia walked down the sidewalk, firm, unafraid, unyielding, her pert body moving beneath her loose jersey—one of Quentin's?—like muscles beneath the skin. Mindy could see the curve of her inner thigh gathering the moonlight with every long, supple step. She felt herself stir with attraction for Lucia. But for the first time, she found herself thinking of it not as beauty but as a kind of camouflage. The red on a black widow was pretty too.

*Why the hell am I following her, then?*

Mindy guessed some people just liked spiders.

She slid from house to house, always around the corner, behind bushes or cars, trying to never ever be in Lucia's line of sight in case she stopped, turned around. But Lucia never even slowed down. She kept walking, walking, like a robot, almost, if there weren't something terribly *alive* about the way she moved—almost a caricature of life, those swinging hips, that sinuous motion.

She didn't seem to be following a path, but Mindy eventually noticed that every few meters, dogging her footsteps like a friendly corgi was a mushroom so white it almost glowed in the dark. Had Lucia left them behind on some prior *Paranormal Activity* sleep-walk, or were they guiding her now?

*Or are they just fucking mushrooms, Mindy, damn!?*

Despite the late hour, the streets weren't completely deserted. As much as Carfax might want to pretend otherwise, it was the twenty-first century, and the sidewalks didn't roll up at nine p.m. There were those who stumbled from bar to bar, alley to alley—bleary-eyed from spending the daylight in bed, still not awake now, but having a nightmare on their feet.

The street ended in a wishbone intersection, and parked on the curb was a red pickup scarred with rust, hubcaps grimy, bumper dented. It wasn't parked for the night. The dome light was on, its stale glow capturing the man inside like a spotlight. Daryl Koontz.

Mindy had read about intrusive thoughts. Everyone had them. You held a baby, you thought about dropping it; you drove a car, you thought about running someone over; you saw someone pretty, you thought about... It happened to everyone.

Most people, Mindy thought, backed away from those thoughts that scuttled over their brain like a cockroach on a bathroom floor. And the thought left them be. The immune system of their mind racked it up and overcame it, and whoever it was cooed at the baby instead, listened to the car radio, struck up a polite conversation and went on a date.

Some people leaned into it, though. They picked up those little cockroach-thoughts and fed them. And the thoughts lingered. And the thoughts rotted, until you could tell they were at home. Smell 'em. Some people you couldn't tell; they hid it well. But a lot of people—they didn't bother hiding. They let it fester like it was something to be proud of.

Daryl Koontz—you could hear the music pumping inside his skull, catch snippets of it through his leering eyes and his grinning mouth. "Hey baby," the grizzled old man called, leaning out the open window of his truck, "how about a nice smile to go with that nice ass?"

Mindy ducked behind a transformer box. Lucia stood in the middle of the road. The nearest streetlight was flickering, but Mindy could see her smile.

Daryl wasn't running. Couldn't he see it?

Lucia's bare feet on the asphalt, tiny, white, their whiteness somehow making the black road even darker. Making her walk on shadow as she went up to the truck. The streetlight finally gave up the ghost. No light but the moon; so quiet they could've been on the other side of it.

Lucia stopped a foot away from the door. The football jersey was molded to her. "You're right, it is a nice ass. Want to go somewhere and talk about it?"

Daryl looked her over, she looked Daryl over. Windbreaker, cotton shirt, Longhorn hat that was mostly camouflage pattern. Nothing stained, nothing frayed, but all of it wrinkled, ruffled, pitching shadows that inundated him. Just like the crags in his face. "How old are you?"

"Sixteen," Lucia lied. "But I talked to Mavis Quinn. She said that wasn't a problem."

Daryl's head tipped down. The shadow of his cap soaked into his face. "That what she said?"

Lucia leaned forward, the folds of her jersey dropping, dripping off her. She put her hands on the window frame. "You know how it is. She can't say she wants it. Not in public. She's a good girl." From her tone—it was so like Lucia, which was a crazy thing to think because it *was* Lucia—Mindy could imagine her rolling her eyes. "Deep down, though, us girls don't want foreplay or cunnilingus. We want it hard. And we want some beer, too. If you have any."

The cap pitched back up, his face came out of the dark like a great white came out of the depths. He was smiling. "Got some riding shotgun with me. Why don't you hop in? We'll go someplace private. Talk about that thing we discussed." His laugh sounded like a machine breaking down. Lucia circled the truck as he started it up. Headlights came on, shot through Lucia as she flounced through them. Turned her jersey so white, Mindy thought she could see her skeleton.

Mindy moved before she quite thought what she was doing. She zipped across the street, down under another car parked behind the truck. She saw Lucia's feet next to the truck's right front tire. There was a broken beer bottle in the gutter of the curb. Lucia stepped on it after she opened the passenger door. It broke under her foot like she was wearing army boots.

Mindy had her cell phone with her. *Typical teenage girl, never go anywhere without my cell phone, not even investigating X-Files.* She knew the number for 911. She should call them. Get the cops here before something happened. She crawled forward, out from under the car, still crouched behind the truck. Right in front of the license plate. *CS1-H821.* She read it, repeated it, repeated it, had it in her memory. She could call the cops on him. Make this stop.

But the truck's engine was growling, Daryl was wrestling his way through the gear shift, he was about to go and take Lucia with him, and Mindy couldn't lose her. Couldn't keep losing her.

*Don't do anything stupid, Mindy.* She put her foot on the rear bumper and threw herself over the cargo gate, hit the truck bed with its litter of wood chips and small fleet of empty beer cans. Mindy pressed herself to the cold metal; it sent chilled shocks up her body, had her shivering like she was electrocuted, but all she could hope was that Daryl hadn't seen her.

She could see him through the cab's rear window. He was bent over, turning on the radio. Country music. It was like some people didn't care about being a cliché.

Two turns and they were on the highway. Mindy hit 811, saw her mistake, cleared it, dialed 911. It rang, rang, rang. God, you'd think if anyone would pick up on the first ring, it'd be 911! *Klik*: "911, what's your emergency?"

Mindy was not good at lying. "Hi, uh, I saw a driver in a red truck, red pickup truck, he had a license plate—" She gave the operator the number, reciting it like it was the first fifteen digits of pi. *CS1-H821.* "Yeah, he was driving really erratically, swerving and I think he was driving and drinking, drunk driving, driving while drinking—beer... He got onto North Bell headed...north. *Bye.*" She hung up. Ugh, terrible. Why couldn't 911 take texts like a normal person?

Daryl turned them onto Carfax Lane, an ancient subdivision that was more trees than house—every yard was something like a quarter-mile. They hit Prize Oaks Drive, and halfway down that bumpy road, Daryl turned off onto a half-mile of rut-worn gravel. A driveway, but Mindy saw the foreclosure sign they passed. No one was in the house up ahead, and they stopped far short of it anyway. Daryl shushed the engine, the radio and lights went off with it, and the forest rushed in. Cicadas, frogs, a barking dog somewhere. The quiet kind of noise.

Somehow the quiet in the cab was loudest. Mindy looked through the rear window and saw Daryl dig up a beer from a cooler in Lucia's footspace. It took him a long time; Mindy imagined him touching Lucia's bare leg as he straightened and she thought she might punch through that safety glass just to get to him. *What am I doing?*

"Here. Have some," Daryl said, pulling the tab like he was about to throw a grenade.

Lucia stared at it like she was looking through a microscope. "I don't drink...Bud Light."

"Well, I got something you will drink."

The little slap of him working his belt leather out of his loop to work the buckle. The chime of the buckle springing loose. The hiss of his zipper coming down. Mindy thought she would do it. She would throw his door open, haul him out of his seat, toss him right down on the ground where he belonged. She could do it. If she moved fast, took him by surprise—sure she could do it.

"Why don't you get down there?" Daryl asked. "See if you can relieve my condition?"

"But you're so hard—all that blood down there. I really would prefer it up here." She brushed his cheek. Her touch cold, clinical. Lucia didn't touch that way. Not with Mindy. "Do you think you could blush? Maybe if I told a dirty joke?"

"This shit ain't funny, little girl. You had time to play coy on the ride over, now get on down there and put those cocksucker lips to good use!"

"You want me to suck you?"

His voice roughened, gravel mixing into it. "Woman, do I have to stop asking nice like I been doing?"

Lucia just smiled at him, head cocked fondly to the side like he was a puppy doing something cute. "Hey, you know how us teens are always doing crazy shit like rainbow parties and sex bracelets—donkey punches?" He nodded testily. "Wanna see what all the cool kids are into now?"

Her head drifted back, *fast*, like a cobra preparing to strike. All of a sudden her eyeteeth were longer, a pair of switchblades flicking out, tapering to razor-sharp points. They were fangs; so white they could've been diamonds.

Daryl stared at them. He was more confused than afraid, but his body was rearing back, like he had smelled something foul, heard something loud. It tried to get away while his mind was still working through the torpor he'd been lulled into.

"Don't worry," Lucia said, as the whites of her eyes bled red, the irises bled black, the two almost oscillating they were so vibrant. So alive. "I'm just gonna put in the tips."

Then she struck, so hard she jammed all Daryl's two hundred and sixty pounds against the door. Her fangs dug into his throat, pulled in a killing stroke like a Marine with his KA-BAR, dragging through his jugular, carotid, windpipe. The blood exploded out of him, but Lucia was a cap on an oil well, latching onto the deep gorge she'd torn, her throat already working greedily.

Daryl's hands flailed, slapping at the steering wheel. Lucia patiently collared them at the wrists and pinned them over his head. Her cheeks were blooming, a rush of blood to the head, just not her own.

At some point, Mindy started screaming, and at some point, Lucia pulled herself away from her prey to look at Mindy through the blood dripping down the rear window. Red painted a grisly smile on her from cheek to cheek and down her throat, down to the tops of her breasts.

She looked past Mindy, out the windows, out the windshield. Lights were turning on, little match points in the windows of the houses next door. Rolling her red eyes, Lucia opened her door and got out. "God, Mindy, way to player-hate. Now there's gonna be cops, guys with guns, torches, pitchforks—"

It all made sense now. It made no sense at all, *but it all made sense now.* She thought she'd woken up from the nightmare of Lucia being a monster, but all this time, thinking it was impossible was when she'd been asleep. "You're a vampire!"

Lucia shook her head condescending, her eyes rolling so far back in her head that Mindy wondered if it was a Bram Stoker thing. "I'm not a vampire, Mindy."

"You have blood dripping from your fangs!"

Lucia closed her open mouth. Then shrugged. "Okay, I'm a little bit a vampire."

"And you have fangs!"

Lucia huffed. "*Okay,* you got me, I'm not a werewolf! That doesn't excuse you being a little B-word and letting everyone know there's an episode of *Supernatural* going on in their backyard. Things get a little PG-13 and you scream? Wow, Minz, *wow.* What are you even doing out here?"

Mindy stood on shaking legs. She could barely keep herself from slipping right out of the truck bed. She held onto the top of the cab like a little old lady without her cane. "What am I doing out here? You're drinking someone's blood!"

"Yeah, but I, like, need blood or else I start to rot and stuff. You were watching me drink blood. That's a lot weirder."

"That's weirder? *Weirder?*" Mindy sat back on the cab, Lucia casually climbing onto the truck bed, sitting down cross-legged at Mindy's feet. Talking to her like they were friends.

Were they friends? "Are you gonna kill me?"

Lucia's shock broke right through her Bela Lugosi impression. "Kill you? God, Mindy, *no.* We're besties! I know we're going through a rough patch, but once Tera and I liked the same boy and we didn't kill each other!" She laughed.

"But you—but I saw you kill him—I'm a witness. Oh God, I could go into witness protection!" Mindy's mom watched a lot of *In Plain Sight.* It did not look fun. And, Mindy belatedly realized, perhaps she shouldn't be pointing this out to the murderer.

"He's not dead!" Lucia giggled, flopping her wrist exaggeratedly. "I just took a little." She glanced at the blood-smeared rear window. "Okay, maybe a lot. It's that O-negative blood. Makes me such a pig. But yeah, he'll be fine. It turns out, you don't need all that much blood! Besides, I have it on good authority that guy went no-daddy-bad-touch on Mavis Quinn, so maybe that was the molesty part of his blood. I heard in history class that doctors used to put leeches on you to suck out the bad blood when you got sick."

Lucia rose like she was weightless, suddenly sitting down beside Mindy on the cab. "That's kinda what I'm doing, only I'm, like, sucking out the *bad blood* of society? It's like a metaphor. Wow, I'm totally applying all these English class teachings to my real life. You think I'll use calculus next?"

Mindy couldn't think, couldn't process. All her mind was taken up with the memory of Lucia biting Daryl, like a shark, teeth rending flesh, blood flying, the very stuff of him being ripped apart by Lucia, by her mouth, by her teeth… It wasn't like *The Walking Dead.* It was all skin cells and blood vessels and real. "So, you—so, you—you just drink people. You just—"

Lucia reached out to Mindy, straightening her wind-blown hair, brushing her face. Her hands were warm now. Warm with stolen blood. "I know what you're thinking. If you were a vampire, you'd just eat murderers and racists, jerks like that. But it's not like people advertise they're scumbags."

From somewhere in her haze, Mindy found herself replying "Not unless they're on Reddit."

"Yeah, not unless *nerd humor.*" Lucia shook her head with a smile. She looked out into the distance. "I'm forgetting something—" Below her, in the cab, Daryl gave a gurgle. "No, not that." She tapped the rear window with her heel. "Keep pressure on it, up-skirt shot, you'll be fine." Lucia snapped her fingers. "We need to make a thrilling escape, or like, they'll probably put us in prison. I can hear sirens on the highway. My hearing's really good now. I'm like one of those kung fu masters who go blind, but train their senses so they can still fight."

Mindy didn't know what it was. Maybe it was just that she'd gotten used to the sight of blood after she got her first period in the girls' locker room. But something went *ping* and suddenly she was in survival mode. Lucia was a vampire, molester van guy was bleeding out, okay, fine—but she was not going to jail. "We should run! We'll go into the woods and if we find a stream, we can wash off our scent so the dogs won't find us!" she babbled.

Lucia stood, a casual finger on Mindy's shoulder keeping her sitting. "Easy there, Jason Bourne, no need for a hike. Just open your legs."

"We have time for that?" Mindy asked unthinkingly.

Lucia huffed a sigh. "Quit the lesbian act, I'm not playing soccer with you. Wrap your legs around me before I slap you."

"We have time for *that*?" Mindy persisted, feeling like being a little bit of an asshole. But she opened her legs.

Lucia stepped in, pressing herself to Mindy. Mindy knew without being told that Lucia wanted her arms around her. She wrapped herself around Lucia and Lucia returned the favor, one hand at the back of Mindy's neck to support her head like she was a newborn.

"Your hair's really soft," Lucia said. "Did you finally stop using that store-brand conditioner?"

"I splurged."

"It shows. Now you might wanna close your eyes."

Mindy did. Well, it was more like she blinked. Suddenly, her stomach *lurched*. She felt subzero air on her skin. Wind chill, pushing on her with physical force. She opened her eyes: Lucia was carrying her, she was facing backward, and the world was ripping past her in a blur. So fast she might as well have been flipping channels on her grandma's TV. Woods, road, woods, road, grass, suburbs, turn, house, house, driveway, side-yard, *stop*.

Lucia set her down.

Mindy promptly vomited.

"That's really gross," Lucia said, "but it'll probably be good for your dress size."

Mindy fell to her hands and knees and managed to land to the side of her spew when she fell over. She was dizzy—completely discombobulated, and disconnected from her body, gravity, the world at large. Her vision swam like a kaleidoscope. Nothing was straight anymore. Someone had mixed all the paint together.

Lucia knelt down beside her, her hand massaging Mindy's back. "Yeah, I don't think you're meant to travel at warp speed like that, puny human. We were going Mach 5 or something—shaving razor speed." Lucia patted Mindy on the spine with her joke. "Pretty cool, though, right? And how about me supporting your head so no whiplash?"

Mindy rested her forehead against the grass. It was cold. Damp. Real. "How'd this happen to you? What…what's going on?"

Lucia lightly scratched between Mindy's shoulder blades. "Something bit me, now I'm superstrong and really fast… I think it's obvious what happened. I'm Spider-Man now."

"Oh God…oh *God…*" Mindy pounded her head into the soil. "We killed someone! We—I should've—what if he dies?"

"Mindy, it's cool."

"It is not cool!" Mindy turned over, scrambling backward until she backed into the wall of her house. She pressed herself into it like she could pass right through the brick. "What if he recognized you? What if he tells the cops, what if he comes looking for you?"

"It's cool," Lucia insisted. She reached into her mouth and drew back her lip with her forefinger. Mindy could see the petite point of her canines, still sharp. "I hab thib g'and…" Lucia let go of her lip, realizing she was muffling her words. "This gland in the roof of my mouth. Really hard to stop touching it with my tongue. Anyway, it's full of this venom and, this is cool, it basically gives people amnesia. Like tequila, only much cheaper. So, yeah, he's not gonna remember any of it. Oh, I can milk the venom out of my gland. It's just like they do with cobras on YouTube, and it feels *really* good…"

"Are you high?" Mindy shouted.

Lucia canted her head. "There's a bit of a sugar rush, I suppose. Blood sugar rush. Ugh, that was horrible, forget I made that joke."

"You're a vampire!"

"Keep your voice down."

"You're a fucking vampire!"

"People are trying to sleep, Minz, it's a school night."

Mindy looked at Lucia. How had it taken her this long to notice—really notice—that Lucia's entire jaw was smeared with blood? It stood out, black in the moonlight, but still a little red, vivid on her pale face. Real.

Mindy thumped her head back against her house. "Okay. Okay, I know what to do."

"Do you, Mindy? Do you know what to do when you're BFFs with a vampire? Because that is going to be some very useful knowledge now."

"We need to get you cleaned up before someone sees you." Mindy turned on the garden hose, cupping her hands under it, washing Lucia's face with the water. Lucia knelt on her hands, leaned forward like she was going to have her first kiss. "We'll go to the police, we'll go to the FBI. Maybe someone knows about this and it's just classified, maybe there's a treatment or a cure…"

Lucia rolled her eyes. "Or maybe they'll dissect me in Area 51 to figure out how to get a superspeed pill on the market. I've thought of this, Minz. The government can't even keep the Obama girls getting bukkaked a secret; if they knew about this, it would be out there. People would tweet about it. But nobody knows, so… Plus, I need blood or I turn into Sarah Jessica Parker without makeup."

There was so much blood on her mouth. It wasn't just a bloody nose, a scraped elbow. It was like stripping *paint*. Mindy practically slapped at Lucia, getting it all off. "They'd give you blood! From hospitals! Not from—people!"

"I know I'm white, Mindy, but I'm not that white. I'm a twentieth Cherokee, so I'm not trusting The Man here."

Finally, Mindy thought she had all of it off. She just held Lucia's face. The spigot kept running. "What about animal blood?"

"I tried that, and I don't think my little brother's guinea pig is ever gonna forgive me." Lucia saw Mindy's look. "Tidwell's fine! I just used a little syringe and did a taste test."

"Yeah, on the guinea pig you use a syringe, on the *dude*—the human *dude*—"

"Tidwell never raped anyone, Mindy. Except my shoe once, and it was pretty adorable."

"This is crazy." Mindy felt her mind going again. It was a weird sensation—being able to pinpoint how insane you were going. "This is crazy, it's crazy. Please tell me that it's a prank. You're the best at pranks, okay Lucia? You really got me, and I've really learned whatever it is you meant to teach me by pretending to be a vampire, but let's just stop and—El, please."

It was so serious the way Lucia looked at her. So sad. "Alright, you're taking this a lot better than I have, but I think we've hit peak Mindy, so let's get you to bed and in the morning we can talk more about it. I'm actually kinda glad I can share this with you now. It's not like this is the sort of thing you can blog about. Start telling the Internet you're a teenage vampire cheerleader, you get real weird e-mails real fast."

"Oh, fuck...fuck, Lucia." Mindy ground her hands into her head. "This isn't happening, this is—I'm having a nightmare. Or some really bad acid trip. So bad I don't even remember taking acid. But it makes sense. I mean, we have this lesbo thing between us, vampires are historically known for their queer sexuality, it's in *Carmilla*, *Dracula*..."

"Oh God, when you get high, do you seriously start talking about literature? Sometimes I can't believe we're friends." Lucia reached over and turned off the spigot. "Okay, beddy-bye and a couple Ambien for the party girl. Climb onto my back, I'll take you up."

"What?" Mindy said flatly.

"I can stick to walls too. I told you, I'm Spider-Man. Well, at least as much Spider-Man as Andrew Garfield. God, those movies." Lucia stood, turning away from Mindy. "C'mon, little monkey, hop on. Unless *your* parents don't care what you've been doing out this late either, which would be a pretty big coincidence."

What a wonderful morning Mindy woke up to. She could think it had all been a dream. And it had been. Had to have been. Vampires? In Texas?

Maybe in Austin, *maybe*. But not here. Not Lucia. It was just a combination of Tex-Mex before bed, Lucia's goth phase, and a fetish or two Mindy was just finding out about herself.

Then Mindy looked out her window. Lucia's blinds were up. The girl had a Sony Handycam aimed at her, the view-finder flipped around to display its screen to Lucia as she filmed herself…applying foundation.

Noticing Mindy, she waved at her with a white hand. Mindy was so relieved. It-was-all-a-dream-or-was-it? She could even put up with the cliché, if she could finally be on speaking terms with Lucia again.

So she waved back. Even if Lucia was a vampire.

Her best friend, the vampire.

She washed up, put on something mildly flattering and went downstairs. "Hey Mom, Dad, what's for breakfast?" The casual words sounded like a foreign language to Mindy.

They were sitting at the breakfast nook, talking in the hushed tones of the adult world. There was a third person there, a blocky man in a seersucker suit, bolo tie. She thought the white Stetson on the table was his as well. He looked familiar to Mindy, but she couldn't place him. That was going to bug her.

"We were just going to get you, honey," her mother said, then: "The police are here."

*Well, every mother wanted to say that to her daughter.* "Hi, police," Mindy replied. Still too in a state of shock to be nervous. It was her last set of finals all over again.

The man stood. "Lou Card, Texas Highway Patrol. I'm here about the attacks we've been seeing lately in this county."

"The animal attacks?"

He looked at her coolly. "Some people say that." He picked his hat up off the table, held it in his hands as he circled his chair. "Last night, 911 got a call from your cell phone reporting a DUI. Did you place that call?"

*Be cool, don't look like you're being cool, be uncool.* "Yeah," Mindy said readily, "I couldn't sleep, I saw a car…um, pickup truck, driving all weird, so I called it in. See something, say something, right?"

"Right." Card perched the hat on his head. "The driver of that vehicle, Daryl Koontz, was found last night. He'd been attacked—something practically tore his throat out."

"That's horrible," Mindy said. No acting required. "Is he okay?"

"He's lost a lot of blood," Card said noncommittally. But present-tense. Card took a notepad from his jacket pocket and prepared a pen.

"Mindy." Her father held his cup of coffee like a talisman. "Now, you don't need to talk to this man if you don't want to."

"I know, Dad, it's fine," Mindy said, like a liar. "I wish I could help you, but I just saw his truck."

Card's pen scratched at his pad like he was chipping ice. "You saw him turn onto North Bell?"

"Yes, sir."

"And is that your room upstairs with the window over the garage?"

"Yes."

"So how is it you saw him getting on North Bell, to the North, when your bedroom faces south?"

Mindy shrugged. This was easy. It was like he wasn't even trying to crack her. "I couldn't sleep, I was walking around. I saw him out of a back window."

Card nodded agreeably. He clicked his pen, drawing the tip back in, and Mindy saw Lucia's fangs disappearing into the shadows of her mouth. "Two things. One, we did a blood test on Mr. Koontz. He had a 0.02 BAC." He looked to Mindy's parents. "That's about what you would get drinking some table wine out on the town. Not something that would impair driving."

"Maybe he was a lightweight," Mindy said, and instantly regretted it. Defending her story—that made it a story.

"Second," Card said, "I've been asking around, and no one else saw Mr. Koontz driving erratically."

*Did they see me?* "It was pretty late."

"Yes, it was. Do you always stay up that late on a school night?"

"I had trouble sleeping."

"Bad dreams?"

"Trouble sleeping."

Mindy's father stood, his hands on the table like all the times she'd asked for a puppy. "Mr. Card, I'm not sure what the point of badgering my daughter this way is. She's told you all she knows; if she knew anything that would help you figure this thing out, she would tell you. Wouldn't you, sweetie?"

Her mother broke in. "But if you're not telling the detective something because you think it'll make us upset, you don't have to worry. Just be honest. Whatever it is can't be as important as solving the case. Is it a boy? A girl?"

Card's eyebrow raised.

She thought she recognized him now. Less shaved, less preened, but she'd delivered a pizza to him. He hadn't tipped. She wondered if she could report that to Internal Affairs. "I couldn't sleep, so I walked around the house, I saw someone driving weird out the window, so I called it in. Then I went back to bed."

Card tapped his pen against his lip. "That's what you want me to put down in my report? Nothing else?"

"There's nothing else to put."

The pen and notepad slid back into his jacket. "All right then. Thank you for your time, Miss Murphy." He nodded stiffly to her parents. "And the coffee, Mrs. Murphy. If any of you think of something you'd like to share, be sure and place a call." He gestured to the business card he'd left on the kitchen table. "Take care now."

# CHAPTER 12

Mindy wasn't surprised when Lucia called soon after. "What did that loser want?"

Sitting on the toilet, she put her phone on speaker and set it on the counter next to her. She wasn't dropping it in like that time at Barnes & Noble—with the plumber. "He was a cop, El. He was asking about you."

"*Oh.*"

"Not you, specifically. Just…last night."

"Oh, okay." Lucia sounded blandly relieved. "You listen to the new Britney? It's super-gay, you'd like it."

"Are you not worried that I'd tell him…something?"

"Nah, I trust you. Besides, what would he do, go up to a judge and say 'Give me a warrant, this girl's a vampire'?"

Mindy bit her lip. "I could stop you. If I had to."

Quiet on the line. "Wow, Mindy, I'm feeling really attacked right now. I'm not going to respond to that, because it's not what Jesus would do, but you're really lucky you didn't tell him anything. I'm saying this as a friend."

"Fine, whatever. You still wanna meet up?"

"Yeah, but I have to babysit my dumbass little brothers. You mind hanging at the dog park with the fanny pack set?"

"See you there."

"Later, hooker."

But Mindy wouldn't be going to school. She had shopping to do.

Most reputable gun stores did not carry crossbows. Totally overlooked market.

You *could* fill an empty Ozarka bottle with holy water at St. Margaret Mary Catholic Church, but the priest gave you a look and asked if you had something you would like to confess in a really insinuating tone. If they sold crucifixes there, Mindy certainly wasn't going to buy from them after that.

Stakes were easy. Go to the junkyard, find a sturdy chair leg, and then whittle a stake out of it. Though whittling was a lot harder than it looked. It took Mindy about an hour and a half to get a good one done—so much for the bandolier of stakes she had planned.

It turned out Wal-Mart *did* have UV flashlights. Mindy had thought she would have to trick Lucia into one of those UV manicure lamps. Not that she thought an ultraviolet light would do much good when she'd *seen* Lucia walking around in the sun, but it had helped in the *Blade* movies.

So did silver, even if Mindy was pretty sure that was werewolves. Still, she took a photo of her Grams in a silver frame with her.

Box cutter, pepper spray, her mom's stun gun, a rape whistle, and fuck it, a good-sized rock. She emptied her purse of everything, including way more candy wrappers than she would've thought, and filled it with an arsenal.

She didn't *want* to hurt Lucia, or slay her, or whatever, but she wasn't going to talk to a vampire armed only with the sharp Hello Kitty knucks on her keyring.

Mindy decided to wear a scarf as well. Just in case.

"You look like fucking Harry Potter in that scarf," Lucia said.

"And you look like a Tim Burton movie. Do a British accent, I'll think you're Johnny Depp."

Lucia wore Keds Royal Hi Canvas sneakers, Ray-Ban aviator sunglasses, a white V-neck beater stenciled with a Sex Pistols logo like spray-painted graffiti, with her prize black leather jacket and a set of black skinny jeans. Even as a vampire she had a better fashion sense than Mindy. It was frustrating.

The dog park was a fenced-in quarter mile of pond and grass. It was sparsely populated today. Mindy and Lucia sat on a bench under the shade of a cypress tree. They were supposedly watching as Lucia's younger siblings ran around with their dog, a young scrapper of a Yorkie that Lucia referred to as Malty with a bit of a wince.

Mindy had her purse in her lap. She held onto it tightly.

She'd been on the school paper, she knew how to interview someone. *Okay, what first, what first—a simple question, to put the subject at ease.* Yeah, she could do that. "So, as a vampire…can you, like, stand garlic?"

"No, but I couldn't before either." Lucia ran a hand through her darkened hair. "Don't try to bullshit me, Minz. You wanna know how it happened."

"If you want to talk about it."

"Of course I want to talk about it. Who wouldn't want to talk about it?" Lucia asked dryly. "It's such a cool story, I can't wait to break it out at parties." Her nails tapped on the slats of the bench. "Ever had one of those nightmares it seems like you can't wake up from? You know you're in it, you know it's not real—just keeps happening to you? Well, mine's still happening. It just used to be less…" Lucia stared straight ahead. "I remember being with you at Lake Travis. You left, I stayed. Next thing I know, I'm at the bottom of the lake, chained up, wrapped in plastic."

Mindy's hand twitched to her mouth. "Jesus."

"Don't think he's too interested. It was very hazy. I was scared. So I thought I'd go to your place. And I must've done that, because then I was there and you were trying to help." Her eyes shifted under her sunglasses. "Thanks for that, by the way. Appreciate ya."

"What happened then?"

"I was sick." Lucia held up her hands, staring at the dappled shadows the cypress leaves put on her pale skin. In the bright sun's shade, they were almost their usual tone. "Really sick. I almost thought everything that'd happened was some sort of fever dream. You visited me, you know how it was. But I was hungry. Really hungry. And eventually I figured out what I was hungry for." Her eyes went back to Mindy, who felt her veins throbbing under her skin.

"I know," she said. "I know you didn't want to hurt anyone." Mindy's voice sounded different, even to herself. Grown up.

"Yeah, well—nightmares about being bitten, sudden thirst for blood, sensitivity to light. I may not have your grade point average, but I got it figured out."

"Lucia." She was still looking at Mindy, but those sunglasses were like an impenetrable barrier. She seemed to look through her. "The sun didn't kill me. It purified me. My skin came off, Mindy. Hell of an exfoliation. Then I realized that I couldn't leave Abe and Artie and…everyone. I had to stay, and I had to take care of this. So I went to Quentin." Lucia's eyes focused briefly. "I'd sucked plenty for him. Why not for me?"

"You…drank him?"

"I let him live, didn't I?" Lucia scooted where she sat, adjusting herself. She held onto the bench on either side of her legs. Looking down now: "Do I get to ask a question? Are you gonna kill me?"

"What, no, Lucia, I wouldn't—"

"I can feel the cross in your bag. I'm not offended. You bring protection when there's a predator on the loose." She held up her right hand, palm facing Mindy. "Yeah, the thing about crosses is right. First day I got sick, I tried praying to God." Mindy could see it now. On the heel of her hand, the imprint of a small crucifix was burnt into a faded scar, almost like a brand. "Oops." She lowered her hand. "God doesn't want me anymore."

Mindy made a choice. She set down her purse between her legs, kicked it under the bench. "I don't *want* to hurt you. I just have to be able to defend myself."

"I would never hurt you, Mindy," Lucia insisted. Her voice finally sounded strained. "We're BFFs forever."

*Yeah, that is part of the acronym.* "So why'd you say it was a good thing I didn't say anything to that cop?"

Lucia took off her glasses. "Oh, you thought—no, no, I just meant it would look bad. But they'd probably figure out you're not guilty, like, eventually."

"Not guilty? You mean, of the attacks? Why would they think I was involved?"

Lucia had turned away. "Oh my God, look at that dog with the Frisbee, he is going *nuts!*"

Mindy's brow furrowed. "El, why would they think that? Why is that a thing they would think?"

Lucia stood, holding her elbow in her opposite hand, looking so sheepish and yet somehow *exuberant* in that sheepishness that Mindy could see the old Lucia in her. She wished she could pull that Lucia out of…all this. She paced to the cypress tree and leaned against it. "Have you ever heard the expression 'ain't nobody fucking with my clique'?" she asked Mindy.

"Yes, El, I'm not that white."

"So, you're in my clique—congratulations—and if people fuck with you, they're fucking with my clique. And then it's on! I have to serve them!"

Mindy stood up slowly. "Who's fucking with me?"

Lucia gritted her teeth together nervously, hemming and hawing with her head. "Okay, Mindy, you know those receipts you keep of bad tippers in your glove compartment? And you know how you don't lock your car, which is really pretty irresponsible. I mean, my cousin did that, went to Atlanta once, *bam*, no speaker system, and he had a *great* speaker system…"

Mindy held up her hand. For once, Lucia was silent. "Are you drinking the blood…of people who stiff me on tips?"

Lucia kneaded her hands together. "We roll deep, Minz. We roll deep."

For a split second, Mindy looked around to see if anyone was looking. Then she had Lucia by the lapels. "The cops! Check on that shit! They connect things! To people! Haven't you ever seen *Law & Order*?"

"I have basic cable, I've seen like a million *Law & Order*. And it's okay if you want to keep Batman-grabbing me, that's fine."

Mindy growled in frustration, giving Lucia a shake. "I could get arrested, Lucia. I could go to jail!" Lucia's eyes brightened. "And do not even think of making an *Orange Is The New Black* joke, because you are being enough of a slag without taking this seriously! Un-seriously. Either one!"

Lucia took Mindy's hands where they were fisted in her shirt. "Mindy, come on, I bet those people never tip, ever, so if the cops want to check out people they've stiffed, there's Starbucks and China Café and like a million other places that could've attacked them just as much as you did." Now Lucia reached up to Mindy's face, petting her cheeks, twisting her bangs between her fingers. "And let's say the cops do finger you." Lucia didn't say it, but she cracked a small smile, clearly at some private 'fingering' joke. "So what? If they send someone to arrest you, I'll just drink him. I'd drink a whole SWAT team for you. I'd chug 'em like I was at a frat party."

"That's not very reassuring," Mindy said. Yet her lungs let in a deep breath. "Why couldn't you just *tell me* what was going on? I could've helped."

Lucia spun Mindy around, wrapping her in a hug. Her arms were like steel bands around Mindy's chest, but that was reassuring in a way. She wondered how much Lucia had missed—them. "I didn't want you involved, okay? If you knew how close I'd come to—"

Lucia was looking out at the dog park's pond. Malty had taken a dip and now was shaking himself off, splattering Artie and Abe with water.

Lucia's voice turned hard: "It's not gonna come to that."

Her body was cool but not cold, soothing after the heat of the Texas sun. Mindy could've melted into it, like an open refrigerator door on a hot day. "I know it won't. But you've gotta stop biting people, Lucia, I mean, even if they are bad tippers, what if one of them has AIDS or something?"

"What is this, *Rent*?"

"Promise me."

"I need blood, Minz. If I don't get it, I start to burn."

"And if you do get it, people notice. Let me look for a cure. Or someone who'll let you feed on them willingly. Hell, I'd be okay with—"

"No," Lucia said suddenly, her whole body stiffening.

"It's not a big deal, El. I've had my blood drawn before. You wouldn't even have to bite me, I could just get a syringe and—"

Lucia let go of Mindy, backing away so fast the air rippled. When Mindy turned around, she was in the light. Pale as ever. "I am never drinking your blood, Mindy."

Mindy nodded, suddenly okay with the distance between them. She understood. She got it completely. After all, drinking a dyke's blood—you might as well be fucking her. And Lucia West didn't fuck women.

They walked back home from the dog park, which was just a part of the Maxwell Bakula Community Park, built with funds left over from the new stadium.

"Hey, Ewoks, listen up." Mindy pumped her legs to catch up with Abe and Artie, leaving Lucia in the dust. "Me and some of my girls are thinking of starting a club, and we wanted to know if you'd like in."

Abe looked up at her suspiciously. "What kind of club?"

"Sort of a monster club. Horror movies, creature features, slashers, thrillers, chillers, that sort of a thing. It's mostly just girls. Oh, and Kimberly's in it. You know Kimberly? Wears glasses, has those *Star Wars* T-shirts?"

Abe elbowed Artie in the ribs. "Doesn't sound too lame."

Lucia was begrudgingly catching up to them. "Do you want in or not?" she asked. They nodded like she'd offered them free chocolate.

"Okay, but first you gotta pass a quiz," Mindy said.

Both groaned. Even Malty seemed about to howl.

"Hey, you little monsters, just wait until high school. Essay portions. Get ready for that bullcrap."

Lucia linked her arm with Mindy's to whisper in her ear. "I know what you're doing."

"You want to know about monsters," Mindy whispered back, "who would know better than a ten-year-old?" She raised her voice. "So what are a vampire's powers?"

"Easy," Artie said. "Standard-issue speed and strength. They can throw cars around or run circles around you in the blink of an eye."

Mindy looked to Lucia for confirmation. "Why would I throw a car?" Lucia mouthed. "But I am pretty fast," she added, with a pelvic thrust. Mindy rolled her eyes.

"Transmogrification!" Artie continued. "Vampires can turn into wolves and mist, and…what's the other one?"

"Bats! Duh! How do you even miss that?" Abe demanded.

"Sorry! It's not like anyone cares about vampires anymore. Not when there are zombies."

"Zombies are so played out! And half of them are fast, so they're not even zombies anymore, they're basically retarded vampires—"

"Anything else?" Mindy interrupted; God help her with adolescent fan boys.

Abe tried snapping his fingers, which he couldn't quite manage. "Mind controlling!"

"It's not called that, he puts people in his *thrall*. You look into his eyes, bam, he's got you. Goodbye cross, goodbye garlic, you're done."

"And bats, he turns into a bat."

"Can he control mist too, or does he just turn into mist?" Artie asked.

Abe shrugged eloquently.

"That's nice. Fine," Mindy said. "What about telepathy?"

"Like *X-Men*?"

Artie put his hands to his temples. "To me, my brides!"

Abe gave him a push. "If you've been bitten by a vampire—or if you've drinken their blood—"

"Drunk," Lucia corrected.

"Then there's like mind reading, but only for two people."

"Yeah," Artie agreed. "Dracula bit Mina and made her drink his blood, so they were connected and she was turning into like his love slave, but *since they were connected,* she told Van Helsing where Dracula was going, and that's how they got him."

Mindy almost stopped. Some of the dreams she had felt like she was connected to Lucia, felt like they were one, but Lucia hadn't bitten her. She *hadn't.* "What about curing someone who's been turned into a vampire?"

Abe mimed holding something in his hands, then plunged it into his chest like he was committing seppuku. "Gak!"

"That's not the only way," Artie said. "All you have to do is kill the vampire that sired them—the head vampire."

"Sired?" Mindy asked.

Artie held up two fingers. "Drink someone dry, then feed them your own blood. It's how vampires reproduce."

"How do you kill one?" Lucia asked. "A vampire."

Mindy stopped walking. Abe and Artie kept going.

"Well, stake, obviously."

"What else?" Lucia pressed.

Mindy caught Lucia's elbow, wishing she'd stop. Lucia ignored her.

"Cut their head off," Abe said.

"Fire," Artie added. "And sunlight."

"Not in *Dracula.* Sunlight just weakened him." Abe disagreed. "Oh, and silver."

"Silver, that's *werewolves.*"

"Not in *Blade!*"

"*Blade* sucked—"

"—you suck!"

"Wait, I got it, running water!" Artie stopped, turning around to regard his audience. "Vampires can't cross running water. I think it's like holy water to them. And we all know what holy water does to vampires; something to do with the moon and the tides or something."

"So what, if a vampire tries to cross a river, he'll melt?" Abe asked.

"Maybe."

"You idiot. Vampires just can't do it, the same way they can't enter a house uninvited. That's why they need to be in their coffins and get some schlub to move them across."

"No, that's just a comfort thing. A vampire can fly over water or walk over a bridge, but if he tries to swim across—"

Abe threw up his hands in exasperation. "That doesn't make any sense! You can kill a vampire by cutting their head off, impaling them through the heart, setting them on fire, or *making them soggy?*"

At the end of their walk, Lucia came up to Mindy's room. Mindy didn't know what to say. Lucia had to be thinking about the head vampire, right? How to kill him?

Mindy drew the blinds and turned the lights down low, wanting Lucia to be comfortable. Not that Lucia noticed. She moved around Mindy's room, examining the posters Mindy had swiped from her old job as a theater usher, picking up some of the books stacked around. Mindy tried to remember if Lucia had ever been in her room before. She couldn't picture *this* Lucia there.

The silence between them grew larger and larger. Mindy picked up her laptop, sat on the bed, had a split second flash of Lucia closing her laptop for her—crawling over her on the bed, getting closer and closer until…her fangs.

She shook it off. She had work to do.

Then Mindy felt Lucia blowing in her ear. She looked up sharply. No, Lucia wasn't. She was at Mindy's desk, notebook paper spilled over the desktop. Lucia had borrowed Mindy's textbooks, assembling a stack of them beside her chair. Lucia wrote like a fiend, stopping only to shake her pen when it ran dry or to pick up a textbook and flip through it at warp speed. Every little supersonic movement sent a gush of wind through the room. Each little gale carried Lucia's perfume with it.

"Are you doing homework?" Mindy asked. She didn't mean to sound so shocked, but she did.

"Yeah." Lucia paused, scratching her pen on the header of her notebook paper. No ink came out. In a flash she had the pen unscrewed and eyed the ink level. Next to Mindy, her waste bin shook with the pen parts dropped into it. When she looked back, Lucia had a new pen and was at it again. "Check my answers?"

"Yeah, sure," Mindy agreed, and a finished homework assignment was on her chest, just like that, right in the middle of a closed Calculus text. She opened up the book and started matching the questions to the answers. Her laptop hummed beside her, faithfully torrenting the last *Game of Thrones*.

"So you're trying to get into college? Vampire sorority girl?"

"Only if they have sororities at dentistry school."

"You want to be a dentist?"

Lucia tapped her pen on her knee as fast as ever. Nervous. "It pays well. I could put Abe and Artie through college. Get Mom into rehab, if she'd ever agree to it. Hey, wouldn't you go to a vampire dentist?"

"I think we'll get you better *sometime* before you graduate college."

Lucia stopped the pen, holding it still as a stone in her hand. There was a crack through it. "I am better, though. Kinda." She broke into a grin. "How about controlling the mist? That could be fun. I'll just put big misty dongs everywhere!"

Mindy giggled. "And you can hypnotize people? I wish I could hypnotize people! If someone's being rude to me, I want to make them sing the theme song to *Shaft* instead."

Lucia's smile froze. "I, uh… I think that's what the venom's for. After I bit Quentin, he kept screaming, so I told him to stop and he did. Hey, Minz, take it from me, your room is *dead*. Where's the boom box?"

Mindy pointed to a lone shelf her father had nailed into the wall. It held a few books, one photo, but mostly a pair of speakers and an iPod docking station. Lucia picked up the iPod, looking it over, trying to figure it out. It was weird for Mindy to think she'd never worked one. It was new, sure, but it wasn't that new…

"Ah!" Lucia cried, selecting something and plugging the iPod back in. The petite speakers began to vibrate with sound. A gently warbling voice over a jaunting, trotting beat. Lucia swayed her way to Mindy's bed, doing a hip roll that pulled up her shirt (her belly had an underlying golden warmth) before she crashed down beside Mindy.

It took Mindy about a minute to recall the song she was listening to from the depths of her iTunes account. "Really?" she asked incredulously.

Lucia was on her back, hands folded over her belly (where her shirt had ridden up). She looked like a girl in a coffin. "What, you don't like Vampire Weekend?"

"Don't you think that's a little on the nose?"

"Hey, I liked Vampire Weekend when I was alive. Wait—feel me."

"What?" Mindy asked. Not quite incredulous.

Lucia held up her arm. Mindy put her hand near the elbow. Lucia's muscle was subtle, a little giving, but mostly hard to touch. And for a dead girl—undead—whatever—she wasn't room temperature. It wasn't a lack of heat, it was an absence. She had a chill, like metal at night.

"I liked Vampire Weekend before I was cool," Lucia said, already giggling her way through her own joke.

Mindy laughed, more out of what a nerd Lucia was than her joke. Lucia nudged her head under Mindy's arm, like a kitten asking to be petted, setting her skull on Mindy's shoulder and forcing Mindy to wrap her arm around her. Mindy thought Lucia's skin was less cool after a moment. Like Lucia was warming to the touch.

"Hey, you know how on *Buffy*, the vampires' faces go all Klingon? Does my face do that?" Lucia asked.

"Happens when they pop their fangs out, right? Show me."

Lucia shook her head immediately. "I don't think that's a good idea. C'mon, you saw me with Daryl. Did I have…ridges?"

"No, you were beautiful." Then Mindy clamped her mouth shut. *What did I say? Why did I say that? Am I hitting on Lucia? Why am I hitting on Lucia? And why is she nuzzling me?*

Lucia's claw of a fingernail clicked over Mindy's belt. "If I show you something, will you promise not to laugh?"

"Not laugh at *you*? That's a big ask, El."

Lucia grinned ruefully. "Pretty please? With sugar on top?"

"Okay. I'll try."

Lucia pried Mindy's arm off her shoulders, brushing her lips across the back of Mindy's wrist as she set it down on the bed, then she went to the window and opened the blinds. A pillar of sunlight shot in all the way to the bed, turning the room white. Mindy shielded her eyes from the sudden glare.

Lucia laid back down on her back. She knotted her hands at the bottom of her shirt. "Uh, as long as we're computing data or whatever, my skin isn't white. Didn't turn white. It's still the same, I put on foundation to make it look this way."

"Okay. Why?"

Lucia pulled up her shirt an inch, thought better of it, then pulled it down like she was trying to hide her whole body with it. "And obviously, I don't burn up in the sunlight. Abe said that, right? That in Dracula, the vampires are just weakened by direct sunlight, they don't—*fwoosh*. I don't know, I have a hard time doing the speed thing during the day, but I don't feel like I've skipped lunch or anything either."

Mindy reached over and put her hand on top of Lucia's. "Lucia, c'mon, you can tell me. I really won't laugh."

Lucia took her hands away. Mindy tugged at her shirt, sliding it up the tight, compact girl-warrior stomach all cheerleaders had. Without the makeup, Lucia's skin was gold as ever, but it was also something else. Iridescent, multi chromatic, like a snake's almost. Mindy had gone through a snake phase; she could remember the names. Iridescent Shieldtail, Brazilian Rainbow Boa, but more so, more of a *sheen.* In fact, when Lucia breathed and the light rippled over her, she almost seemed to…sparkle.

Lucia rolled over, turning onto her side away from Mindy and pulling her shirt down. "I look so stupid! No wonder vampires only go out at night!"

Mindy slipped in behind her. "No, you look glamorous."

"I look like a Katy Perry video!" Lucia pouted. "Only Katy Perry has more class!"

"No, you look like—David Bowie's lovechild. That's a good thing!"

Lucia looked up. "You think so? Promise me from here on out we will never talk about *Twilight* getting things right. Ignorance is no longer an excuse."

"I won't even say the *T*-word."

Lucia nodded gratefully. "So that's the secret of my goth look. It really isn't a phase."

Mindy smiled at her. She put her hand on the back of Lucia's, sliding her fingers between Lucia's, dropping her fingertips to Lucia's palm.

Mindy's laptop pinged. She gave Lucia's hand one last squeeze and rolled over to it, checking her e-mail. A message from the Austin Yacht Club.

"Okay, what is it you're working on?" Lucia asked. "Because there's no way your *Supernatural* fanfic is more interesting than a real-life vampire."

"There are fifteen marinas around Lake Travis, I've either called or e-mailed all of them, trying to find out who the *Persephone* is registered to."

"The *Persephone*?"

"The yacht where you…died."

Lucia slipped up, slipped back down like a yo-yo, laying her head down on Mindy's leg. "Smarty. You're such a little smarty-pants."

"Save it for when I actually find this asshole. Then praise me excessively and give me candy."

Lucia put her hand on Mindy's knee, rubbing it in her palm. Her brow furrowed, the warm look on her face going away.

"How do you know the boat is named *Persephone*?"

Mindy stared at her laptop like Lucia was a predator and if she just didn't make eye contact, she'd be safe.

"I remember now," Lucia said. "There was a boat, and I got on it before everything went black. But I didn't remember that until you said it just now. So, how'd you know?" She lifted her head off Mindy's leg. "Minz?"

Mindy shut the laptop. "I've been having these dreams."

Lucia was already shaking her head.

"And in them, I'm…I'm you. That night, I dreamt I was you, swimming out to that boat, being attacked—"

"No," Lucia said firmly, finally, but to no avail.

"I dreamt you being sick and you being burned and—I wasn't really sure the dreams were real until you told me about the sun, but now that I know… Now that I know, I can use it."

On her hands and knees, Lucia crept forward an inch, staring into Mindy's eyes. Hers were very small, very white. "Did it hurt? What happened on the boat?"

Mindy nodded. She didn't want to talk.

Lucia looked away. "What was it like?"

"You were…afraid and in pain and alone. You said—" *Don't tell her that. Please, let her stay happy. She deserves to be happy.* "El, it's going to be okay. We're going to find this guy and make him pay, we're going to make it right."

"You shouldn't have had to go through that. It was me. Not you. You shouldn't—"

"It was just a bad dream, Lucia. That's all it was to me. I'd go through it again if it helped us find him."

Lucia looked at Mindy as if all of her being was trained on her, loaded and aimed at her, her eyes shrinking in a veil of tears. "Okay, but…how'd it happen? How can you see what I see?"

"I don't know…but Abe said that…if someone were bitten, if they drank blood…"

"No!" Lucia moved up so fast that her feet slipped on the bedspread, then she shot forward, almost colliding with Mindy, only stopping because she slammed her hands on the headboard. "I would never do that to you! I've never bitten you, never slipped you my blood—how would I even *do that*, you would taste it, right? You would know, so you know I haven't!"

Mindy felt herself swept up in the storm of emotions bursting out of Lucia, trying to calm the waters, trying to perform a miracle. "I believe you, I believe you!" She put her hands on Lucia's cheeks, cold, so cold, and tried to press her warmth into Lucia, tried to infuse her cool unmoving body with any of the life she had to offer. "I know you, Lucia. You would never do that to me, not to someone you—"

The doorknob opened, and Lucia *flew* off Mindy like a scared cat, flipping instinctively before she hit the ceiling so she dug her nails into the plaster and held herself there. And the door began to open, and while Mindy was still staring upward in total bafflement, Lucia must have realized how she looked and let go, landing on the mattress just as Mindy's mother walked in.

"You kids want some chili?" Mrs. Murphy asked. "We're having chili for dinner." A little trickle of shredded plaster landed on the still-creaking bed. Mrs. Murphy paused. "What are you girls doing in here?"

"Having sex?" Mindy offered.

# CHAPTER 13

The hamburger pizza, Dragon Pizza's new contribution to the world of Italian cooking, was boxed and placed on top of the restaurant's conveyor oven. All the drivers and in-stores were invited to take a slice to familiarize themselves with the taste. Mindy sneaked two, putting them on a paper plate and carrying them out atop the hot bag her order was in. She carried the order slip in her teeth.

Mindy didn't drive, though. Once out the door, she went across the grass that divided the Dragon Pizza parking lot from that of the pawn shop they neighbored. Parked behind the storefront so it couldn't be seen from the road or Dragon Pizza or anywhere except out the backdoor of the pawn shop, Lucia laid on the hood of Mindy's car. She wore her own khaki pants—much better fitting than Mindy's—and Mindy's spare Dragon Pizza shirt. The hat they traded off, Mindy planting it on Lucia's head as she slid beside her on the hood.

"It's 818 Sycamore," Mindy said, handing her the hot bag along with the order slip. "But Sycamore Cove, not Sycamore Lane. It's gonna be the cul-de-sac."

Balancing the hot bag masterfully with one hand, Lucia tossed her a salute and blurred off, leaving Mindy's iPod atop the hood. Mindy picked it up, slotted one earbud in, and switched over to her audiobook. A few minutes later, Lucia was back, and Mindy switched back to their music—Kanye West, Nicki Minaj—holding out the other earbud for Lucia to take. They both plugged in.

"This is so good for the environment," Mindy said, taking the signed slip from Lucia.

The order slip had directions to every address for those not blessed with a GPS system, and included with that was a laughably inaccurate count of how long it would take for the driver to get back to the store. The computer never seemed to account for the fact that running red lights was frowned upon.

Still, at the very earliest, it would take eleven minutes for Mindy to get to 818 Sycamore and back. The system wouldn't let her clock back in until those eleven minutes were up. Since Lucia had made the run in four minutes (literally), they now had nothing to do but relax under the evening sky.

"Here." Mindy spun the paper plate between them, a still-warm pizza slice onboard. "Our new hamburger pizza."

Lucia eyed it. "Is it a hamburger or a pizza?"

"It doesn't belong in either world. It has no place. Take pity and eat it."

Lucia picked it up, turning it this way and that—eyeing the 'burger sauce' that replaced the familiar marinara. Then there was the ground beef and dill pickles. There were also Roma tomatoes. All in all, Mindy didn't think Lucia found it trustworthy.

Mindy suddenly snatched it back from her. "I'm sorry, I should've asked. Do you have to eat?"

Lucia shook her head. "Nah, I think I can get by just on blood, which is great for my thighs. I'm thinking of writing a book. The All-Blood Diet."

"But can you? Eat?"

"Sure. This is almost pizza, after all." She took it back, had a bite. "This… is not as good as blood."

Mindy checked her watch. Five minutes until she would supposedly get back from her run. She didn't want to appear too eager—she liked hanging out with Lucia. They'd rigged the system three times this week, which had already saved Mindy a metric buttload on gas money, and left her lots of time for watching cat videos with Lucia on her phone.

But sometimes, she felt like Lucia was a time bomb. Somehow, the ticking was soothing, but Mindy didn't want to chance setting her off. She wanted to be close, this close, in fact, but she didn't want to send Lucia into another panic.

Lucia picked off a pickle, flicked it away. "Okay, not so bad without the pickles."

"But then it's just a pizza."

"Exactly." Lucia finished off the crust in an uncomfortably large bite. "Hey, Mindy?"

"Yeah?"

"I'm hungry again. No, not hungry. *Thirsty.*"

The pawn shop's sign shot up over the store, standing vigil, its LED scoreboard flashing red to passing cars. GLOCK 17S – HALF OFF.

"Okay," Mindy said slowly, wondering what Lucia was suggesting. "How often do you need blood?"

Lucia blew a brief raspberry. "It's like my period. I just *get it* and then I have these cravings and I need some fucking blood, okay?"

"Okay," Mindy said again. Her arm was coming off her Taurus's cold, dead hood. "So… what do you need?"

Lucia gave her a look. The whites of her eyes were almost as bright as the fangs protruding ever so slightly from behind her upper lip. "Well, since my needs aren't a secret anymore…I was thinking you could…"

"Yes?" Mindy's heart was pounding, trying to get out of her chest, up to Lucia's mouth. She'd had her blood drawn before—you had to make a fist, pump it. That was if Lucia bit her *arm*.

"Pick who I bite."

Mindy blinked. "Who you…bite?"

Lucia opened up her wallet, pulling out some of the receipts she'd collected from Mindy's glove compartment. All bore signatures, but no tips. "Who would you like me to go after? How about Lawrence Roberge?" She pronounced the name with a school-play accent. "I delivered to him last night, got him his pizza halfway across town in ten fucking minutes. He gave me a tip as big as his dick. Want me to eat him?"

"No!" Mindy turned off her iPod, which put Lucia in a pouty mood, slumping down the windshield and crossing her arms. "I told you, no feeding! We're about to find the guy, you don't need to—"

"Vampire!" Lucia interrupted. "Pretty sure I do."

"Are you sure you do? What if you're just bored?"

"You sound like one of those weird bulimia people right now."

"Models?"

"No, listen—" Lucia seemed to teleport, she moved so fast, now perched on the chain-link fence that separated the pawn shop's lot from the wilderness behind it. "I'm a growing girl. Blood is my calcium. My mother's milk. I was *sick* until I drank from Quentin. And every time I've drunk since then, I've gotten faster, stronger, cuter… What if I need so much blood because my body's still changing? Making me a better vampire?"

"Is that a good thing?" Mindy asked. "Being better at…that."

Lucia walked off the fence, bobbing down to the ground with a lazy tug of gravity. "You don't have to choose if you don't want to. But c'mon—how many times do you get a chance to inflict emotional trauma and bodily harm on people who were mean to you, all for a worthy cause?"

"Making you cute?"

Lucia flashed her a smile. "You don't have to pick for me, just, like, blink once for yes, twice for no." Suddenly leaning on the Taurus's cab, she flipped through the receipts. "Oh, this one I know, you *complained* about her! You were going to make a blog post about her, but you were worried you'd get fired." Lucia gave Mindy a pout. "Netsanet Hopkins of Skyview Terrace… I know her. 'Five chins that all come together to form a whole greater than the sum of its parts—sorta like the Jackson Five.'"

Mindy finished for her, standing. "And just like the Jackson Five, it would be better if there were only one of them doing its thing and the rest just faded away. I remember. That was me venting."

"This is why women don't run the world—we *vent* while men wrestle each other and shoot each other and run each other over with cars."

"And I'm pretty sure that's why Florida doesn't run the world. Come on, El, I need to get back to the store—"

"Worried I'll step out on you?" Lucia teased, but with the almost-seriousness that she was easily master of.

"I'll get you some blood, okay? Tomorrow. Just don't do anything stupid."

"Stupid?" Lucia repeated. "You don't know what it's like, Minz. Needing something to live and hearing that you can't have it."

*The hell I don't*, Mindy went back to the store.

That night, Mindy spent an hour watching videos of blood being drawn on YouTube to get it right. She even checked the comments, before realizing that some people had really, *really* weird fetishes. Then she phoned Seb to see if his host family would be working tomorrow afternoon.

They would be.

"Mindy, Lucia, come in, come in! Come all over my home!"

Seb's house was one of those homes that papered the walls with crosses and *Home Sweet Home* type signage, like a parish church run by TGI Fridays. Lucia kept her distance from the crosses, eying them like an ex-boyfriend whose appearance made her want to be better dressed than she was at the moment.

"So-ing… What assistance may I be helping you with to-Monday?"

Mindy opened up her purse, digging out a shrink-wrapped syringe needle and a rubber hose, plus an empty cream soda bottle that she'd washed out. She had, stuffed into a Ziploc bag, blood collection tubes, cotton balls, *The Lion King* Band-Aids, and alcoholic wipes. "We're gonna need some blood."

"Yes, that is what I thinking you said last tonight. But…why?"

"School project," Mindy said. "Extra credit."

"Which class would needing blood?"

"Buddy, try all of them," Lucia sighed.

"We'll pay you twenty bucks," Mindy said.

Lucia showed the twenty.

Seb bobbed his head, thinking about it before he drew a chair from the dining room table and sat down. "How much will you needing?"

"Just a pint," Mindy assured him. "You won't even know it's gone."

"Not…two pints?" Lucia asked.

"Just one," Mindy said certainly. She mouthed *don't be a pig*.

Lucia scratched her nose with her middle finger.

Seb rolled up his sleeve. Mindy set his arm on the dining room table and tied the hose over his elbow. "Make a fist."

He did. Veins began to come to the surface, Mindy tracing them with her finger like Wikihow had told her to. Lucia slunk in to observe, but Mindy shooed her with a look. She told Seb to wait while she washed her hands. When she came back, Lucia hadn't ripped Seb's throat out.

Lucia nodded to her. "Your friend's a real Chatty Cathy."

"I am not this named," Seb interjected.

Mindy gave Lucia a look. "Be cool."

Faking a yawn, Lucia squeezed her thighs together before opening them up. Mindy ignored her pumping her legs. Seb didn't. Mindy prodded him with the needle, making him wince, then undid the tourniquet. "Okay, this'll just take a minute. Pump your fist like you're holding a squeeze toy."

"Or your dick," Lucia added.

Seb nodded. "Your friend is seeming nice."

The blood slid through the needle and down its tube, into the glass bottle. "She can be," Mindy said, too low for anyone but Seb to hear, but she knew that wouldn't stop Lucia. "When she wants to be."

Looking away, Lucia flipped up the piano's fallboard and plinked a random note on the keyboard.

"The bottle actually holds three hundred and fifty-five milliliters," Mindy told Seb, "so it won't be quite a pint. Does this hurt any, by the way?"

"No—it pinched a littles." Seb pumped his fist. "Are you friends with her again?" he whispered.

"It's complicated."

"You are not friending with her? Just—study mates?"

Mindy did not want to have this conversation with Lucia in the room, in the house. She lowered her voice more out of politeness than thinking Lucia wouldn't hear. "She needs me. For the assignment. And I need her to be okay."

Seb nodded along before smiling. "I am thinking you will work things out."

"Wish I had your confidence, partner."

"She is friending you, you are friending her—y'all are liking each other too much to stay mean."

"Y'all? Really?" The bottle was about to overflow. "Open your hand." She drew out the needle, popped a cotton ball onto the puncture mark, and folded Seb's forearm up against his upper arm, pinching the cotton in between.

Lucia stood, bouncing on her heels with anticipation. She tried to play cool. "Where'd you get all this junk?" she asked loudly.

"Amazon," Mindy said. "Overnight delivery. I had to sign up for a free trial of Amazon Prime, so remind me to cancel that before they actually start billing me." To Seb she said, "Could you give us a minute?"

"Suring. Would you like some bites of pizza?"

"Yes," Lucia said. "Bake them in the oven. Take your time."

Mindy pulled away the cotton ball and slapped two Band-Aids on him. "Tell me if that starts bleeding. Plan B is a handful of cotton balls and duct tape."

Nodding uneasily, Seb slipped away. Once he was gone, Lucia blurred onto the dining table, knotting her hands in front of her face. "Hey, Minz?"

Mindy tapped on the tube, getting all the blood out into the bottle. "Yeah, El?"

Lucia took a deep breath, out of habit. "How do we know Seb isn't the vampire? He's from Transylvania."

"He's from Romania," Mindy corrected gently.

"Romania, Transylvania, same thing. He's a transperson."

"I don't think that's the right word," said Mindy, who knew it wasn't the right word.

"No, I've seen it used a lot on my Facebook feed, it definitely is. You know that really tall woman on *Orange Is The New Black*? She's a transperson, from Transylvania, that's why she's so mannish."

Mindy held out the bottle. "Drink your blood."

"Chug?" Lucia asked teasingly.

Mindy shook her head. "I don't care."

"You don't care because you *don't think* I can chug this or…"

Mindy put her finger on the bottom of the bottle and tilted it. Lucia threw her mouth under the rim before it could spill, filled her mouth, only a little spilling onto her chin, Mindy held the bottle still as she began to swallow. Then she spat, wheezing, sticking her tongue out, flecks of blood hitting Mindy's face, the mass of it slapping her shirt and dribbling toward her pants. Mindy didn't care, concerned as she was for the spitting, heaving Lucia.

"What is it? What's wrong?"

Lucia fell off the table, onto all fours, hacking now like a cat with a furball. "Prune juice—" She forced out. Mindy slapped her back. "Tastes like prune juice!"

Hearing the commotion, Seb rushed back, finding Mindy holding Lucia's hair as Lucia raspberried out the contents of his veins onto the carpet. The dining room looked like a cross between a slasher movie and a cooking show. The bottle, set down in all the confusion, teetered on the edge of the table. Seb ran, catching it before it fell. Lucia's lipstick clung to the rim of the bottleneck.

"Did you…drinking my blood?"

Lucia aimed a finger squarely at him. "*You* have the Peach Schnapps of blood!" she told him, wiping her mouth off. "You actually have this running through your body? God! I've drunk Mexican people who taste better than you!"

"Okay, that was racist—" Mindy remarked.

"They eat spicy foods, Mindy!"

"You're drinking blood! Why…" Seb half turned, almost hiding the bottle behind his body. "Is this a sex thing?"

"No!" Mindy said.

"Yes," Lucia said at the same time.

Mindy looked at her, got *a look* from Lucia, and said, "Yes, it is. This is very…" Lucia hocked out a loogie with the last of Seb's blood in it. "Sexy."

"Maybe it's the bottle," Lucia said. "Did you wash it out?"

"*Yes*, I washed it out—"

"Because that tasted like—like blood mixed with bug spray…"

"I am taking medication for sleep apnea," Seb said.

"You have sleep apnea?" Mindy asked.

"One in five Americans have it," Seb told her. "It's nothing to be ashame from. Wait." His face darkened. "You couldn't come in. You couldn't come in before I invited you!"

Mindy gave Lucia a panicked look, which Lucia was already ignoring. "Dude, stop changing the subject from your skank-ass blood."

"And you drank it! And you couldn't come in without an invitation."

"I told you, I'm just very ladylike," Lucia said, before burping.

"You are the *wampyr!*"

Lucia chuckled, slapping her thigh. "Your friend is so funny, Mindy!"

"Yes, he is, we should go."

Shielding his blood in the crook of one arm, Seb lanced out with one finger. "Creature of the night! Nosferatu! Undead!"

Lucia rolled her eyes. "Like, whatever. I'm out during the day, I can't be a vampire."

"Sunlight only weakens the *wampyr!*"

"Oh my *God*, does everyone know more about vampires than me?" Lucia stood. "Look, you can't prove I'm a vampire, so I'm just gonna go. Don't tell anyone your dumb theory."

"Or what?" Seb demanded. "You will kill me?"

"No, you'll just be that weird kid who thinks the head cheerleader is a vampire. In social terms, you might as well start wearing Crocs. C'mon, Mindy, let's leave this loser and his weird blood alone."

Seb puffed his chest out. "I revoke your invitation!" he bellowed.

It was like someone had hit *rewind* on a remote control. Lucia was suddenly walking backward, almost being dragged along by an invisible force, until she hit the front door, swinging it open to be deposited on the porch.

Mindy watched in complete shock. "That was... Seb, invite her back in! Invite her back in, right now!"

Seb looked at her, mystified. "But...she is *wampyr*. She drank my blood!"

"Yeah, after we paid you twenty bucks for it! And baked cookies to give you so you could get your blood sugar back up!"

"They were going to be a surprise," Lucia said, standing back up and dusting off the grass clippings from her outfit.

Seb's head shook. "She is *wampyr*! Undead fiend! She drinks the blood of the living to revitalize herself!"

"Yeah, I'm not a vegan either. Let her back in or I am never speaking to you again."

"Fine! But if I am killed—!" Seb pointed an angry finger at her, then he sighed. "Lucia, I invite you in."

Lucia stepped back through the door. "*Thanks.*" She fixed Seb with a look. "You're never going to get a green card with that attitude, buddy."

"You really...*had* to leave?" Mindy asked her.

"Yeah, I backed out of this place like it was a commitment."

"That is so damn weird. Can anyone do it or just someone who lives here?" Mindy looked at Seb for confirmation, but he just shrugged, so she said, "Lucia, I revoke your invitation."

And Lucia was skating on wet ice, her legs flopping around under her as she tried to resist the sudden force field pushing her back, pushing her out the front door to pile atop the door mat.

"*Wow!*" Mindy enthused. "We gotta put this on YouTube."

"It is very interest." Seb set the bottle down, seeming to slowly come to terms with both the existence of vampires and their presence in his house. "So you say she is...friendly *wampyr*?"

"I'm a bad bitch vampire who's gonna kick your asses if you don't invite me back in!" Lucia shouted from outside.

Seb opened his mouth, but Mindy planted her hand across it. "Wait, let me see if I can. I invite you in!"

Lucia stomped inside. "That is not funny, okay? It is very hurtful and insensitive and—you don't see me making fun of Seb's English or Mindy, your..." She gestured at Mindy. "Okay, bad example, you're perfect."

"Aw." Mindy locked her hand onto her heart.

"Except your wardrobe. That could use a little work. How many shoes do you own?"

"Two. One for each foot."

Lucia clicked her tongue. "Okay, if we're done being grossly insensitive to my medical condition..."

"One more, one more, *please*?" Mindy pleaded with her hands clasped.

"If you're okay with me being totally pissed at you—"

"I am!" Mindy said cheerfully. "Seb, revoke your invitation on three, okay? One, two—"

"I revoke your invitation!" Seb cried, just as Mindy threw out both her palms, joined at the heels.

"HADOKEN!"

Lucia reeled backward, flung by an invisible force until she toppled out the front door. She landed on her feet this time, immediately throwing her fists down her sides.

"You guys suck!"

# CHAPTER 14

Mindy helped Seb Febreze the shit out of the carpet, while Lucia pouted unhelpfully from the top of the piano. As they washed up, Mindy explained the situation. It felt good to get it off her chest, for both of them, she thought. As she told the story, Lucia went to the bathroom to clean herself off.

Then the pizza bites were done. They gathered around the dining room table to eat, Mindy and Lucia next to each other, Seb across from them. He stared at his plate. Mindy and Lucia ate. He picked one up and stared at Lucia. "Does your lower jaw split open into claws to grab people?" Seb asked.

"No," Lucia said in between pizza bites. "Just one piece."

"Do you have a spear-tongue that shoots into people to drain their blood?"

"No, I just swallow it."

"Do you have little suckers on your hands that drain people when you hold—"

"No, I am just a normal, everyday vampire. I have fangs, I move fast, I wear a cape and sleep in a coffin. Okay?"

Seb nodded, backing up in his seat.

Mindy felt bad for the guy. He was dealing with the existence of the undead pretty well, considering. "She does sparkle, though."

Seb swiveled to her. "What, like in the *Twilight*?"

"We don't say the T-word," Mindy said.

"How about we just stop with the questions? Like, why are you so obsessed with me? Doesn't Wikipedia have a page on vampires?"

"What about…do you have a soul?"

Lucia pushed her plate away. "Whoa, personal…"

Mindy felt compelled to step in. "Seb, maybe you could just send her an e-mail, some yes or no questions…I don't know, maybe she has some questions for you, maybe there's some things Lucia would like to know about you."

"N-ope," Lucia dryly enunciated.

In the neighboring room, there were a half-dozen crucifixes on the wall. Seb took one down and brought it back into the dining room.

Lucia visibly tensed, but Mindy could also see how she was trying not to.

Mindy freaked on her behalf. "Would you put that thing away, alright? She's not a science project!"

"I just want to see if it push her back, you know, like the force field." He held it out to Lucia before Mindy could stop him, and the vampire shrunk back, holding a hand in front of her face like she'd stepped out of a theater into a bright summer day. She didn't hiss, though. Just grimaced.

"*Seb!*" Mindy pushed down his arm. "You are being really uncool right now! Do they have that in Romania? Being uncool?"

"Yes." Seb lowered his arm, then put it behind his back. "Sorry—she is being my first *wampyr*."

"Just…other room, okay? She's not a toy." Seb went to the other room to drop the crucifix on a sofa, and Mindy followed him, hating how haranguing she was being but feeling an intense need to defend Lucia—like she'd failed her by letting it escalate this far. "Imagine if you were allergic to, like, shellfish, and I came in and started waving around shellfish and asking you how big you would bloat up if you ate shellfish and…wearing a shellfish T-shirt!"

"Alright! I am sorry," Seb said submissively.

"She's sensitive about this stuff, man. And she didn't even get to drink your blood, so she's hungry too."

Biting his lip, Seb picked the cross back up and replaced it on the wall. "Why not just go to a hospital? They have blood there."

"Yeah, they also have drugs. You still don't see junkies breaking in there. Hospitals have guards and cameras and alarms and locks—" Mindy gave up on it. She wanted to check on Lucia.

Lucia was standing, pacing aimlessly, her arms wrapped up in herself. A trickle of blood ran from her nose. She caught it with her finger, wiping it away, then looked at her fingertip. Licked it.

"Is that like masturbation for you?" Seb asked from the other room.

"Seb!" Mindy cried in exasperation. "I swear to God, no more questions! I revoke your questioning status!" She went to Lucia. Stopped with her hand in the air, almost touching Lucia, but her mind suddenly overwhelming her body's instincts. She thought for a split second of Seb standing there watching, of who Lucia was, of what she was. Then she put her hand on Lucia's arm and felt a small voltage in her fingers. "Are you alright?"

"I'm fine." Lucia smiled without meaning it. A little blood remained on her teeth. "God and I aren't on speaking terms right now." Mindy could hear her depression, the little tone change that spoke of hours before Lucia would be able to strip herself of the funk she was in, let things touch her again. She shot Seb a fierce look, and he raised his hands apologetically.

"Uhhh… Would you girls like some of chocolate?" he asked.

Lucia blurred—no running start, just the rush of her pushing air out of the way, the snare drum crackle of her feet striking the floor in rapid succession. She stopped next to Seb in the passageway between rooms, eyebrow raised, then blurred once more. They heard the snare drum sound zip to the kitchen, then the creak and whoosh of cupboards being opened. Lucia came back at normal speed, holding a medicine cup full of a clear liquid.

She set it down on the dining room table. "Drink," she said, looking at Seb.

"What is it?" Mindy asked.

"My venom," Lucia explained. "I don't know exactly what it does and I want to find out, so—"

"But…why am I drinking now?" Seb asked.

"Because Mindy's pissed at you, and this will make you friends again."

"I wouldn't put it that way," Mindy said.

"I want you to do it," Lucia insisted, looking at Seb with eyes that weren't quite imploring, weren't quite demanding. Seb went to the table. Picked up the medicine cup. The liquid sloshed—a little thicker than water. He looked at Mindy, who wasn't sure where she fit into this. She didn't think Lucia would do anything really harmful, even to get back at him. She didn't *think*…

"Do it! Drink my venom! Peer pressure!"

Mindy nodded, and Seb drank the venom. He cleared his throat, coughing a little—tugged at his collar.

Lucia blurred and was back with a glass of water to wash it down. He took a drink and cleared his throat again, seemed to get whatever it was he wanted.

"How'd it taste?" Lucia asked, gleeful to be asking questions of him.

"A little bitter—but not really…a taste." Seb blinked rapidly. He moved his hand to rub at his eyes. He got it right the first attempt, but then he hit his nose instead of his eye. He made a noise like a leaky tire. "My tongue is numb."

"How do you feel?" Mindy asked, stepping forward with concern.

Seb pulled out a chair and sat. He didn't quite align with his seat. "Little weird."

Sitting down in the neighboring chair, Lucia smiled at him, her grin both genuine and a little—not mocking, but like she was charmed with his simplicity. The kind of smile you'd give a novelty app. "Hey, Seb, do you want to slap yourself?"

"No…"

"Slap yourself."

Seb slapped himself.

"Ha!" Lucia pumped her fist. "I knew it! I'm the smart one, Mindy! You have to be the cute one now. Start wearing skirts."

"El, what are you talking about? What do skirts have to do with anything?"

"It's my venom!" Lucia circled her forefinger around her jaw. "It makes people really suggestible, like my boobs. And the amnesia thing too. That's why no one's reported me for, you know, biting them." She glowered momentarily: "And here I thought Quentin was being nice…"

"Did I do something?" Seb asked. "Why does my cheek hurt?"

Lucia pinched his nose. "Don't worry about it. Slap yourself again." He did. "Harder than that." He did again, the noise louder, his head turning with the impact. Red rose to the surface of his cheek, darker than the bright blush that had been there before. Lucia watched his skin boil with dark eyes.

"Lucia…" Mindy said warningly. "I think we've established that he'll slap himself."

"You're right." Lucia smiled at Seb. "Pick up that pencil and poke your eye out."

"Which eye?"

"Left, I'd think—"

Mindy was struck by disbelief, and when Seb's hand moved, so did she. As he picked the pencil up off the end table, she grabbed his arm with both hands. He fought her, surprisingly strong, dragging the graphite tip toward his eye. Mindy couldn't imagine it looking bigger to him than it did to her, but it had to.

"That's enough," Lucia said.

Seb's arm relaxed instantly, his limp hand jerking down with the force of Mindy's weight on it. She pried the pencil out of his hand before Lucia could say anything else.

"Go," she began, "go lie down on the couch and sleep it off."

Seb got up unsteadily, rubbed his bruised cheek once, and took a haltering step out of the room.

"You're no fun," Lucia told her.

"What was that?" Mindy demanded.

"Just seeing if he'd do it. I was gonna stop him. Superspeed, remember?" Lucia took out her phone, switched it to camera mode, and took a selfie, which she checked out. Off the impromptu reflection, she rearranged a lock of hair. "Don't be so tense, Minz. You'll give yourself a break-out."

*Why is it I'm not allowed to have two friends without them hating each other?* "He's really a nice guy..."

"You don't need a nice guy. You need—well, it's none of my business." Lucia crossed her legs. "Hell, you could do worse, I guess. I sure have."

"El, we're not together. He's just a friend."

"Oh yeah?" Lucia whistled to Seb, who stopped stumbling toward the other room. "Seb, what's up with Mindy? You banging or what?"

"No." Seb took another unsteady step toward the couch. "I would've wanted to, but she is not wanting this. It is good having her as friend, though. Very nice to talk to her. She never makes fun of my wording—" He dropped forward over the couch's armrest and on top of a decorative cushion.

Seb's host family owned a pretty big couch. It took up a lot of their modest living room—didn't even have a coffee table in front of it. There wasn't that much room. There was just a rug taking up the few feet of spare carpet, then a disarray of game systems, cords, and DVDs, leading up to the TV. A big-screen TV, not a wide-screen. One of those rear-projection TVs rich people used to have. Mindy could see the whole room in the reflection of its dead screen. Her on the far side of the couch, Seb on the other two seats, his feet flopping over the armrest. She petted his hair. He seemed alright, just out of it. Nappy, but half-awake.

"Hey Seb?"

"Yeahess?" Maybe less than half.

"I just want you to know that I think you're a good friend too. And I'm sorry if I yelled at you. You were just really putting Lucia on edge, but I guess I probably should've set some ground rules before I sprung the vampire stuff on you."

"Should I slap myself again?"

"No, that's okay." She patted his shoulder. "Hey, listen. As long as you're whammied, you should know that you're a lot cooler than you think you are. The English thing? You talk better than all the wiggers in school. It works for you. And even if I don't like you the way you want me to like you, just keep being a sweetheart, alright? Someday there's gonna be a girl who sees how sweet you are—probably gonna get off on your accent a little—and she is gonna just—*fight for you*. Fight like hell for you. Just don't turn into an asshole, okay? We have enough of those."

"Okay...so no slapping?"

"No, just—I'm gonna get you some water."

She went into the kitchen. It was a lot like her mom's—different selection of utensils and cookbooks, but the same underlying concept. Like Spock with a goatee. She found the glasses two cupboards down from where her mom kept hers, filled it with water, and turned to see Lucia was standing in the doorway.

She dropped the glass in surprise.

Lucia caught it, handing it back to her, smiling bashfully at how close the save had brought them. "I don't think I've said thank you."

"Thank you?"

"For helping me. And not, you know, putting a stake through my heart."

"El, I wouldn't even know where your heart is."

"I appreciate it. The help, not the—anyway, maybe you could draw some of your own blood? Like you did for Seb? I mean, there's this book where a vampire keeps drinking from one person and she develops a taste for it, but if you're not worried about that—"

"I'm worried that you'll starve to death."

"Thanks."

"You said that already."

"Not for the help." Lucia stared at her feet. "For caring if I starve to death or not."

The glass clinked as Mindy set it down on the counter, then she had Lucia wrapped up in a hug. Lucia burned so cold. It was almost like Mindy was hugging an ice sculpture. But that was okay. Texas was too damned hot anyway.

Mindy's cell phone beeped. She broke away to check it. She had an e-mail. Another marina had gotten back to her. They had the *Persephone* on record.

"I found it!" Mindy cried. "The *Persephone!*"

Mindy clicked through to the attachment—a copy of the registry of the *Persephone*. "Oh God—it's owned by Coach Bakula."

Lucia's head tilted slightly to the side. "Okay. When do you want to kill him?"

"We cannot kill someone because they own a boat!" Mindy said for the fifth time. "There's no way of knowing that Bakula is even a…a goth, let alone a vampire!"

There was a second place to sit in the living room, not that Mindy was sitting. An easy chair next to the couch, beside a little fireplace—one of those pot-bellied, cast-iron things with a slim flue leading up to the roof. Lucia had her feet up on its cold metal.

"I remember my blood went everywhere. You don't forget a thing like that. Say someone else just happened to decide to chase me onto his little boat to tear my throat out. He *kills me*, dumps me in the water, then he leaves. Bakula comes back from practicing with the Vienna Boys Choir or whatever innocent people do and finds his yacht's covered in blood. *Why doesn't he call the cops?*"

"He doesn't know. The vampire cleans up after himself. Just like he hid— just like he tried to hide your body."

"He wouldn't have cleaned that mess up, not if he didn't have to. I don't."

Mindy hated hearing Lucia compare herself to him. "Even if Bakula did it, we don't even know how to kill a vampire."

"I get as many guns as I can and I shoot him as many times as I can. I blow him up with a bomb in his car. I rip his goddamn head off and set his ass on fire. If none of that works, I start experimenting, because I've got nothing but time."

Mindy shook her head. "El, I know this man, he's my friend—"

"*I'm* your friend," Lucia gritted out. "We put crosses around his house. Doors, windows. We set the place on fire. We don't let him get out. He can't get out."

"*We?*"

"You and me. He *bit me,* Minz. He dumped me in the water!"

"We don't know that for sure."

Lucia slammed her fist on the chair's armrest, ripping it. Then she covered her mouth with her hand, looking angry at herself for her own anger. "I need him gone. I need him gone, I need him gone, I need him gone…"

"We will," Mindy promised her, kneeling down in front of the chair. "When we're sure. Could you live with yourself, El, if you got the wrong guy?"

"Living isn't a problem I have at the moment." Lucia took her hand away from her mouth, fisted it on her brow instead. "Remember that metal door in his basement, the locked door? He has to have something down there. Maybe he keeps the bodies in there. Maybe I'd be in there, if he hadn't run out of room…"

"Okay then." Mindy clapped her hands. "We go in, we check the basement—if it's a coffin and blood then…we'll get him."

Lucia scoured Mindy's face for the truth in her words, and Mindy looked up at her, trying to be as sure of herself as possible, trying to assure Lucia with her own confidence. Lucia took out her cell phone. Checked something. "The Dragons have a game tonight. Bakula will be out all night. While he's at the stadium, we go to his house, we break in, we *find out.* But we have to go right now."

"Okay," Mindy nodded. Her hand was on Lucia's knee. "Okay, you got it, it's on."

She stood, her hand slipping off Lucia, and went back to the dining room.

"Where are you going?" Lucia asked, standing after her.

"To get a tourniquet ready. I still have to draw some blood."

Lucia shook her head. "It's him. We'll kill him, and then I'll be normal. Everything will go back to normal. So you don't have to…"

"Do you want me to?" Mindy asked, wondering why she even cared, what she had to prove, and still wishing Lucia would just—this one thing, couldn't she have *one thing?* Lucia needing her in one tiny way… But Lucia shook her head again.

Mindy heard a long, shuddering yawn from Seb in the other room. He was up, leaning in the passageway, a finger hooked in his mouth and pulling at it like he was adjusting it. Mindy didn't know what that was about.

"We're going to slay a *wampyr?*"

"No," Mindy said just as Lucia said "Yes."

"Good. I'll get my crossbow."

"Why do you have a crossbow?" Mindy asked, instantly regretting it.

Seb had already turned to go. "My nana gave it to me," he said over his shoulder. "For the punks."

"Punks?"

"That better not mean black people," Lucia added.

"No, punks, of all races. They wear leather jackets and mohawks, drive motorcycles, terrorize people for wallets and gas!"

"Like Mad Max? That was a post-apocalyptic movie. Seb, you know there hasn't been an apocalypse in America, right?"

Lucia shrugged. "Well, the Baby Boomers…"

By default, Mindy drove, taking Seb back to her place to pick up her vampire-hunting kit from when she thought Lucia was a vampire…well, more of a bitch about being a vampire, at least. Lucia promised to meet them there, and when Mindy finished gathering her things in a black duffel bag, she came out to find Lucia by her ride, shadowboxing a little and cracking her neck.

"Okay!" Lucia said, sounding vaguely like she was launching into a cheer routine. "You've got your go-bag, Seb's got his crossbow, now let's girl up—Seb, you can man up, at your discretion—and go get our *Buffy* on."

Mindy tossed her bag into the trunk. "Let's say for a moment that Bakula is the vampire. Do you even know how to kill him? Because I'd like to know that before we piss off a vampire."

"*Do I know how to kill him?*" Lucia whined mockingly. "While you were being all dial-up, I've been on broadband, whittling stakes, gathering silver, experimenting… Don't be jealous…" Lucia held up her hand. Mindy just now noticed that it was inside a mitten. She chided herself for being a bad friend. Hermione would've noticed.

Lucia took the mitten off. Her fingers had that melted plastic look people got from being in fires. "Holy water's not much fun. Garlic doesn't do shit. Natural running water is like acid. So, after we cut his head off, we're tossing him in a river just to be sure. If that doesn't kill him, at least it'll *really hurt.*"

"Well…at least you've still got garlic bread," Mindy joked, trying to lighten the mood.

Lucia pulled her mitten back on. "Never mind, game's starting, let's go."

They listened to Rihanna and Eminem sing "The Monster" on the ride over. Sang along to Rihanna's vocals, beatboxed over Eminem, parked on the gritty gravel a fair distance from the house. In the evening, with the lake so low, they didn't have much company. Just a family in the picnic area, using the public grill to fry some burgers. Mindy had already thought up a plan. Seb, dressed in a spare Dragon Pizza shirt of Mindy's, would go up and ring Bakula's doorbell. If he were home, for whatever reason, he'd say, "Oh, I didn't order any pizza," Seb would apologize for getting the address wrong, and they'd call the whole thing off. If he didn't answer the door, then the mission was a go.

Seb gazed at the huge lakefront property as he tucked in his borrowed shirt, seemingly embarrassed that Mindy's size fit him. "When is moat being put in?" he asked sardonically, earning a grin from Lucia.

"Remember," she said, "if he answers the door, whatever you do, do not go into that house. Leave as quickly as you can. If at all possible, turn and run."

"Do not worry," he told her. "I am protected." He fished a crucifix out of his shirt collar, making Lucia wince, then gathered up the "delivery" and started through the trees. His red shirt didn't pick up the light for long.

"And I always thought it was dumb in those old movies when the vampire hunters went to stake a vampire at night," Mindy thought aloud. "Guess it doesn't make much of a difference." She looked over at Lucia, who was lost in deeper thought than Mindy had ever given her credit for. "So, you and Seb…"

"Yeah, he's cool. Not as cool as me, obviously. There's this girl in Theater Arts he has a crush on, so if you want him—"

"I don't."

Lucia ducked her head like she was hiding her teeth. "I can't wait to have this done, Minz. I feel like I'm having a tumor cut out of me or I'm getting liposuction or something. All this bullshit, I'm just gonna crap it right out. I'm gonna be *normal* again. I'm gonna wear dresses and have big fluffy hair, and my kids are gonna ask me about my weird goth phase. I wish this had happened during school picture day. That'd be cuh-razy!"

"I got you a present," Mindy said. "I guess you could call it a good luck charm."

"Great. I love presents," Lucia said listlessly. Then Mindy saw her lift her head, force a smile for Mindy's benefit—she could tell when Lucia was faking. "Is it a pony?" she said, with her smallest smile.

Mindy dug into her purse, took out the velvet box she'd bought that afternoon.

Lucia's eyes bulged.

*She doesn't think it's a ring, does she?* Mindy opened it up before she could make some joke about that. Inside was a little golden heart, attached to two gold chains. Mindy picked up the small piece of jewelry, worked the catch, and broke the heart in two along the crack designed down the middle. So one half read *Best friends* and the other read *Forever.*

"They had a lot of these for sale, but this one—I like the idea, I guess. That getting your heart broken just means you have a piece to give to someone else."

Lucia just stared at it. For once, Mindy couldn't read her. She continued, babbling on, almost wishing she could stop.

"I know how religious you are and how much it must hurt that you can't wear your cross, but—you said God wasn't listening to you. Well, I have one half and you have the other. So you know that—*someone* is always there to listen to you. About anything."

Lucia's lips bunched up, hiding her teeth once more.

"Okay," Mindy said, "please tell me if you hate it. Don't pretend to like it, I still have the receipt, I won't be upset if you get a refund…"

"I love it," Lucia interrupted. "Go ahead. Put it on."

She bowed her head for Mindy to slip one-half over, watched as Mindy put on hers. She was staring. Mindy looked down, saw how the half heart caught the light.

"It looks really pretty on you," Lucia said, her voice heartfelt, but dull somehow. Like it was coming over a bad connection.

"It looks really pretty on you too. Really, really pretty."

A tear slipped down Lucia's cheek. Lucia's hand blurred, but Mindy saw it before she wiped it away.

"What's wrong? If it's not the necklace—"

"I still have it. My cross," Lucia said. "I just can't look at it." Her voice was suddenly so thick, so *strangled* with emotion that Mindy didn't know how she could ever have wished it wouldn't be so neutral.

"Lucia. El…"

"Why doesn't God want me?" Lucia asked. *Demanded.* "It's not my fault—I didn't ask for this. So, why is He punishing me? I took care of my mom, I took care of my brothers—so I slept with a few boys, does that make me a bad person? It's not like I…like I *enjoyed* it, really. It's just what you *do* with him when he's your boyfriend. I tried to be good, Mindy. I really, really tried."

Lucia's hands were flying around, gesturing with each word, each *sound,* so fast that Mindy imagined them coming off or something, hitting herself in the head, hurting herself. So, as soon as they slowed, she reached out with her own hands and laced them with Lucia's. She didn't mean anything by it. She just saw Lucia upset, playing with her hands, and thought how much Lucia needed something to hold onto.

Lucia let out a long, soft breath. She was very still. Everything was very still. Even her eyes, looking at Mindy like she hadn't seen her a million times before.

"I don't think it's God that—hurts you," Mindy said haltingly. "Maybe it's just the shape of the cross—the symbol. Maybe… I read this book where it was a psychological thing. Psychosomatic. The vampires who had faith when they were alive, they saw the symbols of their religion as clean and pure, and themselves as filthy, unholy. That's all it is. Not God. God is love. It's just your head that gets in the way of the love."

In a rush, Lucia was out of the car, spilling out, down, dropping to her knees and the gravel. Mindy got out herself, just as the car rocked with the violence of Lucia shutting her door. Mindy left hers open, the car beeping with some outrage or another as Mindy ran after Lucia, who was twenty feet away, staring out at the dark water like the sight had caught hold of her.

Lucia heard her get close and wheeled on her. Her eyes *shone* black inside the red, black holes in the night. The rest of her was so dark, Mindy didn't know how she could tell Lucia was crying. She just knew.

"You drive me crazy, you know that? I don't know how to…make anything out of you. Where to put you in my head. How is it the most perfect days of my life are being your friend—and now, you're the only thing keeping me sane—but you also *hurt*. I hold you in my heart and it *hurts*. If you were a boy…if you were any other girl…I'd know what you were to me. I'd have a word for it. But you're *you* and I'm me, and I don't know what that means!"

"Does it need a word?" Mindy asked.

"It doesn't feel safe without one." She took off her mitten, massaging her injured fingers. "I'm sorry, it's not you, it's my hand. I have a booboo, I'm acting like a bitch—"

"No, no, it's fine. Would some blood make you heal faster?"

Lucia smiled fondly, tears still flowing. "How do you say shit like that with a straight face?"

"Because you need me to."

"Yeah," Lucia answered her, "it would, but there's no time."

"You could take some of mine."

Lucia turned away.

Mindy took a deep breath. "I can understand not asking me. But I don't understand how I can offer—of my own free will—and you'd rather hurt someone else to get it. Am I that bad?"

"You know that's not it."

"*No*, I don't! I know what I tell myself, try to convince myself, but I want to hear it from you. Please. Tell me."

"It's not…important. I'll be cured soon anyway."

"What if your hand doesn't heal then? What if you're scarred for life?"

"Then I'll be scarred!" Lucia pulled her mitten back on. "Seb's coming back. Guess nobody's home." She walked by Mindy. "Thank you for the necklace."

# CHAPTER 15

In the night, without the lights on, the house was like a glass poured full of wet shadows. Icy furniture swam inside, shifting into view with the waning of the moon, liquid and bony. Looking through that dark glass, Mindy felt like she was looking inside some alien creature, watching its organs pump and beat and breathe. She went to the front door and bent to the lock, Seb and Lucia standing behind to shield her from being seen from the lake. Not that there was anyone there.

She took out the lockpick kit she'd ordered from an eBay seller in China for a buck last year. Mindy has seen this whole thing done in a GIF. She just had to use the pry bar to hold the bottom of the lock down, then try all the tumblers with the toothy thing. She clicked the first tumbler, nothing happened, the second tumbler, nothing happened, the third tumbler…

Where had she heard that the first tumbler in the sequence was always one of the first three tumblers in the lock? Maybe she should start over, try them more carefully. Was there something else you were supposed to do? Maybe she should look at that GIF again. She could probably find it on Google with her phone.

"Have you ever picked a lock before?" Lucia asked.

Mindy ignored her.

"Because when you said 'I'll pick the lock,' I assumed you'd picked a lock before, and that's why you were on lockpicking duty."

"I have the lock*pick,* don't I?" Mindy said, which she counted as still ignoring Lucia because she was stating a fact, not engaging with her.

"You didn't answer my question. Seb, she didn't answer my question."

Seb rubbed his arms against the cold. "Mindy, *have* you ever been lockpicking before?"

"Have you guys?"

"If I had a lockpick, I would've," Lucia answered smartly.

Mindy tried the fourth tumbler. She'd show them. When she opened the door, she'd give them a look right off Natalie Dormer's face and say something clever like—wait, was this the fourth tumbler or the third one?

"Okay, you want to know the truth?" Mindy went back one, tried that tumbler. None of them seemed to do anything. "When I got them, I tried picking the lock on the backdoor of my house, I spent like ten minutes on it, then I got bored and watched Netflix. *The point is*, I may not be the Lockpick Queen of Central Texas, but I know the basics, and now I have incentive."

"Yeah, slaying a vampire."

*Shutting you up*, Mindy silently corrected her. "Uh-huh."

"Can I try?" Lucia persisted.

Mindy quickly prodded each tumbler. *Stupid fucking*—"I can do it!"

"Just let me try, alright?"

The last tumbler wiggled but did nothing. Mindy moved out of the way. "Be my guest!"

Lucia kicked the door open. "Whaddya know, it was unlocked."

Seb and Mindy went in together, inviting Lucia after them.

Lucia led the way. Mindy guessed when it came to night vision, becoming a vampire was better than eating carrots. She tried to follow, but Lucia was going too fast and Mindy didn't want to trip over anything.

"Lucia!" Mindy whispered harshly, bringing her to a halt. "It's too dark."

Lucia extended her hand. Mindy took it, held hers back to Seb. He grabbed it before they took off, Lucia dragging both of them behind her. She looked back at the weight and rolled her eyes. "Like the fucking Hardy boys and Nancy Drew."

"I'm Nancy Drew," Mindy said.

"No, I'm Nancy Drew!"

"Shut up, Seb."

Still, it was so dark that Mindy pulled Seb's hand into the crook of her arm and took out her phone. The meager light was just enough to illuminate the floor under them. Beyond that, it was like walking at the bottom of the ocean. Lucia's skin was a ghastly white in the blue glow. Her eyes electric when she looked back. They came to the stairs, and Lucia finally slowed down for Mindy. She took them one at a time, Mindy following at a snail's crawl.

"I remember everything about that party," Lucia said. "The taste of the chips, the beer, the weed, the dancing, the music. I would've died to hold a party like that. It was *amazing*. But I wasn't having fun. And I remember thinking, what does this party need to be perfect? That's when I called you, Mindy. And ordered the pizza."

Mindy jabbed Lucia's hand with her thumbnail. Lucia gave a tight-lipped smile.

"I remember everything good about that night. Why do I want the bad too?"

At the bottom of the steps, Seb unslung his crossbow from his shoulder and aimed it at the door, ready for whatever popped out. Good to know some of his time in America had been spent watching horror movies.

Lucia tried the doorknob. It was unlocked. She pushed the door open. Mindy held her lit phone up. They looked inside.

"Well, it seems you've discovered my secret," Bakula said, appearing on the stairs behind them, dripping with something wet and viscous and dark that glistened in the pale light… "I use bronzer," Bakula admitted cheerfully, walking down in his bare feet and bathrobe. "Now, why are you in my house?"

Seb silently pushed the door further open. The light feeding the thick leaves of marijuana plants filling the basement from front to back spilled out. Bakula was running a grow operation.

"Why, heck, that's no reason to break my door. I know my middlemen take their fair share of a markup, but you can understand how people wouldn't understand a teacher selling direct. What can I say, I'm a big believer in hemp. Me and Willie Nelson. Frees the creativity, reduces stress, tastes better'n beer—heck, I think if we just let you kids smoke your reefer, our test scores would be up. All this worrying about SAT, TAKS, CIA, DUI… I wouldn't put a stray dog through it." Reaching behind them, he pulled the door shut. "Like I said, can't sell to you, can refer you to a dealer who'll give you a fair price. He's black, so I hope you don't mind the stereotype. Is that boy holding a crossbow?" he asked of Seb suddenly.

Lucia jabbed her fangs into his throat.

"El!" Mindy cried. She saw, out of the corner of her eye that Seb stood stunned, not sure what to do, his crossbow only half-raised.

Lucia pried herself off Bakula's throat, her lips a little wet with blood, but mostly with bronzer. She wiped it off on her wrist. "Uck! Get a real tan or don't tan at all." His eyes were glassy, his body wobbling a little on its heels. "Glamoured, bitch."

Mindy let out the breath she was holding. "For fuck's sake—"

"You want to try your luck with a cover story, or do you want me to use my roofie-spit and make him forget we were ever here?" She jerked her head to the top of the stairs. "C'mon, George Hamilton, let's find out what you know."

"And do you having any ice cream treats?" Seb added. "My host family does not believe in them."

"Yes, I have many ice cream treats," Bakula said woozily.

They sat him down in the kitchen. Seb was digging through the freezer for ice cream sandwiches, so Lucia ripped the crossbow off his back and shoved it into Mindy's arms.

"If he moves, shoot 'im."

"It's clearly not him, El, how could you glamour another vampire?"

"I don't know, how do you turn into mist? This is all crazy bullshit, Minz, why are you expecting it to make sense?"

"My Creative Writing teacher would hate you."

"Fuck creative writing, this isn't high school, this is real life! Real life! Sometimes you gotta arrow someone!" Lucia spun on Bakula, pulled out her own chair, spun that around too, and straddled it backward. "Are you a fucking vampire?"

Bakula talked like he had a bad head cold. "No. Vampires don't exist."

"You lying vampire motherfucker!" She slapped him.

"That hurt," Bakula said truthfully, his voice dull and level under Lucia's thrall.

"I'm gonna kick your ass if you lie to me again! I'm fucking gonna rip your face off with my fingernails, then go for a mani to get your face out from under my nails!"

"I didn't do anything to you—"

"Liar!" Mindy put her hands supportively and restrainingly on Lucia's shoulders. Lucia seemed like she would pull free, but didn't. Her anger was wet and hot, boiling out of her through almost-tears in her eyes. "It was your boat! You were there!"

"Someone broke into my boat," he said, as simple as a child giving a book report. "They took it for a joyride. I really thought they wouldn't, since I'd allowed them to party inside the house and taken the keys with me, but I guess I can't trust the team as much as I thought. I'm thinking next time I'll have to specify a chaperone…"

Lucia slapped him with so much of her strength, his head twisted around. Mindy was amazed his neck didn't break. But she'd only caught him with the tips of her fingers, her rage stealing her accuracy.

"El, stop—" Mindy pulled back on her, pulled Lucia out of reach of him. "It's not him, okay? You have to stop."

"I know it's irresponsible, hosting the team in my own house without my supervision, but I just love those boys. I'm an old-fashioned coach. I can't be ruthless with them; they're not just parts in a machine to me…"

"Shut up!" Lucia pulled away from Mindy, her hands in her hair, pulling it out at the roots. It was dark in her white hands, like an oil spill on water.

"To a coach like me, the pride of my team is my pride. Their glory is my glory! Their fate is my fate! Sometimes I catch myself using the royal we—" Bakula pulled on his white mustache like he was reading Braille off its whiskers. "We Dragons have the right to be proud. Our veins flow with the blood of all the lions of the human race, those who have *fought* as lions. Texas is the whirlpool of the American races—"

"What is he talking about?" Seb asked.

"He's *high*, he's not talking about anything," Mindy protested. "Seb, get a mirror."

"He's in on it!" Lucia sobbed it out, her eyes teary and cold at the same time. Glaciers in the sun. "He knows something, he's playing you, he's playing you because you're soft!"

"And you hate him because he's my friend! Just like you hated Seb!"

"What'd I do?" Seb asked, looking up.

"Seb! Mirror!" Mindy reiterated, frustrated, ready to scream.

"I remember facing the Bishop Huns," Bakula said jovially, smiling to himself, no idea his fate was being argued over in the same room he was in. "Their fury *swept* Texas football like a living flame."

"I don't hate Seb!" Lucia cried, confused now.

"Yeah, because now you know we're not dating!"

Bakula slapped his bicep. "Idiots! What devil was ever as great as Attila? His blood runs in these veins! Huns, indeed!"

"Why should I care who you're dating?" Lucia asked in total exasperation.

"That's right, *why should you?*"

"They say that I think only of myself, but what good are players without a leader? Where does the battle end without a mind and a heart to conduct it?"

"Do you know what he did to me?" Lucia shouted in her face.

"No, I…"

"Me neither."

"Here!" Seb said, holding up the compact Mindy had packed. She grabbed it from him, opened it, held it in front of Bakula.

His reflection neatly twinned him.

Bakula's melancholy oratory continued, the only thing that held. "But now, it's all about safety—they don't let us play like they did in the old days. This winning streak brings me no pleasure. It is a dishonorable victory."

Lucia was still. "That doesn't prove anything."

Mindy turned the mirror on Lucia. No reflection. "He's human, Lucia."

Lucia threw up her hands. "Okay, so let's splash him with holy water, throw a cross at him—"

"We already broke his door and *bit him!* Let's just go, okay?"

Lucia stabbed a finger at her. "You don't want it to be him! Not your friend."

"And you do? Goddamnit, El, remember the last time we were here and I said we should leave? Why can't you just listen to me?"

Lucia's hands were on her skull like she wanted to crush her brain. "You don't care. You don't care about me."

"I don't care?" Mindy demanded. "I just said you can have my blood. *Five. Minutes. Ago.*"

"If you cared, you wouldn't tempt me. Fuck this." Lucia blurred.

Mindy heard the front door slamming before she spotted Lucia through the window, curled up on a stone post of the property's fence.

Seb turned back to Mindy. "You know she is wants someone to go to her."

Mindy shook her head. "Let her stew."

Something scraped behind them. Bakula was pushing a salt shaker around the kitchen table.

"What are you being here anyway?" Seb asked. "Don't you have the game?"

"Opposing team had an injury. They had to forfeit."

"That's too bad," Seb said. "Their quarterback was great. Would've been a good game."

"Don't fraternize with him," Mindy chided. "It's…disloyal."

"To Ms. Lucia?" Bakula asked. He seemed deeply confused, boggled by an intricate puzzle in his mind. "Huh. How can you be loyal to someone who isn't loyal to you?"

"Lucia's loyal to me. She's my friend." Mindy sighed. "Shit. Maybe we should use some holy water—baptize the guy if it'll get Lucia to see reason."

"Wait…go back…Lucia's your friend?" Bakula exhaled slightly. "Oh yes, now I remember. I'd heard she wanted to befriend you. It's really none of my business—"

"Wait, what do you mean, you *heard*?" Mindy sat down with him, close enough to see the grains of salt shift each time he prodded the shaker with his long stalk of a finger.

"Oh, us teachers, we gossip as much as anyone. It's not our concern how you live your lives. We just hear things. I didn't know whether to tell you or not. It seemed like you might want to know—but then again, I didn't think you would appreciate me intruding on your personal life."

"His brain is fried eggs," Seb said. "As you being say, Mindy, let us go."

Mindy put up a hand, gesturing him to wait. "Who said what?"

"The cheerleading coach—Mrs. Fox. Nice lady. Tough, but nice. I don't think she would make up something like that…"

"Something like what?"

"The rumor was that you were bi-curious, bisexual, it's all the same to these kids. Most don't really care, it's not all that interesting these days." He shrugged. "*Glee*, you know? But Mrs. Fox said she overheard Lucia promise

Mr. Morse that if he won the game against the Panthers, you know, in January? That she'd have a threesome with him. He won, of course. Quentin's a great runner, I think he'll go college ball. So, to keep her promise, Lucia needed a bisexual woman. Someone who would be so grateful to be included that she'd do, well, anything. Anyone." Bakula gave a loopy smile. "I never believed it myself. You just don't strike me as that type of girl. I think you're waiting for the right man to come along."

Mindy felt like she was going to throw up. But she couldn't, she wouldn't, not until she talked to Lucia. She didn't think she could do anything without asking Lucia if it were true. She barely felt like she could breathe.

She rammed out the front door and stalked to Lucia to give her the attention she wanted so badly.

"Are we having a threesome?" Mindy demanded. *"Are we having a fucking threesome?"*

Lucia looked past her to Seb, who had followed her out. "Whoa, Seb, my man, what moves did *you* pull?"

Mindy spun around. "Seb, go back inside the house, tell Bakula that we were never here and that a deer broke his door, some shit like that. Go!"

Seb hurried away.

"I think I should let you know," Lucia said jokingly, so easy for her to cool down, to turn on a dime and make everything into a joke, "that I don't believe in orgies before marriage."

"Not him." Mindy didn't recognize her own voice—tight and controlled and throttled down somewhere deep in her gut. "You and me and Quentin. Because he scored more goals than the other team and you wanted to *reward* him. And why wouldn't I do that? I'm such a great big *bisexual slut*, aren't I? You probably could've paid me to do it, like a whore, but you thought you'd save a few bucks."

Lucia's eyes flashed. "Who told you that?"

"It's true, isn't it?"

"No, no it's not!" Lucia leapt down off the post.

"Then swear it. Swear it's not true, El, I'll believe you…"

"It's…" Lucia's head dropped to one side. "It's complicated."

Mindy felt like she was being strangled to death. Like she had wire wrapped around her throat. Like a guillotine was coming down.

"It was…a little bit true, but just for a little while!" Lucia tried to smile, assuage Mindy like a lion tamer with an angry animal, but she didn't know what would work and what would make it worse. "I was going to see if you were interested, but then Quentin and I broke up and you were so nice to me, Minz, you were such a good friend—" She reached out…

Mindy punched her. It hurt, felt like slamming her fists into brick, but Lucia jerked away.

"You punched me in the tit!" Lucia cried. "Who does that?"

"Stay away from me." Mindy didn't know how she got the words out. It felt a little like her throat had been slit and what she said bled out. "Don't call me, don't e-mail me, just—I don't want you in my life!"

She ran for the car. Lucia blurred in front of her, stood there as Mindy went past her. She did it again and again, never saying anything, and Mindy fled from her each time, until she was in the car, waiting for Seb. She honked the horn and he came rushing out of Bakula's house with a box of ice cream sandwiches.

A last little whoosh of air, like a sigh, and Lucia's face was outside the driver's side window. Finally, words: "I'm sorry, I am so sorry, I never ever meant—"

Mindy looked at her. Her eyes shut Lucia up. "I would've given you every drop. Every last drop."

Seb climbed into the passenger seat. They left Lucia there. She didn't follow them.

Next day, the morning radio show, *Up For The Count With Jack & Gil* reported another animal attack. A local lady, Tammy Smith of Trench Street, was found in a pool of her own blood.

# CHAPTER 16

Mindy set her food in the microwave, covered it with the dish that kept the hot juices from splattering everywhere, then started the nuking. There was a knock at the door, overpowering the noise of the movie her parents were watching.

"Mindy, can you get that?" her father called, and Mindy left the microwave humming to loop around the house to the front door. The knock kept beating at the door as she approached, slow but regular, like maybe it was just a branch blown by the wind.

Mindy unlocked the door. The beating stopped. She opened it and there was no one there, just a little white shape out on the lawn. Mindy turned on the porch lights. It colored in the figure a little—small and hunched over, shriveled up. "Hello?" she called.

The shape moved, and Mindy thought she saw a leg extending from out of the huddle of clothes. But it could've been a cane. It was so thin, so white. It moved again and Mindy could make out a little tail of white hair fluttering out from a head that canted down and seemed lost in the shadows that the light cast.

Mindy stepped outside. Her socks hit the damp grass of the evening's sprinkler, and the cold ran up her legs like a bunch of tiny needles. "Hey!" she said, a bit louder, a bit ruder. "Are you alright?"

The shape was walking in circles making a staccato beat on the grass. The wind picked up, letting her see more of the white hair that seemed so thin, so frayed, and carried words to Mindy. Mutterings, indistinct but not unimportant. Weighted, as if the shape was trying to remember something.

The wind blew the front door closed behind her, cutting off the sound of the TV and the trivial conversation of her parents. She moved to reach out for the shape—it was that close— and was ready to defend herself. It was ridiculous: she could see the shape, see it was a person, a senior citizen, a woman, so what was the harm? But the way her body twisted…the way it lost itself in the shallow darkness… It wasn't right. Mindy kept looking at her as if she were a Magic Eye picture and she'd made a mistake, but in her mind, she wasn't thinking of it as a little old lady. She didn't want to think about it at all.

"I'm gonna go get my parents," she said, backing up. She took a step backward, *I should turn around.* Another step back, *I should run for it.* Another step. *Now, now, now!*

The shape reached out a hand, but it was more like it sprouted it from some abyss within itself, a skeletal tendril with claws for fingernails, bone-white for skin. It grabbed the sleeve of her shirt and it hung on.

"They let it in." The voice was old and it was tired and it was defeated, words from a soldier about to be overrun or a prisoner on death row. "They let it in. They let it in."

*If I try to pull away, I'll die.* The thought was so clear in Mindy's head, like a bell ringing in a quiet space. It could've been a prophecy, for all she knew. Yet she inched away, her body recoiling from that clawed touch on a biological, an instinctual, a molecular level. The long fingernails frayed her shirt sleeve, and Mindy imagined them in her skin. She thought of them cutting like razor blades.

"What'd they let in?" Mindy asked.

The woman looked at her. She turned, and Mindy saw the patch of blood on her neck, spreading onto a nightgown almost as white as her skin and becoming a second shadow, a darkness that encroached on an entire half of her body. Eclipsing her. "The Devil."

Then Mindy pulled away. She ripped her hand free and she turned around and ran for the door as the distance narrowed and stretched and refused to let her pass. But then the door snapped into focus, and she was there, she was home, and she threw the door open and fell inside and she slammed the damn thing closed with her entire body.

The door slamming echoed through the house. Her parents looked at her. "What is it, sweetie?"

Mindy turned the lock before she answered.

Of course her father unlocked it, and of course he and her mother went out to put a blanket around the woman and bring her inside. And of course, in the light, it was just a frail old woman who'd hurt herself.

The police came while Mindy was up in her room sitting on her bed. Wishing she could feel foolish, but it'd been so real. That deep-bone certainty you have as a child that there's something under the bed or in the closet and only pulling the sheets over your head could protect you. Mindy was too old for that. She was eighteen. About to graduate!

Her door opened without knocking, setting her teeth on end. She'd heard the muffled conversation downstairs, the police interviewing her parents, but hadn't expected anyone to talk to her. It was just someone's grandmother, right? Someone who'd gotten confused and escaped the retirement home— cut herself on something. Couldn't be anything else.

Detective Lou Card came in, the lumbering bear, but he didn't have that lazy heft now. He was on point, a soldier's bearing, and he focused on Mindy hard. "Quite a shock, huh?"

Mindy nodded.

"I just have a few questions." He moved around her room like he was touring a museum, examining the posters on the walls, the books on the shelves. "Do you know the Shady Rest Retirement Home? Any friends or family there?"

"No."

"That's where Mrs. McCallister—your new friend—was from. You know where it is?"

"No."

"Other side of town. Now, that place isn't exactly Fort Knox, but do you have any idea how a senile old lady on foot could cross twenty miles of suburbia without anyone noticing?"

"No, I think that's your job."

Card smiled at her. Looked at her Emma Frost Sideshow Collectibles statue on top of her bookshelf, picking it up and examining it.

"Could you please be careful with that?" Mindy added, feeling like she was breaking some kind of stalemate. "It's pretty delicate."

"Sorry, sorry—your parents buy you that?"

"No, I bought it. She's my favorite character."

"What's that, life goals? Thinspiration?"

Mindy rolled her eyes. "It's a school night."

Card set the statue down. "Where have you been the last few hours?"

"Here. In my room. Playing Tomb Raider."

"Any witnesses?"

"No. It's a single-player game."

Card nodded. "Seems your style." He reached into his pocket, taking out a notepad, and it suddenly bothered Mindy that he hadn't had it out before. He took his time, opening it to a dog-eared page, then working backward. "Alright. Five o'clock, Mrs. McCallister takes her medication, stays in her room. Four hours pass. You're here, in your room, standing on your head or whatever. Mrs. McCallister turns up on your front yard after being attacked by our 'animal'. Grabs you, smears blood on you, you wash it off."

"Yeah," Mindy said, kinda wishing Card would go back to circling. She didn't like how still he stood, how he looked at her like he wasn't sure where he would move next. "That's right."

"So if we find little bits of your skin under her fingernails, it's just because she happened to ring your doorbell and you answered it and, uh, gave her a hug."

Mindy stared at him. Almost too confused to be angry. "Do you always accuse the nearest teenage girl of a crime?"

"I do when the victim shows up on her doorstep. Why don't you come down to the station, let our lab boys run a few tests. I know you'd hate the thought of everyone wondering what you had to do with these attacks when just a few swabs could clear everything up."

"I'm not going anywhere with you."

"You seem like the kind of girl who thinks she's very smart. I wonder if you're smart enough to get the picture before I have to snap the cuffs on."

She wasn't in handcuffs. Mindy clung to that thought. She held onto it, a life preserver on a stormy sea.

The interrogation room—"interview room," which Mindy couldn't think about without putting mincing air-quotes around it—reminded her of a janitor's closet. It was a place where you put things, but without any care or attention. You just stowed them there and forgot about them until they were needed. That's how Mindy felt. Forgotten. They made her wait for what seemed like hours. She'd heard that guilty people slept. She didn't. But she still didn't know what that made her.

She wasn't in handcuffs.

She thought about Lucia. Thought about how much she could've angered Lucia, calling her on her bullshit, cutting her off from "Mindy time." Funny how she'd used to wonder if Lucia cared about her at all. Now maybe Lucia cared so much that... Mindy tried not to think about a cat leaving a dead mouse on the doorstep. She tried harder.

Card came in. He could arrest her, but he couldn't compel a DNA swab or any of that other CSI bullshit. He needed a court order for that. So he'd keep her here while he got a judge to sign off on it. Mindy wondered how long it would take at this time of night.

He sat down across from her, a folder under his arm. It stayed there like a gun in a holster. "I was just thinking about that guy who got his throat gnawed on by a coyote." He opened the folder. There was a crime scene photo. Mindy almost would've believed it was tinted red, except the colors were so normal around the edges. "Remember that? We're the police—we kept investigating it. Obviously, his truck was covered with blood. Covered in it. What's weird is that a lot of it's missing. We have the blood that's in his body, and we have the blood on the ground, and then we have at least three pints of blood that's just gone. So then we had one guy missing blood—" He pushed the stack of photos toward her. They were red too. He spread them around the table like he was setting up a board game. "Now we have a lot of people missing blood. What does that sound like to you, Mindy?"

It wasn't a question. There were no questions. It was like he was giving a monologue, every word precise, calibrated, *sharpened,* chiseling away at Mindy. Only they didn't bite into her. There was a shield around her, a feeling of warmth, a thought of *fuck this guy.* It was talking in Lucia's voice and Mindy repeated everything it said, like an actor with well-learned lines.

"Are you asking me to help solve your case? Because I'm not Nancy Drew. Okay, I'm a little Nancy Drew. I've read all the books and some fanfic online, you know, crossovers with the Hardy Boys. Not, you know, the kinky stuff, they're just good friends...but maybe someday, when Nancy's ready for a real relationship..."

"I don't want you."

"I get that from a lot of guys."

His hand lashed out, fist striking the table, hard enough to jolt it a few inches to the side, the legs squealing on the tile floor. Mindy jumped. Card left his hand on the table, tightening his knuckles. "I want whoever put you up to this. Look at the pictures. *Look at them.*"

Mindy did. She'd known Lucia was capable of all that. She'd known, damnit. "You're still printing out pictures? Ever heard of a smartphone or a tablet? So much better for the environment..."

Card stood. He held the folder at his side, empty. "Let me give you a piece of advice, little girl. You're not smart enough to act this stupid. I've read your file. National Honor Society, no detentions, no absences. You're almost valedictorian. I don't believe you roped yourself into this; I think someone pushed you. Befriended you, seduced you, whatever—and now that you've been sucked in, they're hurting people. They think they're some kind of vampire, and they're pulling this hoax—I don't know why. Some social media bullshit, I'm guessing. It doesn't really matter, to you or to me. You're in over your head, but you think you're just too fucking smart to go under, don't you?

She looked into his eyes. Maybe if she'd seen one bit of caring—just a little bit—she would've given him another answer. "Well, I'm here, aren't I? I hear they only let smart people in..."

Card gathered up his folder. "All right, then. I'll let you think about it. In the meantime, let's see how your parents feel about their little girl being in trouble with the cops."

The door locked behind him. Mindy hung her head, pressing it to the cool tabletop. She closed her eyes. She didn't feel guilty, just tired.

They left her alone for half an hour, but Mindy didn't worry. She almost wished she could. There was a thought growing like a cancer inside her, killing her worry like an Ambien—Lucia wouldn't let anything happen to her. An hour from now, a week, a month, that very night, El could come strolling in. She would tear through the cops not with machine guns or a chainsaw, but her bare hands. And, streaked in blood, she would kick down the door and pick

Mindy up and carry her away, over the dead. And Mindy found that thought so comforting, she couldn't even be frightened of it.

The door cracked. Mindy jumped, her brain screaming *Card*, but it wasn't him. One of the deputies was looking at her. "Come on. You're free to go."

In the lobby of the police station, Lucia was still giving her alibi, declaiming to Card with the boundless confidence of a particularly talentless American Idol contestant. "So yeah, our windows face each other dead on, I have a sweeping vista of the next house over, it's messed up. Who designs a neighborhood like that? Imagine if it were some creepy old guy with a bald spot and shit." Here, Lucia gave Card a smile. "Anyway, she was there the whole evening. Didn't slip out the window or anything. You really thought she had the athleticism for that? Because I've seen her try push-ups. It's like watching Tara Reid count." Lucia put on a nasal voice. "One...*twoooooooooo...*"

"Anyone who can account for your whereabouts?" Card asked, words short like his teeth wanted to grind together more than to open.

"I was on the phone to my boyfriend, Quentin Morse. Well, ex-boyfriend. We're kinda sorting that out. He's seeing other people and I'm crying a lot."

"Can I go?" Mindy interrupted, and Card looked over at her. Eying her like a dog would look at a slab of meat.

He nodded. "Stay safe now. Your parents are—"

"I'll find them," Mindy said, walking right past him.

Outside, Lucia did her Batman thing, appearing in front of Mindy as soon as she'd excused herself from the cops. Mindy automatically looked around to see if anyone had noticed, but this late at night, the place was a blue canvass with light spilling out from the police station. They were at the outskirts of that light, meeting their shadows.

"You're welcome," Lucia said, leaning against the flagpole.

Mindy scanned the parking lot for a parental vehicle. "I don't want to hear it."

"What, you don't think I had anything to do with Aunt May back there, do you?"

Mindy stopped and closed her eyes. She really didn't like being this angry. It made her keep wondering if she was a bitch. "At the moment, I'm really not sure what you're capable of. *Clearly.*"

She heard a single click of Lucia's heels as the other woman stepped toward her. "Not to rain on your parade, but if you're going to be pissed at me, could you wait five minutes for me to do something to be pissed about?"

This, this feeling of being about to scream and cry and possibly do even more things at the same time, Mindy hated it. But she hated Lucia more for bringing it out in her. "There's the usual bullshit you pull, and then there's how you see me. I thought you looked at me as a person, but apparently you just see me as something your boyfriend can get off on!"

"You should be thankful someone can."

*Okay,* Mindy thought. *Okay, okay, okay.* She turned around and faced Lucia, who somehow didn't look pretty anymore, she looked annoying. "My sexuality is not the most important part of me, but it is a part of me. It's not a joke. not a game. It's not a trend or a style or a fad. It's not a girl crush. It's not 'all girls are a little bit bi.' *I'm attracted to women.* And maybe you rolled out of bed one morning and decided to be a dyke, but I didn't! It took me a long time to get here, and I didn't do it just so you could cast me in some porno!"

She said it advancing on Lucia, step by step, inch by inch, until Lucia was backing away from her, into a bicycle rack, the loose metal swaying slightly as she collided with it. She bent backward, and Mindy felt compelled to follow her, to shove her over those looping waves of metal, to grab her by the shoulders and push her back until her feet left the ground. She didn't, but just for that one moment, it made so much sense.

"I'm sorry," Lucia said, as if pushed to that point beyond defensiveness, that point where she was so desperate to keep Mindy that it almost seemed unfair to deny her. "It was before we were friends."

"I was *always* your friend," Mindy said as headlights pushed the black away. Her parents were circling the parking lot, looking for her. When Mindy looked away from them, Lucia was gone.

# CHAPTER 17

For most of her life, Mindy had had no contact with Lucia. Being without her should've been like going back to normal. No more harebrained schemes, no more shenanigans, no more hot-queasy feelings that slid into Mindy's stomach at random times, summoned by the thought of Lucia. But the only thing worse than it was when it stopped.

She should've been glad she didn't have to worry about that now.

For the first day, she felt like she'd lost an arm, or like she was a lost arm. A phantom limb. She had jokes to tell Lucia, lazy thoughts to share with her on text message, dumb YouTube videos to e-mail to her. They got blocked up, crammed into her body by invisible gates, and she felt like she might explode sometimes.

The second day, those gates were wider, taller, locked tighter. It seemed like things—just little things—got caught outside by them. Things that would've made Mindy laugh didn't get through. Things that would've made her sigh, flutter, tear up... They must've been going right past Mindy. Instead, she felt like white noise.

The third day was quiet. So quiet. The white noise had faded, leaving that hum you can hear in those long stretches of the night when dogs aren't barking and cars aren't running. The sound of the moon, maybe, singing a lonely song in case anyone would care to hear it. She thought she was over it.

Day four, five, six, she'd see Lucia swinging out of her house or coming back to it, as quick and irrevocable as a knife jabbing into flesh, and the Band-Aid was ripped off. Sometimes it struck Mindy as hard as a fist in her stomach. She'd go to the bathroom or the supply closet and cry until she found out how many tears she had.

And she was grateful for those minutes that felt like hours, those absences that led to school administrators and safety officers finding her, sending her to the nurse's office for a checkup, explaining to her gently that it wasn't safe for good little students in the boiler room. Because the hurt meant it was real. It had happened.

Mindy didn't get to sleep the sixth night. Part of it was the lingering adrenaline that stayed right under her skin instead of going back to wherever it was supposed to be—being arrested, fighting with Lucia, almost killing a man. Part of it was that she kept hearing weird noises from Lucia's house. Not vampire noises. More like…shop class.

Finally, she put her headphones on and played Enya music until she couldn't help but go to sleep. She woke up three hours later, in the middle of the night feeling perfectly refreshed but with nothing to do because it was four in the morning. And that noise was still coming from Lucia's house…

Mindy got dressed, went downstairs, out the door, across the lawn, knocked on Lucia's door. A silent pause, then the noise started again. Mindy tried the doorknob. Unlocked, of course. She went inside, up the stairs—gathering a few scraps of litter to throw away in passing—and went to Lucia's room. The door was open.

Lucia was wearing eye protection, a rubber science lab apron, and dishwashing gloves. Her iPod—no, it was a Walkman—was stuffed in her belt and she was listening to something on headphones, performing the lyrics sotto voce as she worked a hacksaw through a two-by-four plank of wood. The wood had already been painted in candy cane stripes.

Then there was the papier mâché, the store mannequins, a stereo, and what could be either an IED or fireworks of similar legality and deadliness. Overnight, Lucia's room had turned into one vast, unassembled attempt by Wile E. Coyote to kill the Roadrunner.

"Lucia, what's going on?"

Lucia noticed her abruptly—rather like a cat hearing a vacuum cleaner—and she hit herself in the face with the hacksaw as she moved to take her headphones down. Managed it with the other hand. "Oh, Minz, hi, I was just—it's a surprise."

"I would agree with that. Is that confetti?"

Lucia looked. "Yes."

Mindy nodded and resigned herself that, much like *Lost*, this would not make more sense if it was explained. "I just wanted to come over and apologize for being so upset the other night. It's one thing to be angry, but it's another thing to be angry *at* someone, and I shouldn't have yelled or punched you in the tit or—"

"It's an apology."

Mindy held up her hands. "I wouldn't go that far. You did try to get me to have sex with Quentin."

"No, all this!" Lucia waved her hands around. "It was going to be a big apology, I had the marching band lined up, it was going to be just like one of those movies where Matthew McConaughey screws up with a girl, then gets back with her by making a big crazy gesture! Or running through an airport, but we don't have an airport here."

Mindy put her hand on her heart. "This is all for me."

"Yeah, you kinda ruined it by forgiving me so fast. Can you keep being angry with me for like two more days? I hired an Elvis impersonator, but he is going to take a while to get here."

Mindy smiled hard enough to give herself laugh lines.

"Okay, if you can't be angry with me, and let's face it, who could, can I hug you? I really need to hug you if you're going to be looking all huggy."

Mindy nodded and was all of a sudden wrapped up in a hug. One look at her and Lucia had seemed so small, folded up in herself, lost in her own white skin and dark hair and *fangs*, fucking *fangs*.

Mindy knew she could make it better. Not right, but better.

"I hate fighting with you," Lucia said. "I hate it, I hate it, I hate it."

"I'm not a fan myself. Let's quit doing that."

"Listen, you know how in all those cheesy romances someone says the other person should stay away from them because they're bad news? Well—I really am bad news. New York Times headline—bloodsucking vampire on the loose—that's the definition of bad news. So if you wanna stay away from me, I completely understand. But do it for your own good. Not because of something stupid I did when I didn't even know you. I mean, you knew I was stupid going into this. I never lied about that."

"You're not stupid. You just—don't always remember to be smart." Mindy forced herself away from Lucia's chill. She felt like she had to stay against it. Warm it up. "Our relationship has to change. I can't keep giving all the time and get nothing back."

Lucia nodded desperately. "I don't want you to! You just never ask for anything!"

"I know. That's what has to change."

"What do you want, Minz? Anything. I'll get you anything. I can get other things. How about a scooter?"

Mindy's hands felt like they'd fallen asleep, hanging down beside her hips. They didn't belong there. She wanted to hold Lucia, touch her in some way, not have her hands down at her sides like some useless things. But she kept them there. Still and small and as little a threat as she could make herself.

"I need you to drink my blood."

Lucia looked like she'd been punched in the gut. She fell on her bed, slack as a puppet with no strings, and now Mindy let herself go to her. She slid up behind her, covered Lucia in her arms, was big for her. "I know it's hard for you," she said to the back of Lucia's head, giving her the privacy of not looking her in the eye. "But whatever it is, you have to tell me. Tell me what would be so wrong with you doing to me what you've done to half the people in town? And I'll understand. Just tell me."

Lucia reached back, found Mindy's hand waiting for her. She kept looking away, out the window. The sky was an unhealthy blue, the color of someone drowned.

"He bit me. I don't even know who he is, but he bit me." Lucia's thumb stroked over Mindy's hand, constantly telling her it was still there. "And he killed me, and other things—I can't even remember how he hurt me. I'll never know what happened. I don't want that for you. As long as you don't have bite marks, you'll *always* know that you can trust me."

All throughout it, Mindy just held Lucia. Afterward, she kept holding her. She could feel Lucia shaking at her core, holding something in, and she helped Lucia clamp down on it until it went still. Then she put her fingers on Lucia's chin—felt her flinch, like when you petted a dog that been kicked too many times. She pulled her hand back, but Lucia turned her head anyway. Looked Mindy in the eye and nodded. She could say what she had to say.

"I'll always trust you," Mindy said. "And if you drained your venom, I'd remember the bite. I'd know... you."

"And what if I bit you again when it came back? I could tell you to forget. I could tell you to do all sorts of things and you'd never know. You'd just think I had bitten you the one time, without venom—"

"You wouldn't do that."

"How do you know? How do you know I even have a *soul?*"

"Because you're my friend. You're my Lucia. Bite me. Let me be what you need. I know you'd never take advantage of me. If you think you can't trust yourself, trust me. Trust us."

Lucia's head shook like a broken clock. "It'll hurt…"

Mindy put her hand on Lucia's cheek, bringing her still. "Some people are worth getting hurt for. C'mon, El. Find out what I taste like."

Lucia's eyes gleamed so bright they could've had stars in them. "You're the best friend I've ever had."

"You're my best friend too."

"No, it's not the same thing. I've had a lot of best friends. I've only had one you. You change into an old shirt, I'll—take care of the venom."

"Do you want to do it now?" Mindy asked, still hugging her tight. "Or in a little while?"

"A little later," Lucia said. "I'll be ready soon."

# CHAPTER 18

The blinds were drawn in Mindy's room. The lights were out. The room was dark and that felt better, more right, than doing this with the lights on. This was their secret. It was huge and horrible and terrifying, but it was also theirs. They owned it. It belonged to them.

Mindy wouldn't let herself be nervous. She would be brave for Lucia's sake. She wanted this. She wanted Lucia to know she wasn't a freak. She wanted…a lot of things.

After an eternity in the bathroom, Lucia came out. The light from the bathroom's tiny bulb dipped into the room. Lucia left it on, only partly closing the door behind her, so it was like a nightlight. She held an old Winnie the Pooh jam jar half-full of her venom. She set it down on Mindy's dresser, then hid her hands in her pockets.

"That's all my venom, I think. I tried to get more out, but nothing came, and I started hearing this nasally sound… I think that's all of it," she repeated.

Mindy nodded. She had taken off her bra and changed into a faded pink shirt with the Superman logo on it. It was an old shirt, and had stopped fitting after her last growth spurt, now showing a little of her pudge at the belly. It also had a big hole at the left armpit and a gravy stain on the back—Mindy wasn't sure how it had gotten there.

"What's that?" Lucia asked, indicating the shirt.

"It's my Supergirl shirt."

"No, Supergirl wears the same logo as Superman. I think that's a gay Superman shirt."

"It's not a gay Superman shirt."

"Superman after he's been exposed to pink Kryptonite." Lucia laughed.

Mindy laughed with her.

"It's a nice shirt. Really. Don't know why you'd want to get blood on it…"

"We've been over this…"

Lucia advanced on her. There was something in the way she looked at Mindy—Mindy got that feeling again where she was in the presence of a big cat. It might eat her, it might ignore her, it might play with her a little bit. She was afraid and she hated herself for that. "I've been through this. I just can't understand why you want it."

"I don't want it," Mindy said. "I want you. I'm saying yes to you. And—the fact is, I'm an accomplice. I am helping you feed on these people, and I think I'm gonna have a hard time living with that. So, if I'm going to be a part of this, I need to know what it is you're doing."

"What I am," Lucia echoed listlessly. "Okay then. Your phone have an alarm clock?"

"Yeah."

"Set it for seven minutes." Lucia's voice was confident, experienced, and despite how horrifying that was, Mindy took comfort in it. "I'm going to take a pint of your blood… four hundred and fifty milliliters. I drink about one milliliter a second. Seven minutes, four hundred and twenty milliliters, a little under ten percent of your blood."

"Wow," Mindy said, setting her phone rather than looking at Lucia. She wasn't sure she wanted to know what Lucia's face looked like when she was saying all that. "You've thought this through."

"If there's one person I can't afford to hurt…and hey, I'm not that bad at math." Lucia smiled weakly.

It was meant to be reassuring, but it was as nervy as Mindy felt—and that was okay. They were both anxious about that, and Mindy felt like she'd been given permission to be afraid. Of course she was afraid. A vampire was about to drink her blood. But she was also confident. She believed in Lucia. And she believed in them. Whoever else Lucia might hurt, she wouldn't hurt *her*.

"Where do you want to do this?" Lucia asked. "On the bed or…standing up?"

Lying down seemed too intimate. Too much like…something else. Mindy took a step back, from it and Lucia. "Standing up, please."

Lucia nodded. "One sec." She blurred, and the door opened and closed like it was caught in a hurricane. In five seconds, Lucia was back. She spread the house's firewood tarp atop Mindy's bed. "In case you change your mind."

And she set the first aid kit from Mindy's car on her nightstand. "I'm gonna patch you up as soon as we're done."

"Okay. So, you're gonna bite me on the neck?"

"Yeah. Where else would I bite you?"

Mindy squeezed her legs together. She felt raw. Like gasoline under a lit match. "And I should just—stand—here?"

"Wherever's fine." Lucia was looking at her now, eyes clouding with black. It was disconcerting, seeing the nervousness once there now draining away. Turning into something more like need.

Mindy backed away again. She hit the wall. Lucia stopped. Mindy felt like laughing. A dance. That's what they were doing. She raised her hand and beckoned with her fingers. Lucia came closer. Closer. She knew her eyes were dark, right? Black like a shark's eyes. Mindy could see herself in them.

"Part of me wishes you would run away," Lucia confessed.

Mindy slid sideways. Into the corner. "Nowhere to run." Reaching out, she took hold of a dresser on one side of her, the windowsill on the other. Bracing herself. "You want this?"

Lucia nodded.

"I want this. So what's the big deal? It's just blood. The same as if I were at a blood drive."

"So why don't we get a syringe?"

Mindy's lips were dry, her palms sweaty, but she didn't dare let go to wipe them. "Because that's not what we want."

"I don't want to hurt you."

"I don't want you to think there's something wrong with—wanting what you want. From me. So c'mon. Do it. We've said everything there is to say."

Lucia's eyes were obsidian pools, but they were set in a face that was all warmth and concern. She looked away. "Have you set the alarm yet?"

Mindy set her phone on the dresser. "Just need to start it."

"Okay. Don't do it yet. I'm going to lick you a couple times first."

Mindy's eyebrows perked up.

"My saliva has a numbing agent, like a mosquito's. It's not cuz I like the way you taste. Not that there's anything wrong with the way you taste, I'm sure you taste fine—" Aware she was babbling, Lucia leaned in and quickly lapped at Mindy's neck, accidentally tugging a few hairs in the process.

Realizing they were starting, Mindy tilted her head to the side and held her hair out of the way. Lucia licked her again, longer and fuller.

Her tongue was cool and slick, almost metallic. Soothing in a way. It was like pressing an ice-cold can of Coke to your sweaty skin on a hot day, only a second after the contact, the chill turned to a bloom of heat—a little tingle across Mindy's nerves. Lucia felt it too, Mindy knew she did.

"Wow, your skin is really clean," Lucia said. "Do you use body wash?"

"No. Just soap. I have a loofah, though."

"Oh. I should try that." Lucia's eyes slid over the curve of Mindy's throat offered up to her. Now she licked it from the collar of her shirt almost to Mindy's ear. Mindy could've moaned. The heat set into her skin like a glowing tan. It didn't feel numb. It felt—good. "Tell me to stop and I'll stop."

"I'm not telling you to stop."

Uttering a little, helpless moan, Lucia dragged her tongue over the blush of heat that was now spreading down into Mindy's chest. Mindy thought she tasted good. That Lucia liked her taste.

Lucia barely pulled her tongue in before she came to Mindy's ear. She held herself there—would've been panting if she still breathed, but instead, Mindy felt the *intent* behind panting. The intensity vibrating out of Lucia. The hunger Lucia was slowly letting out.

"I think I can make it feel good for you," Lucia said. "I mean… If I get you ready first… if I take it slow… I don't think it has to hurt." She pressed a sharp kiss to Mindy's cheek. When her lips came away, they were peaked with fangs. "Start the clock."

Mindy pressed the button on the smartphone. The display lit up, the glow sizzling into them, cheap and tawdry. In the dark, the room was vast and expansive. It had room to hide them.

Soon, the screen darkened again. Light came from the cracked bathroom door, the shuttered windows, under the door to the hallway. It touched them with its fingertips, but didn't hold them.

Lucia lowered her mouth to Mindy's neck. Her lips parted wetly. Mindy took a deep breath and thought, *When I am exhaling, Lucia will have bitten me.*

She felt Lucia's fangs for the first time—her skin pinched between incisors. Not broken, though. Just pulled taut. It didn't hurt. It…buzzed.

But Lucia wouldn't—couldn't—bite down. She was shaking, trembling, and though Mindy thought her hands were dead-bolted to her supports, she found them on Lucia's waist. Lucia wasn't sweating. She was. Her mind misfiring, malfunctioning. She thought, *Lucia can't sweat, I have to sweat for her,* and for some reason she was petting Lucia's back, the sides of her body.

And the more she did it, the more her own racing heart slowed. Stilled. Until she thought the next beat would never come—then it did—and that the one after that wouldn't come. It did. And she wasn't nervous anymore. She was aware of her fear, her quite rational fear, but it was a star a galaxy away, the light reaching her ten thousand years after its source had burnt and died. And now all that was left was the adrenaline. She was exhilarated. She was calm. She was ready.

"It's okay. It's okay, El. I want this. I want—"

She thought she would've said 'you' if Lucia hadn't bit down. Mindy's hands tightened on Lucia's body, hard enough to hurt her if Lucia still felt pain. She hadn't had time to brace for it. It was a sudden rush, the downward plunge on a roller coaster she hadn't known had been climbing.

She could feel *everything.* The black silk of Lucia's hair brushing her cheek was a whisper. The pain was a song, an orchestra playing in both ears—it hurt. Like nothing Mindy had ever experienced. She'd never been stung by a bee, never stepped on a nail, never been shot, never stabbed. This was real pain. Real hurt. It left scars.

But it was clean too. A clean hurt, a cleansing flame. It burned away all the itches, all the soreness, the pangs of hunger and the crud in her eyes, the tiredness, the dirtiness, everything that afflicted her body was suddenly behind this vast new *thing* she was feeling—this country of sensation. She balled her fist, put it in her mouth, all she could do to stop herself from crying out, but then it was over. The pain had been wrung out of her body and all that was left—all that was left…

She was short of breath. Floating like her whole body had fallen asleep. The little sting, the little embers of Lucia's fangs were keeping her grounded, but she was still floating. Lucia was sucking on her wound now—her bite. *Her* bite. And Lucia was right up against her, the only thing Mindy could feel, the only other thing in her universe. Making these sated little noises, satisfied and ravenous at the same time. Like Mindy tasted so good, but each new bit tasted even better.

Lucia bit down *harder*—her fangs becoming a part of Mindy. What Mindy felt of her knees went weak. She wasn't tensing up because the pain wasn't hurting her, it was relieving her. She slipped, and Lucia moved in seamless instinct, bearing her down onto the bed. On top of her now. Drinking from her like a river.

Her hands were still on Mindy, cradling her head and lower back. Their bounce onto the bed allowed a little blood to escape Lucia's hunger. It spilled down her shoulder, a hot little shower. Mindy thought it was no wonder that Lucia enjoyed this, if it tasted as good as it felt…

Lucia's breathless wanting had become deep, ecstatic gurgling—a howl deep in her belly—an orgasmic moan. One hand was on Mindy's back—behind her heart—the other stroked Mindy's body lovingly. It traveled over all of her, not avoiding her breast any more than her flank or thigh, but there was nothing sexual in the touch. Or, all of Mindy's body felt so sexual that it didn't matter where Lucia touched her.

She still wasn't where Mindy needed her. Not between her legs, where her clit was so hard it was begging for release. Mindy managed to move—managed to get one leg scissored around Lucia's body. Clinging to her like a life preserver, even as her phone blared distantly. An echo of an echo.

Lucia's fangs left Mindy empty, alone, all her body's little complaints now audible again, if as distant as her phone. Her clothes were chafing her, warm with the heat of her old body—not the new, pleasurable one that Lucia had gifted her with. She wanted to be naked: the release of cool air. But Lucia was pulling away, not undressing her, and Mindy was too weak to move.

"That's all," Lucia breathed. "I stopped. I didn't think I could, but I stopped… Minz, you okay?"

Mindy just stared at her. Just as her hurts were coming back, so were her feelings too. All the ones that weren't warmth. She hadn't wanted Lucia to stop. She would've almost rather died than stopped. She couldn't even feel the bite—what she felt most of all was lead in her belly. It grew heavier and heavier.

Lucia was quick to bandage her—it hurt like a brand, making Mindy wince for the first time. She soon had Mindy bundled up, and only then did Mindy notice Lucia's fingers had become wet with blood. Lucia stared at them, then dropped them to her sides. She didn't wipe them off. Mindy knew she'd lick them clean later. When Mindy wasn't looking.

Lucia whooped a laugh. Seeing Mindy unharmed by the ordeal, unafraid, seemed like a dose of the strongest drug to her. "Thank you so much, Mindy, so much for doing this. I… You're the best, Minz. Just the best."

Her kiss was quick and chaste and tasted of blood, copper and crimson. And it was on Mindy's lips. Even that was more than Mindy could take.

Maybe it was that Lucia's body, once so cold, was warm with borrowed blood—the softness of her lips finally matching their rosy warmth. Maybe it was the bitter taste. Maybe it was the sight of Lucia licking her lips, cleansing them of blood and of Mindy—knowing that if Mindy kissed her again, the taste would just be *her*.

She did. She was. She was kissing her. She didn't know what had come over her, felt like a different person, a brave person. She rolled around to get on top of Lucia, who immediately snaked around to be on top of her—their roll landing them on the floor. Mindy didn't even care. The fall had brought her sex to Lucia's thigh.

It felt amazing: the touch, the contact, some alchemy Mindy didn't understand but that had everything to do with it being Lucia touching her, her touching Lucia. She felt heaven between her legs, on her sex, up and down her spine. She bore down on it. Tried to catch it between her thighs. As they kissed, every movement of Lucia's tongue was a whip-spur urging her on. She made a mortar and pestle of their bodies, mashing Lucia's heaven into her flesh. A few precious seconds transported her by leaps and bounds. She was close. She was close. And then, she was there.

Mindy buried herself in Lucia's body, wet and aching and so sensitive that she thought to move one inch would hurt unbearably. She was ashamed of herself. She was so damn proud.

Lucia was mercifully silent. She let Mindy stop kissing her, just ran her palms under Mindy's shirt and down the back of her pants, not cupping, not feeling, but like she was warming her hands on a fire.

"So, uh," Lucia faltered. "That was kinda hot."

Mindy's head was shaking, grinding like a broken machine. She couldn't think, she couldn't speak. She couldn't believe her pussy still felt so—she shook her head on Lucia's body. Why was she still pretending? Why were they still dancing around this? She wanted to tell Lucia how much she meant to her, how good it had been…the words came out of her like she'd held her breath for a full minute and was only now gulping in air: "I want my first time to be with you."

Lucia laughed, a crackle deep in her throat that Mindy felt shake her. "Yeah, bitch, I noticed. I don't even blame you. I'm pretty fine."

"Don't *joke*…"

"I'm not joking, I'm—I've thought about it. You being a lezzie and all. And it makes sense. You shouldn't just let some Justin Bieber-looking job pop it for you. It should be someone who loves you. Someone who'll make it special for you. So, you know, I'll *do*."

Was this what being high felt like? Mindy felt excited, giggly, ecstatic—happy. "You know, boys do it all the time, according to the fanfic I read. It's not a big deal. So why should they get to have all the fun? It's just, like, our fingers and our mouths, and you don't even have use of those, your leg was just—"

"Yeah, that soggy feeling in my jeans is getting that across," Lucia giggled.

"I just kinda thought you would make the first move. Or that I'd have time to think of some clever way to bring it up. Now that you're a vampire. You could eat some garlic bread tomorrow and be outta here."

"Minz, c'mon, what do you think, that I'm some kind of—okay, yeah, I might. I'm putting you on don't-let-me-have-garlic-bread duty."

Mindy looked up, saw Lucia smiling. It was like looking into the sun. She ducked her head back down, lodged her own grin in Lucia's chest. "Just…do whatever it was you did when it was your first time. I'm sure that'll be great."

"Christ, with the low standards, Needy. I gave it up to Phil Digart because he double-dog-dared me too."

"I *knew* you two had a thing!"

"Anyway, get on the bed. You keep rubbing against me the way you are and I'm gonna get rug burn. And we're not doing anything with you all tensed up like you don't know if *The 100* is getting renewed. I am giving *you* a massage."

And something let the fear in. Mindy could see this going and going and going. She would give up everything to Lucia. Absolutely everything. She'd die for her—sucked dry, dry as the desert. Nothing left but sand and bone. Did Lucia know that? Did she know how special this was? Or—did she care?

Mindy was up, walking on unsteady legs, and the light of the bathroom beckoned to her. "I have to wash up," she said. "I'm all sweaty—I should wash up."

Mindy took off her clothes in the shower, with the water already on. The hot water made it worse. The thing pounding in Mindy's body got louder. It was nearly free. Mindy put her hand on the dial. She was almost turning the water to cold. She was seeing herself doing it, thinking to herself she needed to do it, lying about how good it would feel to wash off the sick heat Lucia had inflicted her with. To bury it in winter.

Her hand slipped off the wet dial and didn't return. It went back to the fire. To Mindy's burning body. It traveled over her skin, but there was only one place it could go. Where Mindy was hottest.

For precious, addictive seconds, Mindy could *feel* what Lucia had done to her.

She sobbed out her orgasm. Her body shook and convulsed with it, came apart at the seams. And she thought—so clearly—that it wasn't *her* that was shaking and pleasuring her body. It was Lucia.

Planted against the tiles, feeling the warm water rain down, knowing there was a heat inside her that had dwindled but would not, could not, go out— Mindy knew. She didn't realize, she had known before; now she just knew she knew.

She was in love with Lucia. Hopelessly in love with her. Despairingly in love with her. Her love wasn't a flower or a swan—it was a tumor and a sickness. It had grown inside her. It had taken her over. She was infested with it. The parts of her that could love someone else, that were not Lucia's to command—they had died off. Flowers in a weed-infested garden. All that was left was this dark, venomous thing that owed total allegiance to Lucia. It was terrible. It was beautiful. She didn't think she could be happy with anyone or anything *but* Lucia.

And she also knew that she could never, ever let Lucia know.

She washed with the bar of Dove soap, the loofah, the soap again—shampoo, conditioner—loofah. Mindy didn't know how good Lucia's sense of smell was, now, but she didn't want her to *know*. She dried herself with the towel and noticed that Lucia had slipped a set of fresh clothes through the door onto the counter. And Mindy knew, *knew*, Lucia had just stuck her arm through, not looked, not lingered. It was a funny feeling—trusting someone. You didn't really think about it until you did.

Her old clothes laid on the floor where she'd pulled them off—Mindy still remembered the rush of the air on her bare skin, wanting to run back to Lucia and… There wasn't much blood on them. She could've messed up eating something with ketchup. Just a dab on her collar. Lucia hadn't let much spill. It was too precious for that.

Mindy dressed and was surprised by how put-together her outfit looked in the mirror. A jade-green knit blouse, a dark brown skirt, a set of black leggings… They looked cute together. Leave it to Lucia to put together a nice ensemble for you after she drank your blood. Mindy walked back into her bedroom and Lucia was on the bed. She was gorgeous. God, how had she ever been human when she'd always looked like *that*?

Lucia patted the bed next to her. It was like a magnet had been turned on and Mindy was made of metal. She took a step forward that dragged on the carpet. "You wanted to take things slow? With a massage?"

"That not how they do it in your lesbian porn?" Lucia asked, head tilted.

"Slow is fine. Slow is perfect. Just, would it be okay if—"

"Mindy, you came on my leg. You can tell me whatever."

Mindy nodded for her. "If nothing else happened tonight, that'd be fine."

Lucia's eyes narrowed. She was suddenly hard to read. But she nodded. "That's what you want?"

"I, ah—" She winced, knowing Lucia must be hating her wavering. Tried to mollify her by taking step after step toward the bed. "I would want it to be special—it's stupid, I know, it's never special—but, like, it'd be special because it's *us*—and tonight is already special, you drinking my blood and all—so I don't want to cram all the special into one night and have it over with, right? I wanna save some. Like with Halloween candy. You don't eat it all in one go, you'd make yourself sick. You eat some one night, then some more the next, then some more the next."

Lucia nodded imperially, like she was a queen listening to a courtier, and then she extended her hand.

Mindy took it, feeling like they were about to dance, and Lucia pulled her gently onto the bed. Wrapped her up in her arms—it felt like being bathed in silk.

"What candy do you want to have tonight?" Lucia asked, another layer of silk wrapping around Mindy.

Mindy said the first thing that came into her head. "Scratch my back?"

Lucia's head went back, a little incredulous: "Specific."

"And my head. You've never had your head scratched? It feels supergood."

"Just…" Lucia reached into Mindy's hair and raked her nails along Mindy's scalp. "Like that?"

Mindy crooned with pleasure. "Yeah. That's perfect."

It was. Just enough Lucia to stop her body from demanding more, to let her relax. She was so tense, so worn out, that the tension was the only thing holding her up. Without it, she'd swoon like a Jane Austen lady. So, as it leaked from her body, she felt less and less grounded. She just slipped away, feeling Lucia's claws travel her skin, marking her with a thousand invisible scratches. She dreamed that her blood was singing to her, humming in her veins, but Lucia never let it out.

# CHAPTER 19

Mindy wondered why she kept dreaming that she *was* Lucia. It seemed like something out of a bad Freudian textbook, a shitty explanation of why a woman was the killer in some bad eighties slasher movie. *You keep picturing yourself as Lucia, because by dating another woman, you wanted to become another woman. Self-loathing!* Christ, what horse piss. Yet her subconscious just kept on giving, showing her Lucia's view of her own body sleeping.

As Lucia, she bent over her own body, examining the bandage on Mindy's neck like it was a slide under a microscope. Her fingers brushed over it, feather-light against the texture of the tan rubber and Mindy's own soft skin. Like some phantom limb syndrome, Mindy could feel the lightness of Lucia's touch back in her own body—mail from the home front. Then Lucia's fingernail ticked over the adhesive borders, maybe seeing if they were sticking properly, maybe playing at peeling them away. The downside of being Lucia was that Mindy could see everything but Lucia's face. Mindy wanted to know what emotion she wore as she lowered herself to Mindy's wound like a fawning worshipper. Regret? Lust? Or nothing at all?

Apparently satisfied, Lucia pulled away, leaving the bandage alone. She drew Mindy's blanket up to her chin, gingerly tucking it about Mindy's shoulders and just under her sides to make a sort of Mindy burrito. Then she took Mindy's pulse—Mindy hadn't even known that she knew what a pulse was. While she did it, her thumb rubbed softly against Mindy's chin. She took her hand away, and Mindy felt weirdly wrong without the phantom chill of her touch. Then Lucia bent again, the static strangeness of her unbreathing lips moving on Mindy's forehead in the gentlest touch of all—*What are you doing?* Mindy asked.

"Nothing!" Lucia replied, jerking upright. "Are you…talking in your sleep?"

*Don't change the subject. You were going to kiss my forehead!* Mindy cried, overjoyed, and then even more overjoyed at Lucia's mortification. She noticed, at the same time Lucia did, that she *was* asleep and her lips weren't moving. *You're like the first gay Disney princess.*

"So, like Elsa?" Lucia went to Mindy's nightstand, taking her phone and puzzling out how to take a picture with it, then holding it out as if to take a selfie. Mindy was able to see herself—correction, *El*—in the phone's screen. "I think we have a psychic link! This is awesome! If I ever turn into a serial killer, you can help some loose-cannon cop who plays by his own rules to hunt me down!"

*Uh-huh. Still wanna make out with my hairline?* Mindy asked—weird without a voice. She wondered if it was weird for Lucia, hearing without her ears.

"There was a bug! I was trying to get it."

*With your face?*

"Hey, you're the one dreaming about me. You make *me* look butch. And I'm so girly, I can name every single reason it doesn't make sense for Dan Humphrey to be *Gossip Girl*."

Lucia looked back at the sleeping Mindy while Mindy tried to look at the phone screen in her field of vision. Weird sensation, having her "eyes" not focus on her even when she looked. A bit like not wearing her glasses.

*Stop looking at my body. I look so dumb while I'm asleep.*

"No you don't!"

*I'm drooling!*

"You drool so sweetly and innocently." In a flash, Lucia was leaning over the sleeping Mindy, wiping the corners of her mouth with her sleeve. "Yeah, a lot of people do that around my tight ass."

*Oh God*, Mindy could see herself blushing in her sleep. "Cut it out," she growled sleepily.

Lucia sighed. "Why won't you let me love you? Hey! How about I take you hunting?"

"Absolutely not."

"Why not? Don't you just love *being inside me*?" Lucia asked dolefully, running her hands over her body.

"I'm not gonna love drinking someone's blood, Hannibal. No matter how long your legs are."

"Oh yeah, I forgot." Lucia poked a finger into her own shoulder. "You're usually around here, aren't you?"

"Only cuz I don't wear heels."

Mindy felt herself-as-Lucia reaching down and pulling her shirt over her full, sated belly. "How about we take a shower together?"

"Can't we just cuddle?"

"Tease," Lucia said, even as she laid out on the bed, resting her head on Mindy's shoulder.

She took Mindy's hand and put it on the skin of her tummy. It felt warm. A chilled warmth, like—hot water poured into a cold bowl. Odd, feeling herself against Lucia's feeling her. It was like the 3D bit in a Magic Eye picture, but it wouldn't come into focus. She was coming awake a little, in that haze where she wasn't really tired but didn't have to get up. Just luxuriating in the comfort of her bed, the comfort of Lucia.

"Feel that?" Lucia grinned. "That's you. Your essence. You're inside me."

"I wouldn't put it that way."

"Like, I've never had a guy come inside me. I've always used a condom. I haven't even swallowed!"

"Your Wikipedia page suddenly has too much detail."

"Oh, what, scared of a little gay? Since when? I'll tell you what, you'd know this if you had friends, but all the best friendships have a little gay in them. Watch me hug you with my legs in friendship."

Lucia scampered on top of Mindy, snaking her legs around her waist. Lucia's thighs were cool and hard around Mindy's middle, almost like stone, but there was an aliveness to them that was hard to explain. Sort of like a tree, or fur instead of carpet. You could just tell it was real.

"There now," Lucia said, now wrapping Mindy up in her arms. Mindy could feel a deep-seated warmth in Lucia's chest, a tinge of it in her extremities. The blood. It was warming her. "Isn't that good friendship?"

"For a koala, maybe."

"It's just a hug," Lucia said. Her face was over Mindy's, her hair falling down around Mindy's face on all sides. They were in their own little world.

"It's spooning."

"No, this is spooning." Lucia moved around so that Mindy was on her side, and Lucia behind her, arms and legs shifting, tightening around Mindy.

It should've been less intimate, Mindy staring straight ahead now, Lucia at her back. It felt warmer, though. More dangerous. She was trusting Lucia not to bite her—maybe Lucia was trusting her not to be bitten?

"That's good spooning," Mindy admitted. She wasn't sure what else to say.

"Yeah…" Suddenly, Lucia started pumping her hips, as if dry-humping Mindy. "Yeah, take it bitch! You love my hard dick!"

The sweet romantic moment was gone before Mindy had fully realized they were having a moment. "You don't have a penis, El."

"You love my imaginary penis!"

Mindy yawned. "I'm still asleep a little. Quit it before you wake me up."

Lucia stopped. "You got me. I'm a two-pump chump. You know, this is useful, we should think of a way to use this. Maybe if we're taking a test, you could pop into my brain for a minute…"

"Lucia! That would be dishonest!"

"Or maybe if some guy is bothering me, you could jump into my body and drive him off with your awkwardness."

"Hurtful. Although…"

"Is this the shower idea again? Don't steal my shower idea. You could really benefit from knowing my routine, but it wasn't your idea."

Mindy spoke through a yawn—so weird. "Okay, so we know that rest home attack wasn't you, it was the vampire stirring up shit. You could check it out with me riding shotgun in your head—we'd be like a fusion of your vampire badassness and my all 'A's report card."

"Alright, but then I'm taking a shower."

It was a simple plan. Lucia would speed to the rest home while Mindy synced up their minds. Then they would check it out without Mindy's fleshy vulnerabilities in harm's way. Lucia liked that part. She was very keen on Mindy not entering a vampire's 'hunting ground' and made her promise that if something went wrong and Mindy had to play cavalry, she would get Seb to back her up.

Mindy waited in her room, turning on the ceiling light as well as her lamp. It didn't help. The light pushing out of her dark window into the night, with its flicking street lamp, just underscored how alone she was. Her parents were gone on another retreat, the hour late enough for the roads to be clear except for the occasional ghostly car that only emphasized her isolation. After the shocking intimacy of her connection to Lucia, being apart gave steroids to her nervousness. The seconds ticked by like hours, as she wondered when Lucia would call, worrying for her. "Hunting ground," Lucia had said. *Christ!*

Her phone vibrated. Mindy snatched it up, *I'm here. Come inside me.*

They really had to get a move-on for coming up with some hip lingo for this stuff, like they had in sci-fi movies. Maybe when Mindy was using the psychic link, she was "riding" Lucia? No…

Mindy tried to push herself back into Lucia, but the connection was difficult and she was unskilled. She thought she got flashes of what Lucia was seeing, but it could've just been the colors inside her eyelids putting on a clever disguise. Her phone buzzed again: *What's taking so long?*

Mindy snatched it up: *It's not as easy as it looks!*

She emptied her mind and did a breathing exercise she'd seen on YouTube, and Lucia just came to her. Filled her.

The rest home was a squat, homely sort of building. One story, spread out like an unwashed rash, surrounded by a fence. One side hunched against the ever-diminishing woods of Carfax, the other open to the highway. Lucia was in the trees, surveying the barred windows, the tiles atop the roof. Then she looked down at her cleavage. "Nice."

"El, I'm here."

Lucia's eyes jerked up. "Oh, Mindy, you surprised me."

"Sure I did. Ready to go?"

"Oh yeah. Creepy old people, here we come."

Lucia hopped the fence like she was doing nothing more than stepping on and off a curb, crossing the lawn in casual haste, going to one of the windows she'd obviously selected earlier. The window pane was up, but iron bars still divided the view inside. Lucia grasped two bars and fed her head through them, then her shoulders, then bonelessly shimmied the rest of herself inside.

"Okay, didn't know you could do that," Mindy said.

"You should see some of my jeans."

The room was waiting to be a coffin. It was maybe seven by seven, with a toilet like a Porta Potty stapled on. Making it more cramped was the amount of detritus in the room. It wasn't unreasonable, the inhabitant wasn't a hoarder, but in a space this small, there was simply no room on the walls for so many clippings and photographs, no room on the floor for the precariously stacked books that longed for a shelf.

Mindy's poetic mind supplied a backstory: the old man earnestly moving these possessions from his own house to a single bedroom with one of his children, then into this smaller still room, and next he would die. His prized possessions would be reduced to his burial clothes, and his space would shrink to the scale model of this room's prototype. She reminded herself to call her Grandma next chance she got.

Quickly and silently, Lucia bypassed the heavy sleeper in the room's cot and went to the door, tried the knob. Locked from the outside.

"Got a hairpin?" Mindy asked.

"Of course. What do you think I am, an animal?"

"Here's what you do," Mindy said and walked Lucia through picking the lock. It was easy; the locks were old and Mindy had just read the Wikihow on her laptop. The door swung open, and Lucia slipped out into the hallway, closing the door gently behind her.

The hallway was made up of black and white tiles, and though they'd been mopped recently, that couldn't clear the cracks that grew like mold along them. The florescent lights were all either cut off or the color of jaundice. And the sounds—the rest home was like a remix of an insane asylum. There were shouts, moans, groans, but all pitched low, hidden under the PA system's whispered playing of Beethoven. *Moonlight Sonata* which merged uneasily with the sound of a floor buffer going in the distance. Lucia moved with purpose, following the wall signs to their victim's room: wing B, room 24. She kept to a subtly rapid speed that reminded Mindy of riding a bike, hugging the walls and placing her feet carefully to make not a sound.

"Here we are," Lucia said as they came to a double door, closed and locked. The sign above the doors was a simple *B*. She bent to the lock and went through the routine Mindy had taught her, easily halving the time of her previous attempt. Mindy whistled in admiration as the door swung open—

then wondered how a whistle could translate over a mental link. Certainly, their psychic power seemed to transfer whatever Lucia heard, as well as whatever words Lucia thought "loudly" enough.

"I said we're here," Lucia reiterated, stepping through the doors. "You still here?"

"Yeah. Just still getting used to, ah—being psychic."

Lucia went from door to door in B wing, setting her palms against the wood and then seeming to ease her senses through that contact. Mindy suddenly felt the volume of whatever was in the room turn up, hearing the rubber-padded feet of a walker tip-toing along the floor. Lucia went to the next door, now hearing phlegmatic sounds of sleep.

"I didn't know your hearing was so acute," Mindy said.

"Everything about me is cute."

Lucia gave up the perusal, proceeding directly instead to Room 24. Police tape barred the doorway, the sickly yellow like a tumor of the maleficence cast by the coldly humming ceiling lights. Lucia nestled her hand between the tape on the closed door, listening through it. Nothing. She tried the knob. The door seemed to pop off its hinges, swinging inward like there was a pitched imbalance in the air pressure. Looking inside, through the police tape, Mindy could see no real difference between this cubicle—she hesitated to call it a room—and the one they'd come in through. The bed was neatly made, the dresser drawers shut, the door to the bathroom closed.

Lucia picked at the police tape like a guitar string. "There's *nothing* here."

"There must be something you can smell or hear or—"

"A message written in invisible vampire ink? The cops couldn't find anything; why should I be able to?"

"Keep looking. There has to be something."

Rolling her eyes—Mindy could see, suddenly, the fringe of Lucia's hair—Lucia went to the next door and the next, palming them, hearing only labored breath after labored breath, until she laid her hand on a door and it swung open.

Lucia blurred backward, giving Mindy motion sickness as she retreated into the darkness at the end of the hall. An orderly poked his head out through the open door, checking right and left. Satisfied, he pulled the door back to nearly closing. All of Lucia's senses focused on him as he turned around and stepped deeper into the room.

Another burst of speed that twisted Mindy's insides up like a roller coaster, then Lucia was lurking outside the door, fingers gently settled against the wood, peeking through the keyhole. Another room like an archaeological excavation of a life, a few curios nestled on particleboard furniture. The orderly was seated on the bed, caressing the offered arm of the old man holding onto the bed's lift button with a kind of hopefulness, like it was a lottery ticket about to be called.

"Must've been the wind," the orderly said, giving the old man's arm a second quick going-over. There was a tourniquet near the elbow, making the veins stand out on his skin like paper would warp after it had gotten wet and then dried. "Sorry to keep you waiting. This won't take a minute."

Lucia's eyes fixated on a vein worming through his arm, watching without the slightest distraction as the orderly's syringe neared it, neared it, then punctured. Dark blood oozed inside the syringe and all Mindy could hear through Lucia's ears was the thrumming of the blood as it still vibrated with the heart's force.

"Damn, woman!" Mindy called. "I just gave sweet blood to you five minutes ago."

Lucia snapped out of it, backing away, the sounds of the rest home in remission washing back over them. "Sorry. Kind of a habit."

"What are they doing drawing blood this late?"

"Probably want to run some test or another. Make sure he's dying on schedule. God, I hope I die before I get old." Mindy felt Lucia's brow furrowing. "Oh, wait, I did."

The orderly finished, applying a bandage to the old man with a few quiet words, putting the vial in a stout small cart nearby. After moving the old man's bed back down to a reclining position, the orderly pushed the cart to the door. Again, Mindy felt more than saw Lucia's withdrawal. The orderly emerged from the room, pushing the cart ahead of him, then turned and carefully closed the door. It clicked, locking automatically.

"Follow him," Mindy said, and had the experience of Lucia condescendingly tilting her head to the side.

Lucia crept after him with the instincts of a born hunter. She waited behind each corner, watching every little movement, listening to the echoing footsteps

He visited another two rooms, repeating the same procedure. Exchanging a few doctorly words with the resident, then drawing blood. It was so innocuous, Mindy wondered if there wasn't some reasonable explanation for it. Maybe some of the residents were night owls, and preferred being examined at night when they were awake, anyway?

The next stop proved the exception. This door had a newer lock, with a keypad mounted on the wall. The orderly punched in a number—Mindy writing it down in case Lucia couldn't recall it—and a little buzzer rang and a red light on the keypad went green. He stepped through the door, pushing his cart. Door closed behind him. A few moments passed. Then he came out again.

No cart.

He walked off, hands in his pockets, whistling even, but Lucia's attention was bolted to the door.

"Um," Mindy said.

"Yeah."

Lucia waited for the orderly to move away, then slid to the door. Punched in the code her eagle eyes had caught. A buzz, and the door unlocked with a weighty clang. Lucia pushed her way in.

The room was empty. It looked like it had begun life as a janitor's closet— exposed concrete, water heater, little ankle-high tank for a mop bucket to be filled in—but now, Mindy couldn't tell what it was. There were no cleaning supplies. Not much of anything, except a row of carts like the one the orderly had pushed along the far wall. On the near wall were plastic bins, filled with a small selection of medical equipment. Needles. Vials. Rubber tourniquets. And a large chrome refrigerator, the kind restaurants used, the sleek door as featureless and imposing as a monolith.

"Well," Lucia said, the high-ceilinged room making her voice echo slightly. "Guess that's where they keep the blood."

"You need that big a fridge to keep blood samples?"

"Only one way to find out."

Lucia took a step. Another. Another. Each one cemented her further inside the thick concrete walls, blotting out the music from outside, the hum of the fluorescents—everything but the burning noise of the refrigerator's activity. She reached for the thick handle—the heft of it filled her hand. Then she gave a tug, putting a jiggle of motion through the slab of a door. Otherwise, it did not move.

"It's stuck."

"El, are you sure—"

Then Mindy heard someone whistling, through her own ears. It was an odd difference, like hearing something on a pair of headphones versus hearing it in surround sound. She felt herself *yanked* back into her own body, sitting up in her bedroom. She stood, heart beating hard as if to remind her she was in a living body now. She could still hear the whistling and, no, it sounded like the wind, but louder, more intense, almost *willful*.

Outside her bedroom door.

Her parents wouldn't dare leave her home alone without a baseball bat beside her bed. She picked it up, cocked it over her shoulder, almost pointed like Babe Ruth as she went to the door. Hand around the doorknob. Smaller than Lucia's, fingers, slenderer, more delicate. Turned the knob, threw the door open.

The window was open in the hallway, curtains gently rustling.

Dragging the baseball bat dejectedly across the carpet, Mindy went to close it, at the same time trying to retrace her steps to Lucia's mind. A bit like walking and chewing gum at the same time. She heard snippets of Lucia's mental voice as she wrestled the sash back down: *Mindy? Mindy?*

"I'm here, Lucia." Mindy said it out loud as well as telepathically, figuring that might strengthen the signal. The window sash plunged downward, cutting off the sound of wind. "It's fine. What was in the refrigerator?"

Like she had seen a bright light and was now battling the afterimages of that, Mindy saw the inside of the refrigerator—a vast and mostly empty space clogged with caked ice more than anything else. "Nothing. Just a bunch of blood samples and some guy's lunch."

Mindy turned back to her bedroom. She spent so much time on the second floor of her house, she could get around with her eyes closed. "Okay, so it's weird, but it's not vampire-weird. Probably just one of those stupid little things every business does—"

She heard whistling again.

Mindy turned around.

The window was opened.

Fear jerked Mindy wholly into her body like a dog on a tight leash. She wasn't alone, she just knew suddenly. *Not alone.*

"Lucia," she whispered, trying desperately to summon up the connection once more. "Lucia!"

Something crashed behind her. Mindy whirled around. Another window had been opened, its sash banging against the lintel. The wind rushed in, curtains flaring up, reaching for her. Mindy backpedaled so fast her feet skidded on the soft carpet, almost slipping up from under her, pitching her against the deck railing of the stairwell that led from the first floor to the second. She looked down into the first story of the house to see that every window was open, curtains snapping like angry whips.

The knob of the front door began to turn.

*Don't scream,* Mindy told herself. Screaming means panicking, and you can't afford to panic. She pulled herself to her feet, running for the stairs at the end of the railing. Something brushed the skin of her upper arm, and her mouth opened to scream, mind blanking with fear until she forced, forced herself to realize it was just a curtain.

*This time,* her terror said. *Thistimethistimethistime.*

She ran down the stairs, taking steps two at a time. The front door's hinges creaked. Mindy hit the landing stumbling, the baseball bat flying from her hand. It landed close to the door, too damn close. The door was yawning open now, like a rip between the world of safety and sanity inside her house and whatever was out there that wanted *in.*

Her breath wailing out of her like it desperately wanted to be a scream, she ran to the kitchen, her knee banging on the island, then her feet slapping on the cool tile, her hands scrambling upon the counter, onto the knife block, ripping a butcher knife from it.

She heard the stolid thud of the front door against its stop, the little rattle of the doorknob settling back into place. She held the knife up high, trying to remember how you were supposed to hold it. There was some special knife-fight way you were supposed to hold it and she knew it wasn't high up in the air like she was Norman Bates about to murder someone in the shower, but she couldn't think of any way else to do it, of anything else to do.

She didn't hear footsteps. Was it inside? Too quiet for her to hear? Or was it still outside?

Had to be outside. She hadn't invited it in. Lucia was a vampire and she needed to be invited in.

Unless it was someone she knew. Someone she had invited in already. Someone she'd seen a thousand times, never knowing, never suspecting—

"I know the rules!" she shouted, choosing to believe that it was a stranger, someone with no invitation inside, because that was the only choice where she survived. "You can't come in unless you're invited! And that's not happening, asshole!"

She heard the door banging against the doorstop, caught by the breeze. First the creak of the hinges, then the pop of the doorstop. Again and again.

But it couldn't come in. *It couldn't.*

Mindy screamed, rage and fright and frustration tearing her throat raw, *screaming* at the top of her lungs to fill the house with sound because it was better than the unknown that had crept in from the night, replacing all the comfort of the place with fear.

The door creaked its way into the doorstop.

Mindy couldn't take it anymore. She had to see, knowing the thing was waiting for just that, daring her to do it. She threw herself out of the kitchen, facing the front door, the gaping open wound of the doorway.

There was nothing there.

"FUCK YOU!" Mindy cried, clutching the butcher knife so tightly in her hand that her knuckles hurt.

Then she heard the backdoor crash open behind her, the footsteps on the tile floor. She whirled, arm in motion, knife swinging, and sunk the blade deep into Lucia's chest.

For a moment, they stood there, stunned by the impossibility of it. Mindy looked down at the expanse of shirt over Lucia's pectoral muscle, bloodlessly interrupted by a short length of steel and then the long brown handle that itself led, inexorably, to her hand. As if this were about to infect her, contaminate her, Mindy ripped her hand away. The handle quivered upon Lucia's chest, rattling with her as Lucia took a long, sodden breath.

"It's cool," Lucia said, reaching up tentatively to try for a grip on the knife. Successfully, if gingerly, wrapping her hand around its handle. "It's cool," she repeated, then gave the knife a pull. It jostled a half-inch. Then, as the muscles in Lucia's arm carefully strained, the blade began to slide free. "Ouch. Owwie. Ow. Oouch. *OWWWWW*—and we're good!" she proclaimed, the knife now held aloft.

Mindy wondered how feminist it would be to faint, under the circumstances. She stumbled to the living room, the couch, mumbled "sorry," and proceeded to do just that.

She came to a few minutes later. Lucia had closed and locked all the doors and windows in the house, which brought an instant sigh of relief to Mindy's lips. Then Lucia showed her the skin under the tear in her shirt. "Don't worry, okay? Just like new."

"That's good to hear," Mindy mumbled, her head still spinning, her lungs only beginning to get as much air as they needed. "For a second there, I thought you were dead."

"Well…yeah. Only now my shirt is too."

"Sorry," Mindy said, feeling an impalement was grounds for more than one apology.

"It's okay. Makes it look vintage. You don't think this is like pre-ripped jeans, do you?" Lucia asked, fingering the cut. "I mean, a stabbing's normal wear and tear. I'm not a poser."

"Definitely not." The wooziness was rapidly passing. Mindy sat up. "It was him. The vampire."

Lucia nodded. "I know."

Mindy supposed she wouldn't have wanted Lucia to see her scared out of her wits either. "I don't think he could come in. Just open the windows, the doors—like he was trying to flush me out. Scare me into making a run for it so he could—"

"Hey, your dad keeps beer in the fridge?" Lucia came out of the kitchen, holding two Shiner Bock bottlenecks between her knuckles. "*Nice.*"

"I don't drink," Mindy said, taking the bottle Lucia offered her anyway.

"It's medicinal," Lucia replied, picking the bottlecap off with one fingernail. "Now, drink. Doctor's orders."

Mindy took a gulp for peer pressure. It tasted bitter as hell—like biting into a lemon without the Vitamin C.

"Finish the bottle," Lucia told her without enough assurance that Mindy didn't think to question her. Didn't want to. "Then you're going to bed. You'll feel a lot less like shit after a good night's sleep."

"Stay with me?" Mindy asked, unable to meet Lucia's eyes while she felt like a little girl, asking to sleep in her mother's bed after a scary dream.

"Yeah," Lucia said, flicking open her bottle. "Of course."

They lay beside each other like a TV Land married couple, Lucia even holding Mindy's beer for her, tipping it to Mindy's mouth with some preternatural awareness of when she wanted a sip. Which, it being beer, was rarely.

*I wonder if Lucia can read my mind,* Mindy thought.

*I can totally read your mind,* popped into her head.

It was a good thing Mindy hadn't taken another sip yet. "You can read my mind?"

"Only just now," Lucia replied. *I think you have to be trying for it to work. Like holding down the button on a walkie-talkie.*

*Holding down the button,* Mindy thought. *That's actually a good metaphor.*

"Don't think so surprised."

"So is there like an echo when I think into your head…?"

*Bitch,* Lucia thought. Her eyes glowed with a playful dare. "Dude, let's get you drunk. I wanna know what it's like in the mind of a lightweight."

*I am not a lightweight.*

One beer later, Mindy was asleep.

But not for long. Dreams of coming around that corner and there *was* something coming through the front door or inside the retirement home's refrigerator. A shadow the color of blood. A darkness as deep as the depths of Lake Travis.

She woke up and there was Lucia, sitting cross-legged on her windowsill. She offered Mindy a reassuring smile. Mindy began, for no particular reason, to cry.

There wasn't much to it. Lucia walked to the bed and sat beside her pillow and pulled Mindy's head onto her lap, petting her hair with long, languid strokes of her hand. She didn't say anything. Not that it would be alright or that it was okay or even something mindlessly calming like "shush." She let Mindy cry into her jeans until something tense and coiled and so thick that it had filled up Mindy's body was finally unwound, leaking out of her, leaving her empty. But with a kind of numbness, a strained and ragged calm. Still Lucia petted her hair.

She went back to sleep and dreamed of nothing at all.

When she woke next it was morning, an ungodly early aspect of morning that she tried hard to avoid whenever possible. The light was a pinched red glow, and Mindy saw that Lucia's body makeup had run in places, leaving glimmers like veins of mineral within a rock. Lucia sat at the foot of her bed, leaning against the bedpost, legs parallel to Mindy's.

Mindy's nose was stuffy and her throat felt dry. She got up, went to the bathroom to blow her nose and splash her face with water and to pee, and when she came out Lucia had a glass of Sprite for her. Two ice cubes floating at the top.

"Thank you," Mindy said, meaning it so hard she didn't think it was possible for Lucia to catch all of it.

"You would've done the same for me," Lucia said. "If I'd let you."

Mindy hugged her impulsively, only wondering in the middle if Lucia would mind being touched, would feel awkward having her body against Mindy's. And by then, it was all alright. Mindy pulled away and drank her Sprite.

"I wanna go back to bed," Mindy said. "I'm still tired."

Lucia nodded. "That's normal. As normal as any of this is."

"I want you to—" Mindy stopped, chastised herself for beginning to ask, chastised herself for stopping, chastised herself for not going through with it. "I want you to hold me. When I woke up, the scariest moment was thinking you were gone and—I just don't want to think you're gone. Not for a second."

"Alright," Lucia said.

Mindy woke up cold. Cold like the AC was on the fritz, cold like she was spending Christmas up north with her grandparents on the Great Lakes, where people actually *froze* to death. She opened her eyes and was surprised to find her breath not fogging the air in front of her. Her mind worked slowly, jumping from being cold to Lucia having left, then she looked and saw Lucia was still there. *She was* what was cold. It was like Mindy had been cuddled up to an ice cube.

Mindy untangled herself from Lucia, fleeing for the warmth of the comforter and trying not to wake her, but Lucia's eyes snapped open. They focused on Mindy like she'd only been blinking. "What's wrong?"

"Nothing," Mindy said, but her teeth were chattering. "It's cold. It's you. The warmth from the blood—" Had worn off. Lucia pulled away from Mindy, seeing the goosebumps where they'd touched.

"Five seconds." Lucia said it, then she sped off so fast the bedsheets held her shape for a moment. A ghost.

She came back in forty-five, moving so slow Mindy could actually see her legs moving instead of being one steady blur. She knelt down beside the bed, pressing a cup of hot chocolate into Mindy's hands. The warmth of the mug instantly helped. Lucia was everywhere, pulling the covers up and wrapping them around Mindy, rubbing her hands together and stroking heat into Mindy's body—Mindy stopped her before she could burn anything for warmth.

"It's fine, El. I'm okay."

"Are you sure?"

"Yeah. It's blood. It has to cool off sometime." Lucia had that new look in her eyes, that sadness she'd had ever since being attacked. Mindy felt ridiculously selfish, demanding to be pampered when Lucia was still so... alone "You can have some more if you want?"

"No. I should go."

"Please don't?" Mindy sipped her hot chocolate, finding little marshmallows in it. "We can do something together. Anything together. Just keep my mind occupied—whatever you want to do."

Lucia grinned, and Mindy suddenly got all sorts of ideas about all the sorts of ideas Lucia might be having. It wasn't any of them.

"Call Seb," Lucia suggested. "I got him a present, and I want to see if he liked it."

They started up Skype as Lucia wandered Mindy's room, shamelessly going through her stuff. She opened a junk drawer and found a pocket Bible—a little leather-bound copy of the New Testament with a cross embossed on the front. Mindy had kept it because it reminded her of the Grail Diary in *Indiana Jones And The Last Crusade*. It tended to migrate out into the open whenever Mindy's grandparents were visiting.

Lucia eyed it with a challenged look, then held her hand above it as the Skype feed resolved from a series of Tetris blocks into a collection of smaller, finer blocks. When Lucia tried to bring her hand down, it was like she had a magnet in her palm and the Bible was of the same polarity. The stream finally fixed itself, becoming Seb sitting at his desk, left hand propping up his chin. "Hello ladies! You want to see package?"

"Don't," Mindy said firmly to Lucia, who pouted and went back to pressing down on her right hand with her left. The Bible stubbornly resisted her, exerting a kind of force field that pushed her hand back. She tried wiggling her fingers.

"Go ahead," Mindy said. Seb reached down to his feet, coming up with a paperback still in gift wrapping. No postage on it. Mindy guessed Lucia had delivered it the old-fashioned way. Through the torn wrapping, two things could be discerned. One was a sticker for Half-Price Books. The other was the title. *Eating Delicious, Feeling Delicious: Bubba Sawyer's BBQ Guide To A Whole New You.*

"I worry about this," Seb said, agreeably enough.

"Yeah," Lucia put in. "Have you tried legumes? Legumes have a lot of protein. You should eat lots."

"I am thinking you are also saying I should stay away from garlic?"

"Hey, it's a peace offering. Not everything I do has an ulterior motive. And that apnea shit is nothing to fuck with."

"No, I am not to be fucking with it. But I thinking I am still eating garlic, yes."

"Okay, now you're just…being hate speech. Great, ya got me doing it. If you offer me blood, I just don't want to be rude and have to refuse it."

"I am not offering you blood."

"So, hate speech. You're lucky Mindy isn't reading you the Riot Act right now."

"Is this rap song?"

There was a sudden commotion outside Seb's room, picked up by Mindy's tinny speakers. The door to his bedroom opened up and an elderly lady came in, her housecoat pulled tight around herself by blue-veined hands. Mrs. Ferguson of Seb's host family. "Sebastian! What are you doing on there?" He turned the gain on his microphone down all the way before they could hear more.

"What are they saying?" Mindy wondered after a few moments.

Lucia said, in a fair approximation of Seb's accent, "'It's not porn.' She asked if it was porn," Lucia explained. Then in an old-lady voice she said, "'Then why is she dressed that way?'" Mrs. Ferguson was pointing at the screen. "I think she means you," Lucia stage-whispered to Mindy.

Seb's lips moved, and Lucia spoke for him, her words lagging an instant behind his mouth like they were in an old Godzilla movie. "'This is just how American teenagers dress, it is your country, you should know. Can you please go? It is being a private conversation!'"

"'Are they pedophiles? A lot of people online are pedophiles! Grown men pretending to be women! You have to be careful, Seb!'" Lucia channelled Mrs Ferguson again.

"'I am being careful, Mrs. F, please be going, we're about to do homework!'"

"'The pancakes're almost done!'" Lucia lip synced Mrs. F headed toward the door, casting a wary look over her shoulder at Lucia and Mindy.

Seb turned the gain back up. "I'll be down in a minute, thanking you, Mrs. F."

"Be careful," Mrs. F instructed gravely as she closed the door behind her.

Lucia shrugged. "At least she closed the door."

Seb faced them. "Have to go. Blueberry pancakes. Most important meal of the day."

"Yeah, be careful," Mindy told him. "We think we had a vampire last night, trying to get in or get me outside—something. Stay on your toes."

Seb tapped his temple. "And to you. And come be seeing me around lunch, I'd like to talk about nurses."

"Sure thing," Lucia said. "And you excuse us, we have to go jerk off."

Mindy Xed out of the window. "He's never going to learn idioms if you keep fucking with him, y'know," Mindy said..

"He was giving me attitude."

Mindy shot up from her chair, relieved in a way to have the old frustration back. The push-pull with Lucia that so often ended up being worth it. "Oh my Christ, are you still mad at him for crushing on me?"

"No!"

"Because only one of you has saved me from a vampire."

Lucia plopped herself down in Mindy's office chair. "But what if he saves you from two vampires, huh?"

"I'll still like you more."

Lucia winced. "Yeah, but I'm not so easy to like. Lots of complications, lots of baggage. Him, he's easy. You don't realize, but if you did—I wouldn't date me if I were you. I would date someone simple."

"Well, I like a challenge."

Kicking against the carpet, Lucia spun herself in place. "There's challenging and then there's impossible."

"So don't be impossible." Mindy bit her lip. Wondering how far she should go. Remembering Lucia watching over her all night. "We can talk about it, you know."

"You can talk with Seb too. After a fashion."

"About the…" *The kissing?* "The sex."

Lucia's foot skipped on the ground. Turning her around. Facing her away. "It's funny. I can talk all the shit in the world. I don't care if people think I'm racist or homophobic or that I hate men. But when it comes to the things that really matter to me, I can't say shit."

"I don't want you to say something you don't mean or that you're not comfortable saying… I just want you to be comfortable saying what you feel. You do feel something, right?"

"Of course I feel something. I didn't just start kissing girls because they're not boys—or not a vampire." Lucia's head drifted back, and Mindy could see something of her face, staring up at the ceiling. "I don't want to say anything that would ruin this."

"Ruin *what?* What do we have?"

"You." Lucia turned just enough to look over her shoulder at Mindy. "Being my friend."

Sitting down on the bed, Mindy stared at Lucia as the girl whirled around like a top, using her strength to spin herself so loud the chair whined. "So how far can you hear?" Mindy asked, curious. And something else.

"Never really measured it," Lucia said like she was speaking through a fan. She stopped herself, forehead knitted, concentrating. "Guy in the house at the end of the street is watching porn."

"You're guessing."

"It has a *Lord of the Rings* theme."

"Okay, you can stop there."

"Love to." Lucia cracked her neck like she was turning off a radio.

"So you can hear someone in the other room no problem?"

"No problem whatsoever."

"Like, if you were in my bedroom and I were in the shower…"

"I heard you moan," Lucia interrupted. "And I wasn't *listening*, I just heard."

*Oh. Oh God.* Mindy felt like beating her head against the wall. *Nice, Murphy. Real nice.* Here they were building a relationship and Lucia had heard her jackin' in the shower. *Goddamn. Son of a bitch!*

"I'm sorry—I was very tense and I needed a release. Really, I do that pretty much whenever I shower. I have a problem, I know. I wasn't even thinking about you!"

"You weren't?" Lucia asked, and the look she gave Mindy made her feel six inches tall.

Christ, now she was lying. "Okay, I did, I'm sorry! I really didn't mean to sexualize you or anything, it just happened—"

"First time?" Lucia stood. Her manner was insistent.

Mindy didn't even think about lying to her. "That first night, after the… after the lake? I had a dream you were standing over me. Where you were going to bite me, but you didn't. When I woke up…"

"So when I don't bite you, you touch yourself, and when I do bite you, you touch yourself."

"I'm sorry, I am so sorry. I promise, from now on, I will only masturbate to pornography. I'll buy some if I have to. Lucia—God, I can't imagine how this makes you feel."

"It makes me feel like fucking your goddamn brains out."

All of a sudden, Mindy couldn't breathe. It was like Lucia was in her head—making her think things. All the sex scenes she'd ever watched, all the fantasies that had ever heated her... They were flashing through her eyes like a life before dying, but she was seeing them with Lucia and...her. Plain old Mindy Murphy.

Lucia walked by. Her body sleek and strong. Nearly brushing against Mindy as she passed, but not. The brisk little hairs of her skin touching the brisk little hairs of Mindy's. She ran a fingernail over the print-outs. It was short. Since when had her fingernails gotten so short?

"I phrased that bad." Lucia's voice was casual, slinky, grinning. It made it easy for Mindy's mind to register them. They slipped right by her defenses. "Lately everything makes me feel like fucking your brains out. Or I just feel like fucking your brains out all the time." She turned. Her eyes on Mindy. Burning black. "But I'm not really experienced at this lesbian stuff, and so, faced with a choice of binge-watching *The L Word* and learning that shit like a second language or just seducing you and figuring it out as I go, I'm gonna go with seducing you. I'm good at that."

And she was kissing Mindy. Mindy was kissing Lucia back until the woman was away from her, leaving Mindy's lips stinging. Half-charged.

"Here's how it's gonna play out," Lucia said, her words ringing out boldly. "I'm gonna come on to you, while you do whatever's next on the agenda, and when you're so crazy turned on that you can't stand it, we're gonna fuck. That sound okay?"

Mindy spoke so numbly, she almost wondered if she'd had a stroke. "Yeah. Okay."

"Unless you want me to stop." For a moment, Lucia's voice was almost concerned, her eyes beseeching. "Do you want me to stop seducing you? I started already."

"No. Don't stop."

Lucia seized her. Pulled her off her feet and into a bridegroom's hold. It seemed an effort for Lucia to keep herself at normal speed as she effortlessly paraded Mindy up the stairs and into her room. As soon as Lucia dropped Mindy on the bed, she blurred and was on top of her before the bedsprings had finished bouncing.

They were kissing again. Lucia's lips were cold, but they were burning her. Mindy was moaning, sighing, her hands ahead of her, prying at her own clothes to make way for Lucia's body. She barely stopped herself before Lucia had all of her.

"Wait, wait, wait—"

Lucia was quick to pull away. She actually wrapped herself around a bedpost. "What is it? Did I do something wrong?" She sounded so worried, so instantly contrite, that Mindy just had to put her at ease. She caught Lucia with a hand on her cheek and Lucia unclenched.

"No, that was great. Perfect. I just need to check something before we—" Mindy laughed. "You really wanna…do that with me? The sex?"

"Yeah." Lucia grinned and her teeth were all teeth. No fangs. "I want to do all the sex with you."

"Because I might not be very good."

"I'll be good enough for both of us."

Seeing the look in Lucia's eyes—the relief, the love—Mindy felt her lips yearning to be met again. God, it was like trying to eat just one piece of chocolate. She quickly turned onto her stomach, not finding the desire any easier to bear just because Lucia was out of sight, and jerked open the drawers of her nightstand, traipsing through the scraps of a hundred half-finished projects for what she was looking for.

Lucia reached down to Mindy's jeans, peeling their waistline away from Mindy's lower back and hovering down to lick the crest of her spine. Mindy was shocked at how pornographic her moan sounded—going with the feel of Lucia's cool saliva warming with her own body heat like a massaging lotion.

Then she laid hands on it. The crisp cool cover of the trade paperback *So You're Ready To Have Sex*, with the nonthreatening illustration of the boy bathroom sign and the girl bathroom sign holding hands. She pulled it onto the bed with her and flipped to the bookmark she'd put in on that first bus ride to high school. She'd expected a boy to ask her out her first day there.

"What's that? *Fifty Shades of Grey?*" Lucia asked. "Because I don't mind eating you out while you read porn, but that's more of a second date kind of thing in my book."

"Hey, this is your first time with a girl, right?"

"Oh no, I fucked Scarlet Johansson once, didn't I tell you? *Yes. It is.*"

Mindy held the book up to her face, hiding her mouth behind it. "Then this'll come in handy for both of us. It was written by Dr. Melody Friedman, she's this really great therapist, she had her own column on Huffington Post during the Aughts all about respecting your sexuality and stuff—she said Israel should be nuked once, but nobody's perfect."

"The Aughts?"

"2001 to 2011… It means zero."

Lucia floated over to Mindy's ear, tongue flicking out to trace the lobe before she spoke. "When we fuck, do you want to ride my leg again? You came really fast the last time. I've been thinking about it a lot. I liked it. Kissing you. Making you come. But I also really wanna eat you out. Find out if your pussy tastes as good as your blood."

Mindy's nipples were so hard she could *feel* them being hard. They hit her bedspread like it was a bed of nails. "It's just a little cheat sheet… This'll make it really good for both of us." Mindy caught a glimpse of Lucia's sultry smile out of the corner of her eyes and forced herself to look at the book instead. She'd highlighted all the stuff she'd meant to consult before a date where she would lose her virginity.

She read out loud, "Feeling tense and nervous can lead to less than optimal memories, as well as making the vaginal muscles clench, leading to unnecessary pain."

"Do I make you nervous?" Lucia cooed in Mindy's ear.

"Read up about what an erection is and how to—not a problem. 'Know your body, especially what you enjoy and what you don't enjoy. Masturbation can—"

"I don't think that's a problem either…" Lucia pulled at Mindy's jacket. "I want this *off.*"

Mindy held out her arms one at a time, letting Lucia strip her. "Approach sex with a positive attitude, knowing that it is your own personal choice to have sex for the first time. If you feel guilty or stressed out, it's okay to wait until your feelings are in order…'"

"You don't *smell* guilty. Or stressed out. You smell *wet*." Lucia's fingers slid along Mindy's hips, around and down to her belly like they were going to keep going until they were under Mindy's body, down at her *cunt,* but they didn't. Her hand went away and Lucia was still hovering over Mindy, waiting to devour her. Waiting patiently, but not without hunger.

Mindy flipped through her dog-eared reminders, skipping whole chapters at a time. "Condoms, not an issue…lubricant…"

"*Definitely* not an issue," Lucia commented.

"'Discuss your concerns with your partner…'"

"Worried I'm going to make you come too hard?" Lucia teased.

"Not at all," Mindy breathed. "Hymen… probably just have a partial hymen, shouldn't bleed very much, won't be too painful as long as you, I, don't clench my muscles."

"You can bleed all you want, Minz. I'll clean it up."

Mindy swore under her breath. Why did that turn her on? Why was she thinking about how anything she could confront Lucia with, any misgiving or weirdness, Lucia would just *accept?* Why did she feel so safe with a fucking vampire?

Mindy forced herself to focus. She stared at the book until the words swam back onto the page, only picturing herself turning over and pulling Lucia down to her crotch a grand total of ten or twenty times before she was able to resist the fantasy.

"Set a relaxing mood." This, at last, seemed important. "Shut off your phone."

Lucia blurred into motion. Mindy heard the high-pitched beep of her phone being put to sleep, and the sound of what must have been Lucia's powering down. They dropped into an open drawer and were shut away.

"'Lower the lights, play some soft music, and keep the room temperature at a warm level.'"

Lucia swept through the room like a tornado, tuning Mindy's iPad dock to a mellow set of acoustic guitars playing nuevo flamenco. The lights went off, but Lucia opened the blinds a little to let a warm glow in. And Lucia pulled Mindy's comforter out of the closet and set it at the foot of her bed, ready to cover them if they got too cold. Mindy had to laugh at Lucia's thoughtfulness. That El actually wanted her to think she was being seductive.

"Would you believe there's a Pandora station for make out sessions?" Lucia asked, sweeping back down over the bed. Like Peter Pan, Mindy thought, only played by a woman. So—like Peter Pan.

"Consider grooming yourself beforehand to feel more relaxed and at ease. Do whatever makes you feel attractive and self-assured. Take a quick shower."

"Fuck that." Lucia took the book. "Can't I just *tell you* how pretty you are? Don't you believe me?"

Mindy grabbed for the book, which Lucia let her have. "C'mon. Let's do this right. I want it to be perfect."

"It's *us*. Of course it's going to be perfect." Lucia smiled thoughtfully. "Perfect as it can be when one of us is a vampire—I'm not pointing fingers…"

"Sex is a marathon, not a sprint." Mindy checked the number of dog-ears left to go more than what she was reading. Flipped to the next one. "Communicate with your partner… Leave your expectations at the door… Consider making an appointment with your gynecologist now that you're sexually active…"

"Oh my God, are you going to start naming our adopted babies next?"

"Almost done," Mindy promised her. "Birth control…condoms…STDs… Damn, I thought I was so fucking straight back then." She shut the book. It seemed quite thin now. "That's, uh—that's the book. Oh, it says if you don't feel very confident about your body, candlelight can seem more romantic than electric light or darkness."

Lucia kissed her again and Mindy felt like she was *engulfed,* just covered in Lucia's desire for her, a warm glow that pierced her body in so many places, so many ways. Then Lucia broke and blurred away. In a moment she was back, a scented candle burning on Mindy's nightstand. The blinds closed a fraction more, leaving the flickering flame almost the only light.

"It was all I could find," Lucia said apologetically. "And I took it out of the downstairs bathroom, so be careful who you follow in there." Her eyes traced over Mindy's body, as physical as a caress. "You really don't feel confident about that?"

"Not next to you."

Lucia frowned as she put both hands on Mindy's cheeks. "Always remember, babe. All this?" She ran her hands quickly over her own body. "It belongs to me, and you're the one who takes *my* breath away. Now, unless that book has a sequel…" She took it and tossed it over her shoulder.

"It does say," Mindy said, "that if one partner is nervous or…or more inexperienced, they should be the one to set boundaries. So that everyone's on the same page."

"It does, does it?"

"Is that okay?"

Lucia took Mindy's hand, exceedingly gentle, and led it to her lips. "Everything's okay if it's what you want. What do you want, Minz?"

"I was thinking…" Mindy hated herself for this, for doing anything that might make this goddess feel unwanted when every molecule in Mindy wanted to be touched by Lucia. But she'd promised herself a thousand times that she wouldn't rush into this when it finally happened, and now it was finally happening and—Lucia loved her, and the woman Lucia loved didn't know if she was really ready or just thought she was ready, so Mindy would trust Lucia's trust in her. She'd be honest, knowing Lucia loved her no matter what. "I was thinking that I'm not quite done being a virgin yet, so maybe we could just kiss? You don't mind just kissing me, do you?"

Lucia was kissing every tip of Mindy's fingers, every knuckle, every joint. "No. It's like someone saying you can't have donuts, you can only have all the pizza you want."

"Kissing me is like pizza—" Mindy almost laughed, but she quickly turned serious, realizing, "that's the most romantic thing anyone has ever said to me."

"You want romantic? I can be romantic. I'll feed you poetry… I *had* a poem memorized but, uh, not now."

"Oh no." Mindy bet any poem Lucia had almost memorized would've been pretty good.

Lucia flopped down onto Mindy, burying her head in Mindy's shirt. Mindy didn't think it was a coincidence that her next words brushed at Mindy's neck.

"It was Keats! I would've been so suave!" She gave Mindy a quick kiss. She couldn't seem to go a minute without doing so. "Can I take off my clothes?"

"I think that would be a good idea," Mindy stated.

Lucia's long legs parted. Mindy felt the very light weight of her settle on her waist. Lucia was straddling her. Mindy felt herself clenching up. The book wouldn't be happy with her.

Lucia reached behind herself. A little fiddling and her dress top fell away. Her breasts were so *big*, but at the same time not big at all, perfectly fitting to her perfect body, not overinflated beach balls like you were supposed to go to the plastic surgeon for. Bra a wisp of black smoke hiding them.

Then Lucia popped the button on her denim shorts, tiny to begin with, unzipped them, and slipped them off—down to even tinier panties hugging her hips. As Lucia hovered around to get her pants off, Mindy could see the narrow band of cloth that barely, *barely* separated one petal-soft buttock from the other. She didn't know what she wanted more: to touch or to be touched.

Lucia settled back atop her, licking her lips, her whole body a pristine snowfield broken only by the patches of black, like dark waters Mindy could be sucked down into. She put her hands lovingly into Mindy's hair, playing with it like a cat with yarn, and from the laugh she gave she'd been wanting to do it for a long time.

"I love your short hair," Lucia teased, giggly.

It took a while, but Mindy remembered to breathe. When she exhaled, words came with it. "Okay, I'm ready."

"Ready?"

Another deep breath, sucking air down to the deepest chasm of Mindy's body, where it brought up her next sentence. "Maybe we can do more than kiss? If you want?" A minute ago, Mindy had said she'd just wanted to kiss. But Lucia hadn't been naked then.

Lucia smirked smugly, as if she knew why Mindy changed her mind. "We could touch?" she suggested, but it wasn't a suggestion at all.

Like a snake—a big, self-satisfied snake—she slunk around Mindy, wrapping around her. Her lips merged with Mindy, and Mindy was almost shocked by the slip-slide of their tongues together: how could it be so good, so right, so natural when she didn't even know what she was doing?

She felt Lucia's thumb, then her forefinger, spread to either side of her belly button. They rolled together, pinching together the material of Mindy's shirt—God, so hard to focus on it, on anything when Lucia's tongue was slipping up the roof of Mindy's mouth with the same languid, uncomplicated inevitability as the wetness coiling in Mindy's sex and dripping-literally-dripping down the crack of her ass.

And Lucia pried Mindy's shirt up, almost to her bra, and left Mindy's soft belly exposed. Mindy almost wanted to pull her shirt back down—it was so white and pudgy, where Lucia's was all taut and sexy like a marble pillar or something—but then, that would mean Lucia wouldn't be touching her.

Another kiss—was it the same kiss?—Lucia's hand was splayed on Mindy's belly, almost to the start of her panties and skirt. Clever fingers made a lazy spiral, playing the sheen of sweat that was gathering on Mindy like you'd play music on the rim of a half-empty glass. Lucia steepled her fingers around Mindy's navel and Mindy thought of what those long, straight fingers would feel like inside her. She'd never been much for using fingers on herself, not when God had invented showerheads, but Lucia's fingers had to be as wonderful as the rest of her, right?

Then those wonderful fingers spread out as Lucia's hand flattened to Mindy's skin, the outspread fingertips teasingly moving down Mindy's body but never actually *going* anywhere. Lucia's hand always stayed in the same place, just opening and closing—

Lucia stopped kissing her, and now Mindy could hear herself pant and moan and make all kinds of noises she didn't know she could make. Those dark lips went back to her ear like they were meant to be there. "Is this okay? Are you comfortable?"

"Yeah, yeah, uh-huh..." Mindy kept saying yes until she was just nodding and making nonsense words and Lucia finally, mercifully caught her lips again.

The kiss was so familiar now. Still new, still exciting, but somehow it felt like home at the same time. Like wherever Mindy went, she wouldn't really be *there* if she wasn't kissing Lucia. It made no sense, and a little voice whispered over Lucia's, saying, *Love doesn't make sense.* But all wanted to think about was Lucia.

"What about you?" The words were easy. So easy. As hard as it was to think, she just had to imagine Lucia not feeling what she was, and she snapped to like a soldier. "You want to stop?"

Lucia shook her head. The very thought was not to be voiced.

Mindy smiled. It felt like it would break out of her face. "Would you like to fuck me?" she asked, very politely.

Lucia smiled too. "Yes I would."

Her hand went away from Mindy's stomach, just for a second, just long enough for Mindy to spend an eternity wondering where it would go, then it slapped down on Mindy's thigh, hard, gripping the muscle, her thumb rubbing at—*shit*, was that an erogenous zone? It felt *a lot* like an erogenous zone.

"I really like touching myself here." Lucia's voice was dark and dangerous again, just not to Mindy. Dangerous to everyone else. Made Mindy feel special, like you were supposed to your first time. "When I'm *fucking* myself." She drew the word out. "Work for you too?"

"It works," Mindy gasped. Lucia's thumb felt like it was burrowing right to the nerve, and bringing an electrical cable with it. "Works…"

"It's not awkward? Or weird?"

"Mm-mmn." Mindy shook her head desperately. Words were beginning to be a problem for her.

"Because my first time was both. I don't want that for you. I want your first to be as special as you are."

"Keep touching me like that—and kiss me one more time—" Mindy's breath *shook* her body like a dog with a toy. "And it'll be the first of many."

Mindy laughed when she saw Lucia's sudden wired grin. It was so *doofy*— not seductive at all, but it made Mindy want to be with Lucia even harder, wrap herself up in her and never let go.

"Touch you like *this*?" she asked, all rhetorical, her whole hand rubbing at that special spot inside Mindy's thigh.

"No," Mindy said, and guiltily enjoyed the pouty look on Lucia's face. "*Higher.*"

"Are you sure? Because we could stop? It's no trouble, if you have any misgivings, I will go and I will join a convent before I hurt you."

"As much as I like picturing you dressed as a nun, I'd rather you just stay here. Be my first. Make me a woman." She landed kiss after kiss on Lucia's stony lips. And the realization came to her that she wasn't the one that needed reassuring. She wasn't the only one who needed to feel wanted. They were the same. They were together. "C'mon baby. Take my virginity. I want you to be the first one who can ever say they had sex with me. The first and only. I want to be able to tell people that you popped my cherry." Mindy stopped short, biting her lip. It tasted like Lucia's Chap Stick. "Not that I would tell anyone that, but, like, I'll write it in my diary."

"You have a diary? Nerd."

"Your nerd," Mindy retorted.

"Yeah. Mine." Lucia's hand moved. Her face was still, her lips gently parted as if opening to suck in something of Mindy, her eyes fixed with Mindy's. Mindy felt her panties move. Pulled down out of the way. Then Lucia's fingers. On her thigh. On her groin. Her labia. "All mine…"

Mindy sighed gently. It went right through Lucia's open lips. And it didn't hurt. Not at all. Not even a little bit.

"I slipped right into you," Lucia breathed, sounding amazed, divine, powerful, weak.

And all it took was one finger. Mindy felt her pussy do things she hadn't thought it could do. It was pulling tight on that one perfect finger, getting wet, burning and exploding and it was all Lucia's, all of it, something only of her body being injected into Mindy. "Kiss me, kiss me!" Mindy begged and she was coming and Lucia was kissing her and she hadn't known life could be so beautiful. How had she not known?

Lucia stretched over her, hovering, the barest, most scintillating contact between them. As if she was afraid to touch Mindy, afraid she'd break her like spun glass. Amazed by the long pleasure that held Mindy, and slowly, Lucia took her finger away.

Mindy moaned, too satisfied and sore to want it back. Her sex clenched on nothing for a moment, then started to relax, unkink, little tumblers of gratification unfurling all through her, like sparks in a fire.

Mindy opened her knotted eyes just in time to see Lucia's finger in her mouth, ruby red sucking on the pale digit. It seemed endless as it came out of Lucia's lips. Tapering off her tongue.

"Okay, not questioning anymore," Mindy said. "Definitely a lesbian."

"I felt you come apart," Lucia said belatedly, with an equally stunned laugh. "You liked it…"

"How could I not?" Mindy shared Lucia's disbelieving smile. "With the finger of the most amazing girl in the world…"

She didn't finish her sentence. Lucia was kissing her again.

"*Again*," one of them said, but Mindy wasn't sure who. Not that it mattered. The important thing was that they were in complete agreement.

This time, two fingers.

# CHAPTER 20

The sheets were tangled in a Gordian knot. One of the two pillows that Mindy needed, at a minimum, to sleep comfortably had turned into an uncategorized collection of feathers. The mattress pad was ripped. And Lucia *gleamed* with sweat, not her own, but what had been laved off Mindy and onto her.

As softly insistent as a cat wanting to be scratched, she had beached herself on Mindy, one arm thrown over her, head draped over the ruins of Mindy's bra, one leg intertwined with both of Mindy's. Mindy wasn't quite able to move, but she wasn't paralyzed. She could move her hand, rubbing the patch of Lucia's back that it was next to.

She was hopeful that her recuperation would grow to include possibly smelling Lucia's hair at a later date. It looked great, all tousled and sheeny and growing out again. Mindy thought of Lucia going to school like that. *Where did you get your hair done?* All her friends would ask, and Lucia would just smile and say, *Oh, Mindy rocked my world, my hair's been doing this ever since.*

Shit, she probably would, though.

"Yeah, bitch, I totally womanized you. I *totes* womanized you." Lucia was smug, but then, she had a right to be. Mindy lay under her, all spooned out, and thought, *You big dumb. I love you, you big dumb. How could it feel like that if I didn't love you?*

Mindy felt her throat clear, the power of speech return to her. Now if she could just feel her legs… "I really think I might be gay."

Lucia clapped her on the shoulder. "Oh, good. I was thinking you eating my pussy was a big accident."

Mindy wasn't Catholic, but she wondered if this was what confession felt like. Being able to tell the truth and have it come out so pure—no judgment. "Like, capital-*G* gay. I've never really been much for boys—I always thought they were sorta weird."

"Honey, we all think that."

"Yeah, but at a certain point girls see a dick and think 'I want that in me.'" Mindy shrugged. "I never got that."

"I still do." Lucia's brow furrowed.

Mindy could feel the little change in her skin where Lucia's forehead was burrowed into her chest, and it felt a little like an underwire poking into her. But she relaxed quickly.

"But not at the moment...maybe I'm bisexual. All the cool people are bisexual. I can be like Megan Fox!"

Mindy lifted an arm, rotated a kink out of it, and brought it around to hold Lucia tight. To assure herself that Lucia didn't want to go anywhere. "Hey, not to—not to rate it or anything, but was I much worse than a dude or about the same or... Don't tell me I was amazing or anything, I'll think you're lying. Just, you know, hold your hand up about where I was."

Lucia's hand had been on Mindy for so long, it was warm when it touched her face. "Minz, you're *always* amazing. Even when you're eating me out."

It was a silly thing to be worried about. Mindy knew it, she *knew it*, but still... "Yeah, but like—how does me...giving you the frick-frack compare to the *D*?"

"Let me put it this way," Lucia said, kissing Mindy three times in almost the same spot, her lips moving at the speed of a glacier, but not quite as cold. They dragged over Mindy's skin when they weren't pursing together, sucking, bringing a smidgen of Mindy's blood up to the surface of her skin. "I've been with a lot of guys and I've been with you. And they weren't bad, but they weren't special either. You were...you were really special, Mindy."

The way Lucia said it, some defense mechanism went off in Mindy's skull. Long years of cruel jokes and TV shows where girls like her were never the ones in love, just the ones the person in love stopped from being bullied to show how worthy they were of being in love. Mindy wasn't worthy. She was just a joke. So she joked, "What, are you in love with me?"

She hated herself for saying it and was afraid of hating Lucia for how she answered it. *Please, I know you should make fun of me for that, but not too hard? Please, not too—*

"Yeah. I think I am," Lucia said. Her voice as plain and natural and simple as the darkness all around them. If one was the absence of light, the other was just the absence of—of bullshit.

"I think I love you too." Fear and bullshit. The only things that could keep you from being loved. Mindy thought she should write that down. It'd make a good senior essay.

"We should probably start dating then," Lucia muttered sleepily. "I wouldn't want people to think I'm easy."

Fat and lazy with the blood she'd taken, Lucia shifted protectively over Mindy, gathering her up in her arms and wrapping her up in pale flesh. Lucia's eyes were glassy, and her voice was slurred, and Mindy's life sloshed in her belly as she held Mindy close, saying, "My girlfriend, who I love. My Mindy, Mindy mine…"

And Mindy dreamt she was Lucia holding Mindy, feeling the warmth that could only come from Mindy, since Lucia was cold. And it was like bathing in sunlight.

Mindy woke up slowly. Contentedly. Still feeling Lucia's body on her own. It took her long moments to realize that the warmth couldn't be Lucia. It was just her sheets, tangled up with her. She opened her eyes, and the bed was empty.

"Eat and run?" she asked the air, and a bat flew down from the ceiling. "Ahh!"

It flitted around, not panicked, just leisurely flapping around her ceiling.

"Bat! Bat!"

It alighted—lit? alit?—on her bed. "Chill out, slut. Why so tense?"

Mindy was aware of a large breath taking up residence in her lungs. "Lucia?"

"Yeah!" the bat said. "I'm a bat! Ain't it cool?"

"It's…batty."

Lucia spread her wings. "Leave the lame jokes to me. I'm cute enough to get away with them."

"You are cute," Mindy said. As a bat, Lucia was about the size of a small kitten, with a vulpine face of big black eyes and a body that was mostly chubby fluff, and an impressive wingspan that made it look like she was asking for a hug.

Lucia assumed an indignant expression—as much as a bat was able. "No, I'm a creature of the night! I am the mistress of darkness! Fear me!" She scratched herself with a little foot.

"Aw...." Mindy oozed. "Wait, *why are you a bat?*"

Lucia jumped onto Mindy's belt and climbed up her body, somewhat to Mindy's chagrin. "I was just lying here—very well-fed, thank you—thinking how bullshit it was that I was a vampire but I couldn't control wolves or fly or do anything cool. So I thought I'd try changing into a bat. And I'm thinking, 'Hey, how do you turn into a bat, Lucia?' Then I remembered how they did it in *Animorphs* and *bam*, I'm a fucking bat."

"Wow, I read *Animorphs* too! Who was your favorite?"

"Rachel. You?"

"Tobias."

Lucia's expression, perched on Mindy's shoulder, soured. "Second favorite?"

"Marco."

"Me too! Twinsies!"

Mindy's brow wrinkled again. "But where'd your clothes go?"

"Oh, they transformed with me. It's magic."

"So, now magic's a real thing?"

"Well, we're going with God and vampires, right? Magic's not that big a deal."

"What's next, aliens?"

"Are you kidding? That would be so lame. I mean, did you *see Indiana Jones and the...* whatsit of the *Crystal Skull?* They had to go to another dimension to do it, but they finally found something that annoyed me more than Willie Scott."

"Okay, turn back. I wanna..." *look at your pretty face while I talk to you,* "see you."

Lucia paused. "How do they turn back in *Animorphs?*"

"Wait, you turned into a bat without knowing how to turn back?"

"Don't yell!" Lucia chided. "I'm definitely not going to be able to turn back if you make me tense up, you know. I think I'll just be a bat for a while. Bats don't have to go to high school."

"That's terrible reasoning."

"Well, I learned it in high school, so another good reason not to go. C'mon, Minz, let's just hang out." Clutching Mindy's blouse with her talons, Lucia hung upside down. "Ha! I'm so funny."

"I am not going to ditch school to babysit a bat!"

"Please? I'll let you pet me?"

Half an hour later, Mindy had faked grievous illness under Lucia's tutelage and was in bed, laptop topping her lap, doing research. She wore a hoodie with Lucia tucked behind the zipper, watching as she browsed.

"You're cutting class to use Tumblr?" Lucia asked.

"I know, right? I feel so alive!"

"You are the worst person I have ever ditched with. Let's get krunk! Drag race! Smoke some weed!"

"I'm not even sure you can get a bat high?"

"Sure you can, it's easy. I'll just flap my wings a lot."

"*Stooop*," Mindy protested.

"If all else fails, you can go to the top of a really tall building…"

"Noooooo!"

"And throw me off!"

"You're the worst at telling jokes," Mindy complained. "You tell jokes like the American economy. It seems like you're trying to be funny, but you just aren't."

"That was way harsh, Minz."

Mindy ignored her, clicking through the vast repository of Google's bat pictures. "Oh my God, Google, I want pictures of bats, not someone's shitty drawings of Sonic characters screwing—alright, here we go." She clicked an image that looked close to Lucia's form, though Lucia insisted it wasn't as cute as her. "Hunh. That's funny."

"Must not be me then," Lucia griped, digging her head into Mindy's zipper.

"You'd think that you would be a vampire bat, but you're not. You're just a cute little fruit bat."

"You really gotta bring the gayness into everything, don't you?"

"An Egyptian fruit bat, to be precise." Mindy loved playing the Willow to Lucia's Buffy. "Native to Transylvania, actually."

"How does this help our situation?"

"A little knowledge never hurt anyone."

"There's knowledge and then there's finding out your idol and personal hero is a vampire."

"When did I say any—"

"I thought you'd be running for a cross by now. Telling everyone how the evil vampire tricked you into letting yourself be bit…"

"I'm not the kind to run for the hills."

"I am. If I could, I'd run like hell. But I can't. Run from this… I'm glad you're okay, Minz. Most of all, I'm glad you're okay."

Mindy just petted Lucia, running her finger along her back, its soft downy fur. "*Of course* I'm okay. It's just—it's just blood, you know? Listen, you're not…what happened to you. You're you. What you do doesn't have to be what happened. It can be…it can be everything you are. You know?"

"Yeah—hold on, I'm gonna try being human again." Lucia flapped off Mindy, landing beside her on the bed. She held out her wings, beady little eyes fixed in concentration. "Human—human," she chanted. "I had the cutest, flattest little belly, arms harder than Vin Diesel, boobs… You remember, right, Mindy, I had great boobs…"

"They were not bad," Mindy said blankly.

"Hey, maybe it works on frog prince specs. I have to get a kiss from a princess to turn back."

"Hold on, I've got the Queen's number somewhere," Mindy joked.

"You could always try."

"Not sure I want to be on first base with anything that can't drive a car."

In a rush, Lucia was sitting beside her. All homo sapiens again. She clasped her breasts and laughed uproariously. "Ha! *Beauty and the Beast-ed* that bitch! Don't let anyone else call you a beast, though."

"Pet names already…"

"Already," Lucia confirmed. Then she hurried to the window, working at the stiff locks. "When are your 'rents getting back anyway? I don't think they'd believe there's such a thing as a clothing-optional sleepover. And once every leap year my mom checks up on me, so I should be all tucked in for that."

"Alright. I'll see you tomorrow? We'll work on, you know, the thing?"

"Your vagina?" Lucia asked hopefully. Some of her old humor sneaking in. She always bounced back so quick. Maybe she was just getting better at hiding it from Mindy.

"Finding our vampire sonuvabitch who needs a bad case of heartburn," Mindy corrected her.

Lucia nodded absently. The window gave. She slipped past it, though her head stayed inside the room for a moment. "Actually..." Lucia elongated the word, her insinuating voice pulling Mindy to join her on the windowsill, leaning on her end while Lucia crouched on hers. "I was thinking that if you've had enough of vampires that aren't me for the foreseeable future, maybe we could do certain girlfriend-girlfriend things."

"Yeah?" Mindy asked, taking Lucia's hands, the sudden chill of her grip a welcome relief in the Texas afternoon. She poked at the inside of her cheek with her tongue, loving the way Lucia's eyes ran over the little gesture, as thrilling as her fingertips on Mindy's wrists—ice cubes on her skin.

"I want you to go to the school dance with me Friday after next."

Mindy stood straighter, Lucia's fingers tensing on her waist, wanting to hold her in place but letting her break away. "Seriously?"

"I know it's unconventional, but it is a Sadie Hawkins Dance. Girls are supposed to ask their dates there."

Mindy laughed—thinking *you dork, you big dork, you're my big goddamn dork.* "I'd love to go with you."

Lucia smiled back at her. Not one of her coy, elusive smiles. One that was like watching the sun coming up. "Okay, then. Okay. Cool."

Mindy held up her hand, wanting to live in Lucia's innocent glee. "Let's rock this school dance!"

Lucia interlocked their fingers, her hand already starting to warm with Mindy's borrowed heat.

"I was just going for a high-five, you big gay."

# CHAPTER 21

Finally, it was the weekend. They crossed Tate's Creek Bridge on the way to the mall. Lucia leaned over and kissed Mindy's cheek.

"What was that for?" Mindy asked.

"We had our first kiss here," Lucia reminded her. "Have to keep the tradition alive."

They rolled on, thousands of sleeping bats hanging underneath them. Rain ghosted down in a little drizzle, offering a respite from the drought but no relief. Mindy enjoyed it anyway. Like many, she loved the big thick gales of rain, the storms that came down, and it was like the clouds were physically touching you—as long as she wasn't wearing her glasses.

The drizzles were more annoying, but for Lucia it was an excuse for them to cry out in roller-coaster horror, hide themselves under a magazine cover, make a dash from the Taurus, and grab a cuddle under the awnings that lined the mall entrance. Lucia pressed her to an empty window and mouthed her pulse point, first lips, then teeth, the blunt ivory grinding down on Mindy's skin like she was testing it.

"No biting in public," Mindy said, giving her a little push away.

Lucia let herself be moved. Teased Mindy by chomping her teeth behind Mindy's neck when she started for the door. Mindy turned, walking backward as she gave Lucia a good-natured middle finger, pulled it back when Lucia chomped at that too. Then they were through the automatic doors, in the reverse oasis of the mall. The drizzle steadily tapped at the ceiling, the skylights, politely asking to be let in.

They weren't the first ones inside. The early morning exodus of mall security and wage slaves setting up shop had tracked dirty footprints across the first stretch of tiling, like kindergarten fingerpainting, and for a patch after that, it sparkled with moisture. But Mindy and Lucia didn't slip, didn't fall down. The mall was deserted except for old people getting in exercise, and Lucia treated them like an obstacle course, darting around them with Mindy's hand locked in hers. They lifted their joined arms like a drawbridge to get over a doddering 'Nam vet with a cane.

Mindy knew she was a hell of a dork, but shopping with Lucia felt like being on a quest. Only instead of getting the Amulet of Triforce from the wizard, or the Bracelet of Hephaestus off a Minotaur, they were retrieving a Bonsoir Samira clutch or a pair of dangling crystal Cobblestone earrings. Finally, Lucia was dragging her into a vintage store, slipping right between an old couple like the Millennium Falcon between asteroids.

*Damn, I am such a dork.* "You'll love wearing a dress, Minz. It's the only socially acceptable way of not wearing pants in public," Lucia said, her voice so excited, she might as well have been cheerleading. If she started shouting letters, Mindy was out.

"I'm not sure," Mindy replied, but Lucia was already zipping through the store, going so fast that she might as well have been doing her Wally West thing. She held dresses under Mindy's chin again, again, again, like a hacker in a movie running through every password a computer might have.

"You can't wear blue. I'm wearing blue—couples that go all matchy-matchy are so lame—black, too funeral. Orange, with your complexion, I don't *think* so—pink... Do you like pink?"

Mindy jumped out of her own head as she realized she was being consulted. "I'm okay with pink."

Lucia ripped the dress away from Mindy's body. "No, don't think so." Another dress flapped against Mindy, so fast it was like Lucia was trying to fan her for heatstroke. "You don't want to be too slutty—that's my job—Wait. Wait! I saw it, last month, they might still have it..." She disappeared into the back of the store, Mindy following after she didn't immediately rush back. She found Lucia digging through rack after rack of dresses, a Viking raider set on loot. Until finally, she came up with what had to be the Holy Grail of dresses from the way she clutched it. "This is it! This is your dress!"

It was strapless cream lace dress, short but not too short, thin but not too thin—Mindy expected it to be tight but not too tight.

Lucia almost did a somersault, seeing it pressed under Mindy's chin. "I saw it a month ago, wasn't right for me, too expensive. But it just stuck in my head and I thought maybe if I saved up, maybe if I sewed around it a little… But I guess it was never for me at all—it was yours."

"It's…" Mindy checked the price tag, already starting to wince. She knew Lucia thought she was rich, but it wasn't like she could fly to Barbados on a whim. The universe showed mercy. There was a $299.99, but it had a blood-red slash through it, and $129 was written under it. "Cheap. And strapless. Sleeveless…" She looked over at Lucia. It would've looked great on Lucia. "I usually favor clothes that conceal this region." She ran her palm in a circle over her body, "below my neck."

"What? Fuck that, you'll look cute."

"If I had some *Star Trek: The Next Generation* spanx, maybe…"

Lucia circled around Mindy, pressing the dress to her back and pulling it taut so she could see how it looked from behind. "Minz, who do I date?"

"Football players."

"Don't be racist, I've dated lacrosse people too. So, who do I date?"

"Umm—"

"Hot people!" Lucia explained, sounding out the words like she was teaching Mindy English. "And I'm dating you. You're hot. Sorry, it's the rules, can't change 'em."

"Well, I guess… I suppose it could be a bit…flattering…"

Lucia turned her around and frog-marched her toward the dressing room. "Try it on, try it on, try it on!" Lucia's chant had the disturbing urgency of a cannibal tribe. *Kill the pig, drink its blood, give us a twirl…*

Inside the dressing room, opposite the unforgiving mirror, Mindy stripped. For once, Lucia was enamored with something else—she held the dress up to the light and examined it with a jeweler's eye before taking it off the hanger and jamming it into Mindy's arms. Mindy stepped into it, scooted it up past last week's desserts and Nacho Day at the cafeteria, and stopped with the back gaping open, the smooth expanse of her back unveiled. She *felt* Lucia notice her dishabille. Eyes traced the curve of her spine like a wet tongue. She felt them lower down to Mindy's boy-shorts at the base of her tailbone.

"Zip me up?"

"That's one way we could go," Lucia quipped. Without her reflection in the mirror, Mindy couldn't see her eyebrows jog up, but she knew they had.

"I'm not having sex with you in a dressing room."

"Okay, but for your information, if you only use one finger, I'm pretty sure it's not sex." Lucia pulled the zipper up Mindy's body, brushing her fingertips over Mindy's skin in as restrained a fashion as she could—which was to stretch her fingers too far and, almost politely, skirt the outside of Mindy's breast.

It made Mindy smile. Being touched like that by her girlfriend.

Lucia finished the zip, massaging Mindy's shoulders before taking her chin and bringing her face up to the mirror. The dress nipped at her waist—smaller than Mindy would've thought—and flared out at her hips—their wideness not as unflattering as Mindy feared.

Both their eyes were drawn, helplessly, to the long stretch of legs left bare by the dress's hem. Mindy had known that it was a beautiful dress, but she hadn't realized that *she* filled it out where she should, that her lines were so good, that her bone structure was that of a girl instead of an Uruk-Hai.

"I'm…I'm beautiful," Mindy said before looking away from her reflection, embarrassed by her own narcissism, but Lucia had a hand on her cheek and was bringing her back to see it again.

Lucia wore one of those flickering grins, like her smile wanted to jump out of socially appropriate girl-grimace and stretch across her whole face. "Yes. You still are."

Mindy paid for the dress and a pair of matching satin pumps. They left the store with Lucia keeping up a comforting racket about the spa day she would take Mindy to before the dance, all the different sea creatures that would be involved in making Mindy look ten years younger (so…eight), when they saw Principal Heywood holding a giant-sized pretzel.

Principal Haywood was one of those middle-aged women that were too harmless to dislike, but made you want to try. She had a "Can I speak to your manager?" bob, had pictures of her kids on her desk, and thought the *Divergent* series was good reading material. Usually, she wore a pantsuit or a long skirt with a business jacket, but outside school, she was in a borderline-appropriate minidress with suede pumps, Real Housewives of Carfax stuff.

As she always did when seeing an educator outside of school, Mindy felt maybe half-awake, like she was dreaming, and a talking fish had shown up. Also, more nerdishly, she felt vaguely like she had done something wrong.

"Ms. Murphy!" Haywood greeted, with a nod to each of them. "And Ms. West. Good to see you—all your homework done? I kid."

"Hey Teach," Lucia said. "You got all my papers graded?"

Mindy chortled and elbowed Lucia in the ribs. "We're just shopping for the school dance," she said, feeling some deep-seated need to explain.

"Oh, you asked someone!" Haywood said in the kind of voice that usually went with a hand up against her cheek. "And they said yes," she added unnecessarily. "About time the boys found you out. Almost slipped away to college without one. A lovely girl like you should have someone to dance with."

"Couldn't agree more," Lucia said, but she was suddenly stiff, a million miles away.

"Well, you two remember the school dress code: no one's allowed to look better than me!" Haywood laughed at her own joke, moving off, and after waiting a moment to make sure the clack of her heels wouldn't let up, Mindy gave Lucia's hand a pull.

"What is it?" she insisted. "You're acting like you've just seen a ghost."

"Did you see her wrist? The paper bracelet?"

Mindy hadn't. "What about it?"

"That was a visitor's pass for the Shady Rest Retirement Home."

# CHAPTER 22

Mindy lay on her bed, feeling ridiculously Hammer Films. No clothes on under the sheets, and she should've been comfortable, but she wasn't. She was so nervous about part of her showing if the sheet slipped, if she didn't keep it wrapped around her. She was nervous about Lucia seeing her, because it would lead to Lucia touching her, and that would lead… She didn't quite know anymore.

The door to the bathroom opened. Mindy craned her head, expecting Lucia— it wasn't Lucia. A parody of a penis hovered into the doorway, right at waist height. "Hello, Mindy!" Lucia said in a gruff voice, hosting the world's least age-appropriate puppet show. "I hear you like big black cocks!"

"Not really into dicks?" Mindy replied. "Maybe you noticed?"

"But those are *boy* dicks," Lucia corrected in her own voice. "This is *my* dick." She poked her head around the door, apparently just to show off her glowing smile. The rest of her followed to show off the rest of her. Lucia was right—it was worth seeing.

Now that she bought her body paint in bulk, Lucia gave all of her skin the Goth look. It wasn't totally white, but a milky, creamy hue that seemed *real*. Not cold or dead, but ethereal. Mindy felt guilty about her urge to just *look* at Lucia: so goddamn gorgeous, even with a big ugly hunk of silicone strapped to her crotch. "Did you take off your underwear or were you wearing any at all?"

Lucia rolled her eyes. "I've never minded being naked."

"Yeah, why would you?" Mindy took a deep breath and gave into her chill, wrapping her arms around herself to warm up. She rubbed at her upper arms. And there was Lucia, not cold at all—her skin as pure and pale as paper waiting for ink. Waiting for Mindy to write on it with kisses and touches and fingernails—and make the otherworldly *earthly* once more. Mindy barely felt qualified. "Would you take it personally if I were nervous?"

"No. People get nervous. I used to be nervous all the time. It was scary being human."

"You still are human."

Lucia cocked her head toward the bathroom mirror, where her reflection was just the vacant makeup on an invisible face. "I think I only get partial credit on that one."

"Were you nervous your first time?"

Lucia sat on the bathroom counter—Mindy thinking better of pointing out that she didn't want her butt that close to her toothbrush. Lucia's dildo poked up from her lap like a toy poodle. She almost looked like she was thinking of petting it. "This isn't your first time, Minz. You're not a virgin. All that stuff we did—I still think about our first night together. You were really perfect." She snapped her fingers, a thought coming to her. "That must be what it's like to have sex with me…"

"Look, I know it's a meaningless distinction, but it's my meaningless distinction. I'm sure you were nervous the first time a guy ate you out or whatever, but wasn't there a different nervous when you…got the *D*."

"I didn't get eaten out before I took the *D*."

Mindy frowned. "You didn't?"

"Nope."

"Fingers, then?"

"Nuh-uh."

"So, your first just—shoved it in?"

"He didn't pull out an IKEA manual and say 'Congrats, you're a slut now,' but yeah. I had a penis inside me before any other body part that wasn't mine."

"Didn't it hurt?"

"Yeah. And I bled like a rat stole my tampon. But I don't even give a shit now, I'm so next-level these days. Like, why should I care what happened in junior high when these days I'm dating you, and it's like we're in some lesbian Nicholas Sparks porno?"

Lucia was babbling. She always seemed so confident, but Mindy could tell now that when she babbled, she was putting up a wall of conversation to keep anyone from thinking about her too hard. So Mindy sat up. The sheet fell down her body.

Mindy blushed—Lucia's eyes were so eager, drinking her in like she'd never seen anything so beautiful. Lucia walked out of the bathroom like she was spellbound, climbing up onto the mattress with one step, walking over Mindy, then pulling her to her feet, pressing her to the wall above the bed. kissing her, pinning her there, hands petting her face and losing themselves in her hair, soothing Mindy until she'd let Lucia do anything to her.

Mindy let Lucia suck at her neck—she did that even without a cut, loving the scent of the blood almost as much as its taste. She felt pampered, comfortable, and unafraid of the dildo. She cared more about what was going through Lucia's head. "I just don't want you to think I'm about the cock. I'm not about the cock, I'm about you. This isn't about that, it's just something I thought we could try."

"I want to, Minz. I've wanted to for a while... Never thought to say something because I've done enough to scare you off for a few years. But I *really* like the thought of taking you just one more way. Just like I was the first one to feel you. The first one to taste you."

As if sensing her reluctance, Lucia kept kissing her, burning away the chill of her body on Mindy's warm flesh, the friction growing intoxicating. Then she rubbed the head of the dildo over Mindy's labia, her teeth cold and hard on Mindy's collarbone. Mindy wanted them both.

"Let them kill me," Lucia said, her words on Mindy's chest a steady breeze of cool air, no heat, like Lucia was just blowing on her. "Let them get you when you're done mourning and you move on. Date a man or a woman, I don't care. Because whatever they do, I'll have done first. And whenever you come, you'll think of how I made you come harder. Lie down. Spread your legs. I'm your boyfriend now."

"I... I can't."

"Yeah?" Lucia turned around, immediately backed up, offering her back to Mindy like she was the one that would bite her. An arm coiling up around Mindy's head, she undulated her belly. Her entire body working and flexing, clenching and coiling, Mindy's eyes pulled to the dance. Lucia was giving her a lapdance where she stood. "What if you're on top?"

"On top?"

Lucia bent over double, touching her toes with her ass up in the air against Mindy's crotch, rippling and swaying and letting Mindy *touch*—then she slowly drew herself back up, swaying to the beat of her own music, but never fast enough for Mindy's hand not to keep up.

"I lie down. You, cowgirl up. You can do it nice and slow. Ride me like you stole me. Which ya did."

God, that was just not a fair fucking offer. Lucia turned to the side and cocked a grin and wink over her shoulder, hip waggling against Mindy's groin in a slow grind.

"Do you even do that?" Mindy asked in an inappropriate moan before she managed to get her voice less squeaky. "Be the…bottom?"

"I don't want you just to have orgasms this one way because it's my thing, Minz, I want to find out what works for you. It'll make me feel like such an awesome girlfriend when you're one big puddle of satisfaction."

*Puddle of satisfaction* echoed in Mindy's vagina—she could just see herself lying there, all fucked out, Lucia with a saucy little smile like Mindy was just a cute kitten that had amused her. Mindy felt the leather of the strap-on on Lucia's waist bucking over her groin, and fuck, that was worth the pain. Lucia was worth the pain.

She was kissing Lucia, she was touching her, she was pushing her down onto the bed and if the leg she threw over Lucia wasn't a perfect slender pillar of alabaster flesh, it was one-half of the pair Lucia had chosen to get between.

"Don't go too fast," Lucia warned, concern freeing her eyes from their sultry stare. "I know. I'm super-hot, but slow and steady, Minz."

"You want me to fuck you like a tortoise?" Mindy had a hold on the strap-on, keeping it pointed upward. She lowered herself down—okay, okay—*don't fucking freak out*—it touched her, just like it had before, but this time a fresh wave of anxiety hit because she was doing it to herself. Mindy could've laughed; she trusted Lucia more than herself. Okay. Okay, okay, okay. She bit her lip, bent her legs another half-inch—oh! She just opened right up for it. Like it was a tampon. A really big tampon… Yes, that comparison was helping.

Lucia petted her thigh, reached up to stroke her face. Touch light, tempting. Every stroke downward. Motioning her in. To where Lucia was waiting to turn her into *one big puddle of satisfaction.*

Another half inch. Mindy gasped. It wasn't totally weird, it reminded her a little of Lucia's fingers, but they'd been like her own fingers (only more so), and Mindy had gotten used to that good-weird feeling back when Robert Downey Jr. was a cokehead. The little—*protuberance* wasn't her fingers but-with-extra-Lucia, it was much more, the shape strange, the feel terrifying. It couldn't be fingers; her body quailed like it was an entire fist.

Lucia's honeyed voice started in. "You're okay. You're doing great. Go as slow as you want, okay? Don't think about it—it's just a part of me, okay? See? I'm touching you here." She ran her fingers down Mindy's chest. "And I'm touching you here." She gave her hips a miniscule rock, jogging the dildo's head inside Mindy. A twitch that was neither pain nor pleasure made Mindy wince. "It's just me, Minz. You can let me in, can't you?"

Mindy kept going—down, down, down, into an abyss. Only, she wasn't falling, the abyss was inside her. She was letting something fall into her and she had so much *room*... All the while, Lucia tickling, teasing, poking, and prodding, keeping Mindy seeing her. Only her. The dildo was just part of Lucia, pulled into her like the blood they'd stolen, and now Mindy was consuming it, her needful body devouring it. A second-hand vampire.

When she was straddling Lucia, the dildo *in* her, that heft and weight and length and hardness all hers, it came as a shock. Her body clenched at the realization that it was all inside her, and Lucia saw it, exploited it, an owl diving for a midnight mouse. She worked her hips in a slow, unfurling pump, and Mindy crested the wave of her body and wrung an orgasm from something *else* that she had made *herself.*

Mindy fell, catching herself on two hands in the long raven hair spread across the pillow, leaning over Lucia, drawn down to her like she was bowing to an idol that someone had erected just underneath her. Lucia's hands were on her hips, holding her tight, holding her around *it* but not moving yet. Just letting Mindy stretch and open and be *fucked.*

Another motion. Mindy's arms gave, and she crashed down onto Lucia, being kissed hard enough to draw blood. Lucia sucked hard on the needling cut in Mindy's lower lip. A moan started in one of them and continued in the other. Lucia was beginning to buck and writhe. The dildo in Mindy began touching places, striking up sparks here and there, making Mindy ride to keep it between her thighs.

She swayed and danced to the beat Lucia's hips set, rocking up into her. Mindy kept kissing her, and Lucia kept being so damn good to kiss, and Mindy finally just had to stop, ripped herself up from Lucia and hung back in the saddle, just letting Lucia throb into her.

"You need to come," Lucia said hoarsely, as Mindy floated weightless, thoughtless—her husky voice making Mindy's toes curl, shackling her to an orgasm that Mindy knew would rip right through this serene give-and-take pleasure. "I want you to come for me right now."

Mindy stared into Lucia's eyes as the other woman pumped into her, holding her in place with her hands and driving into her with her hips. Somehow, the eye contact made it feel better. It couldn't possibly hurt when Mindy could look into the endless blue of Lucia's eyes and see nothing but love and affection. She reached down, cupped Lucia's cheek, put her thumb in Lucia's mouth—she felt Lucia kiss it, suck it, her whole body aching for Mindy, wanting to pull her inside. Then there was a sudden, sharp pain in the pad of her thumb and Mindy yanked it back; it was now bright red with blood.

"Shit!"

"Sorry, sorry!"

"Don't stop!"

Then a halt. Full stop. The dildo burning inside Mindy, Mindy exploding around it, but not flying apart—just continuously *exploding* like that was actually possible.

Lucia drew herself out, hands on Mindy's hips to hold her up as Lucia denied her their fuck, pulling it away from her, painfully slow. Then, still agonizingly *not-fast-enough,* she went back into her. Deeper. Deeper. Little ridges and bumps, but no friction, just a sweet slide inside her. Mindy was coming by the time it was halfway in, whatever muscles she had inside her pulling at what Lucia was giving, Mindy needing it to make her whole. Her ecstasy lengthened like a shadow at sunset. Drawn out by the small eternity it took Lucia to hit home between her legs.

Lucia smiled like the sun. "I'm so proud of you—you got it all in—you took *all of it.*"

Mindy actually found herself blushing. Really didn't seem like the matching pair of facial expressions to have while dildos were being used. "It was you, right? Just a part of you —like the fangs and the skin and everything…" She looked at her thumb, a nasty cut on it, but nothing a Band-Aid wouldn't cure. "Goddamn…"

"Sorry," Lucia said, "I just…"

"It's alright. Just a little warning next time?"

Lucia nodded, but couldn't resist smirking.

Mindy could just tell it was because Lucia could feel her slickness coating the fronts of her thighs. Mindy worked herself off the dildo, that simple motion setting blood pounding in her ears, and she collapsed back down to Lucia's chest. Skin cool as the pillow's flipside. She took deep gulps of air, smelling the slight coppery scent of Lucia.

"I'm sore," she moaned. It didn't really hurt, but she played up the lingering discomfort. Let Lucia pet her and tut "poor baby" and get her cold bottled water off the nightstand. Lucia had *colonized* it before going to the bathtub. There was even a box of Band-Aids, one of which Lucia applied to Mindy's wounded thumb followed by a little kiss.

Lucia put her thigh between Mindy's legs. The chill was like a cold compress. She uncapped the bottle, the outside dotted with beads of condensation, and held it to Mindy's lips. She drank greedily, thinking she must've sweated out at least a liter. Lucia canted the bottle away so Mindy didn't drink too much, petted her sweaty hair, fed Mindy a little more as she sucked the sweat off her fingers.

"Still sore?" Lucia asked, and Mindy nodded. "Let me kiss it and make it better."

She wiggled down the bed like a snake in reverse, thoughtfully pulling the sheets up over Mindy before she ducked under them. Mindy instantly gasped. Lucia was massaging her thighs, kissing her labia, setting up a gentle lapping motion with her tongue that drove all the aching out of her tightly pinched sex.

"Right, you're bleeding a little," Lucia reported, Mindy holding up the sheet to look at her. "But *a little*—a little. Jerry Steakley bled more when he lost that tooth in the third grade, and you're not crying like a little bitch, so…"

Lucia licked but didn't seem to even care about the blood, just dulling the ache. She was *with* Mindy, holding their eye contact, touching her gently until

Mindy let the sheet drop and felt nothing but her soreness receding, a cool constant comfort filling her body.

"What did you mean?" Mindy asked, feeling sweaty and blotchy and perfect and puffy and beautiful, "'let them kill me'?"

Lucia's head raised under the covers—a ghost haunting Mindy's vagina. She kept up a soft rub on and over Mindy's legs. "I don't know… Vampires don't age, right? And I don't have to worry about accidentally opening a window during sun-up. So, the only way I'm going out is if someone stakes me. And I think that's more likely than me living it up until the zombie apocalypse. Is this really the best time?"

"Well, you're not going anywhere."

Lucia grinned, just visible through the sheer bedsheet. "True enough." Then, still smiling: "I'm a vampire, Minz. I'm going down. I just don't want to take you with me."

"Maybe I want to go down with you."

Lucia snickered.

"You're thinking about sex, aren't you?"

Lucia gave her a look like *Can you blame me?* The look she used to try and get away with everything. Then she broke into more laughter. "Are you sure you don't want to get off instead of going down with me?"

"Honestly, it's like dating a dude. I am so hetero right now, I should run for president."

"You've got my vote." Lucia did something with her lips that Mindy couldn't adequately describe but that left her cross-eyed. "And my big, black cock…"

"El…" Mindy muttered, though she didn't know if she was giving a warning or—Lucia was licking at her sex fast, not comforting Mindy anymore but arousing her, starting her up all over again.

Lucia threw the sheets off them, rising up over Mindy again in all her splendor, all her perfection, a blinding light in the darkness. When she asked, "Wanna keep going?" It was almost anticlimactic. Goddesses didn't ask you whether you were up for round two, they just—had you.

"I don't think I can move," Mindy said apologetically.

"I'll do the moving," Lucia replied and turned Mindy over. And just *looked* at her, so hard Mindy could feel it. Lucia's voice shook with sudden seriousness. "If you're going to ask me to stop, you'd better ask now."

"Will you be able to later?"

"I don't know. I don't want to…"

"I trust you. Do it. I trust you."

Mindy didn't find out what would happen if she asked Lucia to stop. She never thought to.

# CHAPTER 23

Mindy woke up to a fingernail raking over her shoulder. It'd been going on for a while and she'd gotten used to it—the feeling bleeding through into her dream, where she was a pile of leaves being raked. But this time, it'd been too hard and blood had been drawn.

"Sorry," Lucia said unapologetically, leaning over to lick up the scant blood.

Mindy blinked awake, taking in the mellow dawn light. Downstairs a coffeemaker chugged, and cereal poured from the box into a bowl, but up here, in her bed, she heard the soft thump of a heartbeat that wasn't her own.

"Is your heart beating?"

"Huh?" Lucia looked at her rising, falling breasts, pausing to admire them. "Oh yeah. It does that when I have fresh blood." She leaned in to nuzzle at Mindy's face, all kittenish. "Good dreams? Maybe about your super-hot girlfriend who loves hardcore fucking?"

"Yeah. I dreamt you had two heads."

"I'd be twice as pretty, but I'd have to spend twice as much on makeup." Lucia's lip curled. "Tough call."

"Hey, were you watching me sleep?" Mindy asked, beaching herself further up on her pillow as she came more awake.

"Yeah. It was super boring. I'm not sure how Edward Cullen does it." More blood beaded on the small cut, and Lucia kissed it away.

They were under the sheets, only some of the dim light making it in. It landed on Lucia's body, where sweat and touch had smeared her makeup, sending little sparkles rippling around her skin. Mindy followed one with her fingertip, plucking at Lucia's skin with her nail. Nothing happened. No white line. She felt like she couldn't break the skin if she tried.

"Can you even feel it?" she asked.

"For now," Lucia replied. She responded in kind to Mindy, drawing a cross on her skin in the white carvings of her fingernail. As soon as it was complete, Mindy felt Lucia stiffen. "You think it's all in my head?"

Mindy turned over so it couldn't hurt her. "If it's a choice between it being some trauma and you being some kind of…" Mindy winced just thinking of the words she might use. "I don't feel like you're unholy."

"Sometimes I do." She drew a cross on Mindy's arm, then another, then another. Their sudden presence made her shake. "I had a dream that you didn't want me anymore, so you got them tattooed all over your body."

Mindy took Lucia's wrist with one hand, rubbed at the marks with the other, massaging the crosses back into her skin. "I would never do that. I wouldn't even need to—you'd stay away if I asked."

"How can you trust me, Minz? I don't even trust myself." Lucia's hand went back to work, picking at the Band-Aid on her neck to examine the bite marks. With Lucia's saliva at work, they had healed fast. "I wish I could be human for you."

Mindy pulled Lucia into a tight hug, breaking her cold with body warmth, feeling Lucia give in and rub her back, beginning to kiss her chest.

No knock, the knob just turned and the door opened. "Sorry to bother you, Sleeping Beauty, I just need to borrow your car…" Her mom froze. Mindy froze, feeling like she'd just swallowed an ice cube tray. And Lucia smiled politely.

"Hi, Mrs. M, me and Minz were just having a sleepover."

A look of profound disbelief interrupted her mom's shock. "You're naked!"

Lucia shrugged. "I sleep in the nude."

"You're wearing a strap-on!"

Lucia laughed and waved her mom off. "I was having intercourse with your daughter!" She paused. "That was such a bad excuse."

Her mom managed to move enough to point a finger. "Both of you, dressed, downstairs, *now.*"

The door slammed shut behind her. Mindy wondered if she still needed her keys.

Downstairs, they sat at the breakfast nook while her mom explained things to her dad. Mindy could hear their "discussion voices" through the kitchen door. She felt angry, but not in any discernible direction. Usually when she got in trouble—which *did* happen—there was a sense of shame. For all that Mrs.

Murphy was a mom worthy of Austin, she could swing a guilt trip with the best of them. But what did she have to be ashamed of, sleeping with Lucia? It was her choice. What, were they expecting her to wait for Texas to legalize gay marriage, then marry Lucia, *then* sleep with her?

"I'm hungry," Lucia said, looking all-around disgruntled at being forced into a flannel shirt and some of Mindy's mom's jeans. "Do your parents keep any Pop-Tarts around? Maybe an Eggo?"

"Not a great time, El."

"It's before noon. I think breakfast is still an option…"

"They caught us *having sex,* Lucia!"

"Don't be overdramatic, they caught us after we had sex. Can you imagine how frustrated I'd be if they had interrupted during? Unless they'd let us finish before they started yelling. That's what I would do if I were a parent. Like, what, are you not gonna be a slut if there isn't an orgasm? No—"

"*How can you be so calm?*" Mindy interrupted, having to grind her voice down to keep from shouting.

Lucia took Mindy's hands. "Because it's no big deal! I mean, you were going to tell them sooner or later, right? At least this way, there's no awkward monologue—two girls, in bed together, naked, strap-on. Speaks for itself."

"Yes! Yes, that's what I'm concerned about! I don't know a lot about dating, but I know that you have to ease parents into it. First you say you like a boy, then that you're going on a date, then that you're going to a dance, and at some point, oh, I don't know." Mindy wagged her head about. "'I guess I'm not a virgin, huh?' They still think this is a phase! *They don't even know I'm a lesbian!*"

"Well, it's not like it was the biggest secret in the world. I mean, look at your shoes."

"What's wrong with my shoes?"

"Nothing. I would wear those shoes…if I were a boy…"

Mindy made a noise that wasn't quite a groan and wasn't quite a growl. She had no idea how she could be so in love with Lucia one minute and then the next, Lucia turned into a total asshole that drove her crazy. It was like watching *Once Upon A Time* or something.

Lucia opened her arms wide. "Come here. Come to my bosom." When Mindy didn't come to her bosom fast enough for Lucia's satisfaction, Lucia embraced her anyway. "Listen, here's what they're talking about right now: 'Yeah, sure, Mindy's a lesbian—but look at how cute her same-sex lover is!' I'm a *cheerleader!* But like a cool goth cheerleader who reads Proust or some shit!"

"You don't even know who Proust is."

"He invented Tic-Tacs. *Anyway,* if you were his firstborn son and he caught you naked in bed with me, your dad would be pouring you a shot right now. You'd be smoking cigars and going trout-fishing... I don't know, I'm not good at boys, I'm a lesbian now. *Point is,* yeah, there's a little cognitive dissonance because we're both women, but if his daughter has to date a woman, there's me and then there's Angelina Jolie. And have you seen how thin Angie is these days? It's kinda creepy. Plus, what's with all the little kids—"

Mindy jerked away from Lucia.

"I want you to take this seriously!"

"I am taking it seriously!" Lucia protested. "You're just overreacting. The truth is, right now, your dad is thinking that if he were thirty years younger and a woman and a lesbian, he'd wanna do me too."

"*Please* don't talk about my dad finding you hot."

"I'm sure your mom's going, 'If I had to do it with a woman'—"

"No, not either of my parents!"

"I'm not saying they're sniffing my panties or anything..."

"I swear to Christ, they are not gonna need to forbid me or ground me or anything, because I am never having sex again. I can feel my ovaries shriveling like a raisin in the sun."

"Oh, I saw that! Did Proust write that?"

"No."

"Darn."

Mindy took a deep breath. "Is that really what they're saying? That you're a catch and they're proud of me and—all that?"

"Uh, no."

Mindy's eyes narrowed. "You're not listening to them?"

"No, I'm talking to you."

"You have super-hearing. Why aren't you listening in on them?"

"Well, I didn't think to, Mindy, I was hungry. Say, do you have any PopTarts?"

"Even if we did," Mindy hissed, "do you really think my parents would be cool with you grabbing breakfast?"

"Hey, I took their daughter's virginity, what's a toaster strudel next to that?"

Mr. and Mrs. Murphy came back in then. They both looked serious and distantly lost—that mix of confusion and bitterness it seemed you only got from parents. It gave them good poker faces. Moving in fumbling lockstep like it was a dance they'd discussed but never practiced, Mr. Murphy filled a carafe with water from the refrigerator while Mrs. Murphy stood before the table.

"Hi kids, I just wanted to apologize for worrying you, we weren't…we're *not* mad. We would just like to have a safe, reasonable discussion about certain matters…of a sexual nature. You might say. So we're going to have a family meeting, which will include our guest." She nodded to Lucia. "And we are not going to yell or fight or make ultimatums, we're just going to talk about what's been going on and what our response should be as a family, and as Lucia." She nodded to Lucia again.

Mr. Murphy brought the carafe and four cups. They all sat down, the girls against the window, fenced in.

Mrs. Murphy reached into her pocket, bringing out a seashell. "Now this is the Talking Shell."

"Mom, not the Talking Shell," Mindy protested.

"*Mindy*," Mrs. Murphy said archly, "does not have the Talking Shell, and so she is not allowed to speak. That's because this is a discussion, and not an argument with everyone talking over each other. Now, before we begin, does anyone have something they would like to say?"

Mr. Murphy and Mindy looked identically downcast. Lucia raised her hand.

Mrs. Murphy passed her the shell. "You don't have to raise your hand, Lucia, you can just ask for the shell."

"Oh. Okay." Lucia took it. "I'd just like to say, first off, and I don't know if this helps, but Mindy isn't, you know…a slut or anything—"

"We don't like to use judgmental words," Mr. Murphy said.

"Talking Shell," Mrs. Murphy interrupted his interruption.

"I can respond without the Talking Shell."

"You should keep it to a minimum, dear, otherwise there's no point—"

"You're the one who's talking now—"

"You said we can respond—"

"Little response, little response."

"Guys!" Lucia interjected, holding up the shell. "I get it, nothing wrong with being a slut, but Mindy isn't passing it around. Just so you know. I'm pretty sure I'm the only one she's lesbianing with..."

"Pretty sure?" Mindy muttered.

"Talking Shell," Mrs. Murphy said.

"Little response," Mindy retorted, and they both fell silent. All eyes were on Lucia.

"Oh, me again? Yeah, and she didn't throw it at me either. We'd been—we have been—dating for a while."

"Can I have the Talking Shell?" Mr. Murphy asked.

Lucia passed it to him. "This is working out well, I like this."

"So, how long is a while?" Mr. Murphy asked. "A year, the better part of a year, more than a year? How long have you been keeping this relationship a secret from us?" He pushed the Talking Shell to Mindy.

"I don't want it."

"Mindy, take the Talking Shell," Mrs. Murphy said.

Gritting her teeth, Mindy put a finger on the shell. "It's, uh, it's hard to say, because we weren't really officially dating or—it's like, we were really good friends for a long time, and then we kissed, and then we went back to being friends, and then we had a fight, and then we went back to being friends, and then it got..." Mindy spoke like someone was performing the Heimlich maneuver on her, "sexual."

Lucia jumped. "It's like we were having a sleepover, and it was so much fun, we thought if we could just add boning to it, it would be the perfect relationship."

"Lucia, you don't have the Talking Shell," Mrs. Murphy chided gently.

"I'm piggybacking on Mindy's Talking Shell. That's not allowed?" They shook their heads. "But I'm agreeing with her!"

Mrs. Murphy held out her hand. Mindy gave her the shell before sagging back in her chair.

"I think these recriminations aren't helping us get to a place that we'd like to be at… But it's safe to say you have been going out for a while, Mindy and Lucia?"

They nodded.

"So, it wasn't just a fling?"

They shook their heads.

"Or an experiment, because everyone experiments. Abraham Lincoln experimented. It doesn't mean he didn't love Mary Todd…"

Mindy shook her head. Lucia said, "Actually, the dildo *was* an experiment—"

Mindy stomped on her toes. "I think it would be best if you waited for the Talking Shell."

"Yeah, Talking Shell, okay."

"Alright," Mrs. Murphy broke in, "so, we are going to be discussing your relationship and how this family is affected by your relationship. Donald, is there anything you'd like to say?"

"Nope," Mr. Murphy said. His arms were crossed. His eyes were aimed at Lucia. It did not look like he was thinking about what a catch she was.

"Alright then. I'll give up the Talking Shell soon, but right now, I would just like to say that Mindy, we're not angry with you, we're not disappointed, and we obviously support you having whatever sexuality you were born with."

"Thanks, guys." Lucia nodded awkwardly.

"And Lucia. We'd like to talk to your parents about this issue… Do you think that would be safe for you? Does your mother know about your orientation?"

Lucia shrugged. "I don't know that she cares? Like, that I'm a lesbian—or about lesbians… I've never heard her say anything bad about the gays, but it's not like she watches *Rizzoli & Isles* or anything."

"Alright. So for now, we'll just keep this between ourselves, and we'll see about Mrs. West later."

"I can post some gay stuff on her Facebook wall," Mr. Murphy said, "see if she bites."

"Good thinking, Donald."

He poured some water into his cup and drank.

Mrs. Murphy drummed her fingers on the Talking Shell. "Now, Mindy— Mindy, it is just fine and we support you making relationships and expressing your sexuality and just…having orgasms. Orgasms are great, they're healthy. Donald and I—"

"If I steal the Talking Shell, do you have to stop talking?"

"Mindy, that rudeness is not in the spirit of family meeting!" Mrs. Murphy wagged her finger.

Mindy grimaced. "Sorry, Mom."

"That's okay. As I was saying, there's nothing wrong with sex or dating or kissing or whatever you do. However, we are still your parents and it is still our job to…parent you. And that includes first, setting boundaries and second, being aware of what is going on in your life. And you have made that very difficult for us, young lady. And that was a deliberate action on your part, and it doesn't matter that you were lying about having sex or smoking crack or whatever, you were deceiving us."

"I didn't…" Mindy brought herself up short and gestured for the Talking Shaell. Mrs. Murphy gave it to her with a nod. "I didn't lie. It's not like you ever asked me—"

"Are there any gorgeous ex-cheerleaders desperately in love with you?" Lucia finished for her.

"Am I dating Lucia?" Mindy finished for herself. "I'm eighteen, it's my business, and she's great." Mindy turned to Lucia. "Look at her. She's great."

Lucia beamed as much as she was able with Mindy's parents scrutinizing her.

"We don't have a problem with you dating Lucia," Mrs. Murphy said. She'd taken back the Talking Shell. "Or any woman for that matter… You do identify as a woman, don't you, sweetie?" she asked Lucia.

"What else would I be?" Lucia looked around. "A vampire? I'm not a vampire."

"Well, you know, gender is a fluid thing…"

"Mom, she's a woman, okay? And I'm dating her. What's the big deal?"

Mr. Murphy requested the Talking Shell and got it. "Lucia, are you wearing glitter?"

Lucia looked at her arm, which had caught some sunlight and sparkled. "Maybe."

Two hours later, her parents seemed satisfied with Mindy talking about her feelings and having gotten painfully specific on the dangers of STDs and STIs, which were apparently another thing. She didn't get a blanket approval to finger-bang Lucia or anything, but they seemed reasonably certain by the end that Mindy wasn't going to get pregnant during a threesome, get abused by Lucia, get choked out during bondage play without a safe word, or set herself on fire with flammable massage oils. Apparently, flammable and inflammable mean the exact same thing.

Mindy still thought they were watching, having an aftershock discussion in the kitchen while she sat with Lucia out on the porch. But she didn't mind. She couldn't mind much when she was holding Lucia's hands. "I don't think my 'rents like your sense of humor."

"Which is weird, cuz I'm funny as hell."

Mindy nodded. "So, you're pretty sure I haven't been fucking other women behind your back?"

"Hey, I was pretty sure there weren't any vampires in the world either. Never say never."

Mindy squeezed Lucia's hand, hard enough to silence her. "I don't want to fight."

"I don't either! Why am I the one that wants to fight?"

"Lucia…" Mindy picked up Lucia's hand and brought it to her lap, petting her fingers along its wrist, staring into Lucia's eyes. After a moment, Lucia gave in and relaxed. She leaned back against the swing. "Lucia, I know it's been a while since you've slept alone, but would you be alright if tonight you stayed in your own room?"

Lucia stayed bolt upright where she sat, but she kicked the ground so the swing went a little harder. "Yeah, why wouldn't I be? I love sleeping alone. *Love it.*"

"It's not what I want, it's just that after today, my parents are absolutely going to be poking their heads into my room—"

"And so what? What'll they do if they find out their daughter is a little spoon? Call the cops on me?"

"I don't know what they'll do. They're not bad people, I just don't want—I think it's best if we don't provoke them."

"How is it a provocation— it has nothing to do with them, it's you and me and we love each other…"

Mindy squeezed Lucia's hand tighter. "It's not forever, okay, it's just while they get used to the idea."

"*No,*" Lucia said blankly, overpowering Mindy's last word. "That isn't…" She blinked repeatedly. "I need you, Mindy. I can't just *stop* needing you because it's inconvenient."

"It's just for tonight—"

"Oh, don't *lie,* you're not gonna be celibate for one night and then have me bust out the Vaseline tomorrow."

"Okay, maybe a week—maybe two. Just to show them that we respect—"

"*You* respect—"

"Respect their rules, and I am not breaking up with you, Lucia, we'll still see each other, I just can't—"

"*You can't.* You can't…" Lucia nodded fiercely, like Mindy had confirmed some thought in her head. "I can't walk out in the sun without taking a bath in makeup. I can't go to church. I can't be around someone with a bloody nose without wanting to eat them. And you—you can't stand up to your parents."

"I would stand up to them if they were being unreasonable."

"But they're not, are they? *You are.* You're ashamed of me. I made you come like a fucking sprinkler last night, and now you want to put me away like a dildo."

Mindy fixed her with a stare. "You can calm down right now if you want to keep having this conversation."

Lucia was trembling. "I have never been the girl that parents approve of. They look at the way I dress and the way I talk and they think *slut.* And I'm fine with that. But with your parents, I could wear the floral dresses and bake pies and talk all G-rated like a Disney movie, and they will still never approve of me because I'm a girl."

"They're not like that."

Lucia pushed her fist into her face, biting her knuckles as Mindy rubbed at her thigh and tried to figure out how to get rid of the black hole in Lucia's stomach when she still had her own.

"We should just go," Lucia said. "Get our GEDs and *go*. I don't want to be in this town when there's some vampire targeting you…"

"Or we wait until graduation and get into a college that doesn't send their diplomas by mail."

"Or we check out Principal Haywood. See how she likes her stake."

"Lucia, no," Mindy said humorlessly. "I'm not going through the whole Bakula thing with you again."

"I'm just saying, we should check her out. If the opportunity presents itself. We're going to the dance, she'll be at the dance—"

"We'll see," Mindy promised. "We'll go to the dance and we'll have a nice time and after that, if you still wanna drop out of high school and run away together—"

"And join the circus," Lucia suggested wryly. "Don't forget joining the circus."

Mindy smiled back at her. "Yeah. But before we leave, I'm having a nice dance with my girlfriend, just like any other normal high school student."

"Minz," Lucia said, "if you were normal, you really think I'd be dating you?"

# CHAPTER 24

Mindy couldn't wait to see Lucia's dress. She'd bought it months ago, at some sale so good it was practically grand larceny, and kept it in the back of her closet, refusing to let even Mindy look at it. She'd said she was saving it for prom, but that'd died a quiet death. Now she said she was wearing it to the Sadie Hawkins Dance.

Lucia was fashionably late, however. Mindy went with Seb. A text glowing on her phone told her she had no idea how hard it was to apply eyeliner without a reflection.

The theme of the dance was fairy tales. It was done up with all the hallmarks of an enchanted forest. Potted plants lined the floor, poster-board tree branches were taped up to the wall along with string lights. A cardboard castle covered the closed-up bleachers with a plush dragon on top of it. And, of course, Nicki Minaj music.

The tables had flowers wreathed around candles, and actually really looked great, Mindy was very impressed. The boys wore rented tuxes, the girls mostly dresses, with some in masquerade garb as Snow White, Sleeping Beauty, even Pocahontas, which seemed a bit offensive. Mindy was just Mindy. And Seb, as always, was just Seb.

She sent Lucia a text while he got her punch. *No one with superspeed should be this late.*

No reply. She wasn't the only one checking her phone. The boys kept to one wall, girls to the other. Snippets of a conversation about *Call of Duty* came from one side, opposite the pings of texts arriving and being sent. Mindy was in the middle, where the chips were.

"Do you think I'm cool?" Seb asked.

"Mm?" Mindy was checking her phone again. "Yeah. Sure."

"No, for really. Would I be described as cool if you were describing my coolness?"

Mindy put away her phone. "Yes, Seb. You're cool. You're like Jon Hamm with a slightly smaller dick."

"I'm offended by your sarcasm on both personal level and on behalf of Mr. Hamm."

Mindy couldn't get too drawn into the repartee. It was pathetic, she knew, but she opened up her phone again and sent Lucia another text. *I'm turning into a pumpkin here.*

The DJ tried a new song, speakers exploding with Rihanna. Mindy felt the wood floor pounding the beat into her shoes. Boys and girls started to drift together, while Mindy leaned back against the buffet table, staring up at the ceiling. It'd been decorated with strings of silver tassel, florescent stars, and a box of glitter attached to the air vent so that whenever it blew fresh air in, a shower of sparkles went with it. It was great. The perfect, cheesy setting for a high school dance. Only Mindy couldn't enjoy it.

*L?* She sent again. *You're starting to worry me.*

The AC came on again, spritzing Mindy with glitter. She had to brush some off her chip. One of the banners came loose and a chaperone had to climb the bleachers to reset it. A big mural of Rivendell. LOTR Club's contribution to the dance.

"I do trying to be cool," Seb said. "Would I be cooler if I did not trying to be cool?"

"You know what? Dance with me. That's at least cooler than standing around."

"Really?" Seb asked, not sounding enthused, which was, of course, just the reaction Mindy looked for when she asked someone to dance.

"I'm not going to a dance and not dancing with anyone. I'm not eleven years old anymore. I mean, it'd just be as friends, right? No—love triangle stuff, *right?*"

"You're a lesbian, you have girlfriend. I do not think love triangle would happen."

"You don't watch a lot of TV, do ya, Seb?"

She took his hand, leading him onto the dance floor. Pleased that it was sweaty by the time they got there. The speakers were pumping out something hard and dancey, a thudding bass pounding into their skins, hard to get comfortable with. They had to dance it out. On the floor, Seb shook himself off, limbering up, and tried to set up something not too awkward. Mindy followed suit. She wouldn't really call it dancing. But her skirt blurred as she twirled around, her arms and legs sweated silver as she flailed them, and she caught some interested glances from the sidelines. More for Seb than for her.

"I'm pretty sure Mia King is giving you the eye," she told Seb as they shook it out. "When she asks you for the next dance, try to use contractions."

"Why would Mia King wanting to dance with me?"

"*Want* to dance with you, Seb, why would she *want* to dance with you? Nothing makes a girl think a guy is hotter than another girl thinking that guy is hot. I know, it's weird, but that's the whole thing with Benedict Cumberbatch, right there. I think it started as a joke and just snowballed out of control." Seb wasn't paying attention. No one was. He was looking over her shoulder, following the gaze of just about everyone else, out to the open door.

Lucia had arrived.

She'd washed the dye out of her hair like someone panning for gold, turning it into a thick velvet curtain just cresting her shoulders. Her movements, grown bold and aggressive over the past few weeks, were still confident, but now slow and graceful. As she stepped out of the evening gloom, her bronze skin shone half-burnished in the dim light. She wore a white Kaufman Franco column gown. Its floor-length hemline clung to her legs, showing them off, while the one-shouldered jersey side cowl toga loosened into light, airy folds, turning her sexuality into elegance. A dark belt and black gold earrings were the only slivers of night on her. If Mindy had never seen her before, it would've been love at first sight.

She moved heedlessly through the crowd, people automatically moving out of the way, her body swaying and rolling—not so much to the beat of the music, but like the beat was following her lead. She walked right across the dance floor, splitting up couples, sweeping aside suitors, until she was at Mindy.

"Mind if I cut in?"

"Not at all," Seb said, taking a step back. Lucia gave him a smile, maybe out of respect for his survival instinct.

"You came," Mindy said.

"You're mine, so I had to be yours."

That was as long as she could wait. Lucia took Mindy's hand. Her pulse sped up, her breath quickened to bring oxygen all the way to the fingers Lucia clutched. It put a playful quirk on the vampire's lips. Almost exposed her fangs. She led Mindy through the stomping of awkward teenage feet, all the couples doing the sway-and-pray, until they had their own little place. Then she moved one of Mindy's hands to her hip, locked another in her own fingers, and when she danced, Mindy danced. Everything else just fell away. Unimportant next to Lucia's smile.

"I didn't know white was your color," Mindy gasped.

"I didn't either." Lucia dipped Mindy and brought her back. "But I thought—why shouldn't it be?"

With their hands clasping and their bodies pressed together, Mindy thought about how people talked about love. A steamy affair. A warm hug. Hot sex. Always things for the living. But you loved people after they were gone, right? When they were cold. The world grew hot, it *burned,* and you retreated to the shade of memories. To the cold, dark places outside the light.

Mindy didn't *burn* for Lucia. She just needed her. In a world on fire, Lucia was cool relief. Everyone made room for their dance, backed away from *them.* They were so cold, you could burn yourself touching them. And Mindy had never felt so alive.

They didn't bother with small-talk. Nothing about movies or politics or homework or gossip or celebrities or Macy's Day sales. They were embedded in each other. Talking was just a reflex action.

"When I came to your house, that first night," Lucia said, simply, honestly, because there was no need to pretend. "I wanted to die in your arms."

"I know," Mindy replied.

"I thought it would feel like this."

They danced to Beyonce and Rihanna, Maroon 5 and Pink, Lady Antebellum and Shakey Graves—and, begrudgingly, to Taylor Swift. Until Mindy's feet hurt because she'd never broken in those sweet new heels, and Lucia took her to the folding chairs in the back of the gym and laid her down across two of them so Mindy's head was in her lap and Lucia could play with her hair. They watched everyone else try to dance as good as they had.

"Did we remember to teach Seb how to dance?" Mindy asked, watching him do something not quite a seizure with a band geek.

"Shit, I thought you were gonna do it," Lucia replied. She snapped her fingernails in Mindy's hair. "Got a nit."

"Do I?"

"Yeah." Lucia made her fingernails click again. "'Nother one. 'Nother one…"

Mindy grabbed her hand. Kissed her wrist. Lips putting a little pulse where it was meant to go. Wondering if a heart could beat for two people. Thinking she'd never used it much before Lucia came around anyway.

Coach Bakula stepped through the crowd, chaperoning in one of his lighter-duty suits. A bolo tie, even. He nodded to both of them, spoke reasonably. "Girls, Principal Haywood would like to see you."

Mindy felt her blood run cold.

In a few minutes, they were in the principal's office—the only light you could see in the school if you were driving by. Mindy's heart was pounding, sweat beading at her temples, her blood surging inside her skull. She wondered if Haywood could hear it. If it was tempting her. But no, that was ridiculous.

She took one look at Mindy and Lucia, shared a glance with Bakula, and said, "I'm going to have to eject you from the dance."

Lucia said nothing.

Mindy said, "What, why?"

Bakula was settling next to the door.

"I've heard from the chaperones that your dancing was inappropriate, and I can see that your clothing does not meet with the dress code."

"What the *WTF?*" Mindy barked. She'd never argued with a teacher before. It was easier than she would've thought. "She's wearing a floor-length gown, my dress is colored *champagne*."

"I can see the sides of her breasts," Haywood argued, hand moving at Lucia like she was flicking something toward her.

"You can see her armpit and that dumb tattoo she got on her ribs."

"My tattoo is awesome," Lucia said. She wasn't really listening. She was picking up a balancing eagle toy from Haywood's bookshelf, resting the beak on her finger and prodding the wings.

"It's distracting to the male students and inappropriate for a school function," Haywood argued. "We can't be seen to encourage this kind of behavior…"

"Lesbianism?"

"Sex."

"Are same-sex couples allowed at school functions?" Mindy demanded.

"If they follow school protocol."

"Protocol that isn't applied to straight couples."

"It is applied equally and fairly—"

"There were straight kids dry-humping on that dance floor, I don't see them in here!"

Lucia had the eagle balanced on her fingernail. "Do they have these as bats?"

Mindy turned around. "Lucia, could you please support me here?"

Lucia flicked her finger. The eagle went flying. "We're leaving. Your blood is young and fresh and flows as smooth as silk." Her eyes racketed to Principal Haywood. "Yours is old. It moves in your veins like cold syrup. Just pushing and pushing and…" Lucia moved a flattened hand forward in starts and stops. "Never getting anywhere. It's about ready to *stop*." Eyes went back to Mindy. "What more do you want?"

They left. Mindy paused in the doorway, taking out her compact she flicked it open, looking into the mirror but aiming it toward Haywood at her desk.

The chair where Haywood was sitting was empty.

"I am sorry," Haywood said, from beside her now—she'd come out from behind her desk. "I know how much fun these dances can be for young people. There'll be others…"

Mindy dropped her hand to her side. Glanced down to the compact in it, aimed upward. Saw Haywood's reflection right beside her. "Yeah. Can't wait."

# CHAPTER 25

Bakula went out with them, leading them to the front door. "I do apologize for that. It helps, when you're educating children, to know more than they do, but that's something we can't always have."

Mindy reached over to take Lucia's hands. "It's fine, I guess. I mean, we've still got each other."

"Yeah," Lucia said with a glance down at her hand in Mindy's. "This just means we can go home and bang sooner."

Mindy slapped at her.

They were at the school's padlocked doors. Bakula took out a key and unlocked them. "You are very wise for someone who has not yet graduated high school," he told Mindy, letting them out.

It was a chilly night out, but Mindy barely felt it. She didn't even feel Lucia put a jacket around her. She'd been *expecting* this. Expecting some dumb joke or a slur or an obscure rule. And she'd seen herself calmly, coolly shooting all of it down with a mix of rationalism and snark, rallying the proles to her side, having Rachel Maddow come down to interview her. Instead, she'd exited quietly out the back. And now she was walking to her car, feeling angry, and not even at *them*. At herself, for how ashamed she felt. Like she'd been conned into feeling shame.

"It's not Haywood," she said, like that was the reason her cheeks were burning, her ears were burning.

"I know," Lucia said. "I saw her reflection in the pictures on her desk. Think I would let her get close to you if I wasn't sure?"

"Shame. She could really use a stake through the heart."

"Don't worry about it," Lucia said. "School dances are lame anyway. The night is young. We'll drive down to Austin, I'll take you to the Hole In The Wall. I have a fake ID, and I took the bouncer's virginity. They have a pretty good band playing, if their website isn't out of date—Children of the Night."

"What music do they make?" Mindy asked.

"Punk-pop."

"Jesus."

"Don't pretend you're too good for punk-pop. You tried that with Selena Gomez, remember, and it did not work."

"I am not too good for Selena Gomez. I can only dream of the day I am." Mindy pulled the jacket tighter around her. They weren't going to the car. By mutual, unspoken decision, they were just walking around the desolate school. "You're taking this well. Usually you're a bit quicker to defend my honor."

Lucia shook her head. "I don't care about them. I care about you. And you don't care about them either."

Mindy straightened the jacket again. It was way too big for her. Too big for Lucia too, in fact. She checked it, finding it was a letterman jacket. "Where'd you get a letterman jacket?"

"From a letterman."

"El, am I wearing a dead guy's jacket?"

"*No.* The hospital got him stabilized."

"Quentin?"

"Yeah. He never asked for it back, so I guess it's mine now. And I want my girl to wear my letterman jacket."

"You want to be prom king too?" Mindy teased.

"You can be prom king. I have a thing for tiaras."

Mindy leaned over, rested her head on Lucia's shoulder, found Lucia slowing down so they could walk that way. "Take me away from all this."

"To a bar in Austin?"

"To a bar in Austin."

"We have to keep it weird, you know."

They cleared one of the couple of stretch limousines parked around the lot and saw a car idling at the edge of the schoolyard. A bubble light was on top, hitting them with red left hooks, blue right crosses. Card leaned against the car, lit up so thoroughly by the light it was like it was shining out of him.

Lucia trotted up to him, Mindy falling behind. As they came within earshot, Card reached into the car and flicked off the cherry top. Now the only light was from the light poles, burning everything yellow, and Card's cigarette crayoning his shadowy face red.

"Heard you had a bit of a ruckus," he said around it.

"We murdered the dance floor," Lucia said. "No wonder someone called the cops." She looked to Mindy. "Go wait in the car. He wants to talk to me."

"You sure?"

"I can handle 'im."

Mindy nodded and started for her car.

Card reached out suddenly, grabbing her arm, and Lucia tensed, but Mindy held her other hand up.

Lucia didn't relax an inch.

"Where'd you get that?" Card asked, eying the Band-Aid on the side of Mindy's throat.

"Cut myself shaving." Mindy pulled her arm away from him.

Card took his eyes off her, put them on Lucia. "I know Mindy's involved, but you're the ringleader, aren't you? I don't get the sense Ms. Murphy has a lot of friends, unless she's even easier than she looks."

"I have, like, seven hundred Facebook friends, okay?" Mindy protested.

Lucia gave her a look. Mindy walked over, already reaching out to Lucia in her mind, giving herself double vision seeing through Lucia's eyes.

"Got another of those?" Lucia asked, pointing to the cigarette in his mouth.

Card took the pack out of his pocket, rattled the tar around by smacking the bottom with the heel of his hand, then shook one out to offer her. She reached for it. He jerked the pack away, then saw she'd already taken one. Lucia smirked at him, curled lips around the cigarette.

"Got a light?"

Card took out a lighter. As he lit her, Mindy pushed a thought into her mind.

*Since when do you smoke?*

*Since I* died. *Dead people don't get cancer. And I look really sexy. You should watch sometime.*

*Watch you smoke?*

*Yeah.*

*I think I'll not get cancer instead.*

*Your loss.*

Card took the lighter away, leaving a glowing ember at the tip of Lucia's cigarette. She sucked it in, gathering the polluted air into her dead lungs, then spoke so it trickled out of her lips. "You'll want to watch how you talk about Mindy around me."

"You really do care about her, huh?"

"That's me. All heart."

*Be careful with him*, Mindy urged.

*He's fishing. Hoping he can get one of us to confess to something naughty. You haven't been naughty, have you, Minz? I know I haven't.*

"You care about Seb too?"

Lucia held up her level hand, wobbled it a bit, made an "ehh" sound.

"Yeah. I guess Mindy's more into him. You're more into her... I guess it all works out."

Lucia took the cigarette out of her mouth and shook some ash from it. "If I were living on a cop's salary, I guess I would dream of being a comedian too."

Card reached into his pocket, took out an evidence bag wrapped around a smartphone. He took the smartphone out—his lips leering around his cigarette—powered it on, unlocked it, and turned it on Lucia. There was a picture of it. An upskirt.

"That Mindy?" he asked.

"I wouldn't know, can you zoom in? Usually I'm seeing her cameltoe from less of a distance."

Card stared at the picture. "Found this on one of the victims. It seems like people who do wrong by Mindy end up in the hospital an awful lot. Is that why I should watch how I talk about her?"

"Well, in my experience, if a guy takes one photo like that, he takes a lot. So I'm betting a lot of women were on his phone." Lucia dropped the cigarette to the ground, smashed the butt out beneath her high heel. "Maybe he ran into someone who wasn't so photogenic."

*Ask him if the police will be pressing charges against Chester Molester.*

"I trust you'll be investigating him for sex crimes."

"I think he's suffered enough." Card dropped the phone back into its bag. "Don't you?"

"You know when you've suffered enough? When you die. And even then, sometimes…" Lucia trailed off.

Card stopped leaning against the car. Through Lucia's eyes, Mindy saw him tower over her.

"You think because I can't prove anything that I can't get to you." Mindy could smell the tobacco on his breath. "*I can get to you.* I can get to your mother, I can get to your brothers—I can get to Child Protective Services and let them know that the only real parent in your house is an eighteen-year-old girl who dresses like Megan Fox."

Lucia kept her mouth shut. Otherwise he would see her fangs.

"Give me Seb. Give me Mindy. I'll let you walk this time. I think we both know you can find someone else. After all, you must be getting bored of the lesbo thing by now."

Inside the car, Mindy was hugging herself. Hugging Lucia. *Don't give him a fucking inch.*

"I would never do anything to hurt Mindy," Lucia said, speaking with Mindy's calm.

"That's too bad. Because I know you're playing some goddamn vampire game and you're obsessed with Murphy, maybe the same way she's obsessed with you. But two of you means you're twice as vulnerable. I'll keep running at her, I'll keep running at you, one of you will crack and give up the other one. I'll live to see you behind ba—" The vampire struck.

He hit Card from the side, striking him against his car so hard the tires ground a few inches across the tarmac, rubber screeching like the scream Card would have made if his throat hadn't been bit in half. The vampire held Card by the throat, letting him process, his face spasming into confusion, fear, pain, and despair.

Then, as Card's blood soaked his shirt front, the vampire opened his mouth. He didn't have Lucia's petite elongated canines. He had viper fangs that barely fit in his mouth. His jaw had to unhinge slowy to let them out. He clicked like a flywheel as his mouth gaped open and his wet lips kept on stretching, stretching. Card's expression settled on a look of pure panic. His funerary mask.

The vampire's entire skull pushed out of his distorted, peeling, mouth like a newborn shark, born to eat. The soft, flaccid flesh of his face drifted back on his cranium, pushed back like an empty mask, leaving no eyes, no nose, only a stark white death's-head's maw. The Big Bad Wolf teeth of his face clamped onto Card's head, and at last there came a sound. Lucia thought for a moment Card was screaming, but no. It was the screech of his life being pulled out of him. The vampire sucked and slurped and *changed*. His death-pale skin coloring with the stolen blood, tanning, was becoming more human.

It happened in seconds. Card just seemed to decay. His skin sank to his bones, clothes dangling from wire-hanger flesh, his veins standing out as the blood was clawed out of them, so fast that they ripped open, pulled taut and tore through Card's flesh like stiletto wire. Dry, desiccated flesh ripped open and whistled with the force of the vampire's bloodlust.

Card didn't even have time to lift his hands. His wedding ring slipped off a shrunken finger as he went limp. With a snap and grind of bone, and a flutter of dead skin, the vampire bit through his face and skull, leaving a scarecrow's hollow head. The body stood there, not knowing it was dead as the vampire stepped away from it. Then, drained of blood, robbed of life, Card's empty body fell to the ground. A bag of bones.

Bakula sucked his fingers clean. His cavernous skull was a triumph of unnatural survival over true life, his entire being no more than an insatiable hunger with a man's visage hanging off it. He flicked a clot of Card's blood at Lucia, splatting her on the cheek. "They're never going to believe it wasn't you."

Mindy snapped on the high beams. She screamed, hit the gas, and drove full speed right at him. She'd done her best to send a warning to Lucia on whatever mental link they had, but Lucia had been a blank slate, bouncing Mindy's thoughts back at her untouched, mesmerized with Bakula's decimation of Card. Now, finally, she moved, throwing herself aside as Mindy drove at Bakula straight on. She rammed into his outstretched hand with the Taurus's grille.

His arm stayed rigid, but the force pushed him back—dress shoes shredding across the blacktop before he dug in his heels with a crumble of asphalt, grounding himself. He remained upright, holding Mindy's Taurus in place even as she jammed down the gas and sent the tachometer up to 5000 rpm. She didn't move an inch. Then the hood started to crinkle under his grip.

He looked through the windshield at her. Smiled with a mouthful of knives. He threw his arm up, Hollywood style, crooked to cover all of his bloody face, save his eyes. The same man who had watched over her, sympathized with her, cared for her. All of that now leeched away, leaving his true nature displayed in malicious, red-eyed glee.

He said in a mock Bela Lugosi accent, "*I vant to suck your blood.*"

Lucia threw herself into the passenger seat. "Reverse!"

"Oh Jesus, God…" Mindy couldn't think anymore. Her adrenaline had run dry since starting the car and driving it into her English teacher at seventy miles per hour—she'd thought that would *do it.* Now he exerted himself—gently—and the car moonwalked, going backward as the tires spun forward.

"Drive!" Lucia screamed, grabbing the gearshift and dragging it down to *R.* "Get us the fuck out of here!"

The gears screamed bloody murder, but obeyed, and the Taurus lunged backward, smashing into a parked car. Mindy went ass over teakettle, even in her seatbelt—Lucia was the one who shoved the gearshift back to *D.* She ripped the seatbelt away, dragged Mindy over to the side, and vaulted into her seat.

Bakula watched impassively as she hit the gas, threw the car into a 180-degree turn, and sped over the school's lawn to mount the curb and settle onto Outlook Drive. They flew forward, taking off into the night.

"Is he following us?" Mindy asked, when she was able to open her mouth without screaming.

Lucia didn't answer. She just stared straight ahead as the speedometer climbed, hitting sixty, hitting seventy. Traffic was light this time of night, a collection of red taillights practically standing still. Lucia veered around them, took a curve too fast, and slashed the car across the guardrail in a shower of sparks before regaining control.

"El, slow down."

Lucia was staring straight ahead, but it was like she wasn't even seeing the road. She ran a red light, a chorus of honking car horns fading behind them…

"All along…all along… It was him! You said it wasn't, you said!"

"Lucia…" Mindy looked for the source of the sudden chapping noise. It was the steering wheel. It was splintering in Lucia's grip. "Lucia, stop!"

They buzzed past a stop sign, a squeal of brakes as they cut off a truck. Another curve, tires kicking on dirt as they skidded over the shoulder, gravel flying off the tires and sparking off the undercarriage before Lucia got it back on the road. Mindy vaulted over the cup-holders and jammed her foot down onto the brakes, bringing them to a screeching, smoking stop.

Lucia was out of her seat, pushing the door nearly off its hinges, leaving the steering wheel permanently disfigured. Mindy had to turn off the engine, then figure out how to put the car in park before she crawled out of the cab after Lucia, now a spectre in the night with her white dress and her makeup bleeding off her face.

"Lucia," Mindy said calmly as she could manage. "He's not following us. If he'd wanted us, he just wouldn't have let us leave. I don't think he's following us."

Lucia opened her mouth, and a strangled sound came out, like something was being murdered inside her. Mindy knelt down beside Lucia. Tried to reach for her, reach into her mind and found a fountain of words— *So stupid, I should've known, how could I have not have known? It was too hard to remember. I forgot, and all this time, he was with Mindy for months, all this time, I could've stopped it. All this time, he could've done anything to her. She could be dead, dead, because of me, dead* — "Lucia, stop," Mindy said, just like before, only gentler.

*Fucking vampire venom doesn't work on vampires; of course it doesn't. Fooled me, so stupid, stupid—*

Mindy reached out, thought better of touching Lucia, and just took hold of a dangling lock of hair and ran it through her fingers, hoping the steady pressure would lead Lucia back to her. "I'm fine, El, I'm fine."

Mindy felt the resolve coiling inside of Lucia, saw her eyes snap into focus. "Get back in the car. We're driving. *You're driving.*"

"Where?"

"Anywhere but here. As far as we can go. Across the border, maybe. You speak Spanish, right?"

"El, we are not going to Mexico."

"We're going somewhere, we're not staying *here.*"

"Yes. We are." Mindy finally felt confident to put her hand on Lucia's cheek. She was so cold it burnt. "We're doing what we should've done from the beginning. We're going to the cops and we're telling them everything, how we're getting a SWAT team or the National Guard down here, and they are going to shoot him with a bazooka or something."

"Cops? You heard him, Minz, they'll think I killed Card, they're not going to *listen*."

"The Town Council, then. And you can turn into a bat, *they'll listen*."

Lucia shook her head. "I have to keep you safe…"

"Neither of us will *be safe* until he's gone. And I for one am not spending my life looking over my shoulder, El, we're going to have this sicko hunted down and shot in the street. Just come with me. I'll take care of you."

Lucia looked away, digging into her lip with her fangs, and Mindy didn't need the link to know she was thinking of throwing her in the car and driving off anyway. But she wouldn't. Not Lucia.

"You don't leave my sight." Lucia bargained finally.

Mindy took Lucia's hand. "I won't let go if you won't."

# CHAPTER 26

A swipe of Mindy's smartphone showed her that the Town Council was in session at that very moment. They went to the local library, where the Town Council always met in the same side room used for meetings of the anime club and the summer reading program. Mindy walked by that room every time she came to check out a book.

This time, the blinds were drawn, and the door was solidly shut, a patrolman standing in front of it. Seeing them making a beeline for it, he raised his hand.

"Sorry, ladies. Emergency session, closed doors, no admittance for any—"

Lucia snarled at him, fangs extended. He took five steps back, automatically. Lucia tried the door, found it locked, and ripped it open anyway. She and Mindy spilled into the room.

It was a simple, drab conference room. Rows of empty office chairs lined up for town meetings, facing an elevated desk area that *was* occupied. All the names Mindy knew only from voting signs. The county clerk, county commissioner, sheriff, mayor—even Principal Haywood was there. Seeing the two girls, their hushed conversation came to a sudden stop.

Mindy suddenly felt like she was having one of those dreams about having to take a test without studying. At least she wasn't underdressed—she still wore the champagne dress from the Sadie Hawkins Dance.

Wait, what was she worried about? She always got good grades. "Hello… old people." Then again, she had gotten a "C" once. "I need to talk to you about a thing. And it's going to sound crazy, and you won't want to believe it at first, but hey, remember evolution. Think about how that tumbled out. So, yeah, uh, anyway…my friend here, Lucia." Mindy nudged her with her elbow.

Lucia looked at her, silently asking what she was supposed to do. Give a little wave?

Mindy conceded the point by facing the Council again. "She was attacked. Bitten, in fact, by a vampire. She's a vampire now. And the guy who did it, who bit her and tried to kill her—obviously he's a vampire—but he's also Coach Bakula. From football. And I know this is exactly like the part of the horror story where the kids tell some crazy story about zombies or killer dolls or something…but aren't they always right? Don't be the people in the horror movie who don't listen."

"We have proof," Lucia whispered.

"We have proof!" Mindy said loudly. "Wait, why are you telling me we have proof, just, just show them."

Lucia was stock-still.

Mindy reached out, petted her arm. "It's okay. I'm right here. Just…you know."

In a series of blinks, Lucia appeared all around the room. Sitting in an empty seat, crouching on the podium, standing beside the Texan and American flags, at the door, at the water cooler, hanging from a fluorescent light…

Mayor Redfield took off his glasses. "Hon, we believe you."

Lucia sped back beside Mindy. "You do?"

"Well, about you being a vampire."

"But you don't think it's Bakula?" Mindy demanded.

"No, I believe that. It's just—"

"Excuse me, I heard there were some very hardworking politicians in here who needed their caffeine?" Bakula was coming through the door, juggling four trays of Starbucks on two outstretched arms. He nodded at the girls as he passed them. "Mindy. Lucia." He set the trays on the podium and started handing out orders to their respective owners. "Alright, freshen my memory: who wanted their coffee black with two sugars? I know someone wanted it, but I can't for the life of me remember who."

Mindy looked at the exit. Now three patrolmen were standing in the way.

"Coach Bakula," Mayor Redfield said. "Mindy and Lucia have been telling quite a tale about you."

"And my ears have been burning." Bakula handed him his cup. "Cream, no sugar, right?"

"That's right, Coach."

"Ah-ha!" Bakula tapped his temple. "Still some charge left in the ol' battery yet. Well, not my most shining moment, I'll admit. But at least now you can see the chicky in question, get where I'm coming from. And let me tell you, she wasn't wearing some toga that first time after school, either." He smiled bashfully at Principal Haywood. "How many times did you send Ms. West home because she dressed like math class was going to turn into a rap video?"

"Too many times."

Mindy realized what was going on. "Don't drink the coffee! He's drugged it! You're all drugged!"

"No," Lucia said. "No, they aren't."

Bakula hopped up onto the podium, sitting facing Lucia. "Now, before anything else, I just want to say it's mighty solid of you to come down here and 'fess up to what's been done. Mighty solid. But, you needn't have bothered. I already told them everything. I've taken full responsibility for my part in it."

"Your part in it?" Mindy asked. "You attacked her! You assaulted her!"

"Whoa now!" Bakula held his hands up. "Easy on the trigger there, missy. Lucy was old enough to know what she was doing. After all, she did it with half the town."

"You're saying she *slept* with you?"

"You, of all people, aren't going to blame me for that? Just doing what comes natural."

"There is the matter of the Highway Patrolman," Mayor Redfield said. A flash of red came through the windows before the squad car pulling up killed its lights. "Fooling around a little is one thing, Coach, but we had a strict agreement on non-proliferation. *A* vampire in Carfax is one thing. *Ten* vampires in Carfax… We never agreed to that."

"I know, I know, I most humbly apologize." Bakula put his hand on his heart. "You probably could've told me, and you would've been right: the girl was a bad idea. I tried to break things off with her. Somehow she got a hold of my blood. Probably got into the footballers' supply—she was getting it on with my team captain too, which should've warned me. Well, we all know what comes of this and that. It's on me, I fully admit. I just didn't think she had it in her. If I'd known, I would've told you back when these attacks first started. I thought, same as you, that it was just one of my kind passing through. But it was Lucia, and she's gotten worse. *Escalated.* Now this poor Card fellow is dead. It never should've happened."

"You're damn right it never should've happened," Judge Rowling barked. "We agreed you'd only drink from the retirement home."

"The retirement home and those that consented to it," Bakula argued right back. "Just look at that little hussy. You're telling me you would turn her away, she wanted you to put your teeth on her?"

Mindy found her voice. "She never consented to anything! He attacked her!"

Bakula held up a hand. "Now, Murphy, I know you're standing up for your friend, but let's not cloud the situation any further. We all know—a vampire can't come into a house without invitation. And we all know you have to drink a vampire's blood to become a vampire. Well, it's obvious Lucia's been drunk and it's obvious she's been drinking."

"She was at a party. You stalked her, you hunted her down." Mindy looked frantically from gray face to gray face all arrayed above her, all looking down with a sort of…disgust. Like she was doing something *rude.* "Why are you letting him even talk to you? He's a vampire! You all know he's a vampire!"

"A 140-game winning streak," Lucia said. She sat down heavily. "He's the coach."

"That I am."

"The winningest coach in high school football," Mindy said, remembering. "He could coach college ball, easy."

"Surely the head cheerleader isn't going to take this town to task for bringing home the Ws," said Bakula.

*We have to get out of here*, Mindy thought fixedly at Lucia.

Lucia was still too quiet. Mindy looked down and caught a tremor in her hand. She covered it with her own hand. *We have to go.*

Lucia turned and looked at her. Mindy could feel her centering herself, feel her pull back from whatever pain she felt—feel her squeeze her hand. *Right.*

Suddenly she was in Lucia's arms, she was being carried through a world blurred at the edges, her racing heart and flushed skin cooled by Lucia's touch. Then she felt a pain so sharp she saw black, wrenched out of Lucia's grip, and slammed down to the floor. Her hair. Bakula had her by the hair.

Lucia skidded to a stop in the doorway, toppling chairs in her wake, sending her hair into a vortex as she stared back, teeth bared like she would gnaw off an arm to get Mindy out of the trap—preferably Bakula's.

"Shoot her," Bakula said, and the guns were loud as a fireworks displayed.

Lucia's arms twitched in front of her. Like catching bullets, only she wasn't that fast, Mindy heard them ripping into her, splitting hardened skin and meat like hatchet blows. One punched right through Lucia, splattering Mindy with blood. It felt like quicksilver on her face.

*Go just go just go*, she thought desperately.

Lucia snatched up a chair, throwing it at the shooter, reducing it to kindling with the impact. He went down, his body butting into the other two. Mindy heard the room's side-door being kicked in, the cops from the police car outside streaming in. *Lucia, you have to go, you can't—not all of them.*

Mindy didn't know which she was worried about more: Lucia not being able to get all of them or her being able to.

Lucia moved so fast, she seemed to flicker like a hummingbird, head swivelling from the downed, rising cops to the ones coming in armed with shotguns, to Bakula and Mindy and the whole room painted with the light coming through the open door, so red, so blue.

She threw herself at a window, hitting it in one agonized howl of motion and then disappearing into the night. The only sound was the tinkling glass of the window breaking and breaking and breaking.

"Nice shooting," Bakula said sardonically. "I'll take the girl. If Lucia's bitten her, she might be infected. I'll see what I can do to fix that."

And as the Town Council thanked him, Mindy's world went black.

# CHAPTER 27

Awake. Upright in a chair. Comfortable, natural, except for the cold at her wrists and ankles. Her eyelids weighed a thousand pounds. She let them stay shut. Her body kept doing what it was doing. Breathing, sleeping… She was almost asleep. Almost…

No. She couldn't let her body keep…slipping from her. She had to focus. Music, there was music playing. A lullaby without a mother. She couldn't make out the words, the tune, just a rhythm apart from noise. Barely awake. Practically dreaming. She was sitting down. She repeated it to herself like a mantra, the few things she knew.

Lucia—Lucia wasn't there. She tried reaching out to her with her mind; it hurt just to *think*. She could touch her, but just barely, just with the tips of her fingers, just brushing her. She heard a refrain like a song stuck in her head. *I'm sorry, I'm sorry, I'm so sorry.*

It was gone.

Her eyelids were getting lighter. She'd almost think she was getting stronger, but if anything, she felt weaker. But she could open them a little ways and see mostly the fog of her own eyelashes and a little of her body. She was pale, the color of fine china, matching the fragility she felt. She could see her pulse pitching in her wrist, a little itch under the skin. Her wrist… There was something there. A band of her skin was another color. A silvery color. She was handcuffed.

Mindy woke up. It wasn't some secret lair with pentagrams drawn in blood on the walls. It was just a dining room—the same furnishing, the same aesthetic as the rest of his house. She was seated at the head of a long table. Empty chairs, except for an antique table mirror, placed in front of her like a dinner plate. She scrutinized her reflection, helpless to do anything else. She wasn't wearing the champagne dress anymore, but a nightgown. Conservative, practically Victorian. Her skin had been cleaned off, her hair combed. She thought some makeup had been applied. Her neck was bandaged and there was an IV stand beside her, the line leading down to another bandage on her wrist.

She remembered bringing pizzas here once, a party—next to a lake—*no*...

Something scratched like a claw. Mindy turned, saw a record player on top of the sideboard. The record needle was scratched over an LP before finding its groove again. The song started again. This time Mindy recognized it. "It's A Fine Day" by Jane. She remembered it from *I Love The 80s*. After she'd downloaded it, it'd helped her get to sleep. "They're playing our song," Bakula said. He was behind her, but he wasn't in the mirror. Mindy craned her head, not far enough to see him, but far enough to glimpse him.

He wasn't human. Whatever she saw, it couldn't have been human.

"Do you remember? The last time? Nineteen-eighty-something. This was your favorite song. You were a little intern, your jacket had those shoulder pads, and you had that perm and those huge glasses. You looked cute, though. Lucy, she was ridiculous. The leather jacket, the Mohawk, the whole punk... thing. Must've thought she was Joan Jett."

"If you hurt Lucia, I'll fucking kill you."

"Now, I don't appreciate that language in my classroom, and certainly not in my home."

Suddenly, he was touching her. She hadn't seen his hand coming in the mirror, but it was against her cheek, turning her toward her reflection. She could see her skin pressed in against *nothing*.

"Just so you know, back in the sixties, we had this conversation. Back then, I wasn't able to get to you so soon, mentor you, and your parents at the time, as it turns out, should not have been trusted with that. You were a very rude girl, very unpleasant company. I tried my best to be patient, but eventually, I had to give up and wait for another try. I snapped your neck and dumped you in a dry well and, I came to regret that, waiting for you to come back to me, but not much. I'm hoping you've learned something since then. I hope this won't be another 1964."

His hand left her. God, it'd been cold. The chill stayed like frostbite.

"Now, can you ask politely?"

Mindy thought that if she tried very hard, if she pretended Lucia was the name of a dog or a painting or anything but *her*, she could ask without her voice breaking into a million pieces. "Is Lucia okay?"

"She's *fine.*" The cold hand patted her on the shoulder. "Long gone by now, I think. Two vampires in the same turf—toes get stepped on. She's a smart girl, in an animal cunning sort of way. She'll see, if she hasn't already, that there's no point in fighting for you. Never fight with someone who wants it more, Mindy, that's something you learn in football."

His hand lingered on the skin of her shoulder, fingers trailing down toward her collarbone. "Take your hand off me."

"What's the magic word?"

Mindy gritted her teeth. "*Please.*"

His hand came away, but he moved it as if he'd only done it to arrange a stray hair from over the lobe of her ear.

"What happened to me? Why'd I pass out?"

"Oh, just a little trick. Vibrating your skull at excessive speed. The brain can't take it, shuts down like a pilot pulling too many Gs. To everyone else, it looked like you fainted. You can really only use it with women, you see. And then I took a little of your blood—no more than you'd give at a blood drive—to whet my appetite. I was feeling peckish, you see. But I've run a saline drip on you, just to be safe. I bet Lucia never did that for you."

Mindy felt like she would vomit. Like she would be sick.

"Look at us," Bakula continued, both hands on her shoulders, like he was pulling the strings of the marionette that was dancing in her guts. "Fighting like an old married couple. Which we were, of course. Are."

He checked the IV. Mindy could see his hands. In the mirror, she could see his clothes. She just couldn't see him.

"Who are you?" she asked.

"Always so curious. You have to be, for our game to be played. Me hiding, you searching, uncovering, discovering…me. The truth. I am your truth, your great truth. 'The big truth,' as a man I greatly respected once said, 'is that you must have an open mind and not let a little bit of truth check the rush of a big truth, like a small rock does a railway truck. We get the small truth first. Good! We keep him, and we value him; but all the same, we must not let him think himself all the truth in the universe.'"

"So, what's the small truth?" Mindy spat.

"The small truth is why you could see me in your mirror. Look."

Mindy looked. She saw in the mirror an invisible man putting on makeup. A cotton swab in a jar of flesh-colored cream makeup. Being stroked across a glass statue, spreading rich fleshy cream. The hovering splotch becoming the eyelids of a closed eye. A cheek, a face, a head. Then foundation. Highlighter, contouring, blush, lip gloss—eyebrows, a wig, something halfway between Mindy's Essix retainers and dentures. It covered up all the sharp points that Mindy had glimpsed. All the jagged edges of that face inside his face. Until there was Bakula. All but his eyes.

"Usually, I wear scleral lenses, but I want to look at you with my own eyes. I want you to see into my soul, wife."

His eyes were hollow. Empty chasms leading down inside some latex appliance, some mask. He crossed from behind her to the seat next to her, sitting down, and that thing in the mirror was now her favorite teacher. Her friend. The coach.

"Who are you?" Mindy didn't know if she could ask again without whimpering.

"I am Wladislaus Dragwlya, vaivoda partium Transalpinarum. Also called Kazıklı Bey. Also called Vlad Tepes. Also called Vlad the Impaler. Also called Count Dracula. Born 1431. Murdered 1476. And again, 1893. And again, 1922. Again, 1931. Again, 1944. Again and again and again, I climb my own corpses like mountains to ascend to you, my angel. My sweet Ilona, my Mina, whatever you want to call yourself, you. Are. Mine."

*Count Dracula. Coach Bakula. It fucking rhymes.*

"We do this same dance, again and again, the music changes but always the same steps. Condemned to Hell, I pull myself free because it holds no interest to me. I find your world of daylight just as I've left it, the stage changed, but the same players as ever. Your friend, the whore. The professor, my nemesis—I've learned it's best to kill him quickly. The doctor, the cowboy, the madman, the list goes on. And you. Always you. My one reason to try, try again, no matter how many times a jealous God denies you to me because our happiness would eclipse his heaven. Yet, still, you did not wait for me; you never do. Your affections are so fickle, but would I be so intent on capturing them if they were not?"

"You hurt Lucia." Mindy's mouth was dry. It felt like it was cracking open as she spoke. "You hurt her because I love her."

"Because *she didn't deserve you.*" Bakula's gesturing hand drifted about him like a spider in the air. "Usually I turn her. I just can't resist. I can take my time with you, I can be patient, knowing you'll understand, but with *her*—the thirst always wins. And she ruins everything. This time I tried to be clever. I had her—and she was satisfactory, as usual, but nothing next to *you*—and then I let her die. If only she'd had the good grace to stay that way. One of life's little ironies. She made herself a vampire. Bit me, came back to you—I suppose I don't have room to talk, as they say."

Mindy was crying now. Was he going to make her like him? Or was he just going to kill her? The man was insane, a serial killer, going through his fucked-up cycle on an immortal time scale. Maybe she really was a reincarnation, or maybe she was just some girl who fit the profile. She was going to die. Lucia had *already died,* because her nose reminded him of his thousand-year-old fucking sweetheart.

Bakula wiped her tears away. Wouldn't even allow her that. The water smudged the caked makeup on his fingertips. He just kept talking.

"It must've been so hard. For both of us. When you were fifteen, your body finally ripening, changing, and you not knowing—*remembering*—what to do with it. I could've shown you…those long, lonely nights, thinking it would never happen for you, when it had already happened! From the day you were born, it was fated to happen. Can you hear me yet? In your mind, in your heart? The same blood runs in us, my love. Are you ready to listen? Can you feel, now, what you've been afraid to feel?"

Mindy looked at him. His eyes were red. Red like the earth had cracked open, red like there was something inside, burning, primordial.

"I don't feel anything for you," Mindy said. He was going to kill her one way or another. She just didn't want to die afraid. For Lucia. She could be brave for her. Lucia had died, and she'd gotten over it. "I'm not even afraid of you. You…" She searched for the right word. Something an English teacher would appreciate. "*Offend* me."

"Don't lie," he insisted, his voice drawing itself out like a cat's seething growl. "It's impolite."

"I see nothing in you worth loving. Nothing even worth liking! You're nauseating! I'm repulsed by you! The thought of you makes me sick!"

"You've been telling me!" His voice was a sudden roar, an explosion. "All day in class, every time I look at you! How much you want me, how much you need me!"

"That's all in your head."

"Then why have you been dressing that way!" He pulled at her nightgown as if she'd put that on herself. She nearly cried out as her nipple poked over the neckline. "Catching my eye, flaunting your body before me!"

"That's just how I dress... Lucia thought it looked good..."

Bakula reared back like the thought burned him, and she realized how to hurt him. She realized how to hurt him enough so he'd hurt her back, kill her instead of giving her a fate worse than death. "I have it with her. With Lucia. I hear her in my heart. She makes me whole."

"Then you can thank me!" His hand came down on the table in a fist, hitting it so hard that the mirror fell over, glass cracking. "I made her! Hate me all you want for her insignificant work, but she's my work! I took a nothing girl who would've grown up to be a nothing woman and I made her a goddess."

"She was a goddess to begin with."

Bakula opened his mouth to reply, but there was only the endless *gaping*, the thing inside pushing out through his mouth in a nonstop smile, the teeth. *Oh God, so many teeth!*

"I want to know what love is..." erupted through the window, and the music continued playing, loud and jarring from the driveway. Bakula stopped, his face half cramped human flesh shoved to all sides, half the thing protruding from his mouth like a vast white tongue obscenely licking the air. He moved so fast, a little sonic boom that stirred the whole room as he went to the window blinds, opened them with his fingers.

But Mindy didn't need to look through the blinds to see. She could look through Lucia's eyes to the idling Taurus outside, the microphone plugged into the stereo system, the iPhone app running beside her as she sat on the hood. It must've taken some CPR to resuscitate the old car; Lucia was smeared with engine oil as she belted out the song like she was trying to embarrass Foreigner.

Bakula's face drew back together at his mouth, hiding the beast safely in his throat. "Don't get up," he told Mindy. "I'll get the door."

All Mindy could do was watch, not daring to probe Lucia's thoughts. Couldn't distract her. Lucia tossed the microphone aside when Bakula opened the door, letting the light from his house razor out onto his yard. Foreigner continued to blare out across the lake as she walked over the gravel, to the edge of the rectangle of light from inside the house, surrounding Bakula's shadow. There, they faced each other.

"Never had a single lesson!" she said cheerfully.

"Ms. West," he greeted her with his civility pulled up as sure as his face was so easily shrugged on. "What an unexpected pleasure. Drop by for another quick bite?"

Lucia toed the light from the door, drawing her bare feet around the dirt like a line in the sand. "I heard your little pitch..." She tapped her ear. "Super-hearing. Useful for more than just cheating on tests. And I gotta say, as a woman who reads three different advice columns, I think I see your problem."

"Oh?" Bakula leaned against the doorframe as Lucia's mixtape progressed to The Cure's "Love Cats." "What does a child like you know about love? About Mina?"

"I know her name's Mindy. Listen, I know you've got a good thing going with this whole reincarnated love thing—very Anne Rice—but have you considered that maybe she's not into you? Hell, maybe you should be with someone else." Lucia plucked at the corsage of her dress. "Let's face it. A life with her would be like having the world's worst dietician. Always telling you what you can and can't eat. You need a vampire chica. Someone who understands your...needs."

"I *need* Mina. She is one of God's women fashioned by His own hand to show that there is a heaven men can enter, and that its light can be here on Earth." He smiled, false face sloughing away a little. "What could be worth more than that?"

She stepped into the light, her white dress hanging off her in tatters, her body underneath camouflaged by blood and engine oil. She looked like a Pict warrior on her wedding night. "Sex? I mean, take it from someone who knows: Mindy wouldn't know what to do with a dick even if our sex ed didn't suck."

Mindy was so engrossed, watching Lucia talk to Bakula, trying to tell her to run, that she didn't even notice the other person in the room until a hand was clamped over her mouth.

"Shush!" Seb whispered to her, "It's a rescue!"

He bent over her, lockpick in his other hand, working at her cuffs as Foreigner bounced off the walls.

"Harder than it looks, isn't it?" Mindy whispered, just as the first cuff snapped open.

Seb moved to the other one; Mindy got a sudden vision like a blaring headache. Bakula beginning to close the door on Lucia.

"You were fun…but Mina is the *ne plus ultra*. You should know that better than anyone. When her crimson blood tastes so sweet on her lips—when all of her tastes so sweet—would you not do anything to have it?"

Mindy could *feel* Lucia's anger suddenly being let out; flowing through her body like fuel injected in an engine.

"I love Mindy for her, not her blood. That's just a bonus. Just like she loves me, not my awesome tits."

"Your tits aren't that great."

"IT'S ON!" And through Lucia's eyes, Mindy saw the nauseous sight of the world blurred at the edges, Bakula's house growing like a balloon being inflated, Bakula looming up to receive her fist—which stopped, like the air had turned to amber around Lucia, holding her still. Her fist quivered over the doormat.

"I'm sorry," Bakula said, "did I neglect to invite you in?"

The other cuff snapped off Mindy's wrist.

"Let's make like a shepherd," Seb said, "and get the flock out of here!"

With a rush of wooziness, Mindy pulled the IV out of her arm. "Seb, you used an idiom right!"

"That's great! What's an idiom?"

The sound of a door slamming crashed through the house. Bakula's booming footsteps bending the floorboards. "That was smart—playing the music so I couldn't hear you. But I still have a nose, such as it is. And your friend wears entirely too much Old Spice."

Mindy rushed to her feet, head swimming again, but she was able to get a handle on it more quickly this time. "I've tried to tell him…" She picked up the table mirror, ready to use it as a blunt instrument. Its cracked surface reflected Bakula's nothing as he came to the doorway. "You want him, then you'll have to go through me!"

"And if you want her, you'll have to go through *this!*" Seb stepped in front of her, holding up a cross.

Bakula's eyes struck it like flints and it burst into flames.

Seb dropped it in surprise. It spat smoke on the floor as Bakula crossed the room, lashing out with his anger to backhand the table. It shredded through the chairs before twisting into the wall with one glancing blow.

Bakula took a step forward, but his foot didn't touch the ground; it became a strand of mist as his entire body streamed like sea fog toward the door at the far side of the room, blocking Mindy and Seb from getting to it. A heartbeat, and Bakula was a swarm of rats scurrying across the floor for Mindy's legs. She backed up, but they were on all sides. Another pounding lightness in her skull; she fell over, and they were on her calves, her ankles. She frantically backpedaled, into a corner. A blink, and he was standing over her.

"Maybe when the thirst burns in your veins." Viper fangs muffled his voice, "then you'll sympathize with *how I need you!*"

Seb was behind Bakula. He pulled open his jacket, and twenty crosses hung around his neck, from tiny rosaries to a wall decoration that nearly covered his stomach. Bakula was physically propelled through the air, forced against the wall where he clung like a spider hanging over Mindy.

"I'm live with a white suburban Texas family. Did you really thinking I had only one cross?"

Pulling his fingers out of the plaster walls, Bakula set himself down almost before Mindy could scramble out from under him and behind Seb. Seb ripped one of the crosses from his neck, held it out like a gun. Bakula was pushed back a half step. Then he concentrated. The cross burnt out of Seb's hand.

He reached for another. "Go! I've got this!"

"I'm not leaving you!"

The third cross kept Bakula in the corner. He looked like he was suffering no worse than a bout of indigestion. Seb didn't yell. He never yelled at her. His voice fell to a plea instead. "I can't be brave for much longer. Please go before you see how afraid I am."

The third cross burst apart. Seb already had a fourth in his other hand. Mindy took a step back.

"Do you see God in that flimsy piece of metal?" Bakula asked Seb, pushing his hand against the air like he was tapping on the glass at a pet store. The cross burned and melted, Seb holding onto it as it scorched his hand. "Would you like to know where I see God? In the mirror."

Mindy ran outside. Lucia was in the driver's seat of her car. The passenger door was open. Mindy threw herself inside.

"We have to go back! We have to go back for Seb!"

"No," Lucia said, eyes on the road, foot on the accelerator.

"You can't just leave him there!"

Lucia's fingers were so tight around the wheel that the red showed through. "There's nothing we can do."

"There has to be something we can do. We can figure something out, just turn the car around and—"

"Mindy! He's gone!" Lucia yelled. "I can hear!" Her voice cracked, but didn't shatter. "I can hear everything…"

Mindy buried her face in Lucia's arm and screamed.

# CHAPTER 28

The digital haze of the dashboard lights made the blood on Lucia look black, and her makeup white. Mindy couldn't look away. Her eyes kept shifting over, like Lucia had her own gravitational pull. The tires crackled like worn leather on the blacktop, darkness in all directions.

"Where are we going?" Mindy asked.

"Your place," Lucia said. "At least there, Bakula can't invite himself in. We can think of something to do."

"Think of what to tell Seb's family."

Lucia nodded grimly. A bullet hole on her breast refused to close. Lucia probed around it, closing her eyes like a little kid about to get a shot as the shell worked itself up, out of the wound, crinkled lead tearing at the edges of her entry wound as it burrowed out. Then the raw punctuation knitted shut, strands of skin holding it closed but a gaping hole just underneath. Mindy could see it trying to fill in. Lucia was *shrinking*, her skin pulling flush around her ribs, turning so pale it seemed translucent, body burning through the last blood she'd had.

"You need blood," Mindy said.

"I'm fine. What about you? Did he bite you?"

"I don't know—he said he drank from me, but he might've used a needle."

Neither of them said that if he'd bitten her where Lucia had, there'd be no way of knowing. But Lucia's hands tightened on the steering wheel like she wanted to rip it off.

Mindy became lost in her own world the rest of the way home. Trying to think of something they could do, something they could bring to bear on Bakula. But her mind kept returning to Seb—thoughts of burning crosses. He must've been so afraid, at the end. He must've regretted saving her... No. No, he wouldn't have. Not Seb.

They pulled onto her street and Mindy's eyes unconsciously darted to the console's clock like she was delivering a pizza, checking to see how fast she'd made the trip. No good. The glass was smashed in. Then she heard Lucia scream.

Mindy looked up. She saw Seb on the lawn before her house, and relief flooded into her. But it was laced with poison. Even as she was seeing him, she was registering how he stood on his tip toes, no, how he dangled, the toes of his sneakers brushing the ground, the pole in-between them. It was jammed into the ground. It started a foot above Seb's open, upturned mouth, and it kept going down. Right through him.

Suddenly Lucia was out of the car, biting her wrist open, next to Seb, pushing her bleeding wound at his blue lips. "Drinkdrinkdrinkdrinkdrink." His lips didn't move, no matter how much Lucia's did.

Mindy's brain kicked back into working order like it'd lost power in a brown-out. And she found herself beside Lucia, unsure how she'd gotten out of her seatbelt and the idling car, and she was noticing the folded-up paper taped to Seb's still chest, and she was plucking it away from the notch of scotch tape, and she was opening it up, and she was reading.

*The blood is somewhat along the lines of Japanese tonkotsu, equals parts gummy and milky, but once the adrenaline hits it becomes a shimmering harvest bouillon with a bouquet aroma worthy of being sipped and scented like fine wine. My compliments to the family. Four out of five stars.*

The paper crumpled in Mindy's fist. Lucia had stopped her chanting and taken her hand away from his mouth. Her wound had closed up. She looked stricken. She reached for Mindy, but Mindy brushed her hand away, moving to Seb. She leaned her head forward until it was against Seb's chest. She could feel the steel rod's hardness on her forehead.

When was the last time they'd talked? Really talked? She'd barely spoken a word to him at Bakula's house as he rescued her. Nothing like goodbye. No, the last time she'd said anything real to him had been at the Sadie Hawkins Dance. He'd asked her if he was cool.

"So cool."

"We have to get inside," Mindy said, seconds, hours later when she could think again, or at least put words to the animal impulse to flee. "We have to get where it's safe—"

"*Safe?*" Lucia laughed, a teetering giggle that sounded nothing like her. "There's no *safe*, Mindy, there's just *fucked*. We're fucked! Bakula's got the whole town in his pocket. He's... You *saw him*, Minz. He's not human. He's not even a little bit human. He's gonna come after us, or he's gonna come after our families, or...whatever he fucking feels like. We don't have a say in it. I can't protect you. I can't do a goddamn thing to protect you. All this *shit* and I can't do *anything*."

She was casting her eyes all around, looking for some new threat, but finally they settled on the oak tree in Mindy's lawn. She charged it, not stopping until she'd slammed her fist into its trunk, the force of the blow splintering wood, shedding leaves from the branches. Lucia hit it again and again, bark flying away from her fists, whole twigs falling as the impacts shot through the tree.

"Lucia, you have to calm—"

She swung her elbow into the tree like a lumberjack's axe, putting a solid notch deep into the trunk. A branch fell, Mindy having to jump back as its clumsy heft splashed onto the ground. Then Lucia dug her fingers into the wedge and pulled, ripping the tear wider, uprooting the tree in places, the entire thing toppling down to a nasty angle, roots pulled up like exposed bones.

It'd been too easy. Lucia's fury was barely spent. She screamed in frustration and it was like steam escaping, her wounds reopened, fresh blood pulsing silver in the moonlight.

Mindy took hold of the hem of her dress, ripped at it, tore, finally taking a chunk out and going to Lucia, embracing her from behind and bandaged her wounds as best she could. "Calm down," Mindy said, willing whatever peace she had into Lucia's body through their chilled contact. "It'll be alright. Everything's gonna be alright."

Lucia was pliant as a doll then, worn out more emotionally than physically. She let Lucia move her around, bring her inside and up the stairs and to her room. There, she sprang back to something like life. She hacked, she hawked, finally spitting out a pursed bullet onto the carpet.

"Too much iron in my diet," she said, clearing her throat as another one came up.

"Drink me," Mindy said. "You need it."

Lucia looked over her shoulder as best she could, her face streaked black and red like warpaint. "No."

"It'll calm you down. It'll help you heal. Then we can think about what to do. Just… c'mon." Mindy moved a shoulder strap out of the way.

Like the cool breeze that rushed in, Lucia's eyes shuttered on the bare expanse of skin, from the plunge of her breast to the curve of her throat.

She moved in, teeth clamping down where her eyes had marked a target, but all she did was rake her canines across Mindy's skin. Just hard enough to leave thin white lines behind her, the ghosts of scars. Her chin set on Mindy's shoulder and she breathed uncertainly, nearly hyperventilating. "I don't wanna hurt you."

"You won't hurt me," Mindy replied, sure, and she pricked her fingernail into her skin where her neck joined her shoulder, making the blood well up until it finally beaded out.

Lucia kissed the cut, kissed it, never breaking the skin, kissing it, just sucking hard on the cut. Mindy hummed, pleasure cut with pain, felt Lucia's tongue dance across the wound, widening it, extracting electric blood from deeper inside. Her hands bunched into fists; she felt Lucia's hands tightly grab her wrists, thumbing her pulse points. Mindy could *feel* her pulse, thundering into Lucia's fingers, those fingers that had been inside her, touched her clit, skimmed her lips before they kissed.

Lucia wrenched herself away, blood cherry-red on her lips. She was shuddering. Mindy could see; simply holding herself still took all the will in her body. "I won't be able to—" She broke off. Her fangs were growing from her teeth; they'd taken her by surprise.

"You'll stop. I'm not leaving you." Their eyes met. Mindy's mirrored in Lucia. Knowing Lucia wanted this just as much as she did. Knowing Lucia was as afraid as she was. "I'm never leaving you."

She bared her throat. Didn't even see Lucia move in, catch her by the neck and whip her around like a dog with a rat, jamming her into the soft abyss of her bed. She stiffened, cold flesh on her body, teeth sinking into her like ice forming in her veins. Her head rolled back, eyes open seeing nothing but darkness. Cool, comforting darkness.

There was no difference between pain and pleasure. Her breath quickened and she was breathing for Lucia, in rhythm with the tattoo Lucia's lungs once set. Her fingers dug into Lucia's back, feeling the heat of her own blood being horded there. Every drop of it sung with the joy of being devoured.

"Fuck me, fuck me," Mindy chanted without air in her lungs, "don't stop, fuck me, don't stop..."

But Lucia's hands didn't move, had no interest in her warm cunt, her burning breasts. They were locked on Mindy's skull, holding her still as she drank. Drank so deep she sucked up Mindy's senses, Mindy's world—the smell of the ruptured engine, the sound of Lucia's gasping swallows, the taste of Lucia's absent kiss. Her sight went last. Mindy closed her eyes, sighing, opened them, and someone had stolen the stars out of the dark sky.

Mindy's wordless chant stopped. She struggled to change it, play a different tune on her one-track mind—"Easy," she begged now, letting her fear show. "Take it easy..."

Mindy couldn't feel anything, just the insistent pulse of Lucia's sensations, burning bright in her mind. And through it, Mindy felt her own love and affection reflected back at her, still clinging to her body like cut puppet strings. It was so pure. Mindy couldn't blame Lucia, killing for it.

"Stop." She gagged on emptiness. "Lucia, stop..."

Her own mind, her own body had stopped. She just felt Lucia filling her up. She felt how much Lucia loved her, needed her. Finally, at last. She was empty enough to know the full scope of Lucia's hunger for her; enough hunger to kill her.

"You're hurting me..."

She felt Lucia's heart beating for her, just for her. A pounding rhythm. A fire set by blood running hot. Roaring in her ears, smashing into her, waves of heat washing over her, beating all the louder to make up how Mindy's own heart dwindled. Tapped, scratched at the walls Lucia had put up. Not able to be heard, not able to be cared about...

The ghost of Mindy still moved, a scarecrow in the breeze that gently ruffled their dresses. Her body was not her own. It was Lucia's hunger, their hunger, the animals in their love so distant from what Mindy had fallen in love with. It confused what was left of her. She was cold. Unthinkingly, she stroked Lucia's head, stroked at the rabid fierceness that was draining her. She asked why as everything turned not dark, but golden. The color of Lucia's soft, warm skin. *Why?*

It was her last conscious thought.

The hospital reduced all her thoughts to a third-grade reading level. The bed was soft. The walls were white. The IV needle was cold. The doctor was kind. He asked her if she was in any pain. He asked her if she needed anything. Then he pressed a cell phone into her hands and told her the Coach wanted to talk to her.

There was only one number in the phone's memory. Speed-dial 1. She held the number down, then put the phone to her ear. Silence.

"I know it's you, Mina. I know your breath, even across the telephone wires.

"You didn't have to kill him."

"You didn't have to run. There's a reason I let you grow up apart from me. This town is full of your friends, your family. Come to me or there will be more taste tests."

"I want Lucia proven innocent. I don't want anyone hunting her."

"Very well."

"Alright then. How long do I have to say goodbye?"

"Oh. Big game tonight. We're taking on the Peniel Pathfinders. After we trounce 'em, I'll swing by to pick you up. Is that enough time?"

"Yeah. I guess it'll have to be."

She hung up. She could still see Seb, how he'd hung there. It numbed her. She supposed that would make things easier.

The police asked their questions. Mindy didn't know why they bothered. They were already pinning it on Lucia, asking about her jealousy, her rivalry with Seb over Mindy. Mindy didn't give them an inch. After thirty minutes, they stopped trying. Bakula called his dogs to heel and she went back home, to sleep in her own bed one last time.

A creature lived next door to Mindy. It lived in Lucia's house, where it wore Lucia's clothes and ate Lucia's food. Slept in Lucia's bed. But it was not Lucia. It did not have Lucia's eyes, it did not have Lucia's smile, and it did not have Lucia's love.

Mindy was afraid of it, and Mindy could never be afraid of Lucia.

She lay awake in bed all day. During the day, she could almost believe it *was* Lucia. But as night fell, and the moon came out. Then she knew.

Mindy fingered the gauze that covered her bite mark. Underneath, the wound was sensitive enough to ache against her touch. It shook her body like the last drip of adrenaline from that old attack. Maybe she wasn't human either. Maybe there was a little beast in her, just like Bakula said. Because she could hear the front door of the next house over creak as it opened.

Lucia didn't come in over the rooftops. Maybe it seemed too intimate a pathway for her to take. Instead, Mindy could hear—she could've sworn she heard—the yellowing blades of Texas grass crinkling under Lucia's bare feet. It crackled, it creased, it shattered. Always louder, always closer. Until Mindy could *feel* Lucia under the second-story window.

Lucia's nails daintily scratched at the house's wood and fiberglass as she climbed up in defiance of physics. She didn't really need a grip to climb. It was more like a gesture. An old habit that couldn't be broken, even in death. Then those long and pointed claws struck the window. The sound was not the shriek of nails on a chalkboard. It was low, musical. The claws moved over the glass, slotted into the jamb. The window opened smoothly. Not with the jerks and heaves Mindy would need to exercise on it. Her and her human hands.

Bare feet touched down on the carpet. The thing that wore Lucia? The thing in the Lucia-suit?

Whatever it was, it padded across the room. No rush. No hurry. Mindy stayed under the covers. She felt the approach; she didn't hear it. She couldn't hear her make a sound.

Maybe it was just her. Maybe she was too loud. The blood rushing in her veins, the adrenaline electrocuting her blood, the sizzle of thoughts in her head as she debated with herself—what *was* it? How could it be Lucia? How could it *look like* Lucia and not be her? And her heart. Her heart pounding, no, thudding, like it was being slammed against a brick wall, again and again and again.

The thing—the void in the world Lucia had left behind, that walked and talked to fill her absence—stood over her now. It looked at her. Mindy wished she could look into those sky-blue eyes and find herself. See the gentle mocking in Lucia's expression, or warm bemusement, fond embarrassment. Nervous love. But she knew all she'd find would be hunger. Just like the last time.

She didn't want to see.

The thing that had been Lucia gathered her blanket in its sharp claws. Pulled it down Mindy's trembling body. Underneath her, the mattress pad was miserably wet. Soaked with sweat. She'd had a nightmare about this before waking up to it happening.

For the first time, Lucia made a sound. The clicking that put Mindy in mind of mechanical pencils, Zebra pens. A small sound for the grotesque process of her teeth shifting, parting, letting her canines *extend* from her gumline like the tips of icebergs being dredged up to the surface. Fangs that were cold and sharp and *true*. The one real thing, the one thing that belonged to the creature and hadn't simply been inherited, *stolen* from Lucia.

Hands set down on the mattress, bedsprings quietly groaning with their pressure. Mindy opened her eyes. Normal hands. Normal fingers. Nails cut short, even. She looked up and her heart stopped pounding. Not a good thing. More like it was finally, steadily being crushed against that brick wall.

Lucia kissed her gently on the cheek before pulling back to smile down at Mindy. Showing every one of her teeth. Even the fangs. "Move over," Lucia's voice said. "I wanna spoon."

Mindy didn't move, so Lucia just flopped down next to her on her side.

"Don't touch me," Mindy said. Her voice was dull and blunt.

Lucia looked down at her hands, dark as shadows on Mindy's pallor, her bandage, and pulled them back. "Minz—it's me. It's not Bakula, he's not gonna hurt you, I'm gonna take care of you."

Mindy sat up. "Bakula didn't put me in the hospital. You did. You hurt me. I nearly died…" She slapped at her bandages, stirring up a faint pain. She let the spark of it be magnified by an anger, be a fire, be an inferno. "I have other people's blood in me! My blood is *gone!*"

Lucia looked back at her. All pain. No defensiveness, no retort, just pain. And fear. "Do you want me to get out of the bed?"

"Yes," Mindy said.

Without hesitation. Lucia moved away from her like she'd been stung. Stood there with her hands on her head, looking panicked.

Mindy felt her fear and almost heard her thinking, frantically thinking. "I'm not angry with you," Mindy said, some absurd part of her wanting to be conciliatory.

Lucia put a hand down on the bedspread, eyes begging for Mindy to take it. "Please be angry with me, please be furious with me, just please don't be breaking up with me. Don't you do that."

Mindy could be so cold, she surprised herself. "You said you would never hurt me."

"I didn't want to."

A hysterical laugh nearly dislodged Mindy's jaw. "You said you loved me!"

"I didn't mean for it to happen!" Lucia said it like she was pleading. "I didn't want for it to happen, it was an accident! Everything was just so horrible and I knew, I knew that if I started drinking you—you were the only thing, *are the only thing*, that felt right and I couldn't stop myself and..." Lucia blurred, all the speed in the world but nowhere to go, fidgeting in place until she fell to kneel at the foot of the bed like a dog. "I never wanted this! You remember, I didn't want to drink you, you wanted that, I was so afraid I would hurt you! And then you said it was okay, *you said*, and we tried it, and I didn't hurt you, and you liked it, and everything was good! I thought I could control it, I swear to God I thought—we never have to do it again, I'll never even show my fangs in front of you again, I don't want your blood, *Minz*, I never wanted your blood! I just want *you*!"

"I said." Mindy repeated the tiny phrase like it was an error in Computer Science II, fucking up her program, keeping it from compiling. "I said. So it's my fault then, is it?"

"No." Lucia got to her feet. Her face looked drawn. Like a dead woman's. "No, it's mine, I hurt you and I have no right to ask for your forgiveness. But I'm asking. I'm weak and I love you and I want to keep being the person you make me."

"You sound like Bakula. The two of you—you're both just obsessed with me. What is it, do I smell good, do I taste good?"

"I am *not* like Bakula!" Lucia insisted.

"No, you're not, because you're getting what you want. *Me.* But if you couldn't have me, would you accept that? Or would you be like him?"

Lucia just stood there.

Mindy thought a piece of herself was dying; the piece that couldn't bear to do this to Lucia.

"You love me," Lucia said. "*You said it,* you don't get to take it back!"

"Just because I love you doesn't always mean I can be in love with you."

Lucia pulled on her hair. "*Fine,* I'm not as smart as you, I don't know what that means!" She felt the tear worming down her cheek and clawed at her own face to get it away. "Just do it. Say you revoke my invitation. I'll go—I don't have a say in it. It's all you."

"I don't want to revoke your invitation—"

"Then don't." Lucia moved on her suddenly, unable to resist Mindy's pull any longer. She took Mindy's hand and pressed it between her breasts. "It's *me*, Minz. Just wait a minute, and you'll feel my heart. How many times have I even kissed you? A hundred, two hundred? I have a million more kisses for you. I make you laugh and I sing to you and I was such a good girlfriend, wasn't I? I loved you. I do love you. Please, Mindy, let me keep being in love with you. I don't know how to stop."

Mindy felt cold air whistling through the ribs where her heart was supposed to be. "Why didn't you stop?"

"I couldn't—at the end."

"And before? Why'd you even bite me in the first place if you knew—"

"Because I didn't want to tell you, I didn't want to say it: I'm a monster, Minz. I was supposed to die and I didn't and that death clings to me. Gets on other people."

Mindy's eyes were too dry. They were desiccated, like a desert dune. Cracked, like a rock under the sun. "You've been tempted to hurt me before."

There was a kind of honesty that burned. "Yes."

"You'd had to stop yourself before."

"Yes."

"You could've killed me. Before."

Lucia's silence was an answer.

Mindy pulled her hand back. She could still feel Lucia's barely beating heart against her palm.

"I get to choose, Mindy. Don't I? If I have these urges but I don't act on them… if I decide that I don't want to hurt people, then that makes me something else. Doesn't it? That makes me worthy of you?"

"So, you can resist your urges? You can choose?"

Lucia nodded like she was saying yes to the offer of a lifeline. "Yes, yes, we can have a safe-word or you can tie me up or wear a cross, anything, anything. I want you to feel safe, Mindy."

"Then leave."

Lucia's head froze, downcast. "I'm here because you let me be here," she said. "You can revoke my invitation anytime."

"And if I didn't? If I asked you to go, if I asked you to stay away—would you? *Could you?*"

"Minz, please—please don't ask me for the heart out of my chest."

"I want you gone." The words were like Mindy's tongue going numb.

Lucia went still, absolutely still, finally so cold that she'd frozen.

It reminded Mindy that she wasn't a living thing; she didn't need to move. She did because she chose to.

She chose to nod. "You didn't have to revoke my invitation. Remember that. You didn't need to push me away."

Lucia didn't flash away. She walked out the door, down the stairs, giving Mindy every chance to call her back.

Mindy didn't.

# CHAPTER 29

Lucia was out there somewhere. On the run. Hunting, being hunted. If Mindy cared, it was with a dull pang. Everything hurt so much that Lucia's pain was just more white on a snow day.

Mindy crossed between the windows into Lucia's room. She wasn't there, of course. Mindy sat on her bed and let the atmosphere settle into her, leave a mark on her. She hadn't been over here much. She wished she had been. She wished it had been their place as much as it was hers.

The bed smelled of Lucia, and for the first time in weeks, Mindy remembered the human Lucia. Wild and alive, careless and cruel, loving and lost. Of course she'd died. If Bakula hadn't killed her, the world would've. She hadn't been meant for it.

The Saturday night lights were blazing out there in the dark.

Enough.

She walked downstairs, the little brothers not seeing her, the mother ignoring her, and walked out to her car. Got in, scratched the key at the ignition, and couldn't put it in. Her hand closed tightly around the car key. The other keys on the fob, house key, postal box key, rested coolly against her fist. She wouldn't need them anymore.

Someone knocked at her window. "License and registration, ma'am?"

Mindy looked up, into the warm pools of Lucia's eyes. She twisted the key in the ignition, rested her foot on the brake pedal to make a quick gear change, and rolled down the window. "Guess I can't blame you for not wanting to leave things that way," she said

"That's not it. Mind if I...?" Lucia indicated with her finger.

Mindy sat back. In an instant, a bat flittered through the window and became Lucia in the passenger seat. "That's better." Lucia put her hands on the warm vents.

"I don't blame you for anything," Mindy said, hoping if she talked fast enough, her words wouldn't trip. "I'm angry with you, but I don't blame you. And I can't be with you."

"I know. Hey, I bought you flowers." Lucia dug into her pocket. "I was going to go to the florist's and figure out some bouquet in flower language and attach a note about the dance, but—here." She pulled a twenty out. "You can spend this on flowers. Whatever you want. I really only knew that I was going to get you tulips… Just as good, right? The same thing?"

"Not really."

"That's us all over, ain't it?" Lucia tucked the bill into Mindy's jacket. "The 'not really' of couples. So, you really think Bakula's gonna keep his word?"

"You heard?"

Lucia shook her head. "He's kind of cliché. The whole 'be my bride or else' thing seems his style. And for a really smart person, you're dumb enough to sacrifice yourself to that… Okay, I know you're sensitive to the mentally ill, but that guy is *not* reasonably excited for Cocoa Puffs, let's just say."

"You can't talk me out of this."

"I know."

"Someday, I just have to get my hands on a stake or a cross and wait till he's sleeping—I'll think of something."

"Yeah."

"And you'll be safe."

Lucia stared straight ahead. "You would've been safe if you'd lost my phone number the moment you found out what I'd turned into. We don't have much in common. But I think we feel about the same way about 'safe.'"

Mindy was crying, finally crying. Lucia had taken everything else, at one time or another. Her blood, her love, her friendship. Why not her tears, too? "What's your plan?"

"My plan? Same as yours. Sacrifice myself for the greater good, have people write songs about me, build a statue, get Elizabeth Gillies to play me in a movie." Lucia touched her nose. "Twinsies!"

"He doesn't want you, El."

"I know, it's *weird*. But he's gonna get me." Lucia took Mindy's hand. "There is one drawback."

Mindy ground away some tears under the heel of her hand. "The whole plan being crazy?"

"No. I have to break a promise to you." Lucia bowed her head to Mindy's hand, drawing it up to her mouth like she was going to kiss it. Mindy knew what was going to happen and still watched as the fangs flashed between Lucia's black lips and the venom flashed into her bloodstream.

Lucia came up for air, a trickle of blood on the side of her chin. She wiped it away. "Drive us to the church."

Mindy obeyed, putting her hands on the wheel, two neat puncture marks on the back of her right one.

Mindy was driving the car, but she was zoned out, doing it all automatically like she was driving home from work, from school. And, with the same hallucinatory attention she'd pay to the radio, she was watching herself from the passenger seat. She saw herself turn the wheel, put on the gas, brake, even signal. Until they stopped in front of the church.

She was behind Lucia's eyes. She was in Lucia's head. Lucia suddenly said, "I know you're here, Mindy. I can tell when you're in me, now. I don't know if you crawl in on your own or if I pull you in, but I don't care. I'm just glad you're with me. I didn't know what this feeling was before, but I recognize it now. It's love."

Lucia reached out to Mindy, fixing her hair—pulling it out of place—fixing it again. "The venom will wear off soon. I can't be here when that happens. I could never leave if you told me not to go."

She turned off the ignition and put the key in Mindy's pocket. "I just wanted another moment with you. But then, I'm always going to want one more moment. So I might as well go. It'll never hurt any less." Lucia's vision blurred.

It took Mindy a moment to realize why—tears. She pushed through the numbness, made herself blink, made her lips part. She shoved the word into Lucia's mind: *Don't.*

Lucia reached out again, putting her hand on Mindy's shoulder, and Mindy could tell she was just barely contenting herself with feeling Mindy's warmth. "I have to. You're going to go inside now. Just lie down on one of the pews and fall asleep. Don't think of me. Just have beautiful dreams. And when I'm gone, you're not going to think of me as someone you love. You're going to remember that I'm stupid and vapid and slutty and toxic and thoughtless and a total bitch who got herself killed. Someone like that, you should be able to get over pretty fast."

Mindy didn't want to forget. She didn't want to get over it. She didn't want beautiful dreams. She wanted Lucia—fucked up trauma case with all the bad wiring in the world. It wasn't a profound decision. She'd made it a long time ago.

She refused to feel the wood of the pew under her, the slight crisp of the church's AC, any of it. She seized onto what Lucia was feeling…the dread, the resolve…and pulled herself into it. Lucia didn't want to share it, but Mindy wasn't giving her a choice. If it was Lucia's, it would be Mindy's too.

The football stadium was teeming, the noise of the crowd and the marching band music audible for miles. It shuddered down right through cement and steel, into the cheerleaders' locker room. Lucia straightened her cheerleading uniform. A long-sleeved crop top, a miniskirt, both blue with gold trimmings, the team logo emblazoned on the front. Her old captain's uniform still fit, better than ever, in fact, on an all-blood diet. It made her wish she could look in a mirror.

*El, what are you doing?*

"Thanks for the loaner, Pammy. I'll try not to get too much blood on it."

"Uh-huh." Pammy was checking over the banner she'd hold for the team to run through. Making sure it was weak in the middle. Once, it hadn't torn, and she'd been paranoid ever since. "So, hey, you're a lesbian now?"

"Oh. Yeah. Listen, real quick, I never really said this, but I think you're doing a great job as captain. As good as me, even. But anyway, when it goes down, I want you to get all the girls back into the locker room. Keep low until it's over, you get me?"

"Yeah, sure. How did you know you were a lesbian, anyway?"

*Is she hitting on you?*

Lucia shrugged. "Dated a girl. It seemed to work out."

"Did you think about kissing girls a lot first? Or, like, the normal amount? Cuz everyone thinks about it a little, right? Like, you see Ryan Gosling kiss someone, you think 'What if I were Ryan Gosling? Is that how I'd kiss someone?' I mean, you'd tell me if you thought I was a lesbian, right?"

*Oh my God, she's hitting on you.*

Lucia took her hands. "Pam, there's a time and a place for this conversation. And it's college."

"Well, yeah, I mean, it just hurts a little. You want to experiment with the same sex, you work from inside the circle of friendship, you promote from within. You don't just grab a nerd and say 'Oh, you're hot now, make out with me!'"

"Pam!"

"I'm not your type, am I?"

"You're not my type."

Unfiltered by concrete, the roar of the crowd came to the locker room door as if through a wind tunnel. Mindy had never realized how loud it was, but Lucia tuned it all out.

*El, you don't have to do this.*

"Cheer, cheer, show no fear," Lucia said as she strolled out of the tunnel and onto the field. No one was paying much attention to her. All eyes were on the coaches in the middle of the field, the referee with the silver dollar, and the coin toss about to be made. Quietness fell as the referee's thumb flicked.

The coin went up, winked silver, and Lucia snapped her fingers as fast as she could. The sonic boom knocked it a few inches away from the ref's outstretched palm.

"Hello, Carfax!" Lucia called, striding out onto the field. She pulled the referee's microphone off his ear. "Let's all give a big welcome to our guest team, the Pathfinders, so they don't mind too much when our boys trounce them!"

Confused but excited, the crowd gave up a big cheer. The referee pulled at his microphone. Lucia held on to it tight. "And how about a big hand for our lovely referee here? C'mon, show 'im some love!"

Another cheer, slightly muted, went up as the referee tried hard to break Lucia's grip. She put her hand dead center on his chest. "The ref, ladies and gentlemen!" She gave him a shove and he went back twenty feet. The crowd fell silent.

Mindy centered herself. She could force her toes to wiggle, she could cant her foot to one side…

The mike squealed with feedback as Lucia spoke. "Coach? Coach Bakula? This concerns you—c'mon, let's get him out here. Bakula! Bakula! Bakula!"

Confused, somewhat intimidated, the crowd took up the chant. It wasn't long before the man emerged from the bench, stalking angrily across the field. Lucia greeted him with a warm grin. "Hey, Coach! We all know Coach Bakula, we all know what he's done…for our town. I thought we could just take a moment to say a few words about the man."

Bakula pushed the microphone away. "You expose me, you're out too. They'll hunt you all the way to hell."

Lucia smiled up at him. Mindy felt the smile she had fallen in love with, from the inside. "We can take the carpool lane."

She stepped up. Lifted the mike. "He's a vampire."

Silence. It took the crowd a moment to decide to jeer, to boo, to figure out whether this was or wasn't part of the show.

"I know because he made me one. Spread it to me like some sort of disease—" Lucia dodged a hot dog thrown by someone with a good arm. "Alright, fucktards, fucking *look!*" And she became a bat. Under the Saturday night lights, in front of ten thousand spectators, she was suddenly a bat fluttering around like she was fresh from hell.

Mindy could close her hands into fists. Squeeze them tight enough to make diamonds.

Then Lucia was a person again. Kicking the microphone up from the ground, back into her hand. "Okay then! I'm a vampire! Weird, right? But hey, I wouldn't be one if it weren't for *this nut right here!*" She jabbed playfully at Bakula's ribs. "You know how it is? He saw me alone, attacked me, and drank my blood, left me for dead wrapped in chains and plastic at the bottom of Lake Travis. The old story. Usually he only drinks from your relatives at the retirement home, but I guess I'm special." She thrust the microphone in Bakula's face. "Coach, care to comment?"

Like a cat shifting for a new angle to pounce from, Bakula lowered his mouth to the microphone in Lucia's proffered hand. "In all my years of coaching high school football, I've never heard anything so—"

"Is that true, Coach?" Quentin was charging back onto the field. "You hurt my girl?"

"We broke up, actually," Lucia muttered.

"What I want to know is why you had to turn me into a vampire? Of all things! They're not even cool anymore, they're so overexposed! It's almost as bad as zombies. Everyone's doing vampires these days, its passé, it's a total borefest! Werewolves are so much better! Hell, the Creature from the Black Lagoon is cooler. He's vintage, he's authentic, and he's a dinosaur man—" Bakula punched her.

Lucia was now no longer standing there; she was whipping through the air to the end zone. Bakula pointed at Lucia and spoke, though his grip was so tight, he'd crushed the microphone in his hand.

"*That* is not a vampire! That pathetic, mewling excuse for a predator isn't fit to sleep in a drafty coffin! Bitching and moaning over the gift I gave her. Look what you've done with it! Played pinochle with your little girlfriend and drunk a little blood, but only from those who don't meet your high moral standards. You can't even kill! You still think you're one of them. You still play by their rules! You're no hunter, you're nothing! You people want to see a vampire? Fine! Let's take off the mask!"

He took hold of his lower jaw and yanked on it, pulling and pulling and pulling...

*Oh, man, this is gonna be gross.*

His jaw snapped off, bringing a slew of skin with it. His jowls, throat, lips tore away, leaving only pale marble cords of muscle and the sharp bone of his maxilla. No lips, no gums anymore, just teeth. And more teeth. His cheek skin hung in flaps, disconnected from the bony and desiccated musculature. He tore them away like chicken skin off the meat. Then he hooked his thumbs under his eyelids and ripped back, and in one sweep, Bakula scalped himself. Nose and eyebrows gone, eyeballs left bloated in recessed sockets. His new cranium was mottled with chunks of fatty tissue sticking to his head like bits of tape. Long, clawed fingers plucked a piece off, and he casually flicked it away.

His skull seemed nothing but teeth. One massive outcrop: row upon row of needle-sharp teeth. A cancer of teeth, a tumor of them, no ears, no mouth, no nose in this death's-head. Just jaws like a shark's: Mindy imagined when the first set of teeth broke, more just moved into place. Always *more*.

"Hey, you're bald! Is that a vampire thing? Am I gonna lose all my hair?" Lucia leapt back on her feet. "Wouldn't that make bikini season simpler."

"Impudent child!"

"Weirdo stalky-creeper-fuck!" Lucia shot back. She charged at him. Lucia may have specialized in tumbles, but she'd seen enough football practices to know how to block. She jammed her shoulder into Bakula's sternum, sending him flying back toward the marching band.

"Eat brass section!"

Bakula landed on his feet. Blurring forward, his fist connected with Lucia's throat.

For Mindy, it was like watching the field through a telescope as Lucia was pitched halfway across the field, only to be stopped by the goalpost so hard that it nearly ripped out of its concrete mooring. Lucia's battered body fell like a rag to the ground. Her face broke her fall.

*Okay, what's the next part of the plan?*

Lucia spat Astroturf. "Apparently getting my ass whipped."

*Your entire plan is to punch him?*

"To be fair, I've added this clever bit in the middle where I punch him a lot."

Lucia came to her feet in a whirlwind, flying back at Bakula, every stride devouring the distance between them. She threw a punch at Mach 1, and it flew right through Bakula as he seamlessly transitioned into a pile of rats. Off-balance, Lucia went down, rolling across the yard lines. She realized some of Bakula's rats were still clinging to her and casually brushed them off. They scuttled together to reform into Bakula.

"We played a perfect game last Sunday. A perfect game! It was a shut-out! I had a great fucking lineup!" His voice was bones grating together, grinding into dust to escape his mouth. "We could've gone all-state!" Then he simply seemed to step outside of reality, step back into it right next to Lucia, holding her by the throat.

"You wish to challenge me?" he demanded. "I accept." He threw her across the field and the seating so fast that she hummed through the air, a human projectile that abruptly hit home—decapitating one of the stadium's floodlights. Lucia hung suspended for a moment, surrounded by molten glass and sparking electricity, the turbulence of her passage screaming in her ears before she pitched into the parking lot, hitting one car and knocking it into all its parked neighbors. Lucia clawed herself free of the stationary pileup.

"Okay," she muttered. "To the death, then. Again."

Mindy made herself sit up. *Hide, HIDE.*

Lucia hobbled to the visitor's lot, the fleet of school buses that had transported the opposing team, their cheerleaders, the band geeks. She rolled under the first as a cloud of bats shrieked up into the sky over the stadium wall, a dark cloud that rolled over the moon before it narrowed into a more singular monster. Bakula stepped out of the living vortex, examining the debris of Lucia's impact and the blood trail she'd left limping away.

Lucia checked her wounds. Flush with Mindy's blood, they were healing fast. She rolled out from under one bus straight under another, and another, crouching behind a tire to watch Bakula stalk after her through the maze of parked buses.

Casually, Bakula flipped a bus out of the way. "Finally smart enough to be scared, are you?"

Lucia looked at her hands.

*How strong are you?*

She dug her nail into a scabbed cut, opening it up fresh. She scooped up some of the blood, slapped it on a window, and ran.

Bakula strolled among the buses, scraping his nails across the glass of the windows. They'd already grown an inch long. "If you were still alive, I'd wager I could hear your heart racing. Almost makes me regret killing you. But then, you made such a lovely corpse…"

He saw Lucia's blood, black in the moonlight. As one might stop to sniff a rose, he ran his finger through it, then delicately traced his fingertip over the tips of his teeth. "You've gotten sour with age, my dear."

The bus he faced lurched into him, pinning him against the bus behind him. Lucia kept pushing, pile-driving these two buses into a third, the three into a fourth, and the four into a fifth, until the pileup got too heavy for her to move. The cab side had dented into her palm prints. She pushed off. "Step on a Lego, fuckface."

*Yeah, he's not dead.*

"Nah, he totally is. It goes 'stakes, decapitation, sunlight, school buses,' right?"

Glass shattered. Lucia looked up. An eerie mist rose like a storm cloud above her. Streaming over the twisted metal and broken glass. She turned and ran as the mist avalanched toward her.

And Mindy ripped herself fully out of her paralysis. Teetering on sleeping legs, skin flushed, eyes blinking, having to swim through a layer of Jell-O to take a single step…but she was back.

And she had two choices. One, she could go up against a stalkery vampire lord and his bullshit magical powers to save her girlfriend. Or two, she could enter the lesbian dating scene.

Well, that was no choice at all.

# CHAPTER 30

Mindy thought she was going to be sick, riding shotgun in Lucia's head. Lucia was running, pulling the world past her, focusing with eagle eyes on the distant horizons where she'd be in a few steps. Taking the roads of Carfax at a couple hundred miles an hour. Bakula behind her the whole way. *Where are you going?*

"Away from him. You know me. I may not have a plan, but I have a lot of stupid ideas. One of them has to be stupid enough to work."

Mindy forced herself out of the church, into the parking lot, flashing between the parked cars and the speeding ones Lucia was passing—islands of metal that Lucia sailed between. Piled into her own car; Lucia was in a Wal-Mart parking lot. Twisted the key in the ignition as Lucia scooped up groceries, shopping carts, open car doors to throw backward at the coach. The engine turned over. Bakula batted aside the projectiles with ease.

Mindy put the Taurus into gear, but had nowhere to go. Lucia's vision was a DVR on three-arrows fast-forward, a DVD glitching and skipping. Mindy saw cars shrieking past her, felt the wind making her hair whip and snarl like a cat of nine tails, and then Bakula caught her hair—

Right next to a Jiffy Lube. The one on Danish Street. She got her oil changed there, she knew where it was. She stepped on the gas and tried to ignore Bakula shaking Lucia like a dog with a rat, spinning her around to punch a car off the road, whipping her into a minivan.

*Hold on, El.*

Mindy was jerked back to reality—red light ahead, stopped cars; she was about to plow right into them. She twisted the wheel, veering around them, punching through traffic in a flurry of car horns and squealing brakes. Clear road.

She pushed herself back into Lucia's head, saw what Bakula was making her see. Car wreck, bodies sprawled, imprint on the side where Lucia's body had impacted.

The wreck suddenly dwindled. Lucia was thrown off the road and through the wrought-iron fence of Karnstein Cemetery. The rails with their spear-tipped finials were knocked out of the fence by her body, like teeth in a heavyweight bout. When she tried to get up, the rails she had landed on rolled under her scrambling hands.

*This is not funny… Cats doing people things, that's funny…*

The inhuman scream of metal on metal. The rear passenger door and cab of Mindy's car were crumpled inward. She had run another red light, been sideswiped, and was sent into a spin. *Off the gas.* The tires clung to the pavement, trying to stop her, and did it in a huff of burning rubber. When she hit the gas, the car still drove.

She couldn't help herself. She went back into Lucia's head just in time to see Bakula stalking after her, casually ignoring a car as it just missed him, its side mirror snapping off on his shoulder. "You should've been here in the first place, Lucy! You belong dead! You're a born victim, only breathing to make it to the bottom of a ditch. Run, dead girl! *Run!*"

Lucia ran. He followed. Constant as the North Star. They were heading north, and Mindy followed—passing bodies and wreckage and hoping there was something more at the end of the trail.

Lucia ran with the flow of traffic. Mindy, still riding along in her head, felt like she was on the world's fastest motorcycle. Lucia cut between lanes, in front of cars, behind, between cars, past a Peterbilt and a few bikers, putting everything she could between herself and Bakula. He was unstoppable, barrelling after her, right through the cars, crumpling them like tinfoil as he ran them over. Then one side of the road was gone—replaced by a guard rail and a scenic view of the river.

*El!*

"You thinking what I'm thinking?"

*I really hope not.*

Lucia stopped suddenly, digging in her heels to grind her Keds into a smear on the blacktop, and Bakula stopped before her. He looked at the water. Looked at Lucia. His smile made his teeth seem even longer.

"Fancy a swim?" Lucia asked.

He came for Lucia. She gathered herself, fists curled. Fighting angry made him even faster, but he telegraphed everything, swinging wildly—a choreography she could easily learn. She was head cheerleader for a reason.

Watching, Mindy could not even follow the blur of jumbled fists and arms, punches and blocks and counters like jackhammers drilling into each other. Knifing arms meeting each other like steel against steel. Lucia slipping aside, over, under, barraging him, a hundred punches into his ribs as his right hook caught air, another hundred into his face as his left cross went where she'd been a moment ago. But she was a rainstorm chiselling at a statue, and his rage couldn't last forever. He cooled like molten lead, catching her fist as it bobbed for his nose. Then he simply picked her up and swung her out over the water.

Lucia fell, over the guard rail and the steep decline of the riverbank, down to the silvery ink of water at night, reflecting the stars but not her. Like a portal to another realm, the water exploded around her, into her. Her flesh coarsening into crystal, the crystal cracking, the cracks shattering. Thankfully, the water was shallow. She propelled herself out of the battery acid river and onto the riverbank like a scalded cat. She landed on all fours, her body trembling.

"Yes, honey, I'm afraid the swimming lessons were a waste of time." Bakula came down the cliff-side like a spider. "A little running water, and it's all over. Even you should be able to remember that…"

Lucia looked around. She was in a small cove, just a sprinkling of sand and a few cypress trees. Rock walls on either side of her.

Mindy didn't like her chances. Climbing would slow her down, she'd never get past Bakula. She didn't know how he was doing his Spider-Man act and wasn't likely to figure it out before he reached her.

"I'm going to put you in the water, Lucy. Down among the dead things. And let the crabs have you."

*El, you have to run across the water.*

"Okay, Minz, this is a situation where 'What Would Jesus Do?' does not apply…"

*Run as fast as you can when you hit the water, just keep going. You're going to have to slap the water with your foot, creating the support force of a pocket of air around your foot while you kick your shoes through the water to propel yourself forward. The Flash does it all the time.*

"The Flash is a comic book character!"

*Yeah, and you're a vampire! It's just like riding a bike. Don't think, just go!*

"Don't think," Lucia repeated. *Alright, I'm good at that…*

Bakula stepped off the cliff-face and onto the sand. He gestured her closer. Lucia crouched to the ground, ready to run.

*Lucia, no, Lucia!*

She ran, right at him, his arms spread wide to greet her. Two trains on the same track. A sand trail kicked up behind Lucia. She flew to him.

And at the last possible second, she swerved, sweeping back the other way, cutting a scar into the earth with her speed as she burned toward the river, hit it—her foot in the water, no support, no resistance… *Don't think,* she told herself and swung her other foot forward, pumped it into the water, driving herself upward, forward. *Just keep running.* Another step. She was going to fall in. She was going to drown. It would burn like acid. *No!* She made a fourth step and a fifth and a sixth. She didn't think. She just had to do. It was just another routine.

She streaked across the water, as light as the East Wind.

*Oh, El, thank God that worked.*

"You weren't sure?"

*Hell no, I just cited a comic book, for Christ's sake. Get to the shore before you lose any momentum.*

"We're not going to the shore."

*Lucia—!*

Down the river, Tate's Creek Bridge waited, that old skeleton bloodstained with rust.

"I've got a plan!"

*Let me guess, a bad one.*

"Says the woman who dated a vampire."

*Alright, fine, the bridge. Can you get to shore now?*

"I told you, we're not going to shore."

*Then how—*

The bridge pylons waited for her, concrete streaked green with moss.

"I'm going to run straight up it, just like the Flash."

*How do you—*

"I watched the TV show."

She hit the concrete and ran straight up it and heard Mindy laughing in her ear like they were riding a motorcycle together. She took the pylon three steps at a time, came up over the railing, and Bakula was there reaching for her throat. He slammed her into a truss so hard, the rivets popped. Then he ran her through the bridge's pilings, bending them as easily as the tines on a fork before tossing her broken to the ground.

"You're in there, aren't you Mina?" He turned Lucia over with his toe and forced her eyes to meet his by wedging his shoe under her chin. "She's got you locked away somewhere or running scared. You don't have to be afraid. I'm a man of my word. Come to me, and none of your friends will die. I said you had until the end of the game. Well, Mina, the game is over. No more running."

He drew his foot off Lucia's chin, down her body, all the way to her knee. Then he stomped down.

Mindy let out a howl of pain and drove faster.

# CHAPTER 31

She drove like she was still dreaming; everything just flowing by. Even the ambulances, even the cop cars, even the people packing their cars in the residential neighborhoods. There was no thinking to do. She wasn't even afraid until her headlights glinted off the iron trusses. Then she thought, what if Lucia were dead? Mindy wondered how she would die without her heart? All at once or would she just crumble a little at a time?

The trusses cut the moonlight into shadowy slivers. Lucia and Bakula stood in the dark until Mindy pulled up, her headlights illuminating them. Lucia was kneeling before Bakula. He stood behind her, his hands on her shoulders. Mindy imagined him twisting her head right off if she so much as moved.

"You…*children.*" Bakula's voice was almost completely gone, rasping out in a growl so deep that Mindy felt vibrate in her bones. "Raised by television, by movies, by *books* when you bother to learn how to read. You think of life as a playground." Bakula was on a rant. "Everything is love triangles, choice, free will. No. We are what we are. We do what we do. Mindy, you and I are destiny. We are eternity. There is nothing else. Just me."

"You shouldn't have come," Lucia said.

"Silence!" Bakula barked. "Out of the car."

*You shouldn't have come, Minz. Get out of here.*

Mindy unbuckled her seatbelt. Opened the door. She'd done something wrong; the car beeped like a time bomb in a movie. She couldn't care about that right now. She stood outside it, staring at them down the beam of the headlights. "Let her go!"

Bakula drummed his fingers on Lucia's shoulders. "Come closer first."

*Wait a minute… Think I've got an idea.*

*See? Facing the Prince of Darkness not so bad if I get to see that.* Out loud, Mindy said: "What assurances do I have that she'll be safe?"

"Mina. I'm a gentleman. The fact that I didn't rip you out of your crumbling car the moment you put it in park should be proof enough of my good intentions."

"Yeah, you're a real humanitarian," Lucia said. Bakula grabbed her by the hair and wrenched her head to the side.

"And *you* could've had it all, Lucy. Just like you said. We could've shared Mina. You both could've been my brides."

"Dude, you've watched way too much Playboy Channel." *Mindy, I need a very loud noise.*

Bakula flicked Lucia away with a distasteful snap of his wrist. "Enough of this. Mina. You can do this willingly or it can happen another way. All your other lives much preferred the willing way."

Mindy wasn't listening. *A loud noise? El, he's not a cat. He's not just gonna run off!*

*I've got a plan. Trust me.*

Mindy looked at Lucia. Lucia gave her a wink.

"You called my car a junker."

Bakula looked askew. "What?"

"My car. I mean, you're right. It's a P-O-S that's old enough to vote. It needs about a kazillion different repairs. Look, one of the headlights is brighter than the other, what's up with that? And I did spend a little of my tip money on it. I didn't fix the two windows that won't roll down. I didn't buy a new seatbelt to replace the one missing in the back. I didn't even pay to get rid of that smell in the trunk. You wanna know what I did buy?"

Mindy reached inside the car. Spun the radio's volume to the max, touched the number three preset, and finally hovered her finger over the power button. "A stereo system."

Ozzy screamed out "Flying High Again." Lucia raised her fists and slammed them hard down on the asphalt, shaking the entire bridge with pavement-cracking force.

Bakula was thrown off-balance; the bridge creaked and groaned. And the colony of bats exploded out from underneath the bridge like a broken dam.

Mindy threw herself back into her car, shutting the door as the bats blindly slammed against the windows.

"You wanna know what team I'm on?" Lucia asked. Bakula grabbed her, but his hands closed on empty air. She had transformed into a bat—one of the hundred thousand filling the air.

He immediately dismissed her, wheeling on Mindy. He took a step toward her. "Mina…!"

Behind him, Lucia returned to human form. She drew her arm back, twisted her hip, shifted her weight; threw a punch that was worth a million dollars. Her fist stabbed between Bakula's shoulder blades, driving into his body and out his chest. Dry meat hit Mindy's car head-on. And, a small, black, twisted thing that might've once been a heart dribbled down the windshield.

"Team Mindy, you snaggletoothed fuck," Lucia whispered in his ear. Then she realized she had her arm through a hole in his chest. "Oh, shit!" She pulled her hand free. "I didn't know I could punch through people! Sorry! Sorry! You deserved it, though. Sorry!"

The storm of bats passed, and Mindy turned on her windshield wipers. The heart was batted off her windshield. She got out of the car. It laid at her feet, still beating.

Bakula was flagging. Mindy could see his clothes hanging off his body, his skin pulling tight to his bones, his eyes glossing over in a dull maroon. "Alright, Mina, I can see you're not ready for a serious relationship…"

Mindy rested her foot on the heart. It beat against the heel of her Amanda Seyfried Collection ankle boots.

"Maybe we can try this again in a few years, when you're a little more mature…"

Mindy shifted her foot. The heel on her shoe wasn't very long, but it was enough inches for him.

"Mina—Mindy—I have gold…jewels… I can make you a very rich woman!"

Just a little pressure, at first.

"Tell me, *what do you want?*"

"I want you to stay away from my girl," Mindy told him, and drove her heel right through him and his stinking heart. Black sand came spilling out like she'd broken an hourglass.

Bakula screamed and burned and decayed, all the things vampires did. With his dying strength, he threw himself at Lucia, slamming her into a girder headfirst. Then she was tumbling down toward the water. Mindy ran to the side of the bridge, expecting any second for Lucia to turn into mist, to change into a bat—anything but go *splash*.

She looked back at Bakula, saw him as nothing but a state championship ring glinting in a stir of ashes. She looked back down at the water. The white wake of the fall was absorbed back into the milling darkness. Lucia wasn't coming to the surface.

Taking her shoes off, Mindy climbed over the guardrail, took a deep breath. She tried to think of how you were supposed to dive in a situation like this, besides feet first. She couldn't think of anything but reasons not to. So she jumped.

Seventy feet rushed by her, each inch telling her what a bad idea this was.

She hit the surface of the water. Nothing could've been colder, harder, deadlier.

Had she passed out on impact? She'd been wide awake a moment before, but now she was slipping in and out of consciousness, constantly waking up to the blackness all around her—pressed in on all sides by darkly churning cold. A cold made physical, lacing through her clothes and turning them into anchors. She struggled out of her jacket, absently seeing her hands stray into her vision. Glowing white in the blackness, then slowly turning blue.

# CHAPTER 32

She was woken up only by her burning lungs. She hadn't even realized she'd lost consciousness. Which way was up? She trusted it was above her head and swam, every stroke carrying her through thick tar. Her head finally broke the surface. She took a deep breath, another, and another. Her muscles spasming with shock. She had to go back down. *Just go, just go—*

She submerged again, looking around, forcing her eyes to see. *There*—a trail of bubbles streaming upward. She swam for them, lower, deeper, the moonlight abandoning her, the cold embracing her. *Keep going.* She followed the trail, straight down, the bubbles dwindling to a steady trickle, then to drips of air wandering past her. Then to nothing. *Keep going.*

She swam. Bludgeoning the water with the cudgels of her numb arms. She could see the riverbed spread out under her. Rocks and sand and somewhere, Lucia. Her hands tucked into the smooth rocks and her brain rebelled—told her those were Lucia's bones, worn down by the river. *No! Keep going.*

There was a living thing in her lungs, clawing, stabbing at the walls, trying to make her come up, but she couldn't, she wouldn't, she—

*Mindy, I love you.*

*Lucia!* She was like a log that'd burnt down to nothing, every second, another part of her crumbling into ash and pulled away by the current. Off to join the ocean, the dead men at the bottom, the shipwrecks, and the broken hearts.

Mindy kicked hard and brought herself to Lucia. Her arms were numb, lifeless things, connected to her by fraying strings. Her hands seemed impossibly far away from her body, but she made them wrap around Lucia and pull and kick and kick and kick—until the mirror patina of the surface was right above them. Her lungs were screaming as she came up, and the air punched its way into her mouth.

Lucia's eyes were shut.

Mindy felt like she was climbing a mountain, pulling them to shore. It took a small eternity, but her legs finally stopped kicking through the water and instead caught sandy shoal. They were well clear of the river before she let her body collapse and the two of them sprawled out on the green grass.

"Lucia," she said, eyes closed, "now would be a good time to say something inconsiderate. Let me know you're still alive."

Lucia said nothing. Mindy had to force her eyes open. She looked over at Lucia. With her uniform tattered and torn, she didn't look like a cheerleader. She looked like an Amazon from some savage tribe. But her skin... It was charred and seared, smoking in places...

Mindy rolled over, beaching herself on Lucia, holding her arm up to Lucia's vacant face. "Drink. You need it. Drink."

There was nothing there. Mindy slapped at her arm in front of Lucia's face, wiped the cold water away as best she could, rubbed briskly at her skin to get it nice and warm. "Drink! Drink, you bitch! You already died on me once, goddamnit!"

Roaring, she slapped Lucia across the face. It jumpstarted Lucia. A fingernail scratching feebly in the air, toes shifting to seek purchase on the wind. And finally, her teeth baring, her eyes opening, all of it a rictus of pain that she couldn't speak through.

Mindy offered her arm. Pushed the flesh into Lucia's mouth, but the vampire still wouldn't bite down. "It's okay, it's okay, please—*drink*."

And, locking her gaze with Mindy, Lucia bit. The blood leaped into her mouth, surging down her throat. Mindy could practically see it run through her—burnishing her chapped lips, her scratched throat, her ravaged chest, then out to her limbs. Lucia pulled her fangs away, and with renewed strength, she flipped their bodies over so she was straddling Mindy, digging into her throat.

"It's okay," Mindy kept saying, Lucia clinging to her. "Take it. Take everything you need."

It wasn't like Lucia was drinking her blood. It was like she was sucking what meager warmth there was out of Mindy's body, pulling it into her own. As Mindy caressed her, she felt a feverish warmth building under Lucia's skin while a deep chill settled over her. The cold didn't knife into her. Instead it slowly, sweetly, wrapped around her like an old blanket. She let it soothe and seduce her. Her eyelids fluttered shut, and everything became so wonderfully black—

Lucia pulled away from her. "No."

Mindy looked at her through slit eyes. Lucia was still horribly scarred, her face awash with pain, the bone in her broken leg tearing at the distended skin. "It's okay," Mindy said. "You can—"

"That's all," Lucia said firmly. "Hey. " She rubbed at her reddened cheek. "Did you pimp-slap me?"

"No. Must've been somebody else," Mindy said. Then passed out.

Mindy was dreaming about being cradled in Lucia's strong arms. Lucia carried her to an overturned car on the road by the bridge. She shredded her nails on the undercarriage and sparks ignited the spilled gasoline.

The explosion woke Mindy up.

Lucia walked back to her, and they sat down next to each other, warming themselves by the fire. The town was quiet, peaceful—from a distance. The eye of the hurricane was passing overhead.

Lucia put her arm around Mindy, then saw her arm streaked with gore up to the elbow. "Oh, gross, I've still got Bakula on me! Ew, Mindy, ew!"

She waved her bloody hand around, her face as disgusted as a schoolgirl confronted with a worm. Mindy watched for a few seconds before tearing a scrap of fabric from Lucia's skirt. Bit by bit, she scrubbed the gunge off Lucia's arm.

"That was pretty badass, though," Mindy said.

"Yeah?"

"Yeah. Punching a guy through the heart. Very *Mortal Kombat*."

"It didn't work, though."

"I know."

"Killing him was supposed to cure me."

"I know."

"This is who I am now. This is *what* I am."

Mindy watched Lucia turn her arm this way and that, the dawn light dazzling her crystalline skin. "It's beautiful, though."

Lucia nodded. "They're not going to leave me alone."

"Who?"

"Anyone. Everyone. No one'll want to live next door to the vampire. It's what I was counting on when I exposed Bakula."

"Lucia…"

She held up her hand. Her sparkling, shining hand. "I did it for both of us. I didn't want him to just be able to—put it back like it was, if I died. But I can't put it back either. There's a reason I tried to keep you out of it, though. You can go home. You can keep your head down. This'll all pass you by."

"Maybe I don't want it to. Maybe I want to keep chasing the storm."

Lucia shook her head. "You don't. Not really."

"How do you know?"

"Because I don't. I just don't have a choice. But it is a nice thought, Mindy." The fire was dying down, leaving just blackened wreckage. "I think you jumping off a bridge makes us pretty even, as far as favors go, but I'd just…appreciate it if you looked after my mom and the dweebs. I'll be sending some money, but, you know, I won't be there. You will."

Mindy spread her arms. "So we can't—run away together! Alright, we stay and fight! We tell them the truth, we tell them what Bakula was, what he did to Seb." Mindy got up, feeling her second wind. "The Town Council can't stonewall us—we can go to the retirement home, find a player or another coach who knew something. Once they know the whole story, people will see you as you really are!"

"Which is?" Lucia asked distantly, behind her.

Mindy paced. "A hero! My hero, at least…" She didn't look at Lucia. Some part of her knew.

"I've never been good at saying goodbyes," Lucia sighed.

When Mindy turned around, she was gone. Her heart went with her.

# CHAPTER 33

It was a nice statue. Very well-sculpted, very expensive. And from the way the artist had captured Bakula's face, given him a beatific smile, you could tell it was a labor of love. A Dragons fan at work.

Mindy pulled out her phone, turning it on to be able to read the plaque in the dim light of the sunset. The plaque had his name—a lie—his birth date—a lie—and his date of death, one year ago. Hopefully that was true. It went on to list his accomplishments, to commemorate the tornado that had taken his life, and to thank Morgan Biotech for sponsoring the relief effort that had climaxed in this statue, looking over at the high school. Always watching.

Mindy took the spray-can bottle from her backpack. She was glad the plaque was so big. Enough room for all the letters in MURDERER.

Tired and hot in her robe and her cap and tassel, with her diploma clutched tightly in her hand, she got home, went upstairs, and found Lucia sitting cross-legged atop her bed.

"I told you I wasn't any good at saying goodbye."

She wore a two-tone pencil skirt and a black sleeveless top. Both seemed like an extension of the unlit room's darkness, stretching out to wrap around her. Her hair was trimmed to shoulder length, dyed a new chocolate shade. She looked good. Seeing her, Mindy's missing her panged worse than ever, somehow.

"What are you doing here?"

Lucia shrugged. "You never revoked my invitation."

"And I don't think I'm going to. But—you're not dead."

Lucia shook her head. "No. Well, technically—"

"I kinda thought you might be. You didn't text. And you used to text, like—"

"It's not like I never saw anything I thought you'd love or thought of something I'd love to say to you…needed something only you knew how to say." Seeming bored with her own angst, Lucia bopped up to her feet. "Anyway, a clean break seemed best. There's nothing I hate worse than an ex who keeps sniffing around for leftovers."

"That's what we are?" Mindy wrestled her way out of the gown. "Exes?"

"I don't like that word." Lucia leaned against Mindy's bedpost. "You're a college girl now. There should be something more sophisticated—yes. You're one of those things I don't have anymore. Like breathing."

Mindy shut the door. "Sit on the fucking bed and tell me how you've been."

Lucia did, patting the mattress beside her. She waited until Mindy sat down with her to speak. "Austin."

"Austin? That's like an hour from here. Your big escape was moving an hour away?"

"I spent some time in Mexico too," Lucia said defensively. "Learned Spanish, finally. I should go back and get that foreign language credit un-effed. You should be able to do that, right?"

"Alright. Austin. Tell me everything."

And Lucia did. The sun came down, low enough to slant through the closed blinds and catch Lucia's skin, making it sparkle even brighter than Mindy remembered. They lay down beside each other, legs dangling off the bed, kicking at each other's feet. They talked until Mindy had nothing else to ask about but—"What have you been doing for food?"

The smile that Mindy had been kindling froze on Lucia's mouth. "Support groups?"

"What, really? El, no."

Lucia looked over. "They have support groups for everything now. Domestic abuse. Stalking. Rape. You have to be patient—separate the wheat from the chaff—follow someone home, find out who's hurting them, *make sure*. And you wait. You let all connections between the two of you grow cold. And when there's nothing left but you knowing what they've done…when there's some coincidence people can use to explain why he's gone…then he disappears."

"Then you kill them."

"Depends."

"On?"

"Whether they deserve it. I told you. This is what I am now. I'm not asking you to like it. I only came here for three reasons. I'm not gonna stick around in Austin and wait for someone to find a pattern. I'm moving on. What do you think, can LA handle me for a year or two?"

Mindy's gaze was glued on Lucia. Like she couldn't leave if Mindy just kept watching her. "How long are you going to run, El?"

"Until I get away." Lucia went to the window, fingering open the blinds, staring at the moon. It was a full one.

"Three reasons," Mindy said. "What was the second one?"

"I wanted to see your speech, of course, valedictorian." Lucia smiled. "I think Seb would've liked it."

"Yeah?"

"Yeah."

Mindy rolled over on the bed to look at Lucia looking at the moon. Like it was calling to her. "Have you been seeing anyone?"

"Bakula didn't get over you in like a thousand years. I figure I'm entitled to at least a century. I wanna see you all old and wrinkly before I give up on you."

"I'm planning to age like Helen Mirren, so…"

"See, maybe that works for me, I could have a thing for older women…"

Mindy got up. "You didn't come here just for a graduation speech."

"I didn't ask you to come away with me last year, and I'm not asking now."

"I didn't have a chance to think about it. You were right, not wanting me to feel obligated. But I've been thinking about it. And I don't want to have a life without you. And I don't think you want a life without me. Before, I always thought of curing you, fixing you, but I can't. What happened, happened. You are what you are. But you don't have to be alone. Whatever you go through, I can go through it with you. Make me like you."

Lucia laughed, shaking her head. "Have you looked in a mirror lately? You'll notice you look eighteen. I turn you, you'll be getting carded for eternity."

"I don't even like beer."

Lucia took Mindy's hands. "I stayed away because I wanted to prove something. To you and to myself—I'm not your responsibility, Minz. I don't need a babysitter. I didn't go on a murderous rampage without you…even though the Town Council really has it coming. I can feed. I can survive. I can be…content. I don't need you as my therapist or my Jiminy Cricket or…as my girlfriend. I just need you to be happy. And if you can be happy with me…"

"El, you've been here five minutes. And this is the most I've smiled in months."

"Good. Because I love you. I love you so damn much I can barely remember I'm a monster, knowing you loved me."

"You're not a monster, Lucia. Or if you are, then everyone's a monster, and you're just a different breed. If the whole world says you're the Devil, I'll be there asking how that can be true when you're my guardian angel. When you're the woman I love." Mindy took hold of Lucia's necklace, playing with it, letting the pendant catch the light. She used it to pull Lucia close to her.

As she kissed Lucia, the cross was sweetly cool.

# EPILOGUE

She watched as Principal Haywood was awakened by a scratching at the French door that came from outside her bedroom, from the patio of her palatial house. Haywood squinted first at the darkness around her, then at the blazing red numbers of her alarm clock. 5:24 a.m. Then she looked out at the door—maybe expecting a raccoon.

Lucia stood there, still, silent. It took Haywood a moment to recognize her. Then Lucia pawed at the glass panes again before pushing the doors open.

"Oh God, you've seen *Salem's Lot*," Haywood blurted out, before fully coming awake. "What do you want?"

Lucia quit the Stephen King routine, placing her hands behind herself and swaying in her old, insouciant manner. "I'm skipping town. But first I'm throwing a going-away party for myself. It's a long trip. I'll need some snacks."

"I suppose you blame me for what happened to you. Like it was my fault."

"You…" Lucia spoke dreamily, barely paying attention. "Your friends on the Town Council."

Haywood pulled her blanket up almost to her neck. "I had nothing to do with what Bakula did! I had no idea!"

"You didn't want to know." Lucia continued on in the same airy tone, like they were back in a parent-teacher conference, her cheerleader head a million miles away: "You're a teacher. You're supposed to protect kids, not feed us to people like Bakula. Because I know I wasn't the first, and if it were left up to you, I wouldn't have been the last."

"It was the Council's decision! You can't just single me out."

Finally, Lucia focused on her. Gave her that ingratiating smile. "Oh, I'm not. I've already visited them. Don't you always want us teens to be more involved in local politics?"

Haywood sat up. "Alright then. I suppose the others were all stupid enough to let you in—I bet you just tossed your hair and flashed that smile and they opened the door right up. But I know the rules! You can't come in here unless I invite you in, and that is not ever going to happen!"

Lucia shifted and swayed, like a cobra before a snake charmer, her smile bobbing up and down. Her hands still behind her back. "I know. I know! You're all so…fucking…smart. And I'm just a dumb little cheerleader who got a C+ in English, like, *I speak English.* But you're forgetting one thing."

"Which is?"

"We're in Texas, dumbass."

Lucia held the pistol up to the glass and pulled the trigger.

After that, Mindy took over. Tying a rope around Haywood's cooling legs. Throwing its length over the still ceiling fan. Giving the end to Lucia to hoist Haywood's carcass up with her vampire strength while Mindy moved the empty paint buckets under her neck. Severing the jugular vein neatly—now that Mindy thought about it, it was possible Haywood had presided over the frog dissection in biology class. Mindy's hand hadn't shaken then either.

The buckets filled quickly. Mindy sealed them up and gave them to Lucia. They hadn't gotten all of it, but something had to be left for atmosphere. A big dripping puddle of blood under an upside-down corpse—try blaming that on a tornado.

"This is why communication is so important," she said to Lucia. "Imagine, thinking I had something against murderous rampages…"

"The important thing is that we're doing things as a couple," Lucia replied. "You got a smidge…"

She licked her thumb and rubbed at Mindy's cheek, gratified to feel Mindy shudder into it.

"A little wet thumb action turning you on, Murphy?"

Mindy rolled her eyes. "We can continue this conversation away from the crime scene."

"Babe, you are gonna make such a good vampire."

# ABOUT GEORGETTE KAPLAN

It was never easy for Georgette Kaplan. She was born a poor child in Mississippi, where she still remembers sitting on the porch with her family, singing and dancing around her. After learning she was adopted, at the age of twenty-one, she hitchhiked to St. Louis, where she worked at a gas station and in a traveling carnival. After a shooting incident at the gas station, she decided to quit and pursue her lifelong dream of a career in writing. She now lives back in Mississippi with her life partner Marie.

## CONNECT WITH GEORGETTE KAPLAN:

Tumblr: georgettekaplan.tumblr.com
E-Mail: kaplangeorgette@gmail.com

# OTHER BOOKS FROM YLVA PUBLISHING

www.ylva-publishing.com

# First Blood

(Punk Series – Book #3)

### JD Glass

ISBN: 978-3-95533-577-9
Length: 251 pages (98,000 words)

It's in Samantha Cray's blood: she is Wielder, destined to be join the Circle: dedicated to Light, to fight the Dark in every way.

In Europe after tragedy, Samantha learns the secrets of herself and the world. Her best friend, Fran, comes to visit, also joins, and becomes much more than a friend.

Together they must learn and learn fast, not just who but how to fight, for the Dark stops at nothing…

# Good Enough to Eat

(The Vampire Diet Series - Book #1)

### Jae & Alison Grey

ISBN: 978-3-95533-242-6
Length: 223 pages (64,000 words)

Robin is a vampire who wants to change her eating habits. To fight her cravings for O negative, she goes to an AA meeting, where she meets Alana, who battles her own demons.

Despite their determination not to get involved, the attraction is undeniable.

Is it love or just bloodlust that makes Robin think Alana looks good enough to eat? Will it even matter once Alana finds out who Robin really is?

# Driving Me Mad

## L.T. Smith

ISBN: 978-3-95533-290-7
Length: 348 pages (107,000 words)

After becoming lost on her way to a works convention, Rebecca Gibson stops to ask for help at an isolated house. Progressively, her life becomes more entangled with the mysterious happenings of the house and its inhabitants.

With the help of Clare Davies, can Rebecca solve a mystery that has been haunting a family for over sixty years? Can she put the ghosts and the demons of the past to rest?

# Fragile

## Eve Francis

ISBN: 978-3-95533-482-6
Length: 318 pages (103,000 words)

College graduate Carly Rogers is forced to live back at home with her mother and sister until she finds a real job. Life isn't shaping up as expected, but meeting Ashley begins to change that. After many late night talks and the start of a book club, the two women begin a romance. When a past medical condition threatens Ashley, Carly wonders if their future together will always be this fragile.

# COMING FROM YLVA PUBLISHING

www.ylva-publishing.com

# Have a Bite

(The Vampires of Brooklyn Chronicles – Book #1)

### R.G. Emnauelle

Delphine Bouchard is a celebrity chef who also happens to be a vampire. A food critic with a grudge? Sabotage in her restaurant, and a vampire hunter? Cryptic messages, human corpses, and a witch coven that's pressuring her to keep her head down? It's all in a day's work for Del, who must protect her business, her loved ones, and herself, before she becomes the hunter's next victim.

*Ex-Wives of Dracula*
© 2016 by Georgette Kaplan

ISBN: 978-3-95533-410-9

Also available as e-book.

Published by Ylva Publishing, legal entity of Ylva Verlag, e.Kfr.

Ylva Verlag, e.Kfr.
Owner: Astrid Ohletz
Am Kirschgarten 2
65830 Kriftel
Germany

www.ylva-publishing.com

First edition: 2016

Credits
Edited by Joanie Basler
Cover Design by Dirt Road Design

18075686R00210

Printed in Great Britain
by Amazon